OMNIPOTENCE
ENOUGH

Visit us at www.boldstrokesbooks.com

By the Author

Whatever Gods May Be

Shadows of Something Real

Omnipotence Enough

OMNIPOTENCE ENOUGH

by

Sophia Kell Hagin

2017

THIS TRADE PAPERBACK ORIGINAL IS PUBLISHED BY
BOLD STROKES BOOKS, INC.
P.O. BOX 249
VALLEY FALLS, NY 12185

FIRST EDITION: OCTOBER 2017

CREDITS
EDITOR: CINDY CRESAP
PRODUCTION DESIGN: STACIA SEAMAN
COVER DESIGN BY SOPHIA KELL HAGIN

For Susan

To be alive is power,
Existence in itself,
Without a further function,
Omnipotence enough.

To be alive and Will—
'Tis able as a God!
The Further of ourselves be what—
Such being Finitude?

—*Emily Dickinson*
IX.
The Single Hound
Poems of a Lifetime

CHAPTER ONE

After the fog

I admit it. I have a thing about counting. Calms me down, counting.

Which is why this has been so fucked up. Because you can't count without a starting point, right? If you don't have *one*, how the hell do you trust two or three, much less something like $P = F \times d/t$?

But fuck me. I lost way more than an equation about power, force, distance, and time.

I really did lose *one*. I even lost *before*.

Yeah, well, fuck them. I'm slowly stumbling back again through the leftover fog of their pharma, back to remembering *before*, back to understanding that I *need to count*.

Which is a good sign. Maybe if I can keep my head together and count, I can find *one*. And if I can find *one*, I can find *before*, and then I can find my way home.

So okay. I declare this AF1—the starting point, the first day After the Fog, made possible by the woman who once occupied the cell next to mine.

As I listened to her scream and bang out there in the corridor when they dragged her away, a most astonishing thing happened, which I attribute to her, though I don't *actually* know if she had anything to do with it. What I do know is that while she was shrieking, an old audiostick came whizzing under the door with such force that it zinged all the way across the outer cell *and* the inner cell, coming to rest against a tubercle of rust along the back wall next to the toilet.

And neither cameras nor robots noticed.

Maybe they decided it was one of the monster cockroaches always scooting around in here—the audiostick's black like the cockroaches, almost as large, and it moved just as fast.

Took a while to finagle it off the floor. In here, nothing's easy. A multi-lens camera dome has replaced the inner cell ceiling light, and to block the cameras' view, I faked slipping as I got up from the toilet, which turned into a real fall. Couple bruises later, here I am curled on the bunk facing the wall, my hands hidden by the heat-glare of my back so the thermal infrared cam can't detect what I'm doing. Good thing, cuz my hands won't stop trembling.

Could be they're trying to trick me, but why would they? Not like anyone wants anything from me except conspicuous conformity. And sure as hell, there's nothing subtle about them. They pounce immediately when something's perceived amiss. So far, though, nobody's here except me and the cockroaches.

And the audiostick.

The logo on it hints at its corporate party favor origins. Top of the line in its day. Only the very best for MetraGlobal Bank.

So okay. Took a deep breath, pressed ON—and it worked!

Even has a tiny speaker. Soon as I found the playback button, I pressed it and shoved the audiostick's speaker nearly into my ear. At first I thought nothing had been recorded. All I heard was static. Then, spoken in an urgent whisper, this:

"My name is Philippa Flynn. I am—I *was*—senior assistant vice president of investment risk management at MetraGlobal Bank in New York. I've been abducted and I believe I'm going to be killed because I've seen a face I recognize. Robert Strauss—I met him recently at a Georgica Corporation audit board meeting. He was with one of the directors, and he's seen me, too. In this horrible place. But he wasn't a prisoner like me. Dear god, I understand now. It's about—"

And there she stops. That's all she said.

Don't know if this little black stick, Philippa's gift to me, will matter. But at least it works. Has loads of storage left. It'll take a kinetic recharge, too, which means if I'm careful I can keep it functioning in here indefinitely.

So okay. My name is Jamie Gwynmorgan and this is AF1.

Whenever the hell that is. Wherever the hell this is.

❖

Still AF1.

Can't sleep.

Been counting circles—the small hand-and-finger twirls that

recharge Audy the audiostick. Also making sure I stay curled toward the wall, back to the cams, so they can't see what I'm doing. Count just hit a thousand.

Heh. *My* count. *My* thousand.

I wish I could tell you I'd been tough enough to count for myself right from the start. Truth is, I don't dare stop obeying *their* counts. I've been lost in *their* counts for so long that whole stretches of my life *before* have faded into their fog, and I'm left with just my blurry, disoriented *WHY?*

In my defense, counting's hard and memories ebb when you're locked down twenty-four seven in a pair of adjoined galvannealed steel boxes, those prefab things loaded six to a truck and sent off unnoticed for quick installation in obscure abandoned warehouses.

The one that's the inner cell is older, about five feet by ten feet, hot as hell, rusting gray walls perpetually wet with condensing humidity. They run a buzzy hissing sound constantly, too dissonant to harbor figments of voices or melodies. No window in here, either—only a caged air vent above a solid steel door still implacably sturdy despite its rust. An exceedingly slimy shower occupies a back corner.

The attached outer cell—same width, some six feet long—is also windowless. Here resides the elliptical exercise machine on which I'm forced to slog. A small pipe runs from the elliptical's drive housing to the outer cell's side wall. Contains a power line, probably, linked to an inverter somewhere nearby, which means they're forcing me to generate electricity. And, of course, they're forcing me to wear myself out.

The outer cell has a second door with a peephole, always blocked, and a food port autohatch. The entire world lies on the other side of that door, but all I see, blink-of-an-eye-briefly twice a day, is a sliver of the wide gray corridor where those screams, I believe Philippa Flynn's screams, reverberated.

An always-on ceiling light circles the outer cell camera dome and an air vent runs high across most of the wall above the door—larger than the vent in the inner cell, with a fan inside it that puffs weakly at my back when I step onto the elliptical. Despite the louder hissing sound, this little bit of extra light and air in the outer cell makes working the elliptical almost appealing.

In here, the suffocating inner cell, the only air and light come through that undersized vent over the door and the inch-high space underneath. Even so, some things are obvious. Such as, I'm not the cell's first occupant. The scratches on the wall tell me that, though I can't decipher anything in them but misery. Or maybe madness.

Once or twice, I've pick up faint whiffs of something industrial. Diesel maybe. More often I smell salt marsh, which helps account for the corrosion. Add in steel that was never properly galvannealed and certainly hasn't been maintained, sloppy welding practices, poor choice of filler metal, relentless heat—and no wonder the seams of this shithole bubble with pits and rust.

For a few seconds in what I assume is the mornings, I've taken to staring at the cankered weld seam next to the toilet, black in the dimness as it turns and snakes upward to fuse the cell's shower unit to the rear wall, and, in what passes for hope, I succumb to a fantasy about leg-pressing my way out of here.

I imagine my back against the bottom of the steel bunk frame, my legs pushing. I imagine the power I have is power enough and the steel wall bends and I squeeze through into the chase behind the cell—a chase I damn well know is back there; I can tell from how the plumbing's laid out.

Then reality bites. The steel's gotta be twelve-gauge, for chrissake, structurally braced every foot or so, and behind it probably an inch of polyiso bonded to corrugated steel facing. And I'm trying to deform this with my body alone?

I'm reasonably robust—got the long, strong muscles that come with height, plus a decade of using them in rabid daily workouts that've kept me even-keeled first in school and then doing what's mostly a desk job. But even if I managed to kick loose four feet of weld seam, how in this lifetime do I produce the roughly twelve tons of force I'd need to put a forty-five-degree displacement across three feet of carbon steel? Answer: I don't. Not without some sort of additional power which…I…do…not…have.

Anyway, that's all moot, because somebody or something watches and listens all the time. Every minute. Can't tell whether it's bioware or software, but they *notice*. Which I've found out the hard way. As in don't exhibit curiosity about anything.

Curiosity will get you zapped with an electric shock delivered remotely to a small plate on the choke collar around your neck—just like a dog's—that's too snug to pull off. And since once they zap you they have to replace the used-up battery by temporarily removing the collar, they toss in a pummeling for the disruptive behavior of having forced them to interact with you.

And god help you if you then dare to screech what's really on what's left of your mind—like WHO ARE YOU PEOPLE AND WHAT THE FUCK DO YOU WANT WITH ME? That's when they follow up your collar-zap by shocking you with a handheld electrolaser till you're lost in tonic spasms and soaked in your own piss. Then a custodian robot hauls you off—the custodians do almost all the heavy lifting—and you get a lengthy, uncomfortable lesson about their rules.

Definitely not worth it, especially since after all that you can't see anything much from under the hood over your head, only a flash or two of custodian appendages. Actual human beings remain hidden in unmarked black uniforms and surgical masks and wraparound eyewear and boonie hats.

Nor will anyone respond to anything you ask them. Regardless of how much you apologize for losing your cool. Regardless of how pathetically you beg. Only the lesson matters:

DO *WHAT* YOU ARE TOLD *WHEN* YOU ARE TOLD

DO NOT SPEAK UNLESS SPOKEN TO

And then they shoot you up with some kind of pharma. Maybe just so you lose time, who the hell ever knows how much time. Or maybe, if you've really irritated them, they'll get you addicted to something long enough that when they take it away you're sick as shit for who the hell ever knows how much time.

Makes the guards pretty much just another species of machine, irretrievably indifferent like the custodians and the square, squat meals-on-wheels contraptions that deliver what passes for food.

Haven't seen a guard's face yet. At least not that I can remember.

I want to see people, hear people, talk to people.

And god oh god, I want this awful, ugly noise to stop.

It *never* fucking stops. Philippa Flynn's clamorous exit was a rare rupture in the ceaseless buzzy hissing, though occasionally I pick up "natural" sounds—vague rumbles of thunder, rain drumming on a distant metal roof. And a faraway, low thumping—almost an infrasound—that suggests a helicopter. Sometimes I think I hear a guard's passing footfalls while I'm "working" on their goddamn elliptical, but maybe I'm imagining that.

I crave a real live human voice. I crave real live human laughter.

Though I don't lack for the spoken word. A computer-generated voice—almost male-sounding—commands me awake every morning. "DETAINEE, YOU HAVE TEN SECONDS TO STAND AND STATE YOUR IDENTIFICATION NUMBER—NINE, EIGHT..."

Since I've learned too well that they're not fucking around, when the cell voice intones "ZERO," my feet are standing precisely on the worn red footprints long ago stenciled onto the floor.

A few minutes later, the inner cell door clanks open as the food port autohatch swings down and the meals-on-wheels machine rolls up to the outer cell door with the day's first meal-ready-to-eat, invariably one of the cold entrées. (And hey, just so you know, if I ever get the fuck out of here, I will never eat alt-tuna again.)

Too soon after that, it's "DETAINEE, YOU HAVE TEN SECONDS TO PLACE YOUR MEAL PACKAGING ON THE OUTER CELL DOOR FOOD PORT AND ASSUME YOUR WORK POSITION—NINE, EIGHT..."

And onto the elliptical I step. Whenever I'm too slow, I'm threatened. Beeping first—two short, one long, two short. This sequence repeats three times with maybe a five-second delay between each repetition. If I haven't speeded up by the third round, it's "DETAINEE, YOU HAVE TEN SECONDS TO ACCELERATE YOUR PACE—NINE, EIGHT..."

I have no actual memory of the consequences of failing to move the pedals fast enough, but the few times I've heard those words, I react instantly, involuntarily. An electric claw grabs my crotch and I'm impaled, fire tentacling into my gut, down my legs, though my chest, my arms, tightening around my throat.

All in my head, entirely prompted by the cell voice, but I'm sweating, shivering, on the precipice of panic. And I fucking crank those pedals faster, faster, until the fire ebbs and the claw lets me go.

I get a break after, well, I'm guessing more than two hours, less than three. Just enough time to pee, rest briefly on the cell bunk, and refill the water bottle the cell voice commands me to carry to "work" on the elliptical.

Then another shift, another break, another shift, followed by the day's only other MRE, which precedes another three shifts. I'm shut away in the inner cell after that, ordered to return the water bottle to its slot in the back wall's dispensing unit, then brush my teeth with toothbrush and paste from another slot, returning the toothbrush in "... NINE, EIGHT..." By the time it's over, all I care about is sleep.

Periodically, the pattern alters with an announcement: "DETAINEE, YOU WILL SHOWER IN TEN SECONDS—NINE, EIGHT..."

This means tug off the bobos and the yellow spandex top and bottom that are the only clothes I have, scoop up the glop of liquid soap oozing out of yet another slot, and wash and rinse everything, including the spandex, in a few minutes under tepid, sulfurous water gurgling pathetically from a rusting fixture.

Or it's "DETAINEE, YOU WILL WIPE DOWN YOUR CELL IN TEN SECONDS— NINE, EIGHT…" So I scoop up a glop of ineffectual cleanser and a sponge from, yep, another slot, and get it done aysap before returning the sponge.

I have the strange yellow spandex clothes and slip-on shoes. I have the collar around my neck. During my time on the elliptical, I have a plastic water bottle. And that's all. The rest, such as it is, gets dispensed to me for as little time as possible and all utensils must be returned to whichever hole in the back wall they came from.

The worst part of this remorseless goosestep of demand and threat is that I'm clueless about *when*—no sense of day or night, nothing about the date or the day of the week or, god help me, even what year I'm in.

I have no doubt that's on purpose. They want me disoriented. Best way to turn a brain to mush. So they've made sure I have precious little to go by.

Although there's no mirror in here, I can feel how my hair is shorter than *before*. Yet that knowledge is worthless. For all I know, they slipped me a roofie three days ago, cut my hair then, and I just don't remember.

Nor can I get hints from my menstrual cycle, since I lost it years ago and its replacement, a Purple Heart, is less than helpful.

Only option I can think of: count. I've tried counting sleep and MREs. Two MREs, each preceding three shifts on the elliptical, equal one day, which is followed by a chance to sleep. After a few rounds of frenetic paranoia too extravagant even for me, I now choose not to ponder the possibility that they're bothering to dick with the lengths of my shifts.

I've lacked an implement to scratch a count of MRE pairs on the wall, so I've attempted it with my fingernails along the edge of the bed frame. Trouble is, chunks of time are missing—lost to beatings and pharma. And after their lessons about the rules, I've ended up in different cells. I can tell by the disparate rust patterns on the walls.

But this audiostick changes everything. I can keep a reliable count with Audy. Just curl up like always when it's time to sleep, my back to the cams—only now I whisper, a scant whisper low in my throat, as much vibration as sound and hidden from *their* microphone by their own damn buzzy hissing noise.

And I say the day, starting with AF1. Plus maybe I can record what I manage to remember of *before* and listen to it later...

❖

Am I crazy to be thinking so much about my last day of *before*?

I remember kissing Del like always and leaving the house that November morning. I remember where they grabbed me, about halfway between the house and the train station. Lots of bushes along the street—a good place for whisking someone away unseen.

Remembering, I get fucking angry at myself because I damn well should've respected my instincts about that van coming up too slowly behind me. But I'd spent years teaching myself to disregard those old impulses, no longer relevant in the ninety percent safe world where I'd gotten too comfortable.

Even when the van didn't roll on by like it should have, I told myself, "Relax, they're just gonna ask for directions," although I did open the little hatch on my wristcom that protects the panic button from inadvertently transmitting false alarms.

Thank god. Because once they attacked, they moved with stunning speed, and suddenly I was off-balance, barely able to press the damn button before I was shut down by three, maybe four dudes wearing black balaclavas.

Del knew what was happening, more or less, because my panic button raises holy hell all over the place all at once, automatically transmitting and remote-storing everything recorded by every device in my possession. Altogether a paltry trail to follow, but it was the best I could do.

Del's voice—shouting at me to tell her what's wrong—was the last thing I heard. At least, I remind myself over and over and over, I had a chance to warn her.

I know that up to my final instant of consciousness anyway, Del was safe.

I have faith—I *must keep faith*—that when she realized I was in trouble, Del followed the protocol we'd long ago agreed on: secure the house, call in backup, punch an ammo clip into the pistol I keep in a drawer next to our bed so she can defend herself.

And I know the entire clan went into emergency mode to protect her and themselves and to find me.

No luck, though, on that last score. Oh god, how long have I been in this nightmare that won't let me wake up? A month? A year?

❖

AF2.

When I finally fell asleep last night, I dreamed about Del. First time I've remembered a dream since—don't know when. Seemed like a protracted dream, but all I recollect is what Del said right before the cell voice bullied me awake: "Hide it! Hide it well!"

I had tears in my eyes when I opened them because the life that had been real to me for more than ten years is only a dream now.

Then my stomach corkscrewed. Hide it *where*?

Damn. Finding a secret place for Audy should've been my first priority as soon as I got near enough to understand what it was. But I was too busy talking to it. Clutched it in my hand next to my mouth like a kid sucking her thumb and whispered till I faded out. Twice.

Had no chance through this morning's countdowns to locate a better alternative, so I tucked Audy under the skinny foam mattress I sleep on. Out of camera sight, sure, but right the fuck there for them to find just by flipping over the fucking mattress. Spent my shifts today making sure I pedaled fast enough, studiously servile.

But shit—what if this choke collar has more built into it than a zapper? What if it or maybe this spandex crap they've got me wearing does biomonitoring—heart rate, blood pressure, body temperature? How about detecting stress or tension or fear?

I got through today without incident. But what if they've spotted something? What if they're watching more closely now?

So here I am, curled fetal on the bunk facing the wall, whispering to Audy while I scout the weld seam where bunk and wall attach with my right hand. I can feel the grit of rusting steel on my fingers. Think, dammit! Somewhere in here there's gotta be a space just big enough, just invisible enough, just accessible enough, just camera-foolable enough for Audy.

Gotta be.

I guess I must be praying. Don't know what else to call this unutterable *please please please* that won't stop sniveling in my head.

CHAPTER TWO

please please please

AF8.

Finally, I remembered a little crevice I'd spotted some time before Audy arrived—a couple of corrosion-gutted inches along the weld seam on the far side of the sink. Best I can tell, the sink blocks the cameras' view of it.

Blew it off back when I first saw it since it was on the side wall and could never aid my delusion of escape into the chase behind the cell's rear wall. Took me the whole morning of AF3 to recall it was even there. During the MRE break, I checked it out—room enough, not too gritty inside, small entry point, so reasonably disguised. During the following break, I managed to slip Audy into it.

Sounds straightforward enough, but not in this pisshole.

Not if you fuck up like I did and fail to realize that Audy would slip too deep into the crevice and getting her out again would risk everything.

Because they don't watch just me, they watch my patterns. And they forecast my patterns, too.

Nothing else explains the interventions—"DETAINEE, YOU HAVE TEN SECONDS TO…"—every time I do anything for too long or that's even slightly atypical. Like check out a lock mechanism. Or the camera dome in the ceiling. Or the elliptical drive wheel. Or the outer cell door autohatch.

No question they've deployed predictive analytics to sift through detainee video feeds for behavioral patterns. Easy enough to pop an alert at any deviation from whatever parameters they've selected. Hell, the software probably sends alerts directly to the custodian robots, always the first to show up when shit goes down.

Means Audy's gotta be retrievable within the parameters they've set for me. Which translates to sleight of hand, quick and easy.

I knew that.

Knew if I focused too much, too long on that space alongside the sink where Audy's hidden, in mere minutes I'd have a custodian robot in my damn face.

Did I mention how much I despise custodian robots?

Only three feet high when one rolls in—a flat, gray body bristling with cameras and sensors, weapons tucked away, looking like a really big, headless western deer tick atop six legs tightly folded and refolded.

Then it rises up freaky fast, usually on three of its solenoid-driven appendages, while the other three instantly extend into impossibly long, strong, hex-articulated arms with impossibly long, strong weaponized claws ready to deliver an electrolaser shock or pepper gas—or a bullet. Or pin me to the wall. Or fist up to pound me to the floor and then deftly apply shackles that come out of nowhere. When a custodian does three-and-three like that, its "arms" can easily reach higher than the cell's seven-foot ceiling.

Which is the good news. If a human guard shows up, the "incident" has "escalated" into another brutal lesson about the rules, another dose of their pharma. And then I'm lost for god knows how long and have to somehow find AF1 all over again.

To avoid that, at the end of AF3 I crawled onto the bunk without Audy—because I'd begun to appreciate how important avoiding that really is. Thanks to Philippa Flynn, I now grasp what the humans here *really* mean when they're teaching one of their lessons: if you identify anything about us—the way Philippa Flynn identified Robert Strauss— we will kill you to protect ourselves.

Shit.

Years ago, back when Audy was new and leading edge, I was hell-bent, feral almost. I attacked hopelessness locked and loaded—a frontal assault. Because if it's hopeless what've I got to lose, right? So of course I should be dead. And I was, briefly, right around the time that Audy was new and leading edge. But I ended up staying—

And I ended up with a very great deal to lose. I ended up with love. With a family—more than a decade with Del and Lynn and their extraordinarily generous, embracing family.

And I have no idea why that was taken from me. Or by whom. Or why I've end up in this black hole.

But I can tell you it's the sort of black hole that requires capital investment.

Corporate? I imagine Philippa would say so.

Or maybe a government. Maybe a rogue operation or some secret agency enforcing laws nobody's ever heard of.

Whoever they are, they have hierarchy, bureaucracy, robots and surveillance and behavioral analysis apps, guards in uniforms. They have deep pockets.

Maybe they have deep purposes, too, because I'm not the only one here—as Philippa's frantic screams and recorded whispers testify. But I have no doubt whoever, whatever is doing this wants me and anybody else locked away here to feel profoundly isolated.

I'd also bet my life Audy's against their rules.

And there's the rub. I *am* betting my life.

Five days ago, back on AF3 (yeah, I've managed to count that much), I realized I'd bumbled into an opportunity to *unbet* my life when I couldn't retrieve Audy from her crevice.

What the hell, I thought. Maybe some part of me knew to pick that crevice on purpose so I'd lose Audy in there and not have to risk getting caught disobeying their rules.

Just leave her, hope she's never discovered, play dumb if she is. Del and Lynn will find me. They will. They will. Thinking that gave me relief. I felt the muscles in my neck, my shoulders relax a little.

Okay. I leave her there.

Whereupon, on AF3, I should've fallen asleep.

But I didn't.

Fifteen or whatever fucking hours trudging on the damn elliptical and the respite of risk reduced, but I couldn't close my eyes. I couldn't breathe. And some other me just would not shut the fuck up.

C'mon, what if I lose my count without Audy?

C'mon, what if talking to Audy, being able to listen to my own words, is the only reason I'm almost capable again of rational thought?

C'mon, what if obeying their fucking rules makes no difference because they're going to kill me anyway, like Philippa Flynn?

C'mon, what if the words Audy records are the sum of my whole existence from here on in?

Prior to Audy, while I lay on the bunk at the end of my shifts, I'd squint at the wall a few inches from my nose and try to find "my" splotch of rust among all the other splotches. Mostly I couldn't see shit, but I'd make a mark anyway with my fingernail in what seemed like the right place—my meager attempt at a count, an *orderly* scratch, dammit, amidst the insane chaos of scratches and scrapes put there by untold others.

Never mind that my scratches are, so far anyway, inscrutable even to me. Which ones are mine? In how many cells have I done this? And what's the *total* count, huh? How fucking long have I fucking been here?

At the end of AF3, I ripped at the wall same as the others had—to squelch the *please please please* that refused to stop trumpeting in my head.

I'll cop to praying before Audy arrived—if that's what the *please please please* ought to be called. And yeah, sometimes it got out of hand, escalated into furious rage or hysterical self-pity, and, inevitably, a custodian robot check. That last time, somewhere back there in the fog, also attracted a Homo sapiens guard, followed by yet another ruthless lesson about the rules.

I remember it better than the other times earlier because this last time was when I caught on to her—to Caprice, Queen of Vagary, blowing in to remind me of my place. She gave it away when I heard human laughter, a sound I so, so yearned for, while a pair of guards experimented with how high they'd have the custodian hitch up the chain tethering my shackled wrists to the ceiling.

After that I banished *please please please*. But five nights ago when I knew I had to hide Audy, there it was again. I could almost hear Caprice's mockery. *Nah*, she sneers with backhanded disinterest, *you want more than your share. Fortune finds the way to fifty-fifty, fool, and you know neither what nor how to count.*

Five nights ago, when I couldn't retrieve Audy, I got exactly what I fucking wished for. Too bad I wished wrong.

At least I managed not to attract them by wailing in a demented frenzy. But, jeezus, at times I came close, digging along the weld seam in the small area blocked by my back from the camera lenses, a desperate perversion of counting that ceased only when I eventually fell asleep.

This became my nightly ritual. The watchers must have noticed my bloody fingertips, but I suppose they didn't care. And then, on what I believe was AF6, there it was, not part of the corroded area at all, but a couple inches beyond it, still in the area shielded from the cams by my back, still within easy reach of my hand: another crevice.

I lay there, my hand statue-still, in a kind of mental paralysis for, well, who knows how long? I thought I must be hallucinating.

But it was real. A fluke born of happenstance and hornswoggle. And I'm not the first person to find it, either.

Both the cell wall and the inner edge of the steel bunk frame welded to it have very slight deformations that, by chance, more or less align to create a skinny, slightly skewed vesica piscis-shaped gap that the cell manufacturer's robo-welder missed. Instead of rewelding, the manufacturer covered over this gap, my precious Vesica the Gap, with caulk. No doubt the caulk was supposed to be tamper-proof.

I suspect the previous tenant, like me, discovered Vesica because the caulk covering her is not remotely tamper-proof. It's supple, its layer of original gray paint intact, and like my predecessor, I've figured out how to tuck it over Vesica so arcanely that even a guard's finger swipe will very likely miss it. You have to know just where to look, just how to poke and dig to open this secret chamber.

Goddamn, Caprice. *Goddamn.*

On AF6, thanks to Vesica the Gap, I decided to retrieve Audy. Took me five tries over two days—sometimes girls play hard to get. But now, on AF8, she's here, about to be snugged into her new home.

❖

AF11.

Zero dark thirty—that's all I can tell you. The day's countdowns will start soon. I can feel it. So I gotta hurry.

I've just dreamed about Del again. Or maybe I woke into, well, into the memory. Because, dream or awake, I've remembered a crisp, colorful, tactile swath of *before*.

I was home with her, in bed with her in our first-floor part of the two-family she and her sister Lily own at the end of Birch Lane. The display on the far wall read 23:14 hours.

"Where'd you drift off to?" Del demanded, and oh god, I remember her bottomless dark eyes narrowing the intensity of her into a beam. Directed at me.

"Sorry…" I'd missed most of what had led up to her unusually soaring *"…And guess what!"*

Depending on context, I can see the and-guess-what glow before Del speaks—sometimes well before, sometimes only seconds before. And sometimes, like this time, when I see that glow I space out. We both know it's because I want her to come get me.

And that generally happens when Del pushes it. Thing is, Del pushes it a lot.

She relishes her work as an environmental engineer who restores messed-up waterways and wetlands, but her heart lies in a much broader vision: the Wilderness Web Coalition. She even wrangled an environmental economics PhD to help her hone that vision and insulate herself from certain classes of ad hominem attack. "I might be the bitch they say I am," she likes to quip, "but when it comes to the Wilderness Web, they can't call me ignorant or ill-informed."

The Wilderness Web is Del's baby, no question. Its politicking and strategizing consumes much of her time, but it also energizes her.

And I gotta say, Del's energy is a thing of beauty. As well as contagious. You think you're sitting back watching her, enjoying her, and the next thing you know you've volunteered to help her change the world.

After living with her for ten years, I've seen this happen to a fair number of people. How it happens depends entirely on the individual. In my case—and mine is the most impossibly lucky case because she married me—it happened, continues to happen, with her luminous "And guess what!"

"Okay, what?" I asked a bit too reluctantly.

"Monday, Monday," she singsonged as she rolled lightly on top of me, eyes flaring, all her convexes tantalizing mine. "I haven't even gotten to the punch line, Ms. Gwynmorgan."

Del kissed me then and I melted into it, wide-awake at last and defying earth's gravity for hers. "My...apologies...Doctor...Sabellius."

"Mmm hmm." Another kiss, deeper this time.

"You already know...unhh...I'll say yes."

"I want you to *want* to say yes."

I remember caressing the firm curves of her abdominals, richly caramel in the soft bedroom light, then her hips as she pressed against me, pledging a galvanic journey to eruption. "I love when you want me to want to say yes."

She circled, centered, then stilled. "But?"

I closed my eyes. How does she always know?

She kissed me again. "Out with it."

Sigh. And then my truth. "I love that your work is getting the respect it deserves, Del. About fucking time. I know how important it is. And I certainly don't mind playing your butch-tinted eye candy. With the right crowd it's a gas. But god, I have Hazelton project deadlines up the wazoo, and for the last six months these events of yours—" I admit to indulging in a melodramatic groan. "The politicking, especially with the professionals, has been—"

"The price of coalition, my sweet." Her finger traced a delicate path down the center of my chest...down...down. "But I'm keeping my promise not to join any more boards—"

I groaned again, anticipating the worst. "You do get that Lynn Hillinger is the *only* politician I can stomach, right?"

"Of course. Lesbian version of a bromance." Del laughed. I love the sound of her laugh, how it lights her face and sparks her eyes and rolls into her words. "Anyway, Lynn's not really a politician. The senator thing is a disguise—" She put up a hand to keep me from interrupting. "If it's any consolation, everyone will be there, including Lynn. Plus it's not till January. Three months should be plenty of time to work out any conflicts with your Hazelton project. And if you're feeling particularly dour and hermitudinous, we can make it a day trip."

"Everyone" meant the family, so certainly I'd go. "Okay, which night in January?"

"Nope, afternoon." Del straightened up, straddling my hips. "This one's a speech. By me. To the United Nations General Assembly. They want to hear about why a Wilderness Web matters."

"The UN?" I felt my eyes widen along with my grin. "Our very own Adele Sabellius? All by her lonesome?"

"Yep. I'll have twenty minutes to explain why we risk the survival of the planet as we know it without a Wilderness Web. I figure six minutes for that, fourteen to tell the buggers how to finance it on a global scale."

"Wow," I remember saying as I lifted upward to kiss her. "The UN. And the shortest synopsis of your dissertation ever, I presume."

"Yes, ma'am. Wilderness Web for Dummies."

"My god, you won't be able to keep me away." I meant it; watching Adele Sabellius when she's on—and, oh man, will she be on for this one—is a transcendent experience. Every time. Plus she's drop-dead fucking gorgeous; no one on earth is more fun to look at.

"I love you, Jamie Gwynmorgan." Del pressed close to me again, but her words were slipping away. I tried, oh god how I tried to answer her, hold on to her.

Then my eyes opened to claustral, rusting swelter—the cell. And the realization that it was all only a dream of a memory. No matter how real it felt, the most it can be is a memory. I wanted to scream. And cry. Because it was so real. *Del* was so real.

Somehow, though, I've held it all in—the grief, the pain, the outrage—and here I am telling my dream of a memory to Audy. Because if I have a recording of how I remember it, immediate and so vivid, that's almost like being home again, like touching Del again.

CHAPTER THREE

two...zero...seven...six

AF20.

The day following my dream of Del, I passed out. That was AF11.

On AF18, my world turned over. Literally. But in the churn I found a trace of hope. So I'm making sure Audy has a record of the how and why of AF18—a chronology. And that chronology began on AF11.

One instant I'm lumbering along on the elliptical, the next I'm flat on my back blinking at a nausea-inducing dazzle.

Might've been the swelter—the cell's hotter than I can ever recall. Or maybe it was the MRE I'd eaten an hour earlier, which tasted odd. Also—and I don't like to admit this, it's fucking scary—I'd been losing weight, approaching physical exhaustion.

Splatted on the floor, I never even registered the cell's warning beeps and failed to obey the order to resume work on the elliptical. All I could do was roll over, puke, and pass out again.

A custodian's jabs brought me back to full consciousness, but when it demanded "DETAINEE, STATE YOUR IDENTIFICATION NUMBER," I vomited on one of its wheel-foot-claw thingies. Kept my eyes closed, too, hoping to spare myself another lesson, another round of pharma.

Little bit later I hear "Shit" from a distinctly human male voice.

Told myself, *No, don't look.*

When I smelled bourbon-breath, I realized he'd leaned down. Felt his hand grab my jaw, so I played dead and didn't resist as he shimmied my head, which felt like it had been sledgehammered.

"Infirmary?" he asked, jittery. Then, "Roger, on our way."

Did I know already that this joint has an infirmary?

The robot lifted me, dry heaving all the way, and I wanted to resist—my eyes opened, my mouth opened, but my *NO!* evaporated as

I caught sight of a military stretcher basket right before I landed in it. Soon the custodian had me strapped in from shoulders to ankles. Scary how agile custodian claws can be.

God, my head hurt, but I knew enough to mostly keep my eyes closed. Nausea notwithstanding, the basket's movement helped me reboot mentally. A stretcher in motion meant they were taking me out of that fiendish cell into the corridor I'd glimpsed so often through the food hatch. A rush of almost fresh air tempted my eyes open—to a ferocious blaze of lights zooming by overhead. I was in the corridor unhooded and almost fully conscious.

You know how you can see things slitty-eyed, from behind your eyelashes? That's how I counted something like a dozen cell doors as the custodian carried me through what I realized is a huge space plenty wide enough for a row of prefab cells on either side of a center corridor.

Overall, I heard more than I saw. Doors clattered open and slammed shut a moment later, then more smooth motion, more cell doors, more slam and lock. When my head angled higher than my feet, I peeked again. The ever-versatile custodian had tilted the basket to carry me quite smoothly down a flight of brick-and-concrete stairs.

And I thought, *Hey, this stairway's supposed to be open-air*, because, damn, I recognized its red brick and concrete. In that moment, I believed unreservedly I'd been on that very spot before. A back-in-the-day *before*.

At the bottom of the stairs, amid more slam-and-lock racket, the tang of salt marsh suppressed all other scent, and an actual breeze skimmed my face. Low tide, and close by, too. A raw ravening broiled my chest, scorched my throat. I gulped back a kind of delirium as the *please please please* screamed, screamed in my head to go home.

"Got one for ya," I heard the guard say from far away.

Then I heard a female human. "Null Custodian Seven, prepare detainee in bed one."

Soon the robot had me out of the stretcher basket, onto a hospital bed, stripped naked. A shackle clamped around my left wrist, another took my right ankle. I'd gone very still, concerned that they'd picked up on my lemme-go-home freakout and might bring on their pharma. I slit one eye open to see the robot wheel away, leaving me uncovered.

Both the guard and the woman he spoke to followed the custodian out of the room, which gave me a little time to *bree-ee-eathe* and dare a surreptitious glance around. Medical gear, cabinets, several other beds, all empty. So much for making contact with another prisoner.

Next to my bed stood one of those emergency room multi-scanners, the one-stop shop used by medical people to determine what's broken, bleeding, bursting, blighted. On the ceiling, a camera dome kept watch.

Partly because I was still nauseous, partly because I was shit-scared, I mostly kept my eyes shut after that first quick lookabout. Better they assume I'm more out of it than I am.

But I briefly peeked again when I heard someone return—a sound easy to detect without the cell's interminable buzzy-hissy noise. Anonymous behind surgical mask and darkened eyewraps like all the other Homo sapiens, the infirmary woman strode over to me and, without a word, initiated the scanner.

She worked deliberately, thoroughly. She didn't have to touch me, but to my surprise, her fingers lingered almost gently at the old through-and-through puncture scars on my hands as she scanned. When she finished, she removed the shackle on my left wrist and cleaned the area. A quick sting came next, followed by cold liquid invading my forearm, then she inserted a catheter. I glimpsed her adjust the bed herself so my head and knees were slightly raised and, finally, cover me with a sheet.

Carefully, I dared another peek of her departing back before looking at what I feared most—the IV line invading my wrist. I contemplated ripping it out, an old instinct because I simply do not have normal responses to pharma—especially not the pharma these people mess with. Even at low doses, I typically hallucinate.

But I'd pay a horrific price for even touching that needle.

Had to start talking to myself almost out loud. *C'mon, the bag looks like nothing more than water, saline, and glucose, probably really is just for hydration.* Hell, if the stuff was gonna make me crazy, it was already too late. And I'd know one way or the other pretty damn quick.

Do a ten-count and bree-ee-eathe… And, oh god, the last time I felt that comfortable was at home in bed with Del. I fell asleep before my count reached five.

The final fragments of a real live conversation between two real live human beings woke me.

"…Concussion…weight   loss…nutritional   deficits…"   The woman's voice epitomized medical neutrality. Then I heard a man—not the guard who'd escorted me to the infirmary, someone else—say, "…not on the helo list and, according to this, two zero seven six should have been moved to a full sustain protocol more than two months ago…"

Goddamn.

That *means* something.

I know damn well what—who—two zero seven six is, and I soon learned firsthand that "full sustain protocol" means marginally better treatment, more food.

As for "the helo list," well, given the echoes of military cadence and discipline exhibited by the cell voice, not to mention the godawful MREs, I'm betting "helo" means helicopter. Haven't figured out what "on the helo list" means, but the words make my teeth grind.

I admit I hoped for a conversation with Infirmary Woman. Yet in the seven days they kept me in a cell next to the infirmary, I never exchanged a single word with another human being. Infirmary Woman checked me out daily, but the cell voice always prepped me with strict instructions, one of which was to keep my gaze down and DO NOT SPEAK.

I resisted almighty temptation and followed those orders scrupulously when Infirmary Woman entered to conduct her daily checkup.

At least the infirmary cell, constructed of concrete block, was comparatively clean, cool, and dry. No buzzy-hissy sound at all. Brighter, too. One wall even had a window, though the glass was heavily frosted.

I also got clean spandex to wear, which beats being naked in a climate rife with mosquitoes and midges. Also three decent-sized meals a day—one of them hot, of more or less real food. Lots of alt fare, like you'd expect in an institutional chow line, but way better than any MRE. And the cell had, essentially, no regimen other than the lights going on in the morning, off at night. They left me to sleep until I woke up on my own. The cell's shower not only had genuine hot water, I was able to use it once a day.

I took every shower I could.

And did lots of cogitating.

When a power immensely greater than you whisks you out of everything that makes sense and throws you into such disorienting strangeness that only uncertainty is certain, it takes a while to comprehend what a pattern is. That's especially true if the strangeness is stressful and cruel.

But I recognized one pattern. The quiet, cool infirmary cell would be no more than a temporary interlude. Only issue was whether they'd put me back in the cell where I'd stashed Audy or put me somewhere else.

I tried to bracket that worry and mull broader questions—chiefly, where am I and what'll it take to get the hell out of here even if I've lost Audy forever?

Frosted or not, it helped to have a window. I mean, outdoors and real daylight just on the other side of glass I could *touch*! Spent most of my time in the infirmary cell with my hand on that window. Based on the way the light shifted and the intensity of the heat on the glass, I concluded the window faced south.

Useless knowledge perhaps, but knowing anything at all of the world beyond the rusting steel box was so intoxicating that I made myself memorize a list of what else I've learned.

One: I'm treated better if I act broken. Not merely a little broken, thoroughly broken. They relent some when they believe I've surrendered to their absolute dominance. Upside: with the extra food and rest resulting from my collapse, I've had a chance to get stronger; exhaustion no longer completely fuddles my brain.

Two: this place has hardly any guards. They dutifully deploy multiple layers of security, but rely too much on surveillance machinery and automation. Potential upside: automation ain't anywhere near perfect, yet it breeds human complacency anyway.

Three: they're already complacent. For instance, they don't care about the condition of their physical infrastructure. Cuz what the hell, their analytic software will snap an alert way before a detainee can pop a lock or diddle a camera dome, right? So, another potential upside: automation requires electricity; electricity can be cut off. Or short-circuited.

Four: I'm in a coastal location. Maybe a barrier island? Would explain the rust, the mold, the smell of salt marsh. Upside: I have a small clue about where I am.

Five: they're using helicopters. That sound I'd notice through the hissing noise really was helos. Heard it quite clearly in the infirmary cell. And those whiffs of diesel could be the helos' fuel. Upside: maybe I can catch a ride back to civilization someday soon.

Six: they have a helo list that apparently I'm not on. Whatever the hell that means.

Seven: Philippa saw someone in this vile place who's *not* a prisoner—Robert Strauss, who's thus an abductor, a bad guy, yes? And who's connected somehow to Georgica Corporation, the largest agricultural resources company in the world and no friend of the Wilderness Web Coalition. Don't know about the upside (or downside) of this, but it damn well means *something*.

Eight: takes big bucks to run an operation like this one that's large enough, sophisticated enough to have helos and infirmaries with multi-scanners. Operations like that leave a sizable wake. Upside: sizable wakes can be hard to hide.

Nine: I know Del and Lynn are turning over every rock and racket they can think of to find me. Which is saying something. Between them, their connections range from plutocrats to social justice activists to prostitutes and gangbangers, and Lynn's chief of staff, Springer Knox, is a fucking blond barracuda. Upside: sooner or later, they'll spot the sizable wake of this place. I hope. I gotta hope.

❖

On AF18, I heard human voices in the hushed infirmary cell area, which I recognized: Infirmary Woman and the same guard who brought me to the infirmary on AF11. I've nicknamed him New South.

Pretty quickly, I grasped that New South had shown up with a custodian robot to transport me somewhere else and that protocol required me to be hooded, but New South hadn't brought one with him.

Oh so politely, Infirmary Woman made clear who was responsible for providing the hood—New South, not her.

"Nobody's even told me where the hell to find 'em," he groused.

Next, I heard Infirmary Woman speak to the robot. "Null Custodian Seven, locate a detainee hood."

New South didn't like the robot's response and swore colorfully. "Yeah. Great. Hoods in Block A. So, how many sally port unlocks? Six? Eight? Been doin' this long enough to know that'll clusterfuck me right past end of shift," he crabbed. "For a frackin' hood."

Infirmary Woman said, "Your call."

New South griped some more. "Shift's over in ten minutes. Ten or fifteen after that, I get my last shot at some Texas Hold 'em before we cycle out tomorrow."

Infirmary Woman sounded almost resentful when she replied. "Lucky you. You'll be home for Easter."

"Yeah, guess so," New South muttered. A brief silence ensued between them until New South asked, "When's Easter again?"

"Just a week from today. March twenty-ninth. Early this year."

Aaand *pop!*

I realized Infirmary Woman had just revealed what day it was and I immediately succumbed to a brainscream—TODAY IS MARCH

TWENTY-SECOND! SUNDAY, MARCH TWENTY-SECOND!—so I missed some of New South's reply.

"Hell's bells," he was bragging when I managed to tune back in. "I got serious plans for all the cheddar I'll be takin' off Kenny tonight."

I split in two; one of me mutely hollered *SUNDAY, MARCH TWENTY-SECOND!* while the other listened intently to New South and Infirmary Woman.

"You mean Mr. Bouchard?" She offered a skittish laugh. "I guess you like to live dangerously."

"Ooh, *Mister* Bouchard," New South teased her, then diddy-bopped back to his brag. "Ah hell, me an' Kenny, we served together. Hoo-rah an' all that. I give him a good run, f'sure. But I whup his poker ass pretty regular, cuz the guy's got a appetite, y'know? 'Tween you 'n' me, 's how I grabbed this gig. 'Sides, he can afford it."

"Well," Infirmary Woman said, sticking to her neutrality, "it's your call about the hood."

"Great," New South proclaimed. "My call is never the fuck mind, custodian."

Seconds passed, more seconds. By this time I've got a mental chant going: *AF Eighteen is Sunday, March twenty-second, AF Eighteen is Sunday, March twenty-second...*

"Uh-oh. You've confused it," Infirmary Woman said.

"Day-yam," New South whined. "That means a whole reboot."

Infirmary Woman said not necessarily and described a workaround that avoids flipping the kill switch. I couldn't see what she showed him, but I heard her say it isn't a full reboot, instead it clears the robot's cache and resets to pause mode until there's a new command.

"Sometimes I think they don't like profanity," Infirmary Woman said, sounding solemn. "Anyway, the trick is to stick with their limited vocabulary. Stuff like 'Halt,' 'Enter sleep mode.' Anything that's on your custodian command card."

And then she warned New South about something she called slump and lump, in which a custodian's appendages slowly droop into stillness. "Stan over in tech calls it 'controlled upright descent mode.' So they don't, like, drop stuff on the stairs," said Infirmary Woman. "If it happens, call tech. Stan gets them back up pretty quick."

"You sayin' they just quit?" New South asked.

"Oh, it used to be much worse," Infirmary Woman told him. "Usually in summer." She described how the custodians would stop recognizing IDs and treat everyone as a detainee, aggressing if they perceived unwillingness to comply with their command. "A couple people got electrolasered bad once trying to flip a custodian's kill switch," she said. "Had to shoot it."

Something New South said that I couldn't quite hear prompted Infirmary Woman's reassurance. "The humidity, according to Stan. Too much moisture glitching their authentication firmware," she said. "Seems they're not as water resistant as advertised. Took tech a while to figure it out, but after inserting desiccant packs and a new program module, it hasn't happened in, like, a year."

Another silence.

"So, uh," New South finally asked, "how do I wake up this one?"

"Any old command'll do," she said. "I mostly use 'Stand by' or 'Resume prior protocol.' Just make sure you start with its full name so it knows it's being commanded. Otherwise it can get stuck all over again."

They finished up with niceties, then New South got his command voice on and intoned, "Null Custodian Seven, resume prior protocol."

Two minutes later, the robot had me shackled and New South ordered me to keep my eyes glued to the ground in front of my feet, on pain of "or I'll personally beat the livin' shit outta you." He also called me a cunt and clamped his hand hard onto the back of my neck, bending me double as I scuttled along in ankle chains, my hands fettered behind my back.

Several hurried rounds of slam-and-lock later, I was outside. In real, live fresh air. Breathe it, I commanded myself. *Bree-ee-eathe...*

Couldn't see much, but I tried to pay attention, tried to count my steps. I smelled lemon citronella. At the very edge of my peripheral vision I noticed the shade of a few trees dapple what seemed like an old parking lot where straggles of grass claimed cracks in the concrete. I saw security fences, layers of them, cutting through a large courtyard, maybe fifty by a hundred yards, with two-story buildings stretching along three sides, all connected by covered walkways—

And god, even though I saw it all either sideways or upside down, I'd swear I recognized those buildings. Upside down or not, they looked exactly like squadbays. Would've sworn the one dead behind me, just visible between my legs as New South marched me eastward, is the very building where years ago I spent three endless months as a Marine Corps recruit.

I shifted my head slightly leftward to see what I could of the fourth side of the courtyard, hoping to figure out if I'd lost my mind or not.

Which is when it happened, in the nanosecond before New South shoved my head farther down and yanked me forward. In that nanosecond, I glimpsed—or hallucinated—the upper floor of the old red brick recruit depot headquarters building, columns and dormers and all, right where it should be.

Some structures were no longer there, and my hallucination included new features, too: an earthwork that blocked my view of the headquarters building's first floor, a wind turbine rising next to it. Tried for another look behind me at Second Recruit Training Battalion's Echo Company squadbay, "my" squadbay, but that Homo sapienshit New South punched me hard in the gut and shoved me forward again.

Probably because he could get the job done quicker than a custodian, he berated me up a flight of red brick and concrete stairs much like the one I saw from the stretcher basket when I was taken to the infirmary—except this stairwell *is* open to the outside. Like it should be, I thought as I understood he was returning me to the same building I'd come from. I began to hope he might be returning me to "my" cell, to Audy.

And, after a couple more gut punches, he did.

Soon as the outer door slammed shut, cell voice took over. "DETAINEE, YOU HAVE TEN SECONDS TO ENTER THE INNER CELL AND STATE YOUR IDENTIFICATION NUMBER—NINE, EIGHT..."

As I stood on the red footprints and waited until the countdown reached zero—for one never interrupts the countdown—I remembered. Lemony scent means southern magnolias in bloom. Spring. *Makes sense. After all, it's Sunday, March 22.*

More than four months since I last saw Del—146 days, actually. Sixty-one days since Del's UN speech. I think. I hope. Because for all I *really* know, it could be that long plus a year, two years, ten—

But shit, to know whether it's been months or, god help me, years, I need to remember. What day of the week was that November sixth, the November sixth when they grabbed me? A Thursday, right?

Jamie Gwynmorgan abducted near her home on Thursday, November six.

Right?

Or Wednesday. Maybe it was Wednesday, November six...

"DETAINEE! STATE YOUR IDENTIFICATION NUMBER IMMEDIATELY!"

I jumped, startled, and answered loudly in the cadence they demand.

Yet suddenly, inexplicably, that's not what my body wanted me to say. I had an almost irresistible urge to tuck my chin, square my shoulders, align my thumbs with nonexistent pant seams, stare dead-eyed straight ahead, and bellow, "Sir! This recruit's identification number is two…zero…seven…six. SIR!"

Now, no matter how often I tell myself this is confirmation bias gone mad, I keep wondering if I'm back on Parris Island.

But hell, how can I trust that? Dicey combination, tired instinct and faded memory and gnawing fear that solitary confinement and very possibly execution have become my inescapable fate.

Bree-ee-eathe…

You see, the thing is, when I was in the infirmary somebody cleaned in here. It's still the same old rust bucket, of course. But the vomit is gone from the outer cell, the floor isn't so slippery, and the shower looks significantly less slime-green. Plus they've replaced the mattress with one that doesn't stink nearly as much.

So once I roiled through *Oh-my-god-I've-been-gone-over-four-months-or-maybe-more-how-much-more?* and *Oh-my-god-what-if-I'm-on-Parris-Island?*, I arrived at *Oh-my-god-they-must've-found-Audy.*

Yet I hadn't been dragged off, beaten, drugged. A good sign, definitely. So I curled up on the bunk, stroked the weld seam and the scratches on the wall. Stuck to my pattern, what they've come to expect from me, and waited for them.

I waited two whole days.

On AF20, Tuesday, March 24, I gradually permitted my fingers to explore the caulk covering Vesica. It seemed intact. I opened her slowly, carefully. *Very* carefully.

Dry inside. And yes, yes, Audy was still in there.

And nobody's dragged me off.

So I hold on to what I now know, hold on for dear fucking life. Today, AF20, has been Tuesday, March 24. And goddamn, what if this is Parris Island, South Carolina?

CHAPTER FOUR

Why does this keep happening to me?

AF22.

Thursday, March 26.

Been thinking since last Sunday—*ha!* love being able to say that, *since last Sunday*. This really could be Parris Island.

When I was barely seventeen, I did boot camp at Parris Island. And, hell, it was waterlogged then. So I wasn't surprised to read somewhere about how the long parade of storms and hurricanes screwed up so many recruit training cycles that about seven years after my time there, which was seven years before I was snatched, the Marine Corps finally decamped.

Last I heard, Parris Island goes mostly underwater during high tides and, as a longtime Superfund site, is off-limits to all except the environmental engineers cleaning up a lengthy list of contaminants. One thing's for sure: the federal government still owns what's left of Parris Island. Which makes it quite viable for the right someone's below-the-radar detention facility.

And while I have to question the reliability of my nanosecond glances, it's curiously consistent with other perceptions.

Notably the heat.

No question it's warmer now. This cell's become a fucking oven. I can scarcely move on the elliptical. Just like an early spring heat wave in South Carolina.

Then there's what I can smell—salt marsh and magnolias. Parris Island's surrounded by salt marsh and in the heart of magnolia country.

So if—if if *if*—this is Parris Island, at least I know where I am.

And if this is Parris Island, I've been imprisoned by an outfit allowed to use government property for their deep purposes, which is unnerving. Because what's going on here is either illegal or damn well should be.

Sure as hell explains the people hiding their faces. They're operating a hush-hush detention center imprisoning at least one person who wasn't arrested, wasn't charged, has never been permitted to talk to anyone, much less a lawyer, since getting whisked off a Massachusetts street.

But I still don't know *why*.

Which likely accounts for my dream last night of going to Great Hill with Del.

We did that a couple of times a month, on weekends not otherwise occupied with Wilderness Web Coalition events or scrambles to meet work deadlines or the occasional dinner party thrown by one of Del's friends. I love those weekends, which I think of as *our* weekends. Friday night out dancing at Demeter, Boston's only true lesbian club, and then we take the car up to Manchester on Saturday morning, returning to Belmont either Sunday or Monday or even Tuesday, depending on our schedules.

Besides Del, everyone I love in this world calls Great Hill home. I can see it now as I lie here: more than a hundred acres of oak and pine forest north of the city high on a granite hill a mile from the sea, surrounded by nearly another 500 acres of conservation land.

And the house sprawled above the clearing, the entire clan inside. I can see Lynn and Rebecca, happy to be out of DC for a few days. And Rebecca's daughter Dana, who married Del's sister Lily, and their girls. And Rebecca's mother Mary, physically frail but sharp as ever. And Lynn's daughter Robin, too, briefly not at work in one of the ERs that Rebecca loves to tell old stories about.

In my dream, we arrived as usual bearing a large box of pastries from the "good" bakery and were greeted in the driveway first by Lily and Dana's youngest, eight-year-old identical twins, who bounded squealing out of the house—"*They're heeere! They're heeere!*"—to hug us, followed a few seconds later by eleven-year-old Evvie waving freshly picked lilac blossoms.

As had become their custom, the twins were dressed exactly alike, and they immediately challenged us to play their favorite game, "Bet You Can't Tell Us Apart."

Turns out I *can* tell them apart, which delights the twins—and me—but not their big sister.

"How do you *do* that?" Evvie demanded in my dream.

"Alexa has a tell that Remy doesn't," I whispered. When I promised I'd show her, she rewarded me with a lilac sprig.

And then I dreamed the rest of the greetings, hugging Lily and Dana and Rebecca and Robin and Mary while Lynn held back and waited till the others were done so she could take an extra moment to look at me, and me at her. And, like always, she delicately stroked my face, her eyes studying mine, her "How are you *really*?" unspoken. And always, my eyes welled just a little with tears held back—because I am so deeply fortunate that this remarkable woman loves me. And I nestled my nodding face into her lingering hand, grateful, elated.

My recollection of the dream jumbles for a while after that. Fragments of horsing around outside with the kids, of listening mesmerized to Del playing Chopin and Bach and Pachelbel on Mary's superb baby grand, of animated banter while everyone did their part preparing dinner and cleaning up afterward, of helping get the kids to bed with the promise that, oh yes, we'll be here in the morning, of the quieter, more serious conversations later in the family room, part catch-up, part philosophical exploration.

And then, in the dream, I was talking with Mary, just the two of us, up in her bedroom. Although the fragrance of lilac cuttings filled the room, the light had changed.

It was almost like a different dream in a different time. Mary was in bed, pillows propping up her back, a shawl around her small, thin shoulders. She seemed especially pale and tired, yet almost relieved to see me, eager to engage.

And I wanted, *needed* to ask her, "Why does this keep happening to me? It's five times now—*five*. The first time, yeah, okay. I asked for it, really. Fifteen-year-old kid who ends up in the county jail for thirteen days…"

"Right after your mother died, wasn't it?" Mary patted a spot next to her on the bed, inviting me to sit, which I did. "Nicked a car, case continued, got your act together, your record was expunged, and you joined the Marine Corps, yes?"

I nodded, surprised that she knew such detail about a period before she ever met me. "Since then it's happened four more times. Like I set something off."

"All while you were a marine."

"All but one. The next time was brief, part of scout/sniper training. But it was real. That was the first time I was outright—" I couldn't finish; saying the word aloud might jinx me forever.

"Tortured."

I nodded, trying not to wince. "And then Saint Eh Mo's—"

Mary knew to take my hand. "The POW camp, you mean."

"It was bad." I had to clear my throat. "But I survived it. And once Lynn came and we got out of there and she brought me here, well, you saw how I was. Took me a while to unkink my head, but I was getting there, mostly. The plan was for a final boring, go-through-the-motions inspector general gig and I'm out, done with the Corps. But…"

"Mmm, the debrief." Mary gave my hand a squeeze. "Politicians and generals trying to save their wretched little careers. I thought isolating you for four months like that was downright criminal."

She gazed at me, and I knew from her expression that she saw how more than a decade later, a few parts of me are still lost in those four months. But all she said was, "And now?"

"Now—" I felt tears slide down my cheeks. "Now *this*. On the anniversary of when I was taken prisoner of war. November sixth— twelve years to the day."

"Ah," Mary said, and I knew she understood. Dreams can be like that.

"For so many years it's all been fine, normal," I told her. I remember realizing then, right then, how good it felt to be listened to by Mary. "I did school. My master's thesis design won a competition, remember that? Did my apprenticeship, got my professional license. I'm on my way to a partnership at work, just living my innocuous little structural engineering life. I do pro bono stuff, support Del's Wilderness Web passion, work on Lynn's reelection campaigns, pay my taxes. I'm nice to the neighbors. Nobody's accused me of anything. I just don't get it."

Mary sat quietly for a bit, holding my hand. "Well," she said, then stopped herself, her flagging eyes focusing on my hand in hers. Another long moment passed.

"Well," she repeated, her voice soft, thin. She spoke slowly. "I don't know what it means, either. But I find I want to tell you about something that happened to me. It's not anything like what you're experiencing—except perhaps it is." She looked up at me. "That'll be for you to decide."

"Okay."

"I had two sisters," Mary said, "one of whom was diagnosed with what was then called petit mal epilepsy. She was about eight years old and I was ten at the time—back when epilepsy still carried stigma. So my mother made a point of explaining the condition to me and handed me a leaflet from the doctor's office.

"After poring over that leaflet, I felt extremely grateful that my sister's seizures were comparatively minor. Because in the corner of my mind's eye I kept conjuring images of a person in the throes of a full-blown tonic-clonic seizure: going down in rigid convulsions, head slamming against the floor over and over.

"I read about the first aid interventions, too. Stop her head from crashing against the floor, roll her on her side if possible, and so on.

"I managed fairly well to keep these images way in the back of my mind—after all, my sister's seizures weren't convulsive and I wasn't afraid of them. Then, one day in my junior year of high school, I came upon a boy already in the clonic stage of an epileptic seizure, his head pounding the floor like a hammer.

"I saw this from a distance, and, good citizen that I was, I ran to him to help. But when I got to about four feet away, I froze. I could not move another inch; certainly I did not—could not—help him. Fortunately, a few seconds later, another girl rushed in and kept his head from hitting the floor again, and soon others arrived. I slinked away in shame.

"I spent a lot of time after that—especially right after—in a state of crushing regret. I came to realize the only way I could regain any self-respect was to vow to never again let my fear rule me.

"That's the thing about regret, Jamie." Mary offered me a ghost of a smile. "If you're not a sociopath and you bother to look, you can often see it on the road up ahead. All you have to do is take a breath and ask yourself, 'What, really, will happen if I do or don't do X? Will I regret it? And what is that regret going to feel like in a week, a year, a decade?'

"Of course, as part of my vow I told myself that if I ever again encountered someone having a seizure, I would help. I would not freeze. Then, as time went on and the sting of my shame passed, I thought about it less and less.

"Until one day during graduate school. I was in the old Kenmore Street subway station, waiting in a small crowd for a trolley. Suddenly, about fifteen feet from me a scruffy street kid started hopping erratically backward on one foot while his arms and torso went into an odd twist. He bumped into a businessman type who immediately darted away muttering something about drugs.

"But I thought—" Here Mary sighed, smile strengthening.

"Something about the way the kid moved made me think he might be having an epileptic seizure. I was dumbfounded, in shock, I suppose. I thought, 'How can this be happening *again*?'

"As I thought this, the kid fell down convulsing and his head hit the concrete platform. But I was still in denial. I turned to look up the track tunnel into the dark and said to myself, 'If he's on the ground when you turn back around, you move as fast as you can to get your hands under his head so that doesn't happen again.' Which is what I ended up doing. As I held him, I found the medical alert necklace he wore that indicated he was epileptic.

"About ten years later, I had another encounter—near my house, where someone had gone into a non-convulsive seizure in a car while stopped at an intersection. His passenger waved me down and had me go for help, which I did. But I had to pick up Rebecca and her brother from school, and I didn't return to find out how things resolved.

"It happened one last time after that. I was in my forties, visiting my mother, who lived then in the white cape down the road from here.

"I heard the sound of car wheels spinning in a frenzy and looked out to see a sedan in the neighbor's yard. It had very slowly rolled off the street right over a thick hedge of branch cuttings and jammed into a stand of young pines. Engine screaming, wheels churning up enormous amounts of pine needles, oak leaves, dust, dirt. And I could see quite clearly that the driver had passed out. I knew his foot had gone rigid and floored the gas pedal." Mary smiled again. "You know, gas pedals, way, way back in the day.

"I thought, 'If someone doesn't turn that engine off pretty damn quick, that car is going to catch fire and I'm going to see that man burn to death right in front of me.'

"I knew I had very little time. I ran full-bore through the house, out the door, and across the yard, thinking three steps ahead the whole way. Given how tightly the car doors were wedged against the trees, it took quite an effort, but I did it. The EMTs tending to the driver, who I never saw conscious, said it looked like he'd had a heart attack, but six months later, I learned it had been an epileptic seizure."

Mary exhaled. Relating the story had depleted her. "So, that's it. After the man who drove into the trees, I never saw an epileptic seizure again. Make of it what you will."

"Yeah." A low-grade current, like an itch I couldn't scratch, quivered deep in my gut—her story's strange frequency. I sensed it wouldn't abate anytime soon, and I squirmed some, but I wanted to feel it, hold on to it, contemplate it. "Thank you. I-I can't explain exactly, but I get why you told me. Thank you."

Mary motioned for both my hands, which she clasped in hers before looking up at me. "I'll be leaving soon."

I understood instantly. Tears filled my eyes again, and I leaned closer to her. "Oh, Mary..." For a long moment I couldn't speak; I watched a tear, then another slip off my face onto her hand. "Oh, Mary, I'm going to miss you so, so much."

Mary smiled a so-it-goes shrug, as peaceful as it was wistful, then lay back into her pillows. "Be kind to yourself, Jamie."

CHAPTER FIVE

August Twenty-fifth

AF25.
Sunday, March 29.

Seems they really have changed my regimen. And for the better. Maybe the full sustain protocol that guy in the infirmary mentioned lives on.

Cuz now I'm getting three MREs a day—and newer ones, too. Also, that mind-wrecking buzzy-hissy noise has been turned down. Now resembles an old steam pipe with a slow leak.

Showers are no longer random, either. Since I left the infirmary cell, I've been getting one every third day. Apparently, they want me cleaner.

Best part: they've cut the number of shifts on the elliptical from six to four, and they don't hassle me nearly as much to go faster. Breaks are longer as well. The midday MRE break now lasts maybe two hours. Mostly I use it to sleep, though I also often ruminate about Mary's story. I keep wondering if I'll ever see her again. If I'll ever see anyone I love again.

I try to do my how-do-I-get-through-this-alive thinking during the first two shifts on the elliptical. I'm most rested then. Most clearheaded.

Can't be sure how well my brain's working, but I figure only three possibilities explain why I was taken: I've done something that threatens somebody with deep pockets and deep purposes, or I'm a pawn, or it was a mistake.

If it was a mistake, once they discovered their error why not drug me up so I don't remember shit, then dump my ass on some random street corner? Or if it was a mistake and they believed I saw something that might nail them, why not just kill me? Why lock me up and feed me for, well, what's been close to five months anyway and maybe a whole lot longer? Makes no sense.

So maybe I'm a pawn.

Which implies a connection somewhere, somehow between why I'm here and the people in my life—gotta be either Lynn or Del. As in shanghai Jamie to force Lynn into voting a certain way on a certain bill. Or to pressure Del not to address the UN, which I hope to god she did. Given the cost of running this place, kidnapping for ransom seems a stretch—though I have no doubt Lynn would pay, so if that were true, I'd be out of here by now.

Or it's about something I did myself.

This one's much harder because what I told Mary in my dream is true. I'm a structural engineer who designs new buildings, redesigns old ones. I avoid politics and controversy—Del and Lynn generate plenty of that without any help from me—and I've managed to stay away from the sleazy crap that certain developers are known for.

While I'm doing well career-wise, I work for a very small firm. Our projects tend to be modest, many are residential, almost all in New England. Certainly we don't go after the trophy projects, which is fine by me. I spent some time on the trophy track and ended up thoroughly screwed.

But god, that was over and done more than four years before I was abducted. For more than four years, I've been a committed small fry, happy to stay off the potentates' radar.

No denying, though. My time on the trophy track turned into the biggest mess I'd been caught in since the Marine Corps.

So maybe I should revisit those days, leave a record with Audy of every damn thing I can remember.

❖

AF27.
Tuesday, March 31.

My trophy track sojourn began during my last full-time undergraduate semester when I got accepted into an architecture studio course taught by Burton Neal. Yeah, *that* Burton Neal.

By then I'd become jaded enough to realize people as respected and well-known as Burton don't spend sixteen weeks adjunct professoring just for the hell of it. More likely he was scouting for an apprentice or two. I assumed he'd pick from the architecture students, not mongrels like me going for the new dual structural engineering/architecture degree regarded as sneer-worthy by so many old-school architects and structural engineers.

Truth is, I didn't really expect to get accepted into Burton's studio; once I did, my only goal was to learn whatever I could and somehow emerge with a passing grade.

Despite my checkered past with architecture professors "in studio," I liked Burton right off. He was attentive, fair, and, joy of joys, not a prima donna. I learned plenty. Near the end of the semester, he offered me a job that came with a chance to do my entire apprenticeship at his firm's Boston office.

Accepting Burton's offer meant delaying my master's degree program for an entire year, but here was an opportunity to work directly for Burton Neal at Gravis Kalikova Neal. It was kinda like going to heaven without the dying part. I said yes.

Other than the casual Semper Fi camaraderie we shared as former marines, I didn't see what Burton saw in me. But soon I learned where he wanted my assistance. He'd developed vertigo—the price of making it to sixty, he once quipped—and, to function properly during visits to high-rise building sites, he decided I could help him inconspicuously enough that colleagues and clients wouldn't notice his struggle.

For his part, Burton became my mentor and made sure I got progressively juicier assignments. Which seemed fine with everyone at GKN—with one passive-aggressive exception.

"Maybe I misinterpreted," I remember suggesting to Del after a notably pain-in-the-ass interaction with Isaac Franklin, head structural engineer at GKN Boston and founding partner Kalikova's son-in-law.

"No, I think you're right. Your mere presence bugs him," Del replied. "It may have something to do with the fact that Burton keeps bringing lowly little you along on those high-profile site visits. Plus your degree, your training, is the future. Isaac's is the past. I mean, he can't help Burton design for the new robotic construction systems, but you can. You do. Isaac's jealous and threatened. Which means he's dangerous. Keep an eye on him, baby."

Then, on a hot, humid, polluted day in August—only a week before the start of my year-long leave from GKN to go off and do my master's degree, I ended up on Isaac's shit list for good.

I'd accompanied Burton as he, Isaac, and five others conducted an informal inspection of one of Burton's smaller projects, a net-positive-energy, fourteen-story gentrifier on Morton Street in Mattapan, a part of the city that's been ripped off and run down for decades, yet has an irresistible virtue—elevation—that's attracted developers in search of alternatives to such upscale but increasingly sodden and flood-prone neighborhoods as the Back Bay and Fenway.

Besides our GKN contingent, the inspection team included a honcho from the mayor's favorite construction company, a City Redevelopment Agency guy, and the developer and his two assistants, one of whom behaved a whole lot like a bodyguard.

We were on the ninth floor at the end of the construction crew's shift and done with the inspection. As the floor emptied of everyone but us, the City Redevelopment Agency guy started talking about how to jigger schedules for the next phase of the project while contending with an ugly new scandal involving the developer, the mayor, and the CRA that had put the Mattapan community on the warpath.

Burton immediately signaled me that we were leaving the clutch of men to their machinations, and after departing handshakes, the two of us began walking across the open raw floor toward the construction elevator perched on the outside of the building's northeast side. I made sure to keep myself between Burton and the nearest edge of the unfinished structure.

"I don't want to hear any of their shit," I remember him grumbling when we were out of earshot.

"About that Wellington Hill project, right?" I asked. "Some kind of land trade?"

"Yep." I remember the way Burton shook his head, the contempt in his voice. "Julius's group buys cemetery property from the Church for a song to trade for prime city-owned property on Wellington Hill— along with a couple dozen perfectly fine privately owned structures they persuade the city to take by eminent domain."

It had been portrayed as a good deal for everyone. Julius Vicario's company would clean up the cemetery, removing the bodies and remediating the land before the property transferred to city ownership. A new school would be sited on part of it; the rest would be used to meet the Wellington Hill project's urban agriculture requirement.

Then a whistle-blower revealed that the mayor had pressed the CRA into granting Julius Vicario an exemption from the urban agriculture requirement so his company could develop the bulk of the cemetery property. Further leaks showed how Vicario's company faked the cemetery remediation, how not all the bodies had been removed, how both the mayor and the CRA knew all about it.

"Hell," Burton railed on, "I'm glad they got busted. They deserve a dent in their damn margins." He tossed the group a look as we reached the elevator. "Figures Isaac's back there sycophanting away."

"Ah, well," I reminded him, "don't forget who Julius's father is."

Still get a yucky taste in my mouth when I think of former Secretary of Defense Rafael Vicario. So appropriate that his name's become synonymous with outrageous sleaze—including the fucked-up coup attempt in Cuba that wrecked my final months in the Marine Corps.

Of course, he suffered little more than embarrassment and bloated attorneys' fees. Not even a fucking fine. His significant fortune took a gouge but remains mostly intact because he agreed to forevermore keep his head down and his mouth shut. What're the odds he's groomed his son to front for him?

I stopped thinking about the Vicarios when I noticed Burton breathing too hard as he stared at the rough concrete underfloor. Vertigo, I figured, and stood close in front of him, which seemed to help.

"Yeah, and don't forget Walter Welch over there," Burton muttered as I poked the small screen to call the elevator. "Now a CRA deputy director because his wife's the mayor's favorite niece. Sometimes I hate this business. Ah well, I shouldn't bitch—at least it's not me doing the sycophanting."

And then, before the elevator reached the ninth floor, the power in the building went out. This halted the men's conversation. The construction company exec, Gomes, quickly started barking into a pocketcom, then went silent, listening.

I heard something, too—nine floors below us. Like a crowd booing a lousy high school football play. My stomach clenched. A smallish crowd down there, by the sound of it, but I could tell those people were riled.

"Hear that?" I asked Burton, who nodded. "I'm gonna check it out."

He smiled back. "Stairs it is, then," he said, and began marching toward the dimness of the nearest concrete-enclosed fire stairs while I scampered to the edge of the northwest side of the building and looked down.

Below, some twenty or thirty people scuffled with members of the construction crew and a couple of security guards. They'd already crashed the main gate in the fence around the site and were trying to push into the building. Worse, the crowd was growing. Like a damn mushroom.

Gomes and I both spouted "Oh *shit*" about half a second apart, creating an eerie echo effect.

"Screw this," the CRA guy, Welch, announced grimly. "I'm calling nine-one-one."

"We're taking the stairs," I called to the others, my gaze on Isaac, and I jogged ahead to catch up with Burton, who'd reached the stairwell and descended several steps.

"It's nasty," I told him. "Could be a real live riot by the time we get down there."

Burton continued descending but slowed at the eighth-floor landing. "Well, Jamie," he said, "I can't stay here. I feel like shit."

He appeared almost gray in the late afternoon light coming through the unfinished eighth-floor doorway. "You look like shit," I told him. "How about sitting down for a minute?"

"Nope." He started descending again. Quickly. "Gotta get the hell outta here."

"Burton, wait," I called, scrambling after him. I remember wondering if maybe he also suffered from claustrophobia.

He refused to stop for four floors. Then he sat down breathless.

The crowd's shouts had grown louder and better organized as more people gathered on the Morton Street side of the building. I heard chants but couldn't quite make out the words. Sounds of destruction—metal-on-metal banging, shattering glass, crunching, thudding—seemed to syncopate with the chants. But no sirens.

Getting out would not be straightforward. Though at least I hadn't heard gunfire. And both the building and the site had a rear exit; I pinned my hopes on that.

Above us in the stairwell came the sounds of footfalls, male voices, and, within a few seconds, Isaac's distinctive tenor. I figured the six of them would be leaving the ninth floor only if an escort, better armed and more dangerous than the throng below, had been dispatched to extract us.

Burton probably thought so too, because that's when he stood up. And, oh god, that's when he clutched his left shoulder and slumped sideways.

"Christ," he murmured, staring hard at me, his eyes watering, his face cadaverous. We both understood he was having a heart attack.

I grabbed him to keep him from tumbling and used his wristcom to call for aid; at least this way, the medical emergency people could monitor his vitals while we waited for the ambulance they said they were sending.

"Isaac," I shouted up the stairwell as soon as I finished talking to the emergency aid people. "Burton needs your help. Fourth floor. Hurry, man."

Of course, Isaac did not hurry. But he arrived eventually and after one look at Burton, he did what I told him, which was to help me carry Burton down the stairs. "We can't wait for the EMTs to fight through that crowd and then climb up here with their gear. We gotta get Burton as close to them as possible."

The others stayed well behind us as Isaac and I chair-carried Burton to the second floor. Then Isaac balked.

"I'm not going down there until the cops take care of those fucking thugs." He halted and started bending to lower Burton onto a stair. But I still gripped his forearms, which I pulled upward again.

"No!" I insisted. "We're taking Burton all the way down right the fuck now, Isaac." As I said this, I pulled Isaac's arms forward. He actually trembled, but he acquiesced and we descended to the first floor.

The crowd's chants blared—someone had brought along a bullhorn. I heard shouts of "Hands off our homes," "Wellington Hill land for Wellington Hill people," "Don't let the Vicario Group poison us."

Good to know who they were pissed at. I'd sure as hell have tossed them Julius Vicario before I'd let them put a hand on Burton, who at that point was very close to passing out.

Just as Isaac and I reached the first floor and found a crate next to the concrete wall enclosing the fire stairs where Burton could sit down, a band of a dozen, then two dozen people—mostly teenaged and male—barged through a line of construction crew and swarmed us, bellowing their rage.

"Hey!" I bellowed right back, moving between them and Burton, standing as tall as I could. "Back the fuck off! He's not Vicario!"

The kids hesitated—yeah, most of them really were kids. I hastily searched their faces; who was the leader here? If I engaged the right kid, maybe, just maybe, the crowd might focus on their own social dynamic rather than on Burton. Or me. And after that I didn't give a shit.

The kid I was looking for stood about ten feet in front of me, a lanky almost-gangsta almost as tall as I am. He stepped forward, left side leading, chin jutted, eyes squinting, hand gesturing defiance. "Yeah?" he jeered, his eyes shifting from me to Burton as he strutted to within two feet of me, his buddies right behind him. "We know Vicario's here."

"This is Burton," I declared a bit too loudly, my hand claiming Burton's caving shoulder, "and he's having a—"

"Yo! Stop!" screeched another kid as he began to chase Isaac, who'd used the moment to bolt for the stairwell about four feet away.

A second later, both Isaac and the kid chasing him did stop—because Vicario's oversized bodyguard emerged from the stairwell doorway brandishing a large, sleek pistol.

He looked ridiculous, like a badass from a cheap noir cop melodrama, but the weapon was plenty real and I, for one, believed the dude was itching to use it. Within another second or two, I knew he'd already decided to use it on the lanky kid in front of me.

The kid knew, too, and from the back of his pants he pulled his own weapon, plenty big but older, not so shiny, obviously an untrackable glick, illegal as hell.

So there I stood with Burton in agony behind me on the crate, two idiots an arm's reach from me waving loaded pistols, screaming nonsense obscenities as they jitter-danced five feet from each other in testosterone-drenched hysteria, and all around us people scattered, yelling, running for cover, of which there was very little.

Goddammit, I thought. Which was as articulate as my mental processes were going to be for a while.

I knew I had no more than a second, maybe two before Vicario's idiot would fire his weapon, and, if I do say so my fucking self, he'd have fucking killed that kid and god knows who else if I hadn't seen it coming just in fucking time and been able to move like fucking lightning.

In classic fencing fashion, I lunged between them, one leg bending forward, the other straight back, and grabbed the barrels of both weapons simultaneously, yanking downward as hard and fast as I could. The bodyguard's gun fired, but into a pallet of polyiso insulation rather than human flesh—although a while later I realized my calf had been nicked by his bullet.

The idiots were so startled at what I'd done that I was easily able to wrench the weapons out of their hands. I've spent some time with pistols, so I knew how to juggle them, and I had them flipped and pointing at the bodyguard and the kid before they entirely registered what had happened.

I lowered the kid's pistol first; he backed into a smaller, far quieter crowd and disappeared. Vicario's bodyguard hollered something I took to mean he wanted his weapon back and the kid arrested, but I wagged his weapon at him, inspiring him to shut up.

And that's when, mercifully, I heard ambulance sirens and saw flashing lights. Within a few minutes, a remarkable EMT named—yes, truly—Sapphira Honeyjohn had me and Burton out of there.

Sapphira Honeyjohn reappeared in my life several months later, but on that August day, she effortlessly stood down the quickly rekindling crowd long enough to load Burton into the ambulance, demand that I come too—"Take a gander at that leg of yours, sweet pea, then get your bony ass into my response unit"—and adamantly refused to make room for Isaac, despite his pleas.

Burton survived that day, as did Isaac and everyone else present.

Except for answering the cops' questions at the hospital and handing over the idiots' pistols, I didn't hear much about the incident because I followed Lynn's advice and granted a single brief media interview, then took refuge behind the gates of Great Hill until school started.

Exactly a week later, on my first day of classes, the "almost riot" on Morton Street was overshadowed by an abortive community meeting between Vicario's representatives and soon-to-be-displaced Wellington Hill residents that devolved into a *real* riot. The violence culminated in two separate fires—quickly determined to be arson—that conspired with gale-force winds to burn down most of Wellington Hill and kill a woman as she saved others.

Everyone wanted to know who should be held responsible for what became known, simply, as August Twenty-fifth—the day fire destroyed Wellington Hill and took the life of young, brave, beautiful Artemisia Macana.

Meanwhile, since I was in school, I came to the GKN offices only occasionally over the ensuing months to help out Burton as he inched his way back to work.

So I didn't appreciate how much Isaac hated me until I'd nearly completed my master's degree almost a year later. I got the message loud and clear after Burton died suddenly, unexpectedly of a stroke, which resulted in Isaac becoming the managing director at GKN Boston. He fired me twenty-four hours after Burton's funeral—by email—just before I was supposed to return to work at GKN full-time.

Nor was that the end of it. Isaac pulled all the strings he had to make sure I got professionally blackballed right off the trophy track. Didn't take me long to discover that every architecture, engineering, and construction firm in the area understood their good relations with the Boston City Redevelopment Agency would be at risk if they hired me.

A few months later, I confirmed what I'd already presumed—that Isaac's "good buddy" Walter Welch played an instrumental role on the CRA side to help Isaac screw me.

Haven't seen Isaac since Burton's funeral; last I heard, he's at GKN San Francisco. And even before the Wellington Hill fiasco destroyed the mayor's chance at reelection, Welch moved to Washington to take a job somewhere in the bowels of the Department of Homeland Security.

God, I miss Burton still. Damnedest thing, though. Getting booted from GKN turned out to be one of the best things that ever happened to me.

❖

AF30.
Friday, April 3.

Five days now since I stirred up memories of Burton and those slithering creeps Isaac Franklin and Walter Welch—and Julius Vicario, son of a renowned scoundrel who almost got caught by August Twenty-fifth. Almost.

Distrust of Julius Vicario ran so deep through so many of the city's veins that the truth emerged within a month. "Security consultants" hired by his company—*not* the angry citizens of Mattapan—started both fires. The videos that proved it meant neither Vicario's money nor his political clout could prevent the pregnant Artemisia, who saved thirteen people trapped in a burning building, from becoming a martyr.

Of course, he blamed it all on the usual passel of underlings, whose actions he swore, of course, he never knew about, much less sanctioned. But what really bailed him out was—*surprise!*—money. A whole lot of it and every cent a well-publicized tribute to Artemisia.

With great fanfare, the Vicario Group immediately began cleanup of the cemetery land, having hired a preeminent environmental consultant to oversee the process. Simultaneously, the company launched a sophisticated campaign to persuade the city to place the cemetery land within the boundaries of the Mattapan Neighborhood Initiative—a new legal entity granted land use and zoning authority independent of the city of Boston.

Next, all the Wellington Hill property acquired by the Vicario Group was donated to the charity created in Artemisia's honor. Then, in a textbook sweetheart deal, the charity "sold" about half the donated Wellington Hill property to the Mattapan Neighborhood Initiative, which paid top dollar for it—using a fat personal donation from (ta-*dah!*) Julius Vicario.

These arrangements kept Vicario out of court and out of jail. Also enabled him to upend a local political hierarchy that had attempted to sacrifice him to save their own sorry asses. Classic long game: quietly buy and build alliances with the Mattapan Neighborhood Initiative's nouveau pooh-bahs, then slide back in a few years later for another helping of business deals juicy enough to make up for those substantial August Twenty-fifth losses.

But regardless of how I tilt it, I just don't see what Julius Vicario—or Isaac Franklin or Walter Welch, for that matter—would get out of disappearing me, of all people, all these years later, and then keeping me alive to ruminate about it. Even so, those days are haunting me now.

Did I mention that Del says I have a streak of OCD?

CHAPTER SIX

Power

AF33.
Monday, April 6.

When you apply force over a period of time to displace a mass, you have exercised power.

Julius Vicario's exercise of power—applying the force of his money to displace the mass of rage against him—transformed Artemisia's charity into an influential nonprofit with enough resources to plan a large community-oriented complex on Wellington Hill.

They decided to call it the Artemisia Center. Its design would be chosen by means of a competition—announced near the end of the first semester of my master's program—open to students and apprentices only. All entries to be kept strictly anonymous via use of a submission template identifying each entry only by a number.

The instant I heard about it I went for it. After all, I was required to create a design for my master's thesis, preferably one that also could be entered in a real-world competition, and the Artemisia Center submission deadlines fit my schedule almost perfectly.

The second thing I did—after collecting design specs, building code details, geo reports, and every topographical map of Wellington Hill I could find—was to visit the site.

Less than four months after August Twenty-fifth, Mattapan was still pretty jumpy and I knew plenty of people there would be suspicious of a face as pale as mine, so I planned no more than a quick drive through the area, just for a sense of the place.

Ah well, the day was cold and windy, and once I got there I found a quiet, mostly burned-out neighborhood. Not a soul on the streets, so I decided what the hell, no biggie to take a brief walk through the ruins.

I parked near the edge of the burned-out area and walked up a charred, deserted Ormond Street. I'd already been living ninety percent safe for a while, so soon I was entirely focused—too focused—on figuring out ways to preserve what little was left in the rubble.

"Yo, crackah!" Male voice, probably ten feet behind me. "What you wantin' here?"

I about-faced to find four young guys in a semicircle, close to fully grown but, you know, not really. They glared at me, malice and restless bravado glinting in their narrowed eyes, hands in pockets large enough to harbor handguns.

Quick, I thought, ask a stupid question. "What kind of building used to be here?"

"Hey, *hey*," the largest of them responded, sauntering up to me. "We got us some boojee *poon!*"

One of his hands went for my throat, the other for my crotch. I managed to intercept the hand coming at my throat and twist it while stepping sideways, and HeyHey's right arm ended up in a hammerlock. As he yowled and his clamoring buddies drew their weapons, I sidestepped again to avoid his kick and used him as a shield, jerking his arm savagely upward with my left hand as I hugged him tight from behind and shoved my right hand into his jacket pocket to grab the semiautomatic I knew was there.

"Back the fuck off!" I shouted at the other three.

I was shoving the barrel of HeyHey's gun into his junk to dramatize my request, thus persuading him to cease all struggle, when my peripheral vision picked up someone approaching on foot. And suddenly, without taking our eyes from each other, we froze—all of us except this person, this woman coming toward us.

She marched up to HeyHey without even a glance at me and got in his face.

"You." She poked his chest. "Won't *ev*-vah be fuckin' 'bout it this way, Damian."

Then I sensed her eyes move to mine. The three weapons pointing at me had been lowered, so I chanced shifting my gaze. And blinked. I was peering at Sapphira Honeyjohn.

"Hi," I said, still keeping Damian between me and his friends, still keeping my grip on his contorted arm and his gun.

"My apologies," Sapphira said calmly. "Damian's having a bad day."

I nodded. "Yeah." I let go of Damian's weapon and withdrew my hand from his pocket. "War zones are like that."

Then I released his arm and he pulled away from me to stand with the others, his face a jumble of anger and wariness as he cradled his arm. Sapphira tossed them a Look I recognized, and their weapons disappeared. They quietly but alertly took up positions about twenty feet from us. Like a security detail, I recall thinking.

"Do you remember me?" I asked her.

"I do. You prevented a riot that day, you know."

"Bad combo, bullets and testosterone." I took in her broad, dark face, her probing eyes. "But you were the one who prevented a riot. I got away with swiping a couple of pistols for a couple of minutes. You got forty dudes to tuck 'em back in their drawers with a bow because of that—that Look you do."

Sapphira shrugged. "Wouldn't bet on Vicario's stooge, but our Pethra, yes, they are disciplined." She squinted at Damian. "Mostly."

"I should go," I said, resisting a temptation to ask about her relationship with the Pethra, which I'd recently learned were becoming Mattapan's foremost street gang and had an unusually high number of female shot-callers. "Thank you for bailing me out. Again."

I wanted to shake Sapphira Honeyjohn's hand, but such a gesture struck me as insufficient and somehow inappropriate; my hand hovered halfway between us, asking.

She answered by touching my forearm, then my shoulder, and nodding toward my car about twenty yards away. "Yours, yes? I'm walking that way, so we have time for you to tell me why you're here."

"The Artemisia Center."

"So *not* to practice your disarming techniques." She didn't look at me, but a smile teased her mouth. "I've been using the videos of what you did as a teaching moment." Her smile broadened. "I guess they didn't recognize you."

"Or maybe they did." I remember keeping Damian and his friends at the edge of my field of vision as we walked; they kept their twenty-foot distance. No more, no less. "Somebody didn't get back their glick that day."

"Tuition fee. Thank you for not hurting them."

I remember thinking, *I've done enough of that.* I said only "I came to see where the Center will go. What the light's like, if there's anything that can be saved. Stuff like that."

"So you'll be doing a design for the competition. Interested in perspective from some of the inmates?"

"Absolutely." I stopped walking. "Anytime. Right now if you want."

I suspect Sapphira Honeyjohn was about to tell me to make an appointment, but we were interrupted by a woman only a little older than Damian who loped up to Sapphira's ear and whispered urgently.

"Tell 'em face-to they'll ghost in five. Tell 'em pack small." As the woman pivoted and departed at a run, Sapphira gazed at me a bit too long.

"Am I right in guessing you can go dark, all locates off?" she asked finally. "And, uh, 'take the road less noticed by'?"

When I smiled at her paraphrase and nodded, she said, "I have a favor to ask. I need you to give two women and a child a ride for me."

"Where?"

Sapphira's jaw twitched, her mouth twitched. But no smile formed; she frowned. "Don't know yet. But they must leave here right now and, uh, not by the usual means."

I nodded again; I'd decided almost autonomically.

Later, driving, I did my rationalizing. I owed Sapphira Honeyjohn. I admired her. But the deep down truth is, well, more complicated.

Deep down truth is, I believed saying no would be rejecting an opportunity to pay a little something toward an old debt, to lean slightly in a direction that helps restore a balance I can't really imagine making right, but whenever a chance shows itself, I have to try.

Deep down truth is, Sapphira set something off. Only way later did I realize how much I'd assumed about the favor she asked for. This would be about defying, outwitting pervasive surveillance and those with the unholy power to conduct it and misuse it; this would be about helping vulnerable women escape a dangerous situation. I also assumed Sapphira Honeyjohn was not fucking with me.

A tiny chill prickled up my spine, signal that the old instincts had taken charge. "Where do we pick them up?" I asked Sapphira.

"We don't. You do. I'll give you directions. Then you need to get these people out of Mattapan, out of the city. You need to keep them entirely out of sight. You need to be careful of being tracked, shake off anyone who tries. And no LEOs—no matter what." She looked through my car window. "Is that a blanket in back?"

"Yep. Multispectral-shielded."

She did a double take, then smiled. "Well, of course it is. Keep them under it. As for streetcams—"

"Yeah. Only good streetcam is an avoided streetcam." I didn't mention the dodge-the-cams game I played every time I drove the thirty-something miles from our place on Birch Lane to Great Hill; the angle of Sapphira's smile suggested I didn't have to. "I'll do my best," I told her.

"Good," she said. "I'm counting on it." Then she gave me directions to an auto repair garage not far from Morton Street before handing me a comlink.

"Caged burner?"

She nodded. "Off and faraday-sealed. Keep it that way for at least an hour after you leave the garage. When you're clear, turn it on, single-ping the listed number, then wait for my backatcha."

At the garage on Norfolk Street where Sapphira sent me, the same young woman who'd earlier whispered in her ear directed me into one of the bays and lowered the door. Within a couple of minutes, two guys had removed the backseat of my car; in its stead they laid down a thick foam cushion. A minute after that, my passengers crawled in with a couple of small duffel bags and hunkered low. The young woman spread my blanket over them with soft, reassuring words I didn't understand.

The child was too young to comprehend much, but the two women were shit scared. Didn't help that they spoke barely any English and my Spanish pretty much begins and ends with "hola, amiga."

For an hour, I drove all over hell and gone. Spotting sensors and cams was the easy part, comparatively. I make a point of keeping the offlink maps stored in my eyewraps as up-to-date as possible, so I'm pretty aware of street sensors and cams as well as drone schedules.

Also helps to have a commonplace car, which I quite intentionally do. But to drive entirely unidentified in sensored traffic, you need a probe-and-jam device. Jammed street sensors end up with glared images, garbled records of passing license or vehicle ID numbers, and in sufficient traffic volume, surveillance systems cannot pinpoint who's doing the jamming.

On that chilly December afternoon, however, I was most concerned about drones—cheap and easy to deploy if you don't give a shit about legalities. Unauthorized and unscheduled drones are also difficult to spot and therefore difficult to evade.

You gotta assume anyone committed enough to launch drones

to track you has loaded them with the same multispectral detectors used in advanced LEO surveillance gear—radio, microwave, visible, laser, thermal infrared, ultraviolet, even audio. Those wielding high-end drones can detect very particular minute patterns associated with both you and your car, and the resulting signature becomes a unique identifier.

So successful drone dodging requires a more powerful and longer range P&J like mine—high-end military-grade, possibly stolen, probably illegal for me to possess, and capable of disrupting the various signals that can be patterned to identify an individual.

That day, I ran my jammer pretty much the whole time. Even though the only signatures my P&J picked up were authorized. Even though every drone passed us by without diverting from its normal route. Even though there were long drone-free stretches during which I drove in all manner of convoluted ways to make sure we hadn't been tag-teamed.

After a tense but uneventful hour, I began to relax a little. No certainties, but solid odds we'd gotten out of Mattapan untracked. Found myself fairly close to home, too, even though, arguably, close to home was the very last place on earth I should be. Because hell, Sapphira had been desperate and out of time when she took the huge gamble of enlisting me, an almost-stranger. Plus I had no clue what was going on, who my adversaries were, or what resources they might use against us.

But I didn't want to unseal Sapphira's burner comlink to ping her until my charges were in a safe, preferably out of sight place. Besides, what if Sapphira herself had become compromised? Perhaps I should stash my charges in one location and drive somewhere else to ping Sapphira.

Which is why I opted to go to Birch Lane. Where Del and I live.

Had my reasons, which weren't as imprudent as they might seem.

First, despite modest size and appearance, our place on Birch Lane has solid security. The property sits at the end of a short, private dead end, two lots across the lane from each other. The two-family we share with Lily and Dana and the girls when they're "in town" occupies one lot; on the other sits a two-car garage with a shed attached to one side, a greenhouse at the rear, and a sizable attic that I'd been slowly upgrading into a hangout for Evvie, Alexa, and Remy.

Because Dana and Lily run Callithump, the company formed years ago by Lynn and cohorts and worth a bundle, they attract a fair amount of nasty shit from fucked up people. So the place is festooned with security systems and surveillance countermeasures; nobody gets close to the property without us knowing, and Callithump security people are always nearby. Besides Great Hill, the house and garage on Birch Lane are the safest places I know.

(And yeah, yeah, seems ironic that while I rely so much on surveillance systems to sleep at night I also care so much about defying surveillance—a childhood survival strategy reinforced in the Marine Corps. So let me make it real simple: I resist offensive surveillance that attempts to intrude on my privacy, autonomy, and safety with the same vigor I devote to wrapping myself in defensive surveillance to preserve my privacy, autonomy, and safety.)

Second reason I opted for Birch Lane: once the car's in the garage, my passengers have access to a safe place—the garage attic—without anyone seeing them. There's even a modicum of comfort, since my most recent upgrades included real stairs that meet code, insulation, three mattresses on the plywood floor, and the girls' favorite—a composting privy snugged behind a shower curtain sporting their most-esteemed cartoon characters.

Also, Lily, Dana, and the girls were at Great Hill, not Birch Lane, so I didn't have to explain anything to anyone but Del.

Third reason: I needed to either get the hell home or communicate with Del. Unless I showed up soon she'd start worrying. I'd stayed dark for almost two hours—very out of character. I knew I had only a narrow window left before she'd call out the cavalry. That would mean involving everyone at Great Hill—not only the Callithump security people who protected Lily and Dana but also the security people who protected Lynn as well as the cops and probably the feds, since Lynn's a senator.

And hell, my passengers were likely illegals. They damn well were afraid of something.

Of course, I could open a single commo channel and send Del a message—as always using Callithump's super-whammy encryption and network onion-tunneling/packet masking technology. But I'd received an alert earlier that Callithump tunneling technology was down, and I didn't know if the fix had yet been deployed. I had more faith that I'd avoided being tracked than I had in the security and privacy of my commo.

Fourth reason: Del speaks Spanish.

Thus began what turned into a whole new chapter in our lives. Could it really have something to do with why I was kidnapped five years later?

❖

AF36.
Thursday, April 9.

God, I love remembering the way Del was that December afternoon when I came home with three strangers.

As soon as I buzzed her on the intercom, she besieged me. "Are you okay? Why are you still in the garage? How come you went dark?"

"I'm fine," I assured her.

She exhaled, her relief audible. "God, you play it close to the line, Gwynmorgan. I was about to call out the National Guard. Why didn't you just text me?"

"Didn't know if our commo's secure yet."

"It is, actually, as of twenty minutes ago. But why—?" She stopped herself mid-sentence. "Okay, what's up?"

"Well, it's complicated…"

"Ahh." She laughed a little uneasily. "One of those impetuous adventures, my sweet?" Our last impetuous adventure had been her doing; it overran our lives for the better part of two weeks.

"I'll admit to impetuous. Can you bring your Spanish? And some blankets."

"Oh," she said. In her pause I heard her comprehension. This is about people. In her garage. "Be right there," she said. I knew she was already hurrying.

Meanwhile, my passengers responded to my mostly mimed invitation and exited the car to gingerly head up to the attic. Soon they plunked on one of the mattresses, the child huddled between them, and finally I got my first good look. A girl of about four, a spooked younger woman who seemed to be the girl's mother, a leery older woman very protective of them both. And all three even more frightened than when they'd climbed into my car back in Mattapan.

While I was trying to explain that they were safe, Del came bounding up the stairs. I didn't have a chance to convey much— "Mattapan…they need to stay out of sight"—before she engaged them, speaking gently in Spanish as she offered blankets. I heard her say her name, so I know she introduced herself. A moment later she said my name; I'd been too busy driving and probing and jamming to do that myself.

The women's reluctance to talk to Del lasted maybe thirty seconds. Before long she sat cross-legged in front of them, each of her hands holding one of theirs while they spoke haltingly, barely above a whisper.

I watched her from about ten feet away, ached at the beauty of her as she smiled and nodded and talked so softly, as she cupped the child's cheek and was rewarded with a shy child-smile, then shy woman-smiles.

By the time she turned to look up at me, I reckoned she understood more about what was going on than I did. But all she said was, "I think something to drink for our guests, don't you? And maybe some snacks." She reached back for my hand which, stepping closer, I gave her. "First, though, bring up the space heater, okay?"

When I returned with a tray of food and thermoses, our guests had calmed some. Del juggled English and Spanish as the women expressed what seemed like gratitude and I quickly synopsized my version of events. When I said I wanted to ping Sapphira from somewhere reasonably far from Birch Lane, Del signaled agreement.

Okay then, I remember thinking as I studied her eyes, kissed her, inhaled her exquisite scent before I departed—OCD or not, maybe I *didn't* overdo all the probes and jams and driving in arcane loops.

An hour later, I met Sapphira at the food court in a nearby Watertown mall overrun with Christmas shoppers. She did not come alone. The woman with her—introduced only as Cecilia—appeared to be about forty, but I had an ineffable sense she was older than that.

Cecilia is what people call A Presence. Not beautiful. Not blinged. Not particularly talkative. But her eyes, how she stands, how she moves—Cecilia commands. I took one look at her and understood she was Sapphira's boss and she'd come along to check me out, which she did with an intensity that quickly made me uncomfortable.

"I need to know two things," I announced right after I reached into my pocket and pressed my P&J's AUDIOJAM key. "First, what's going on? Second, how do you want to—?"

Sapphira interrupted. "They're in your car, yes?"

"No," I said. "But they're safe. And they haven't been seen." Except by Del, which I decided not to mention just yet.

"Where are they?" Sapphira's voice carried a razor threat I hadn't heard before.

"Safe. And comfortable." In better hands than mine, actually, but I decided not to mention that either. "And I need to understand—"

Now Cecilia interrupted. And took over. "All right," she declared. "This'll take some talking, but we have to keep those ladies moving." She eyed Sapphira. "We clear?"

Sapphira's gaze snapped to three people—two women, one man—at three separate spots on the periphery of the food court. "Yes, ma'am," she answered after a few seconds.

"We'll ride with you then," Cecilia said to me.

"Talking as we go, right?" I asked.

"Right," said Cecilia.

"And you'll both be dark—no locates." This time I was not asking.

"Right," said Cecilia.

Yeah. Well. No fucking way on earth would I simply bring them to our house. To Del. Not without making damn sure we weren't surveilled or followed by anyone, including Sapphira's cohorts at the mall. And not without information about Cecilia and why the hell the women in our garage were on the run.

So even though Cecilia suggested and I concurred that she and Sapphira travel hidden under my multi-blanket, the ten-minute ride from the mall to Birch Lane stretched to another hour of arcane loops and uninterrupted jamming before I was appeased. And I would sustain that jamming—to damn well keep them dark whether they liked it or not—until they were well away from Birch Lane again.

At least that was the plan. Trouble is, plans get intervened on, plans get discombobulated. I mostly executed this one.

Mostly.

I think.

Damn sloppy, I know. But what Cecilia told me during that hour— and yes, Cecilia did most of the talking—knocked the wind right the hell out of me.

Often as she spoke I wanted to curb the car, yank aside the blanket, and take my time scrutinizing her face when I asked her to say…that… again. Twice, I actually did it. And oh god when I *saw* Cecilia speak the words…*say…that…again…*I knew I'd heard the truth.

The ride back to Birch Lane took me out of time and place, back to—too far back. Once I got the car into our garage again, I remember leaving my P&J on the dashboard clicked to U/MR mode—universal midrange jam—so it would continuously obstruct every fucking signal into and out of the entire garage for as long as Cecilia and Sapphira were there.

But I'm not sure whether I had the sense to run the P&J, which was low on juice, off the car's power supply. So here I am, five years, six years, god knows how many years later, left to wonder how long that jam lasted.

Did it matter then?

Does it matter now?

Shit. I don't like remembering how thoroughly I lost control.

In seconds, I'd plummeted from a hundred to just about zero. Once the car was in the garage, I just fucking sat there, silent, unmoving, split in two. One benumbed me stared at the wall beyond the windshield long enough that Sapphira realized we'd arrived and tossed the blanket aside; the other me—the witness, forever mute and wide-eyed—watched my benumbed self and my passengers and the past.

As it regularly does, Del's uncanny timing rescued me. Before Sapphira could say anything, Del had come down from the attic, introduced herself, and led Cecilia and Sapphira upstairs. Still I didn't move. Not until Del came back downstairs some time later, soothed me out of the car, and urged me to go into the house, which I did.

The rest of that evening—for we'd reached evening—blurs for me. I remember Del coming in at one point to announce that she'd be crowding Cecilia, Sapphira, the two women, and the kid into the car for a meet-up with Sapphira's friends.

I lifted off the sofa in our living room, where I'd been hanging out in a kind of trance with my aphasic, wide-eyed witness. "I'll do it."

"No," she said and made me sit down again. "My turn."

"It could be dangerous, Del."

"It'll be fine. You already did the dangerous part." Her eyes pinned me to the sofa as she said she'd be back soon. "And then we'll talk."

Forty-seven minutes and twelve seconds elapsed between the moment Del opened the front door to leave and the moment she opened it upon returning.

"Everything's okay," she said before I could ask and handed me two warm bags of what smelled like tandoori takeout. Her hand rubbed my back. "C'mon, baby, let's compare notes while we eat."

We sat across from each other at the dining table, but for a while my range was limited to monosyllabic replies—about forks, what to drink, please pass the chutney. Del mentioned the color of the van Sapphira's friends drove, where the meet-up took place, but I remember only nodding.

Eventually, she found a way in. "I don't know who I expected you to bring back here, but it certainly wasn't Cecilia Danta."

I gaped at her. "Hold on. The Cecilia who was here tonight is *Cecilia Danta*?"

"Oh, yeah." Del's eyebrows hiked into a you-didn't-know? affirmative as she toyed with a piece of naan.

We'd heard of Cecilia Danta only because Springer Knox, Lynn's prehensile chief of staff, maintains an acutely sensitive network of political seismometers. Springer's cheeky description of the infamous madam with Mattapan roots made me almost queasy. Too many echoes of my mother. But even Springer begrudgingly respected Cecilia Danta's power to keep her elite clientele so irredeemably addicted to her services that she'd acquired not just wealth but genuine, occasionally extortionist influence among The Hundredth Of The Hundredth.

"Del, are you sure?"

"I am," Del answered, chin slowly lifting, lowering. "She was, well, incognito tonight—no doubt she looks quite different when she's working New York or Washington or Paris. But, yes, that was Cecilia Danta."

Del had seen a photo once and was sure.

"I would never have expected Cecilia to maintain a Mattapan powerbase," she said. "Surely not for the income stream. But, god, still OG after all these years. Explains a few things about the Pethra."

"Yeah, like why my bullet-riddled body isn't floating down the Neponset River tonight."

Del glowered. "Not funny. At all. And, oh by the way, Sapphira gave me a blow-by-blow of what *you* neglected to mention. What is it about you, anyway?"

Did she mean my little waltz with Damian?

She did.

I shrugged, raised my hands in mock surrender.

Del had been patiently probing—sideways, like a crab—since she walked in the door with my favorite takeout food. Elicitation, she calls it—the supple and delicate overcoming of another's fear. She responded to my shrug with a flash of impatience before she reacquired her target—me—and began running a finger along her lip much like Lynn Hillinger does.

"I think I may believe Cecilia Danta," she said finally. "But I wish I had more confidence in *why*."

"Cecilia say anything about what she gets from rescuing sex-trafficked illegals?"

"Not really. She has several 'villas,' including one somewhere in Mattapan. Implied she sometimes uses them to hide the women she's rescuing. And she emphasized more than once she's opposed to sex trafficking."

"Retired, is she?" I snarled.

Del got slitty-eyed but ignored my swipe. "Cecilia Danta says she wants only 'professionals' working for her—by definition, they're not trafficked, they've made a choice. She said it's a job like any other—at least when working conditions are okay, which she made quite a point of saying she ensures."

"So. Not retired." My hands had started to fist; I forced them open, flattened my palms on the table.

"She's heard of me, Jamie," Del said quietly. "Told me she liked the EARTH presentation I did last October. She seemed downright astonished to find me at the end of her car ride tonight. She also knows about the Women's International Sanctuary Exchange's underground transport activities. Actually asked me if I knew anyone at WISE she might talk to. And those two women you brought here—they're Guatemalan, by the way—really trust her."

"Fuck," I muttered. On so many levels I did not want to believe anything Cecilia Danta said.

Then Del asked me if I'd ever heard of Friday's Sister. I had not.

"The Guatemalans told me they escaped a week ago because their 'landlords' wanted to sell the child," Del said. "They'd heard about Friday's Sister, who would embrace them and send them on the road to freedom."

Goddamn, I already knew what she'd say next. Friday's Sister is Cecilia Danta.

I remember how the heat rose from my chest up my neck to flush my cheeks. I remember Del leaning closer over the table. "Tell me what happened tonight," she said.

I popped like a cork. Because I didn't want any of it to be real, wished I'd never gone to Wellington Hill. "Screw the Artemisia Center," I hollered. "Screw school. Screw—"

"Jamie!" Del grabbed my hands. "Talk to me. Please."

For a long moment I glared at her, this magnificent woman who made life worth living. When she reached up and whisked a finger across my cheek, I realized I was crying.

"Please, Jamie." Del's hand stroked the side of my face.

One breath, maybe two, and I began my confession. "I'm afraid Cecilia Danta is exactly what she claims she is," I said. "But that doesn't mean I perceive purity in her motives."

Del smiled. "Let me guess. You think Cecilia's going after sex traffickers to protect her business. Slam the competition. You think Mattapan's not chiefly a source of customers—it's where she has a rich supply of attractive young women with ambition but crappy job prospects."

"Shit, Del. Now you're making me defend her."

"Am I?" Del's eyebrows arched toward the heavens. "Pray tell."

"Cecilia Danta is also assuaging her guilt."

"I repeat: Pray tell."

"She's done some nasty, nasty shit," I said. "Shoulda guessed she's the same Cecilia who's so good at squeezing all those Very Important Testicles."

Del's eyes sparked. "And?"

"She said she knew my mother."

Del took this in stride; she even nodded slightly, though her eyebrows lifted again. "I see."

"My father, too."

"Your *father*?" Del's eyes went very wide very fast.

"Cecilia Danta said she recognized me because I look exactly like him." I almost chuckled then. "She kept repeating 'exactly.' Scared her, I think. The world isn't supposed to work that way."

Del's hands now covered her mouth. "Oh my god," she murmured, then her voice pitched upward. "Who's your father?"

"Dunno," I mumbled. "Neither does Cecilia. Some guy off an LNG tanker, she thinks. Bought my mother for a few days."

"And Cecilia knows this because—"

"She was already pimping. Even back then. She trafficked my mother."

Del's elbows thumped on the table, her hands still covering her mouth, as she stared at me. And stared, because she could see there was more. "What? What else?"

"Cecilia said my mother killed him. Doesn't know why. Maybe an accident, maybe the dude was a maniac, maybe my mother was all drugged up. Maybe all of that. Or none of that. Cecilia found her, cleaned up after her, shipped her to a cop in Hyannis who bought her on an installment plan. A while later, the cop sent word back that my mother had arrived pregnant but he'd decided to keep her anyway. Wouldn't be paying Cecilia any more for her, though." I made a wiping hands motion. "End of Cecilia's chapter of the story. Until today."

Del slowly nodded, her eyes claiming mine. She spoke in a whisper. "And?"

"Cecilia said things about my mother that I know are true." Thank god Del didn't look away. I needed Del's eyes to anchor me. "Shape of the scar under her left breast. That damn 'even the weariest river' line of poetry. The awful necklace with the slanted cross, like the ghost of Jesus is dragging the fucking thing across a desert of fucking freckles. Cecilia remembered all that, some of it from more than thirty years ago. Also knew all kinds of shit about the cop my mother and I ended up with."

"So tonight's meet-up was what? Coincidence?"

I shook my head. "Cecilia saw the videos from that day last August when Burton had his heart attack, and she recognized me. Then I turned up today to check out the Artemisia Center site and ended up helping Sapphira get those people out of Mattapan. Two coincidences—which freaked her out. She said she was impelled to talk to me. That was her word—'impelled.'"

"What does Cecilia Danta *want* from you?" Del asked, her face tightening into a frown.

"If I had to guess from the way she looked when she told me this shit, cuz, dammit, I watched her, I'd say she's haunted. She sex-trafficked for years, Del. God only knows how many people like me are out there with biographies a lot worse than mine. I think Cecilia Danta can't stand it anymore."

I remember the way Del rose, the way she came around the table, the way she kissed me to my feet. "My gut tells me you did a good thing today," she said.

"How will we ever know?"

She volunteered to snoop around her connections to the women's sanctuary underground. Carefully, she noted, so as not to endanger the Guatemalans or anyone else. Then she kissed me again. Kissed away the doubts, the shadows of the mother I knew and the father I'd never know.

❖

AF39.

Sunday, April 12.

After they lock me in the inner cell, I get through whatever crap they demand as fast as I can so I can crawl onto the bunk, close my eyes, and remember. I circle my memories, round and round, over and through certain moments. The more I do that, the more detail I retrieve, the more real it feels. The more real *I* feel, for a little while anyway.

My memories of the Christmas after my impetuous adventure in Mattapan begin with me and Del in the car heading to Great Hill and all the people who'd become my family.

For me, the beating heart of that family is Lynn Hillinger—the cause of my presence among them, the reason I know Del, the woman I could not honestly say, do not *want* to say I love less than Del. Lynn was a first-term senator when I met her years ago; as she neared the end of her second term she'd become influential enough that all kinds of people were saying she should run for president.

Told myself that's why I stalled, why I'd communicated nothing to her about my latest impetuous adventure, even though I'd brought a notorious madam/gang boss/maybe reformed sex trafficker to a place where her grandchildren sleep and play.

Oh, and by the way, my mother killed my father who was, oh by the way, one of the johns who rented her and then she got sold to a cop in Hyannis who kept her even though she'd been knocked the fuck up because his wife wanted a girl baby, but after six or seven years I was already just too damn dykey so I started getting the shit beat out of me like that bitch's sons got the shit beat out of them, but hey, at least the cop had my mother to fuck and a nice little unreported cash income on the side and my mother and I got food and shelter. How do you do?

On the other hand, I didn't want to be responsible for blind-siding Lynn when there's no such thing as a "minor" revelation about the misdoings of a member of her family, even one with a connection as abstruse as mine. The woman's already living under a media microscope.

Plus Lily and Dana and the kids were involved; it was their house, their garage, too. Sometime very soon we—*I*—would have to tell everyone about this latest impetuous adventure that might ripple too much and much too darkly into their lives.

As we drove to Great Hill, I rationalized. Del and I hadn't yet learned the fate of our Guatemalan guests, so the story's unfinished, right? Reason enough to duck discussing it until after we did Christmas cookies, after the Christmas Eve party and the Christmas morning that lasts till midafternoon, right? And hell, let's maybe wait a couple more days, too, okay?

It was at this point that Del's pocketcom pinged. She fumbled with the device in her eagerness to check it and something about that, something—

"Who is it?" I asked.

"Oh thank god" popped out of her, and her whole body seemed to slacken into her seat as she handed me her pocketcom. Its little screen showed our three Guatemalan guests standing with two other women I didn't know in front of a classic poster of Rosie the Riveter. Everyone except the Riveter was grinning.

Did this mean they were really okay? When Del nodded, a tightness between my shoulder blades I hadn't realized was there loosened. I asked about the other two women. "You know them?"

"They're Rosies," Del said. Part of the women's sanctuary underground. And yes, Del knew them. "Earn their living as permanent onsite conservation stewards for one of the groups in the Wilderness Web Coalition."

I examined the image. "Ah. Rosie the Riveter, RR, railroad. Yeah, I get it."

Relief danced through Del's laugh. "I told you I thought you did a good thing."

I'd managed not to cause harm. Out of sheer dumb luck rather than skill or insight, to be sure, yet I'd gotten away with it. I should've been trembling at my deliverance, but I fidgeted.

"Del, did you hook up Cecilia Danta with the Rosies?"

"I did not," she said. "At least not directly. Cecilia tried to persuade me, but no."

"So how'd *this* happen?" I asked, pointing to the image on her pocketcom.

"Cecilia gave me the name of someone she trusts and I passed that name on to someone I trust. Don't know how they credentialed each other—don't want to know. But that image is the agreed signal that it's gone the way we all hoped it would."

I realize now she didn't mention any of this earlier because I didn't ask. I just shut down.

A cold sting shivered up my spine. In a matter of days, Caprice had smiled *twice*. Mmm, pushing it. I was silently vowing to avoid any more impetuous adventures when an icon popped into the lower left corner of my eyewraps. Incoming message. From Sapphira Honeyjohn.

Odd, since I hadn't given her any of my deets. The message: my car's backseat had been repaired, when would I like to come pick it up? And did I want to meet some folks to talk about the Artemisia Center?

"Well?" Del asked.

I remember blinking back surprise. Del could hear no sound, see no light indicating I'd received a message, but she damn well knew anyway. Even now, five- or six-and-something years later, I see her face in that moment as she began to smile, her eyes incalculably black and blazing fire all at once.

"How the *hell* do you do that?"

"Your posture. As always." She winked in that way she has, which turned me on, as always. "Ten-hut, my sweet."

Then she took my hand, kissed it, and, as always, I succumbed with a revelous squirm to the current of her, thinking *god you are* so *beautiful*, sensing an eagerness in her to confirm what she knew already. So I bounced the message to the car's dashboard screen. "How do you think Sapphira—?"

"She asked, so I gave her one of your anonymous secure comlink numbers." After a glance at the message, Del flashed a grin. "Excellent! Sapphira's offering introductions, so you'll get great input for your design. And we sure as hell won't have to worry anymore for your safety. The Pethra will protect you whenever you're in Mattapan."

And with that we pulled up to the house on Great Hill.

Then, once we'd all settled into making Christmas cookies, Del did the heavy lifting. "And guess what happened to Jamie last Saturday!"

She neglected to mention the part where the guns came out, artfully glossed over specifics about who ended up in the garage attic or for how long, zoomed at the speed of light right on past the identity of Friday's Sister—all to play up Sapphira's invitation to meet with local people to discuss the Artemisia Center.

I suspect her performance raised a few eyebrows, but since I busied myself rolling out cookie dough, I didn't see it, only heard the brief out-of-rhythm lulls that followed formulations like "and once in the car, Jamie hustled them from the city sight unseen."

If Springer had been the only one there, she'd have eviscerated us on the spot. As it was, she soon reamed me privately—and all in one furious, lawyerly breath. "I know what the law's *supposed* to do, Jamie, but the fact is that judges typically reject gender-based asylum claims because the harm is committed by non-state agents and is therefore considered personal or random crime rather than state-induced persecution unless you have evidence, Jamie, *proof*, Jamie, and dammit, Jamie, doing this kind of shit is illegal, and if you get caught Lynn is *screwed*!"

After that, I decided to dodge Springer for a while—even though it meant leaving the family room while Del was still playing the piano. But Lynn knew where to find me. When I saw her encased in a thick down coat trudging up the path to my favorite spot on the hill behind the house, I jumped to my feet blurting apologies, which she halted with a raised hand.

"I enjoy an Adele Sabellius tap dance as much as the next person," she said, a faint version of her famous smile twinkling her eyes. "And I'm not referring to the 'Etude in E.' So please, give me the *whole* story."

"I met Cecilia Danta."

Lynn squinted at me. "Did you now…"

I told her the rest, every bit of it, her hand gentling onto my knee as we sat on a smooth granite mound and peered at the gray December sea a mile away.

"Wow," she murmured when I finished. "You must be reeling."

"Yeah. I guess." Actually, I'd been numb since Saturday night, holding on, holding still and tight till I could climb the hill to that spot and *bree-ee-eathe*, and if I was very, very lucky I'd have avoided ruining three lives and be able to blot out what Cecilia Danta told me and Lynn would somehow forgive my recklessness.

As I perched on the cold granite peeking sidelong at Lynn, I was one for three. Which, I figured, was more than I had any right to expect.

"Oh, sweetie," Lynn said, her arm wrapping across my shoulders, pulling me to her. "I wish I could reach all the way back there and change everything."

"I'm sorry, Lynn. I should have said no. Should have never gone to Mattapan again—"

Lynn tightened her grip. "Jamie." She put a finger across my lips. "Shh. You didn't do anything wrong."

And oh god, that's when I lost it. Lynn held me and I sobbed. I scared myself the way I sobbed, but I couldn't choke it off, couldn't calm it down.

When I was able to talk again, I talked about my mother. How

I'd gotten so angry at her so many times, blamed her for the addiction I'd always believed she refused to control, the high she refused to live without. How I resented her helplessness and her messes, how worry gnawed through me whenever she didn't come back to sleep at the ramshackle dump we called home, how abandoned I felt when she finally disappeared forever into the flames of a burning car.

"But it wasn't her fault, Lynn. None of it. Cecilia Danta bought her from some foster care monster when she was twelve years old. Twelve! No wonder she said never let them put you in The System. I'm not sure she even knew her real name. She was 'Neve' when Cecilia bought her, 'Rhiannon' when Cecilia ran her. Don't have a clue how she ended up with 'Alby.' Or 'Gwynmorgan.' Could never get her to talk about any of it."

I was out of breath, hugged to Lynn's chest as she rocked me, kissed the top of my head, and I could hear a kind of moan inside her. I love her for that moan because I know it was for me.

"Jamie, sweetie," Lynn said so, so softly as she nestled another kiss into my hair, "it's not your fault, either."

"I didn't know," I remember mumbling into Lynn's chest. "Why didn't she tell me?"

"I think she was trying to save you. Just like you were trying to save her."

"Yeah, well, I failed."

Lynn lifted my head to claim my gaze. "No, you did *not* fail. And neither did your mother. You gave her a reason to keep trying, and she did. Flawed trying sometimes, but it seems to me she was intent on seeing you escape her fate. And escape you most certainly have."

"Dumb luck. I met you."

"Which would never have happened without your mother. Come on, by the time I came along you were already an officer—and against ridiculous odds. In today's Marine Corps, what you did wouldn't be possible. A year before you enlisted, what you did wouldn't have been possible. But there you were, and what you did was brilliant."

I remember shaking my head. "I was clueless, just trying to—" To get ahead? Fuck, no. "To escape." Clever GED-toting seventeen-year-old that I was, I escaped my ass right into a war zone, and, goddammit, I hated thinking about it.

Usually, Lynn would notice my goddammit and pull back, but this time she circled close, skimming the edge of my red zone.

"You didn't burst fully grown from the head of Zeus, Lieutenant," she pressed, an almost-tease crouching in her earnestness. "You came from your mother, who found a way to give you a shot at the tools she never had. She understood how smart you are and she taught you to cultivate it, use it. She taught you to be strong and brave and true to yourself." Lynn smiled at me. "Your mother had guts, Jamie. Determination. And she succeeded at what she cared about most—you. She'd be so immeasurably proud of you now. Everything you are and do honors her."

"Not everything." I remember pulling my eyes away from Lynn to peer at the sea, which had begun to darken as daylight receded. "My mother was dangerously impulsive." I forced myself to look at Lynn again. "And I am, too. Last Saturday, this *thing* took over, this yes-I'll-damn-well-do-that. And I didn't stop for even a second to consider the ways it might impact other people's lives. Your life. I should've realized I'd put you at risk—"

"Stop right there. You haven't put me at risk."

"Springer made it crystal clear—"

"Uh-uh." Lynn's free hand gestured a foul. "I appreciate why you took those three out of Mattapan, and why you were so diligent for their safety. Doing for others what you hope someone might do for you in equivalent circumstances. And I applaud your act. I like to think that in your shoes, I'd have done the same thing."

"But Springer said if I'd gotten caught you'd be screwed."

"Ah, well. If you'd been arrested for knowingly transporting or harboring illegals, I wouldn't be screwed. I'd be making you a cause célèbre. I'd be railing on about the injustice of how this nation handles asylum cases, defending you to the gills."

"Yeah?" I remember feeling a trickle of relief.

"Hell, yes. The cause can always benefit from a few martyrs. We'll be picking out some soon—" Lynn stopped herself and stared at me almost quizzically. "God, you keep doing this. You have the most preternatural timing, Jamie. It's a little unnerving."

"Timing? About what?"

About the asylum reform bill she tried and failed to get through the last Congress. Eases asylum application processes, especially for women, changes detention rules, reins in asylum-related terrorism watch list excesses. Lynn said she'd be reintroducing it in the new Congress, folded into the Homeland Security Authorization Act.

"And, as before, the horse trading will be a bitch. Hence the value of martyrs." Lynn shook her head. "And here *you* show up in the theater of operations, right on schedule."

I remember my stomach twisting just a little. "You've said 'martyrs' twice."

Now Lynn nodded. "Mmm, yes, should you end up arrested. If Cecilia's crew has been infiltrated by a government informant, the feds are likely to find out about you and attempt to coerce you. You'd be pressured with blackmail and threats to become an informant, too. Your connection with me would ameliorate some of that, but only some. They play very dirty."

My stomach completed one, then another full rotation. Duped by a government informant? Moron that I was, the possibility had never crossed my mind.

Lynn continued unfazed, like she had these types of conversations every day. "We'd appeal, of course, certainly challenge everything. For a year or two or three, your life would be sucked into a vortex of legal bullshit and the kind of unceasing, life-upending media attention you loathe. The price of becoming a cause célèbre."

"Shit." This was looking uglier and uglier.

"Sorry, kiddo. A sympathetic close-up of Jamie Gwynmorgan, past and present, would be critical to keeping you out of informant hell—and out of federal prison. The POW stuff, the Navy Crosses and the Medal of Honor, the Purple Hearts, how close the wounds came to killing you, maybe even leaks about your unsung role in bringing down Lambert. With all that, we might build enough momentum to see charges against you dropped. Just as likely, though, you'd be slapped on the wrist and probably watch-listed, which makes for all kinds of travel hassles."

"So," I grumped, "helping a couple of terrified Guatemalan sex slaves and their endangered child makes *me* a terrorist?"

"Regrettably, yes. And that would be the good news. The people you tried to help would spend all that time in one of those deplorable immigration detention centers and quite possibly end up deported." Lynn's arm, still around my shoulders, gave me a squeeze. "So I'm extremely pleased that you didn't get caught."

"Yeah. Me too."

Lynn hadn't said "caught *yet*," but the potential wafted in the frigid air, an unwanted third party. "If you do," she added, "call me first."

I remember Lynn smiling as she stood up, her hand urging me to rise with her. She nodded toward the last of the light, indication that we had just enough daylight left to get back to the house without using nightvision sensors. Her words, meanwhile, didn't skip a beat. "I'll send lawyers—guns and money as warranted."

"Aw, don't tell me that." I was only half joking. "I want to retire from impetuous adventures."

Ahead of me as we moved down the hill, Lynn threw me a glance and laughed. "So to that end you've chosen to marry Adele Sabellius. Who, besides becoming the fresh young face of the Wilderness Web movement, knows and communicates with people who participate in an asylum underground railroad that violates any number of this nation's more egregious laws. Nope, you've got a love-hate thing going with impetuous adventures. And you do *not* like sociopaths. Doesn't bode well for your retirement plans."

A few days after Christmas, I went back to Mattapan.

At the Norfolk Street garage, the same guys who'd removed the backseat of my car reinstalled it beautifully reupholstered. Sapphira showed up about halfway through this process and took me to a meeting at a nearby church. On the way over, I asked her outright about snitches and informants.

"Yeah, poodles happen. Cost of doing business." Her eyes flicked from the street to me and narrowed. "Just recently had to outsmart one." She dipped her head a little and arched an eyebrow. "Not even two weeks ago. Needed some, uh, last-minute outside assistance to make sure nobody got hurt."

An acidic uh-oh cramped my gut. Had someone else's bullet-riddled body floated down the Neponset River that night? "So what happened? To the poodle, I mean."

Sapphira offered a chilly smile. "We call it atimia," she said. "Total and permanent deprivation of all privileges, rights, and protections. 'Wherefore goest thou also with us? Return to thy place, and abide with the king, for thou art a stranger, and also an exile.'"

"The poodle was banished? In one piece?"

Sapphira nodded. "As Mr. Emerson says, 'Violence is not power, but the absence of power.' Sometimes violence can't be avoided, but it's always a last resort."

"Yeah." I remember how my nod seemed to sync with hers. "Yeah, okay." And I remember what I thought as we drove to the meeting. She'll need help again. I have access to lawyers—guns and money as warranted. I'm a halfway decent camdodger. I still owe plenty. And true atonement will remain forever beyond my reach. So why *not* me?

Over the next few months, I attended several small gatherings of regular folks in Mattapan who talked about what they hoped the Artemisia Center might become. Those conversations drove the design I created. I have no doubt my design won the competition because of them.

And nearly a year after Isaac Franklin so resoundingly trashed my career, winning that competition was what resurrected it.

I didn't see Cecilia Danta again until I glimpsed her in the crowd during the Artemisia Center's ribbon cutting ceremony; we exchanged infinitesimal nods before she receded into the throng. By then, I'd undertaken several more impromptu "shuttles," as Sapphira called them, moving endangered women out of Mattapan; twice, Del and I sheltered them overnight in our garage attic before sending them on. Each time, we soon got photos of them smiling their relief—each time from a Rosie somewhere who Del knew and trusted.

Last time—not all that long ago, really—was near the end of the Artemisia Center project, only a few weeks before the ribbon cutting. I was at the site when Sapphira came to me for help with a "shuttle." She always knew when I was at Wellington Hill, thanks to the Pethra members employed in the building trades training program I'd integrated into the Center's construction processes.

I asked her then who the women were running from—something I'd never done before.

"Cops," she said, tossing me a Look. "I know you know the type."

Never found out who the cops were, but maybe those cops found out about me, assumed I know too much about some damn thing or other. Cops with particularly powerful associates.

Maybe *that's* why I'm stuck in here. Rusting. Rotting.

CHAPTER SEVEN

The recognition of necessity

AF43.

Thursday, April 16.

Might as well face it. Even if I could rely on the precision of memories, even if I believe I haven't been hoodwinked into falsely reconstructing them, memories can't help me now. So the fuck what if I penetrate the fog and figure out why I'm here and who's responsible? Won't get me home again.

Yet all that thinking about Isaac and Burton, about Sapphira Honeyjohn and the Artemisia Center, Cecilia Danta and my mother—hell, now I'm looking backward for its own sake. OCD with nowhere else to go.

My remembering circles the same moments like a hungry vulture, and as I spiral closer the memories gain dimension, color, detail. I'm feeding on the carcass of my own life now—anything I can get.

Yesterday I scavenged scraps more than a decade old—the first days and months and years after the Marine Corps disgorged me.

I emerged numbed and tremulous, but at least the numbness offered respite from my nightmares. Hoping that relief might last, I scrambled as fast as I could, as completely as anyone ever has, into school and all those daunting engineering and architecture classes.

And when, inevitably, the nightmares barged through my numbness, I made school my boot camp, more intense and relentless and consuming even than the flashbacks of killing killing finally killing a six-year-old innocent, or the dire dreams of the POW camp, or the sticky leftover anxiety of that hostile, four-month Corps "debrief" during which I managed to slither between half-truth and omission without ever actually lying, only to explode with blood rancor right after I was discharged.

As long as you respect the process, boot camps have a way of radically reshaping how you see yourself, and school did that for me. Also helped enormously that, thanks to Lynn, I didn't have to worry about how the hell I'd pay for it or food or rent.

Even so, I remained numb, blocked off in a heavy, sluggish self that seemed to belong to someone else, someone dazed and disoriented and deafened, like what happens after standing too close to the giant loudspeakers at a dance club.

More than a year passed before I woke up one morning no longer numb; instead I was lucidly aware of the rage that had engulfed me the day after my discharge—rage enough to kill a man with my bare hands after we'd both tumbled over a hundred-foot cliff.

Del and Lynn and everyone else at Great Hill had known within hours of my deed—because they saw the video of it that my eyewraps recorded. At the time, from my little island of numbness, I watched them cover for me, hide my involvement. When I finally remembered, I glimpsed how I must seem to them. Which is to say, how I really am.

Why they love someone like that is a mystery to me, but I am grateful for it beyond description. And, yeah, grateful to Del most of all because Del came all the way down in here and got me.

She knew somehow that no matter how much I wished it, gentle alone would never reach me. Knew that I need to overcome by enduring and resisting and defying in order to come at all. Too often, that need has taken dangerous form. Violent form.

I suspect Del knew this the first instant we looked at each other. Del doesn't do violence, but the violence I tempt, the violence that tempts me, didn't stop her, didn't scare her.

I close my eyes and see her, thankful for my ten years with her, wondrous that my life could have become so much more beautiful than I imagined any life could ever be.

❖

AF46.
Sunday, April 19.

I keep recalling the first time I ever heard Del mention "Wilderness Web."

A late-winter Saturday, crisp, snowless. We were a couple of miles into a long walk on Great Hill's trails. I'd been out of the Corps for a little more than two years, just about ready to believe the life I was living might actually be real.

Del and her sister Lily were still coping with the news that now both of Lily's mothers (and Del's adoptive mothers), Luce as well as Biz, were facing terminal illness, and it was understood that when the time was "right," they'd take themselves out, probably together.

The Wilderness Web was the first thing Del had talked about in weeks that didn't wind back to Luce and Biz and death. So I let her talk, careful to stay diplomatic; I recall replying with something neutral like "That's pretty ambitious."

"Well, this is long-term."

Thus began a twenty-minute oration that left me, as Del often did back then, on the horns of a dilemma. "Omigod, you are sublime" versus "Jeezus, how could I have missed that you're fucking delusional?"

Sublime won out, obviously, but not without what eventually became a few blazing arguments in which I actually *called* her fucking delusional (and worse) in loud, ringing tones, and she hollered at me to stuff my arrogant, self-absorbed cynicism (and worse) where the sun don't shine.

It's not that I opposed her idea of a Wilderness Web. Hell no, it's a delightful fairy tale. Del, however, is a believer—not merely in the idea of a Wilderness Web, but in making it real. ASAP.

For a while, we agreed to disagree and not discuss it. We were both in school—me slogging through engineering labyrinths, Del doing her environmental economics PhD program while also working part-time as an environmental engineer involved in wetlands restoration.

Then one evening months later, Del tossed me a tablet. "Read this."

I glanced at the first page, then did a quick swipe. "Eleven pages?"

"Just read." She pulled thumb and index finger across her closed lips. "And please keep the peanut gallery quiet till you've finished."

It was the first draft of what would become her dissertation's introduction. And you know what? I ended up memorizing the first few pages. Not intentionally; I just kept reading it. Over and over. Pretty soon I found myself reciting it. Over and over.

Now I'm curious. Do I still remember those words? On AF46, can I recite any of them?

❖

Ah yes, there's this:

> *Despite our myths and our wishful thinking, human beings cannot defy the natural laws that govern all of earth's life forms, including us. There is no such thing as human exceptionalism.*

Kinda have to smile; I always liked that last sentence. So simple. So fucking scary.

Been chanting it long enough—*no such thing as human exceptionalism*—that it's starting to weave into a long-ago memory of the first time I ever held Evvie.

God, I was massively fucked up then. Barely more than three months out of a POW camp and back from the dead (literally), just strong enough to have stomped off in a raving fit and got the shit beat out of myself because, essentially, I wanted to get the shit beat out of myself.

Then I stumble through the night back to Great Hill, and who lays eyes on me for the first time in her life when she finds me curled in a semi-conscious drool near the house? Lily's sister, that's who. Del.

Del, who I'd never seen before the moment she leaned over me with an expression I hope I always remember and asked, "Oh baby, what happened to you?"

For two days afterward, I lay on my belly recovering from my escapade while Del kept a discreet distance, playing Bach and Chopin on Mary's piano downstairs. Serenading me, she joked four years later when she asked me to marry her.

But that morning when I first held Evvie, Del was still asleep and I'd planned to scurry off before she appeared, not ready yet to look again into eyes that had witnessed the cringeworthy truth of me—

And then I held Evvie.

She and her mother were in cahoots, of course.

"Don't want Jamie to go yet, huh?" Lily said to her in a soft singsong voice.

Evvie gurgled a grin and reached for her mother's face.

"Okay, then," Lily responded, "we'll ask Jamie to have some breakfast with us."

Lily's smoky golden eyes slowly lifted to meet mine, and that was that; her follow-me wink foreclosed all other options. "But we're doing a bottle this time, understand?" she said to Evvie. "Mama's tits are on vacation this morning. Now Jamie's going to hold you for a little bit, so you be nice."

A few feet behind Lily, I stood immobilized at the prospect. A sniper rifle, sure, but an *infant*?

"Trust me," Lily said, laughing. "You can handle it."

"Yeah, but—" I had no clue where to put my arms. "Her head—"

"Oh, Evvie's a big girl now," Lily crooned, tickling her daughter's nose. "Almost five whole months. You keep your head up all by yourself, don't you? You can even sit."

Evvie babbled happy assent as Lily handed her over. "That's it. Very good. Not so hard, huh?"

Evvie's wide, smoky golden eyes watched me attentively, seriously, waiting.

While Lily bustled about the kitchen retrieving her chilled breast milk and a bottle to put it in, I did the only thing I could think of. I smiled.

Whereupon Evvie's face lit with her own grin. "Aah," she declared.

"Hi," I said softly, finally working up the nerve to imitate the way Lily rocked her.

"Aah," Evvie repeated, and then she laughed.

I held her while she and her mother ate a leisurely breakfast and the kitchen slowly filled with the rest of the clan. I was nineteen, newly wombless.

"I-I never knew about this," I remember whispering to Lily as Evvie and I studied each other. "About how this feels."

No such thing as human exceptionalism.

Ah. Just remembered more of what Del wrote.

> *For human life to thrive on this earth, much that we have taken and misused we must return. Fortunately, we have such capability.*
>
> *A Wilderness Web is a simple idea born of this understanding. Its goal is to constrain the reach and impacts of the human enterprise's boundless avarice, to realize our necessary place in the dynamic balance that is our world.*

I remember how I closed my eyes after reading that for the first time. Oh dear god, Del, don't make me have to deal with this. Tell me there's more time, please. Enough time for us to just live, to be with the people we love, watch the girls grow up—

I remember opening my eyes to meet Del's gaze. I swear she knew precisely what I was thinking. She gave me a tiny nod. Yes, we'll watch the girls grow up, but into what kind of world?

❖

AF49.
Wednesday, April 22.
I dreamed last night of Del reciting parts of her dissertation's introduction. There were times today when I could hear her in the steam pipe sound permeating the cell…

> *A Wilderness Web begins with what we have. All lands and seas currently set aside for habitat conservation and wildlife preservation are deemed sacrosanct and we expand from there, adding to them and prioritizing the identification and protection of extensive land and sea links between them to create a web of connected wildernesses: a single vast worldwide Wilderness Web.*

My stomach turns now as I hear Del's words in the cell's sibilating whir, just as my stomach turned years ago when I read those words for the first time.

A single vast worldwide Wilderness Web. I knew immediately. Del will spend the rest of her life making enemies. She's smart and charming and wittily clever and so fucking beautiful to look at—people will do more than follow her, people will Receive her. And people threatened by her views and her power to inspire others will hate her. Or worse.

> *These are not new ideas. They have been expressed for generations, and a few have found ways to live according to their tenets. But unless we all embrace the unequivocal necessity of these tenets and act together to apply the powers of society and governments to realize them, the entire human enterprise will fail.*

I realize now how much I saw back then. The Wilderness Web

would become far more than a dissertation. It would become the center of Del's life, the foremost recipient of her vision, her radiantly charismatic intelligence. It would attract many people, plenty of money, and way too much conflict. At that moment, it was nothing more than eleven pages, but I knew, I already knew.

And I wanted to cry, I wanted to grab her and retreat deep into a hidden cave and wrap myself around her and hold on tight tight tight forever and get her to agree to stay there with me always, there where we'd be left alone, where we'd be safe.

Kept it to myself, though. It seemed too much like irrational panic, the bite of leftover PTSD. I offered a smile instead, a nod. And she kissed me, her body following her mouth in a long and hard and hungry kiss that told me yes, she'd heard my every unsaid word, and yes, somewhere deep down where she couldn't look yet, yes, she was, if not outright afraid, then at least a little nervous, but she wanted to do it anyway, needed to give it everything she had.

I kissed her back long and hard and hungry, rising up to her so she'd understand that I'd be there with her.

But when light electric pinpricks shivered up my spine, Del noticed. We were almost three years into living together, and pretty much nothing got by her anymore.

To create a Wilderness Web, we must first believe such a thing is possible. In the face of the objections of the powerful and the weary hopelessness of cynics, we must maintain faith in our ability to show why working for a Wilderness Web is worthwhile.

To create a Wilderness Web, we must change minds long hardened and closed, and we must persuade legal precedent to our point of view—a point of view that can perhaps best be characterized by Hegel's simple phrase: "Real freedom is the recognition of necessity."

Today, now, a Wilderness Web has become a pressing necessity that we deny at our mortal peril. Only when we acknowledge this do we have a chance to achieve the real freedom that derives from living within the means provided by the earth's always finite yet exquisitely diverse resources.

She pulled away to examine me. "What, baby?" she whispered. "Tell me what."

I inhaled again, or tried to, but my gut had knotted. I owned up in a single, breath-deprived wheeze. "They will try to destroy you for this. You know that, right?"

Oh god, the way her eyes sparked. The memory of it makes me ache as I lie here. She took my hands and studied the small teardrop scar on one, then the other as her fingers gently circled the matching nodules of collagen centered in each of my palms.

Yeah, I thought, take a good long look at what happens when a fight gets seriously crazy.

A crease formed between eyebrows skittering with what she didn't say. "You don't need to be afraid for me," she did say.

Like hell I don't, I wanted to yell but managed not to. "It's just—" I remember how my eyes cast down of their own accord. "Aw, Del..."

One hand gentle on my jaw, she urged my chin up, up, until our eyes met. "Oh, Jamie, my sweet, sweet girl." She smiled and pressed her forehead against mine. "I know you still have a foot in two worlds. I see your nightmares—"

"You do?"

My sleep gets slightly physical when it's a nightmare, she said, and I started to freak that I'd hurt her, but no, she said, "not violent or anything," and besides, she was glad when my nightmares woke her.

"I nuzzle up close to you. Face-to-face." She nestled her cheek very delicately, very slowly against my nose and mouth and her warm, sweet Del-scent filled my nostrils, swept my brain. I felt myself exhale, loosen, relax.

"And yeah," she murmured, "that's what you do. Settles you right down. I like to think it changes your nightmare into something else. Something better. Because I see them less now. A lot less."

Goddamn. When my nightmares receded for those few months after I returned from the Corps, I convinced myself I'd beaten them back. Even said as much to Del. When they started creeping in again, mere fragments at first, then full-on epic horrors, I said nothing. Told myself living through them once was plenty. After all, my jittery hypervigilance, which Del endured daily, was sufficient pain-in-the-assery—no need to add more.

Goddamn. I hadn't fooled her one bit. "You knew," I said.

"Of course I did." Del spoke softly, her lips close to my ear. "I also know about that high-frequency tremor you do right before you're going into warrior mode."

"Old habits," I mumbled. "Hyper-reaction is a snipe's best friend."

"I do *not* want you in warrior mode, Jamie." Oh jeezus, Del is sexy when she straightens her back and makes a proclamation.

"I'm okay," I told her, still relaxed by her nearness, her scent. I glanced at the tablet screen on my lap where the last of her eleven pages glowed. Could be ten years, even more, I thought, before I'll have to contend with who this woman needs to become. "But a whole lot of people sure as hell won't like your Wilderness Web."

"How fortunate it's not just *my* Wilderness Web, then, huh?" Del grinned. "*If* I can make those eleven pages into something, mine will be one of many treatises. And if I'm lucky, I'll be that girl engineer in grungy wellies best known for the great course she teaches in environmental economics. After that, if I'm *real* lucky I'll get an invitation to give a talk somewhere moderately interesting. And you and I will live happily ever after."

I remember smiling back at her, wanting so much to believe Del was on her way to a career commuting between polluted wetlands and the towers of onlink academia—periodically muddy but plenty safe regardless of how much fretting she might inspire among moguls of industry. Ninety percent safe.

I smiled because even if this Wilderness Web thing turned into a war, at least it'd be the right war, fought on a bloodless battlefield with weapons of language and law where my warrior competencies—stalking, shadowing, dodging, ghosting, the occasional quick and fatal ambush—would no longer be required.

And I smiled because I'd just found out that Del tends me, loves me, heals me in a way I never knew about.

"Which is why I'm okay. Really truly." I pulled her close and kissed her, caressed her soft into deep. "And please—" Kissed her into undulating. "Let me *show* you—" Caressed her into electric. "Just *how* okay I am living happily ever after with you."

❖

AF52.
Saturday, April 25.

Del was right about the Wilderness Web. It was never just hers.
But the name she gave it in her dissertation stuck. Within three

years of her showing me those first eleven pages, she'd become its face, too. And its lightning rod.

Gotta say, though, the evolution of the Wilderness Web appears precipitous only in retrospect. In fact, none of it happened suddenly; it had been churning for a long time before Del wrote anything, yet what she wrote seemed to bring on a tipping point.

The first rustles of interest in her work came from other academics. Then, almost as soon as the university press accepted her dissertation for publication, she was hired to build a Wilderness Web undergraduate open course, just as she'd hoped. The ninety-minute stripped-down version that got so much attention was her idea, and she had no trouble enlisting that hotshot media designer Gideon-whatever to slick it up for her.

It was breakthrough for the Wilderness Web movement, thrilling for Del. And it was a horror for me.

So much for my ten years to deal with it all. Hardly more than four years passed between the evening I saw those first eleven pages and the morning that the number of hits for *What in the World Is a Wilderness Web?* topped eight figures.

After that, buzz about a Wilderness Web Coalition seemed to pop up in a dozen places at once—as did Del's face. People would stop her in the street to talk with her, ask for a selfie. I hated it. I will always hate it.

I mean, *how* do you trust that? Strangers just invading her space like they have a right to her. Bad enough when she invites it, like at a fundraiser. But they maraud her on the sidewalk, in stores and restaurants, on the fracking train, for chrissake.

It creeps me the fuck out. *Those people* creep me the fuck out.

I know I'm mostly being unfair to them. Mostly. But it's the Not Mostly I worry about; they're the ones who require a vigilance that used to be second nature to me.

Not anymore, though.

Truth is, I fought the wrong fucking war, and its pointless, unyielding cruelty fomented a turmoil I cannot escape. That's what happens when you blow a six-year-old's head off. The immense *NO!* of that irretrievable instant replays in my head every day, its entropy growing inside me. I lose sensation to the chaos it started, I lose my own presence. Over the years, I've twisted and warped into some sort of unrecognizable fractal of the sniper I once was.

Truth is, I can no longer be trusted.

Truth is, doing school took all I had, as has pulling off a modest little life with Del and staying focused enough to design decent structures.

So I worried about failing Del because I believed a time would come when she'll need who I once was. And who I once was won't be there.

I tried to explain this to her.

She tried to soothe me, told me not to worry.

Her battlefields, she's always assured me, are boardrooms, courtrooms, media studios, legislative chambers, auditoriums. Her weapons are sharp, yes, but bloodless: ideas, words, the mighty skills of convincing argument. Hers are the comfortable fights of the privileged. No worries about poverty or violent, untimely death.

Not that there wasn't shit. Not that Del didn't exhibit the occasional high-frequency tremor herself; I've seen her shudder at some of the hate messages, flinch inconspicuously at anomalous sounds when she's in a restive crowd.

But she gets pissed off when people try to intimidate her. Makes her more stubborn, more determined, willing to take more risks.

Which means she needs all the protection she can get. Most of the time, she's been protected well, since we both got to piggyback on all the Callithump security built around anywhere Lily, Dana, and the girls frequent. That covers Birch Lane and Great Hill.

But not the public stuff, which always sent me into a cold sweat.

I coped with the invitation-only fundraisers. Even open fundraisers are generally manageable; they tend to attract like-minded souls. People who dislike the idea of a Wilderness Web generally abhor being peer-pressured for money to support it, so the few who might show up to do a jackass routine are usually easy to spot and neutralize.

What Del calls "affairs" were another matter, though comparatively benign security-wise. High-end, full of well-heeled people worth attempting to influence; Del began to get invited to these because she'd become a fad of sorts—someone others wanted to meet and be seen with.

"People use their causes to compete with each other," Del explained when I initially bitched about Why Are We Doing This? "And, conveniently, people with lots of money do it with donations."

I'd watch her play them off each other. Plenty of those who intended to do nothing more than sniff around her to satisfy their curiosity became converts, even if they had to stay in the closet because of their corporate or political affiliations. Del is that good. Others were steel-hard impenetrable or coolly arrogant or, every now and then, unabashedly hostile.

One of the worst of these was the first of these. I didn't know who he was as I watched him stand as erect as possible—the only way he could come close to Del's height—and loudly, contemptuously declare Del a fool for expecting a man like him to relinquish anything to anyone. He seemed so close to losing control that I figured I'd have to pound a knee into his testicles to prevent him laying hands on her. I positioned myself for a swift kick, just in case, but a glance from Del held me back, and he hectored on. And on.

He wanted her to collapse in tears, which, of course, she did not. Instead, her willingness to wait out his tantrum with an amused smile seemed to inflame his diatribe—until at last he needed to pause for breath. That's when Del, with a quick wink, replied serenely, "Vir triumphalis, memento mori."

Latin, I guessed, but I had no idea what it meant. Neither did the fellow Del said it to or the older man next to him, who'd been smirking and snarking him on the whole time.

But the woman they'd accompanied understood. Her already pallid, over-painted face went even whiter and she pulled both men away before either of them spoke another word. Two or three people nearby, safely anonymous in the hovering crowd, had the temerity to titter.

"Who the hell was that?" I asked in a whisper as soon as they turned their backs on us.

"Warrick van Gelderen and his wife, Marilyn, famous for her jewelry collection. And the unprecedented number of heart stem cell treatments she's had."

"Looks like she could use another one, or maybe it's time for a transplant," I said. "And the older guy?"

Del drew a deep breath. "That's her father. Marvin Este Malik."

"The banker dude they call 'The Trillionaire'?" This explained the three large men in dark suits and reflective eyewraps orbiting them in granite silence.

"Ah well." Del took my arm in a graceful sweep that made my loins throb. "I suppose it could've been much worse. All considered."

What had I missed? "Van Gelderen," I repeated, trying to catch up. "Is he—?"

"The CEO of Georgica Corporation." Del sounded unusually satisfied.

Oh. Right. The world's largest agricultural conglomerate. "The plaintiff in that eminent domain case you've been so worried about?"

"Yes, ma'am." Del had danced around the living room when one of the attorneys called to tell her the Ninth Circuit Court had ruled against Georgica and for the Coalition. "I'm guessing they intend to appeal again."

"Damn," I said, scrutinizing her face. "You knew he'd be here, didn't you?"

"Well, it seemed likely," she admitted. "I knew Marilyn would be here."

And what had she said to him?

"'Man of triumph, remember you are mortal.'" Del's left shoulder, draped in black silk, lifted slightly, defiantly when she told me, but she didn't smile.

Both Marvin Este Malik and Warrick van Gelderen glanced back at her then; they had, I suspected, just been told what *Vir triumphalis, memento mori* means. Their faces remained entirely expressionless, but that's when I understood how easy it is for those with shitloads of money and an appetite for power to snarl a vague "Take care of that problem" at an eager assistant.

Et voilà! People hire other people who hire still other people who find vandals and crazies and wind them up to do the vicious, bloody, untraceable deeds everybody pretends are random accident or the ever-reliable "isolated incident." And anyone who says different is a nutcase.

Del's so-called "affairs" and people like van Gelderen aren't even the worst of it. She also does plenty of what she calls "the missionary sell"—venturing outside the wire to take on skeptics and doubters.

As far as I'm concerned, these events—Del calls them "rallies"—pose real danger. Among the curious, mostly okay throngs skulk the crazies. Including the crazies who might, whether they're aware of it or not, be serving the interests of people like van Gelderen.

Naturally, I went with her to rallies, pistol tucked close; it was the most effective way for me to keep my head from exploding. Del didn't do a single "missionary sell" event without me. No fucking way. A few times I found myself stepping between her and some loudmouth who rampaged beyond debate into profanity-infused ad hominem attack. Once, I shoved a dude who was probably drunk. But that was about it.

As the months passed into years, I watched Del's cause gain ground in boardrooms, in courtrooms, in media studios, in legislative chambers, in auditoriums, even at her so-called rallies. I saw the haughtiest of enemies treat her with chilly politeness. I saw some of the rudest retreat out of grudging respect. And not an assassin in sight.

I began to trust ninety percent safe. I understood we were lucky, of course. But we'd been cautious, too, which had paid off. I guess we convinced ourselves we could scoot back unscathed on our magic carpet of privilege to the ninety percent safe of Birch Lane and Great Hill.

Hell, why not? We were nearly as privileged as it got: lawyers at the ready, guns and money as required.

And it worked. For years. Maybe it's working still. I wish to hell I knew.

CHAPTER EIGHT

Before the vulture notices

AF56.
Wednesday, April 29.

I think something's happening to me. I can hear a kind of frenzied, gasping, almost-panicky edge in my voice even now. Comes with a low-level itchy-burny sensation, like something's alive and on fire and wriggling low in my gut, clawing at my genitals from the inside, desperate to escape. Almost hurts. Almost.

Maybe the vulture wants more of me than I thought.

Out of the chaos born of initial conditions I can't see, my dreams are dragging me where I don't want to go. I'm losing control of the daytime to memories I'd rather not remember, connections I'd rather not make.

And I can't get myself to stop.

❖

AF59.
Saturday, May 2.

My dreams keep on jumbling. The last couple of nights have prolapsed from strange to creepy. I don't want to go to sleep anymore. Don't want to shut my eyes and find my way to *before* anymore.

The chaos swallowing my dreams tries to get me to believe lies, impossibilities; it's all cambering out of perspective, out of scale, out of time. Nobody should be peeking at me from red-tinged shadows that defy the laws of physics. My mother and father and Cecilia Danta should not be coming to Thanksgiving dinner at Great Hill. Sapphira Honeyjohn should not be hitting on Del.

And Del—

Oh god, Del should not be dancing on her birthday without me. Woke up with that dream in my head this morning.

I've been hoping it would pass, but instead it's getting worse. My dreams are fucking with me, betraying me, and I can no longer trust them.

❖

AF65.
Friday, May 8.

Late on AF61, after I was curled up on the bunk and not ten fucking seconds before I was going to nudge Audy from her hiding place for a quick recharge, two Homo sapienshits came storming in here.

No announcement, hardly any noise. I heard the clank of the outer cell door lock opening, but the sound was exceptionally muted, so I didn't grasp what it was, much less that they were coming in here, until they began unlocking the inner cell door. By the time I rolled over to see what was happening, I was staring at custodian digits suspended two feet above me aimed at my face.

From somewhere behind the custodian, a sapienshit ordered me to flip onto my belly, hands behind my back, and within a minute or so they had me hooded and cuffed up, my wrists hogtied to my ankles. Then the custodian hoisted me off the bunk, all my weight dangling from the single point where my hands and feet had been chained together. The robot carried me out of the cell and, mercifully, dumped me on the corridor floor. Close enough to hear the sapienshits—actual human beings—search my cell.

They took their sweet time, during which I tried not to think about what they'd do to me when they found Audy. And then, without a word, I was hoisted again, returned to the bunk, cuffs and hood removed, and they were gone.

I didn't check to see if Audy remained where I'd left her. Not till last night. Intended to wait longer, but I couldn't stand it and let my fingers unfold Vesica…and, yes yes yes, there she was, still apparently undiscovered and untouched.

Took me a while to calm down enough to hear anything but the slam-banging of my own heartbeat. When I finally tried to do a brief entry, Audy was nearly out of juice, so I spent the time hand-charging her. And deciding I need to ration her.

Means I'm having to ration my sanity, too. But rationing Audy will reduce the risk of discovery—and reduce how quickly I consume Audy's storage.

So I'm choosing this grim optimism: a log entry once every four days. One night alone, another night alone, then on the third night, I hand-charge Audy, resist temptation, and give her right back to Vesica. Finally, on the fourth night, I retrieve Audy and listen to my previous entry, or maybe two, before logging a new one.

That's my meager protocol. For the sake of preserving storage space, I considered stretching the cycle to five or six days, but I cannot be trusted. More than four days between Audy log entries, and I worry about flubbing the count.

I'm hoping my very own jody call will help. AF *what*? AF *six five*! What day *now*? It's *Friday* now! What *date* this day? *May eight* this day!

Kinda clunky, but so far it's working. Gets me through as I try to dull the dread I feel when I walk back into the inner cell after my shifts, when that door slams and locks behind me.

❖

AF69.
Tuesday, May 12.

No point in denying it. My dreams have become malicious. Every one begins differently, but they're ending the same way now—someone wants to kill me. I fight back, sometimes I even escape or am absolved. And then I see her.

She stands well away from me, child-small, utterly silent, her face shadowed. I call to her, but she retreats. I try again, beg her stay, please stay, and when she ignores me I pursue her farther and deeper into dark, gnarled places I do not recognize. Until I'm back where I began, and I'm caught again, condemned again. About to be killed again. And this time I understand I have no right to fight for myself; this is how I must do my small part toward paying the debt, restoring the balance.

Each night, my dream-death crescendos a few seconds before the cell voice launches into the new day's first harangue. I'm flung thrashing through the borderland between sleep and consciousness, trying to see what rushes toward me. But there's only darkness. Until I perceive, for barely the blink of an eye, the innocent relief of awake—

Hey, look, only a dream…

For the tiny duration of that blink, I could be anywhere in spacetime. I could be cuddled around Del, I could be sitting on the granite mound at Great Hill watching the sea, I could be seven years old listening to *Canon in D* with my mother. Until the next blink, and I'm trapped in this stifling, corroding abomination waiting to be killed, knowing the shadowed child will be there in my dreams, behind my eyelids, until my final sentient moment.

❖

AF73.
Saturday, May 16.

Heard a helo today. I think. The nightmares continue. The nightmares rule. Every night, all night. They're toying with me now before they come in for the kill.

I try not to stare at the scratches on the wall. They've started to move when they think I'm not looking. Since I haven't quite lost *all* my marbles, I know they're not supposed to do that.

At least they stop when I focus right on them. But when I attempt to track all of their movements, my attention bouncing from one to another like a Ping-Pong ball, I start to trip up on my jody call. I know if I let that go on for very long, I'll lose the count. And whatever else I do, I...must...not...lose...the...count.

So now I shut my eyes when I lay me down to sleep, shut my eyes and work at remembering little bits of *before* as best I can. Small, quick clips of *before* with Del and Lynn mostly, and Mary and the kids, too, bits of memory that I sneak-view before the vulture notices and takes me farther back, too far back. Back to the blood.

AF what? AF seven three. What day now? It's Saturday now. What date this day? May one six this day.

CHAPTER NINE

Do you remember me?

AF77.
Wednesday, May 20.

God, how I detest this inner cell. It's almost too dark for shadows, but I see shadows anyway, and I can guess who lurks in them. I force my eyes to the scratches on the wall, but they mock me. *See how fucking crazy you are, cunt? Looky, looky while we dance for you...*

Sometime last night I saw blood oozing from one of the rusty scratches just above my head. Maybe I was awake. Maybe I was dreaming.

Closing my eyes doesn't help; even before I fall asleep, I'm a prisoner of war again locked away in the hellhole we called Saint Eh Mo's, ready to die again, life instinct bargaining with death instinct as my tormenter, eager for her fun, picks her moment.

Elegant, chilling, Shoo Juh no longer bothers with the pretense of interrogation. She sits back relaxed and watches, directing her silent, rigid men with a flick of a wrist or an eyebrow or a syllable. Now, unlike *before*, I understand every communication. Dreams can be like that. I have time to anticipate, too much time. What'll ten more lashes do to my backside? What'll the electrified baton feel like when her grunting minions truss me up and force me to ride it like a broom?

I beg for it to be over, and she laughs as she taunts me. "It will never be over, hong mao."

❖

AF81.

Sunday, May 24.

Just six years old. Her name was Awa, which means "mercy," and I killed her when I was nineteen and trying to be a good marine. I've never seen a picture of her, but in my dreams, she is beautiful and playful. In my dreams, as I watch her, I sense she's curious about me, but regardless of what I do or say, she keeps her distance; she knows to be afraid of me.

I killed her seventy-one days before I was captured and became Saint Eh Mo's first prisoner, seventy-two days before Shoo Juh began uncovering my truths and colluding with my deepest desire: punishment. All I had to do was resist.

It was a simple enough proposition. Shoo Juh would interrogate me, demand information. I would decline to provide it. She would beat the crap out of me until she beat me to death.

She played along at first, or I thought she did. But she had her own plans, her own desires, and she is—was, dammit, *was*—a genius. Only after she got all the information she wanted from me did I appreciate her special talent: understanding when and how to induce pain without killing her plaything or even doing permanent damage.

And oh god, how she delighted when she knew she had me; the excitement would charge her voice. Took her a while to nail it, of course. For a good long stretch I managed to goad her into overdoing it, which would send me beyond pain altogether, into a limp stupor that often swept me all the way out of my own body.

Ah, but when she got it right…I hated her for that. Hate her still. In my dreams from more than a decade ago, in my unstoppable dreams here, now, in this rusting steel coffin, I hear her. "You deserve this, hong mao. You deserve to be emptied. Scoured."

Shoo Juh owns me once I'm asleep. And as her punishments conclude, she journeys from then to now, badgering me as I crawl toward awake. "Open your eyes, hong mao."

I refuse.

But Shoo Juh knows my fear—that the rusty scratches on the walls waiting to greet my waking eyes have transmuted and I will see the truth of them, see how they drip with Awa's blood, with the blood of all scout/sniper Gwynmorgan's many, many targets.

❖

AF84.

Wednesday, May 27.

If I've botched the count at all since Audy came into my possession, it's been because Shoo Juh's been messing with me.

Last night, she had me yanked up, my hands chained behind my back, my feet scrambling for something, anything to take my weight, and I was screaming at her. "What do you *want*?!"

I heard her answer from far away, "I want to say good-bye..."

Just like all those years ago—

And then I was simply standing, surrounded by green. Awa's nearby, I thought, because often in my dreams Awa is surrounded by lush green. Soon I spotted her, shadowed as has become her custom. She edged away from me, so I followed. And once more I found myself in, yes, a dark and gnarled place: another captivity somewhere. Not Saint Eh Mo's, and not here.

I'd been whisked away chained and hooded, brought to some sort of medical facility, where I was manhandled by machines and masked people doing things with needles and probes. Later, I was in a cage, all fucked up on some kind of pharma.

I woke up briefly. Or maybe I dreamed I woke up. Who the hell can tell anymore?

And next I was outside, heard and then saw a helo's rotors above me and guys in dark clothes dragged me and I was fighting them, fighting them, and they electrolasered me before they jabbed a needle in my haunch.

If that had been the end of it—just wake up and trudge through another zombie day on the elliptical—I'd be sticking to my four-day schedule, hand-charging Audy right now in preparation for logging an entry tomorrow night.

But that hasn't been the end of it. I spent every single shift today wafted involuntarily in and out of flashbacks—not of Saint Eh Mo's but of the place I dreamed about last night.

And yeah, okay, maybe I'm crazy. You know what, though? This crazy dyke believes those flashbacks today were memories. Real live episodic memories from the time after I was grabbed on that November sixth and before the fog lifted eighty-four days ago.

I'm not sure about chronology, but after today's parade of flashbacks I have fragments of different periods very much like now, each one precipitated by a moment when I ceased cooperating in my own captivity and ended up being subdued, hooded, punished, drugged.

I lost, of course. Every time. But at least I fought them.

❖

AF88.

Sunday, May 31.

The nightmares continue and I've slogged through more flashback-riddled days, too. Compared to my outrageously contorted nightmares, however, the flashbacks were solid, fine-grained—and at first I studied them, you know? Had a hard time giving up the notion that if I knew more, just a little more, I'd understand why I'm here. And from *why* I'd be able to reverse-engineer how to get out of here.

But then—

Ah shit, yesterday was awful.

Flashes of being wretchedly ill—nausea, vomiting, shaking, sweating, my heart racing, double vision, too weak to stand up.

Flashes of being in some kind of hospital, four-point restraints, helpless while this gaggle of people—all masked—ogled me during their discussion of my physical condition. Obscure medical details, measurements of the state of my blood, my liver, my lungs, my heart. According to them, I was underweight, in need of some aerobic exercise after too long with too little physical activity, but nevertheless in excellent condition. "Great numbers, damn good match," one of them kept repeating. "Almost exactly what we've been looking for."

And I remember hearing, "We'll need to start weaning her off the cocktail..."

At that moment another person appeared above me, leaned in close. Took me a long time to focus; when I did I saw only surgical mask, forehead, and eyes—a woman's eyes, tired, curious but detached, vaguely familiar.

She gazed at me and nodded, like she approved of a cut of meat proffered by her butcher.

"No need for eyewraps," the woman replied dismissively to someone nearby. "I mean, it's not like she'll be writing a memoir, huh?"

Then the silence of no one bothering to answer an obviously rhetorical question.

I don't like to think about these flashbacks. Am I weaned yet from their cocktail? Have I been sufficiently aerobically exercised? And why did that woman's eyes seem so familiar?

❖

AF89.
Monday, June 1.
    Today is Del's birthday.
    Happy birthday, Del. I love you, Del.
    I realize I don't know how old you are. Or who you're dancing with.
    Do you remember me?

❖

AF94.
Saturday, June 6.
    I think I screwed up the count.
    Been five days, not four, since my last entry. I think.
    The scratches on the wall have stopped moving and they don't bleed so much either. That should encourage me, but it doesn't.
    A few days ago I concluded I was taken a long time ago. I remember beatings, sort of, fighting and failing to stop them from shooting me up with pharma, descents into drug-induced blurs. Sort-of memories that, arguably, could sort of account for seven-plus months of captivity.
    But the flashbacks—
    Oh god, the flashbacks drift by now on a ghostly loop carrying hints that it's gone on a whole lot longer, that my earlier sort-of memories are only the most recent epoch. My flashbacks suggest other, earlier times barely recalled, each layered one over another, each separated by the fog of being drugged all to shit.
    So far, I count four layers. I think.
    Mmm, not sure counting's helping me much anymore. Or if it ever has, really.
    Maybe I should stop and never count anything again.

❖

AF98.
Wednesday, June 10.

No nightmares anymore. Not even sure it can be called sleep. It's vast, whatever it is, and…and…

Why am I still an I? *Am* I still an I?

Hey, maybe I'm dead and I just haven't comprehended that yet.

Somebody keeps yelling at me to count.

Crazy fucking bitch. I go along with it to shut up her relentless screeching.

So okay, AF what? AF nine eight. What day now? It's Wednesday now. What date this day? June ten this day.

Like it fucking matters, bitch.

AF102.
Sunday, June 14.

Here's my theory: sometimes people die and they know it. But not always.

When I died before, I knew. Probably because it hurt like hell as my body failed—riddled with enough bullet fragments and shrapnel to start a scrap metal business. None of that hit my head, though, so my mind escaped. Not forever, of course. Just for the final whatever it is—thought? reflection? the great Oh Well?

I remember finding myself above it all, gazing down at my own shredded, bloody corpse, then upward to behold the bluest sky I've ever seen. And I understood, I welcomed what would come next—a soft, blue fade.

I've assumed the alternative to that is a jolt into nothingness—no warning, no fanfare. Like when a scout/sniper's well-aimed fifty-cal round blows your head right off. Here. Not Here.

Now I suspect there's another route out of living—one where you've died but, well, you don't notice.

Maybe you see the jolt coming and sayonara into denial—nope, not me, must be somebody else lying there.

Or it sneaks up on you by angstroms, 254 million to the inch, and you miss the moment between Here and Not Here. So you continue your routine, the habits of living; you continue and continue, fading as you continue because you're not really real anymore. But you never know that. You simply oh so slowly slide away.

❖

AF106.
Thursday, June 18.

If she screams and screams and nobody shows up to beat the shit out of her, does that mean she's dead?

Haven't tried this yet because—

Well, I heard thunder last night. Or maybe it was the night before.

So I could still be alive. And on the off chance I *am* alive, if I scream they'll hear it, and if they hear it they'll haul me out of here, beat the bejeezus out of me, then drug the bejeezus out of me—and if I'm alive...if...

Would help if I could see Del's face. But she's blurry now. Please, Del, please come back...

❖

AF110.
Monday, June 22.

So okay. Maybe I'm a ghost.

Lots of people believe in ghosts. Might be because ghosts are real in a leftover, energy-of-the-past kind of way—like the wake a boat leaves behind in the water it travels through.

Which explains why ghosts can count even as they fade. And talk to Audy. Even as they fade.

Anyway, guess what? Ghosts dream.

About nobody being able to see them or hear them. At first that freaked me out. But as I floated—ghosts float, too, from dream to waking—I started to discern the advantages of invisibility, of incorporeality.

Incorporeality—is that even a word?

Doesn't matter. Don't know what the rules of ghosting are, but I can see how evaporating out of materiality could be useful. I could float my way into the corridor and outside and then I could float up, up into the blue...

❖

AF114.
Friday, June 26.

Strong thunderstorm out there tonight, lots of rain slapping the roof. I celebrate the rat-tat-tatting of it, this force beyond anyone's control. Beyond *their* control. I hope lightning strikes the custodians, the sapienshit guards, the buildings. I hope it blows this fucking place apart.

❖

AF118.
Tuesday, June 30.

Stupid to whine *please please please* just because four days of lightning and thunder—even close like it's been, close enough to shake the building, shake the cell—might actually have turned into something that could help me.

Hell, not even being dead has gotten me out of here.

The bitch who demands I count snickers at such a notion. Dead? Why should *you* be that lucky?

By the second day of storms, I cheered every rumble, every shuddering thud. And yeah, I prayed. You bet your ass I prayed the lightning would whack something, anything—including me. If lightning strikes while I'm on that fucking elliptical, all my problems could be solved.

Couple of times today it came damn close. During the third shift, something with an almighty tingle rock-and-rolled me right off the frackin' machine, which actually glowed a faint blue for a nanosecond. I'd have landed on my head if my hand hadn't had a death grip on the handlebar.

Damn. The rubber soles of the bobos on my feet and the rubber handlebar grips could not possibly have insulated me from the effects of a lightning strike's hundred million volts, but here I am, apparently unscathed. No burns, no trouble breathing. Nothing broken or even sore. No dizziness or disorientation. Heartbeat's fine.

I got right back on the machine hoping for a twofer, but no luck.

I'll keep praying, though. Don't stop now, lightning. I'm here, right here. Whack me, lightning, *please please please* come back and whack this ghost once and for all!

❖

AF123.

Sunday, July 5.

Thunderclaps and rain rattled the roof all day and into the night of AF121. Then, very late, early hours of AF122, the power went out. Only very briefly. Maybe a minute, two at most. Damnedest thing, though. When the power failed, the inner cell door made its usual clattering-open sound.

No lights, so I couldn't see anything; the darkness was absolute. As was the silence—no white noise hissing, no cell voice droning orders. Only the clank of the inner cell door.

So I felt my way to it. And, by god, it *had* opened.

Made a quick bet with Caprice that loss of power also meant loss of cam surveillance and scurried to the outer cell door. Soon as I reached it and realized it had remained locked, I heard yelling—a man first, then a woman.

He hollered something unintelligible—sounded like, "Eye-mah-zahwah." Then he bellowed, "Anybody here?"

A female voice, farther away, echoed back. "Heeere," she yelled. "Reeel!"

Then other voices, at least four or five. Maybe more.

Took my damn breath away.

By the time I'd inhaled enough air to yell too, the power flickered—on, then off again. I scooted back to the inner cell a nanosecond before the power came back on for good, and as soon as it did the inner cell door started swinging shut.

The outer cell light also snapped on, the white noise resumed, and within a few seconds the cell voice intoned, "DETAINEE, YOU HAVE TEN SECONDS TO STAND AND STATE YOUR IDENTIFICATION NUMBER—NINE, EIGHT..."

So I obeyed and waited, worrying that maybe the cameras and microphones had *not* gone down when the power failed. Which means they'd know I'd ventured all the way to that outer cell door.

But nobody ever came to hassle me, even though the custodians and multiple sapienshit guards went banging and shouting up and down the corridor long enough to delay the day's first MRE and the first shift on the elliptical. Before they boosted the buzzy-hissy noise volume, I heard a guard accuse one, then another detainee of leaving their inner cells. I heard them drag a couple of people off, too—probably those caught by the cams in their outer cells.

Circumstantial evidence, I admit, but convictions—and more than a few immodest prison sentences—have been built on less. This jury's verdict: the cams and sensors and mics in here go down during power outages.

But I'm still sensible enough to avoid taking needless chances. Which is why I waited an extra day to log in to Audy. Just in case.

Meanwhile, I've pondered why the inner cell door opened when the power died. Probably has what's called a fail-insecure locking mechanism, designed so its solenoid-driven bolt needs energy to engage. Whenever the power's turned off—or if the power fails—the locking solenoid disengages and the door automatically unlocks and opens.

No doubt this should never have happened. Surely the backup power supply—a couple of rows of honking batteries and/or a room-sized generator somewhere nearby—ought to have kicked in when the primary power source was cut. But something or someone failed.

Good to know the power supply here has vulnerabilities. And goddamn, there's other people—*real people* locked in here like me. No longer conjecture, real knowledge—grim, but almost exhilarating.

❖

AF127.
Monday, July 9.

Can't be sure what happened to me last night was actually dreaming. Not even sure I was asleep.

Certainly I *felt* awake, or alert anyway, remembering events that did actually happen—reliving them almost—in minute, high-def, 3-D, stereo detail.

Even now, a whole day later, whenever I close my eyes, there it is, bright and real…

Four years almost to the day before I was ripped from my own life. The afternoon's unseasonably warm—no sign yet of the winter to come—and I'm 400 feet above the Big Mystic River, atop the emerging skeleton of the New Tobin Bridge.

I glance southward for a second toward the gleaming towers of Boston, then southeastward to the harbor, then upward to the crisp, blue November sky. I think of Luce and Biz, who just a couple of weeks before said good-bye to us all and…left. A final afternoon nap curled up together on a spacious bed in a room with a beautiful view of the sea.

The last time I saw them, they were smiling. No regrets, they said.

Four hundred feet above the Big Mystic River, the time for regrets and doubts and second thoughts is long gone for me, too. One more breath and I step carefully onto a narrow steel beam, eyeing a half-ton clamp about thirty feet ahead of me.

My task is simple enough: bolt one end of the beam into place, then release the clamp that's been holding the beam in position so the crane can lift the clamp up and away. This requires me to walk unaided across that skinny beam—no railings, nothing at all to hold on to.

I know everyone on the raising gang has stopped whatever they've been doing to watch me, the novice engineer consigned by my old-school boss to an old-school supervisor; they've decided I should play apprentice ironworker for a week in order to see how a bridge *really* gets built.

When I took the job—the only job I'd been offered since Isaac Franklin booted me from GKN four months earlier—I figured I'd have to deal with something like this, but I didn't expect it quite so soon. Or quite so 400 feet high.

For the briefest instant when I first stand on the beam, I quiver as a new and strange sensation owns me body and mind. Suddenly, I'm dizzy, spinning, the contents of my stomach already gushing up my esophagus; the sensation draws my gaze past the delicate boundary of balance to the river 400 feet *down there* and whispers…*Let go.*

I muster all the energy I possess and *will* myself to ignore what's happening to me. To *bree-ee-eathe.* The sensation dissolves and I take my first step.

The guys in the raising gang, brusque and unforgiving, have probably put a few bucks on the odds. Will she be able to walk the iron? Will she be able to walk it if somebody whistles or catcalls, if the erratic breeze decides to slap her with an invisible gust?

It'd be fine with one or two of them if I fail the test and free fall maybe twenty feet before the yo-yo that attaches my sturdy leather harness to the beam catches me and, despite my heavily insulated outerwear, ruptures god knows what inside me, the price of stopping a fatal plunge into the river below.

"Hey, rivet," coos Brunker, the roughest of them, "wanna dance?" There's plenty of scorn in his graveled voice, and I'm pretty sure if I look down at him now I'll find him scratching his balls or miming where he'd like to put that skanky piece of meat dangling between his legs.

"Not with you, Pinky," I reply cheerily, determined to keep my arms casually at my sides. On a whim, I stop abruptly and pivot ninety degrees to face him so he can see my shit-eating grin. "But maybe your wife—long as she's not stump-ugly like you."

My movement jiggles the huge beam, part of the staging needed to construct the bridge's decks, but I know by the frustration on Brunker's face that I've managed to appear unfazed.

Truth is, I didn't expect the jiggle, but my body adjusts itself immediately, automatically, before the adrenalized pirouette in my stomach can quite become fear, and I silently thank the straight-laced high school gymnastics coach who demanded all those balance beam sessions when I'd have preferred to be practicing on the rings.

The other guys in the gang hoot at Brunker, their focus shifting away from me. Count one for the clueless neophyte.

A few minutes later, I have my end of the beam securely bolted and the clamp removed. A few minutes after that I'm off the beam, watching the crane sweep away the now-liberated clamp, and I'm safe again.

Except for Pinky's glower. He's miffed that the gang's foreman has given me such a high-status task on only my second day among them. And my new nickname for him—appropriately ironic for someone so beefy, hairy, and, well, so Brunkerish—has already begun to stick.

"Come back sometime when we got some real wind, Major," he grumbles just loud enough for me, and only me, to hear.

I wink at him.

My head's still buzzing from the excitement of my first time walking the beam, working the bolts. I toy with the notion that I could hold my own on a raising gang; god knows, I might have to if I lose this apprentice slot, too.

My reverie is interrupted by Brunker.

"Hey, minor!" he shouts louder than he needs to. "Move your scrawny ass. I need another choker cable right the fuck now!"

I recognize his challenge. Low as apprentice engineers rank on the hierarchy, they are not subject to the whims of any ironworker. But apprentice ironworkers damn well are, and that's what I am for this week. This week only.

So is this the moment I'll pull rank and expect to be treated like an engineer, or maybe even the Marine Corps major Brunker somehow continues to believe I used to be, despite my telling him otherwise—rather than the gofer, the minor I'll embody for the next few days?

"Yes sir Pinky sir!" I holler back, snapping off a genuine salute before turning toward the manlift. I sense Brunker's beginning to like me in spite of himself. Hell, I like him in spite of myself. And despite losing Luce and Biz, despite the quiet sadness enveloping Del, I haven't felt this good in a while. Not since before Burton died.

Some of it's the relief of having finally found my way around Isaac Franklin's blackballing campaign and into another engineering job I can commute to, even though, building design master's degree in hand, I'm stuck instead working on a bridge.

But most of it comes from something else. Something about the sky, and hell, maybe it's *because* of losing Luce and Biz and my own experience with the blue.

It starts when I descend in the manlift to the barge tethered at the base of the new bridge to retrieve whatever the guys ask for—choker cable, bolts for the connectors, lunch coolers. I'm already anticipating the return trip and that transcendent rush I get every time the manlift climbs, that almost out-of-body release while I'm hoisted skyward, above the river, above the city, above everything.

"And bring me a coffee while you're at it, minor. Nice 'n' hot." Brunker tosses me his empty thermo-mug, which I catch without stopping.

His anger has relented; I can tell from his tone. And I can tell he's going to enjoy the nickname I've just given him as much as I enjoy the one he's bestowed on me.

"Yes sir Pinky sir!" I remember hollering.

Yes sir Pinky sir. I did six months on that bridge—a whole winter. Lots of onsite work, because the senior engineer I belonged to despised the cold. So I was out there instead of him. Actually made friends with Brunker, an old-school ironworker who'd never met a lesbian before and lived in an RV so he and his girlfriend could follow the jobs. He became the only person on the bridge I confided in.

By spring, I figured I was on the road to a career in bridge engineering and should probably be grateful to have stumbled beyond Isaac Franklin's remarkably long reach. And then my design took the Artemisia Center competition.

Heard about it when I was at the bridge, down on my knees checking details of the raising gang's latest efforts. I spotted worn heavy-duty work boots first, then Brunker's grizzled face wearing the biggest shit-eating grin I'd ever seen. He yanked me to my feet and into a bone-crushing bear hug.

"You did it, minor!" he trumpeted. "You fuckin' *won*!"

I actually took him out for a beer after work that day, since beer is the only way Brunker celebrates anything. At his behest I actually *drank* an entire beer, too—some ferocious brew called Aberdeen Armageddon—and had to be rescued by Del, who appeared unamused at her mission. Until she spotted me swaying on a bar stool.

"You must be Pinky," she said to Brunker even before she stopped laughing.

He rose from the bar stool next to me and bowed. "Yes, ma'am. Mr. Pinky at your service. C'mon an' join us. Minor's buyin—" He belched almost delicately behind the back of his large, rough hand. "Cuz she *won!*"

Del patted him on the back and shook his hand, gave me a bear hug nearly as bone-crushing as Brunker's followed by an exceedingly sexy kiss that had the whole place indulging in wolf whistles, then ordered a chocolate ale every bit as potent as Aberdeen Armageddon. Unlike me, however, Del can hold her beer. And get a bar full of ironworkers singing German drinking songs for an hour.

Find myself with a kind of sad smile sensation as I remember. Sad that I won't get any more moments like that. Smiling because I ever got any at all.

Chapter Ten

Local optimum

AF131.
Monday, July 13.

They keep the buzzy-hissy noise loud now. Fucking obtrusive, yet it doesn't seem as intense as before. Probably they don't understand it's not working like they want. I can distinctly hear the helos that have been thwacking overhead for the last three days. Half dozen flights a day by my reckoning.

Single-rotor utility birds, I'd guess; room for about a ton of cargo, combat radius of 400 miles or so, more if they carry supplemental fuel tanks.

Transporting god knows what. Like maybe whoever's on their helo list.

❖

AF134.
Thursday, July 16.

Today everything changed.

Everything.

Started this morning—an eon ago—mere seconds after Meals On Wheels collected the day's first MRE packaging, when the cell voice didn't order me onto the elliptical. Instead, it told me to return to the inner cell.

Definitely an *Oh shit.* I obeyed slowly, reluctantly, scared of what I'd hear next.

Then, "Detainee, you have ten seconds to face the rear of your

CELL, LIE FACEDOWN ON THE FLOOR, AND CLASP YOUR HANDS BEHIND YOUR BACK—NINE, EIGHT..."

The helo list, I thought, and freaked. Flashburn raked across my body, a firestorm sucked the air from my lungs, an invisible giant's thumbs pressed hard into my temples.

"...FOUR, THREE..."

My body obeyed without any help from my paralyzed brain. I was shivering by the time my chest met the floor, by the time the bitch achieved full snarl—"Ignominious!"—and the word's eleven letters, little neon yellow hallucinations, staggered like drunks across the bottom of the rusted wall before me—

I g n o m i n i o u s

The second time she said it, the bitch somehow made it sound like "You piece of *shit*."

Prostrate before Ignominious, I started counting.

Barely made it to three when the cell's doors clanked.

At four, I twisted my head to see, at five, a custodian's appendage roll close alongside my left leg while one of its claws/grippers/whatever-the-fuck-they-are angled fast toward my hands.

At six, handcuffs ratcheted tight around my wrists.

At eight, my ankles were chained—all steps henceforth shall not exceed eighteen inches.

At nine, custodian claws clamped my biceps and, in one swift motion, hoisted me all the way to my feet.

And didn't let go.

As the custodian pulled me backward out of the inner cell, then the outer cell, and began to force-march me in front of it toward the sally port at the center of the floor, I found myself eye-to-eyewraps with a sapienshit leaning casually against a neighboring cell door, obscured as usual behind surgical mask and boonie hat, so I didn't recognize him until I got a whiff of his bourbon and heard his voice.

"Detainee, eyes to the floor," New South commanded indifferently, not bothering to hood me. I only pretended to obey and New South didn't give a hoot. So I saw plenty.

Oh fuck, bleated the bitch.

I tried to ignore her and pay attention. Twelve large, long, gray custodian digits had encircled my biceps—six per bicep and each one designed for both delicate manipulation and quick, efficient control and/or destruction, each one capable of generating enormous force. To my biceps, it felt like irresistible force.

Soon I spotted the thin lines of a diaphragm shutter at the end of one of the digits, then another and another where the tough, flexible material retracts to expose the digit's weapon, armed and ready. Which digit carried pepper gas? Which held the electrolaser? Which bore bullets?

I'd been paying attention up to that point. Counting. A dozen doors on each side of a long corridor, then the sally port. Managed to register all kinda shit about their locks and protocols and the adjacent control center, where only a single sapienshit mostly ignores a bank of screens showing plenty of occupied cells, some with people plodding on ellipticals.

I'm not sure what I expected to see if-when I ever got a decent look beyond my cell's corroding walls, but it was worse, way worse than I'd imagined. I felt daunted.

And then they shambled me onto the covered outside stairwell. The sun hadn't yet risen and the weak overhead stairwell light glinted off fierce rain slashing across the view in front of me, so I couldn't make out much.

Took me several long seconds to spot the tower only faintly visible a hundred yards off my one o'clock. Five stories high, rooftop crowded with commo antennas and dishes, top floor all darkened gun-slotted windows, so they can look out and shoot out but nobody can look in. A second later, directly below us, I saw a courtyard.

A courtyard I *recognized*.

That's when the bitch started gasping. I joined in as soon as I beheld twenty-odd other prisoners in yellow spandex like me, chained like me, unhooded like me, standing in two hunched, sodden rows where they could easily see each other's faces. Every one of them shivered like me but, like me, not from cold.

Seems like we'd all come to the same dire conclusion. This is the day they're going to kill us, so they no longer give a shit who or what we see. As my belly cramped, the bitch's tremulous *oh fuck* ramped into hyperdrive. *Ignominious, you piece of shit*—because I didn't fight them. Like the rest, I obeyed.

How long before they stuff us into a helicopter, take us for a 200-mile easterly flight, and drop us into the Gulf Stream from several thousand feet up? Probably drug us so we'll stay compliant. While the custodian force-marched me in front of it down the stairs, I wondered if maybe I'd been drugged already via the MRE I'd just eaten.

Say good-bye, you ignominious piece of shit.

Well before the custodian conveyed me to a spot at the end of the second row of prisoners, I knew where I was. Yep, this really *is* Parris Island. What's left of it. The harsh, unequivocal knowing—yep, this really *is* Parris Island—seemed like a reason to give up. Because whoever grabbed me has the clout and impunity to stash me and a fair number of other people on federal property less than 600 miles from Lynn Hillinger's Senate office.

Best I could tell in the dimness, everything I thought I'd seen that time when New South frog-marched me across the courtyard was there. I went kinda dizzy for a bit as I took in this darker version of my melded memories, so dark I could make out only shadows.

I wondered if maybe I was dreaming. And I thought, *hey*, look at that. I can choose, like a fork in a road.

In that moment I considered just releasing my grip, letting myself well and truly surrender to what's-the-point? Exhale, let everything go fuzzy, and don't come back ever, no matter what.

Or, what the hell, I could count.

So okay. I was one of twenty-four prisoners who stood in the pummeling rain.

We were flanked by six restless sapienshit guards with the snouts of assault rifles peeking from beneath their orange rain ponchos. Four semi-upright custodians patrolled under the covered walkways that edged two sides of the courtyard, each with a transparent, plasticky-looking membrane covering the sensors on the upper part of its "body," each with three appendages on the ground, the other three aimed at us.

Having grabbed an assault rifle from somewhere, New South now stood about ten feet from me, legs wide apart, knees locked, stifling a yawn, attention wandering. I wondered if I could reach him, shackled as I was, and—?

And what? Wait till he yawns again, then maybe a two-step and a long leap to bite open his carotid artery before he has time to raise his weapon and blow me away? And then what? Hope maybe the others' bullets puncturing my body within seconds will overpenetrate and hit him, too?

Before these notions progressed any further, some dude wrapped in a blue rain poncho strutted out in front of us: New South's nod to him kicked loose a memory from my time in the infirmary. New South's buddy is the boss, right?

An edgy, fretting boss who doesn't want to be here just slightly less than he doesn't want to lose his job. I knew before he spoke a word that he needs our—that is, the prisoners'—help.

So no, we were not to be killed today.

❖

God, my legs trembled as I stood there watching my imploded world suddenly swept into an unpredictable centrifugal spin. I had a little more time. I was outside. *Outside!* Seemed like something I could work with, a sliver of light revealing survival's distant possibility.

Finally, I savored the relief of the rain, the cool, fresh air. I made myself *bree-ee-eathe*.

That's when I remembered the boss dude's name: Bouchard.

Kenny Bouchard, who's addicted to playing poker and sure as hell looks like a double-dipper to me. Kenny Bouchard, who started out issuing stern orders—keep your eyes down, focus only on the tasks you will be assigned, speak only when commanded by "staff or custodians," else we'll beat the crap outta you, etcetera, "because Camp Null discipline *will* be maintained."

Camp Null?

Kenny rattled on, but I suffered a brainbalk. *Are you shitting me? Camp* NULL*?*

I wanted to kill him. Right then. Might've tried if I hadn't been chained hand and foot. If I hadn't glimpsed that sliver of light.

My brain managed to uncrimp as Kenny finished exhorting us about how important it was "for *every*one here, for us *all* to work *together* in the face of Mother Nature's *extreme* challenge."

He meant an imminent hurricane. The "work together" part was about the pile of dirt surrounding Camp Null—actually a six-foot levee that's the only reason this hellhole doesn't flood with every high tide like most of the rest of Parris Island. To cope with the hurricane, the levee needs a boost.

"And that's what *you* are gonna do," Kenny told us. "You will add another six feet of height to that levee, starting now."

As Kenny talked, two more sapienshits—both sporting green rain ponchos—emerged from the old battalion HQ building on the northwest side of the courtyard. I suspect it's now the sapienshits' HQ, since they've erected no less than three lines of fencing to separate it from the courtyard where we stood next to the old squadbay housing the cells where they cage us.

So, eight sapienshits now, all armed, all skittish as hell.

When Kenny finally finished, we were split into groups of four, each group assigned to a sapienshit overseer. A classically clumsy hurry-up-and-wait dance followed. They stood us in single file (hurry, hurry) well apart from each other (wait, wait) and marched us through their fencing via a triple-gated sally port (wait, hurry, wait, hurry, wait, hurry, wait), letting us know along the way that the middle of those three fences is lethally electrified.

Of course, I tried to look around. But no. Eyes down, they demanded, and anyone who disobeyed got a nasty electric shock from one of their electrolasers. Knock-you-to-the-ground nasty. I was the second one it happened to—the price for glancing up at the dome centered about twelve feet above the sally port.

Hurt like hell for an infinite six seconds, but I'd be willing to pay that price again, since I now know the dome holds a multi-sensor CL160—a compound-lens cam (infrared, thermal, and low-visible light) with a 160-by-90-degree field of view, and able from a twelve-foot height to monitor a swath of ground stretching roughly forty yards by ten yards.

Flat on my back, spasms ebbing, I spotted CL160s in other strategic locations while the custodians waved their weaponized digits like psychotic mechanized sea serpents at anyone, everyone in yellow spandex. Soon the same robot that electrolasered me zapped two other prisoners, one because he shook rainwater off his face, the other for coughing.

Even the sapienshits realized the custodians were having a kind of fit when, within five or six seconds of each other, every one of them shot off electrolasers, and down went three more prisoners, though the custodians fired at another three who were unaffected because—to everyone's surprise—they stood beyond small-arms electrolaser range, which appears to be limited by the rain to about ten feet.

Anyway, Kenny intervened at that point, and within a minute the custodians backed off from us a little. A minute later, when the guy behind me sneezed, two custodians whirled their appendages and took aim at him but didn't do anything. After that, head down and scout/sniper careful, I began to look around again.

On our right, ominous behind sheets of rain and those three evil layers of razor wire fencing, loomed the squadbay-cum-cellblock where I'd been locked down for god knows how long.

Looking left was riskier. A majority of the sapienshits were positioned there because not ten yards behind them sat their HQ building—now without any fence at all between us and it. Finally, my benumbed brain recognized the evidence of Kenny's desperation. No way prisoners, and certainly not twenty-four prisoners, were ever *ever* supposed to set foot where we were in fact standing.

Swirls of rain enveloped us, but beyond the clouds the sun had risen enough to at last provide light by which to glean some detail. Amazing how different the world appears in natural light, even when it's rain-drenched.

Straight ahead, several hundred yards beyond Kenny's levee, I was able to make out the old depot headquarters building, its red brick dim gray in the downpour. A small industrial wind turbine rises next to the old building now, and a modest elevated service structure perches just to the west of it.

Inside the levee, a mere forty yards in front of us, one of those modular enclosed power substations has been erected on concrete pillars. No more than ten yards farther right, a long row of elevated solar panels stretches eastward. That area's fenced off, but with just one fence, not three—and, to my surprise, the fence has no razor wire, no sally port. The area with the substation and solar panels is accessed via a simple cam-free gate with only speaker, microphone, and, for some reason, basic numeric keypads rather than autokeyed locks.

I started counting cameras and kept counting once the sapienshits returned to hurry mode and ordered us forward for a few yards before turning us right to scuff about fifty yards eastward alongside the electrified fence that enclosed the cellblock.

By the time we halted again, at another cam-free keypad gate, I'd counted eleven cams to my right in high-redundant panoramic configurations, all targeting the cellblock building and the fenced no-man's-land around it. But I saw no cams at all to my left where the substation and solar panels are located.

That's when the sliver of survival's light got just a little brighter.

Once through the cam-free keypad gate, we stood on the edge of the battalion's old parade deck. Plenty big enough at a hundred yards by a hundred yards to serve as a helicopter pad, it claims the entire east side of this thing called Camp Null.

Around its outer perimeter as well as the outer perimeter of the whole rest of the camp, the fencing goes high-security again: three razor wire–topped layers, the middle one electrified. About twenty yards beyond this outer perimeter fencing, accessed via sally ports, the levee embankment begins.

But cam and sensor coverage of the helipad itself is nominal. So nominal it took me a while to believe what I saw.

Panoramic CL160s mounted at the corners of the outer perimeter fencing focus tightly on the fifteen yards of no-man's-land enclosed by the three-layer fencing. More CL160s sit high on poles along the levee crown to scrutinize the marsh-side levee embankment and the vast coastal wetland beyond.

But nothing covers the twenty-five-yard stretch running from the outermost perimeter fence to the top of the levee's inner embankment. *Nothing.*

I checked, rechecked, so yeah, I'm sure. The sapienshits have left a great big fucking coverage gap—a camera blind spot that continues all around the camp, a kind of blind rectangle.

The bitch had plenty to say about it, always a version of *So the fuck what?*

Because the bitch understands. Besides zappers, these fucking collars around our necks also contain locators—GPS. Unless, *until* we can figure out how to remove our collars, we can't do shit.

My first thought: they'll make us work in ankle chains, but they'll have to take off our handcuffs. So okay, once my hands are liberated I gotta find a couple of thin wires or pins that can be shaped into a pick, then rake the small lock on the collar's dead ring and maybe the ankle chain locks, too. Never mind that I hadn't picked a lock, any lock, in well over ten years, making my skills as rusty as this cell.

Second thought: find a pair of hard-wire cutters capable of handling the collar's four-mil steel links as well as the ankle chains.

Out there on the helipad for the first time, standing bruised and sore in the rain, how I'd pull off raking locks or cutting chain links was not obvious. Nor was what I'd do if the locks are onlink and designed to throw an alert upon being opened by unauthorized means.

But plenty of other things *were* obvious. Like the way we'd be constructing Kenny's six-foot levee addition—with "tubedams" made of vinyl-coated heavy-duty polyester, each one fifty feet long.

And yeah, they're tubes, every last one of them sapienshit-poncho orange. Haphazardly piled and stacked along the helo pad periphery, they'd be traipsed out to the levee crown and laid on top of poly sheets, connected together, then filled with sea water pumped directly out of the marsh. Way, way faster than filling and piling sandbags.

I know from Del, who regularly specs tubedams, that typically two types of specialized robots help with much of the work. Placerbots position the poly sheets, then the ground anchors to which they're strapped down, and can even do some of the tubedam placement and strapping; machines called pumperbots follow along and fill the tubedams.

After my second glance around the helipad, I realized Camp Null's allotment of tubedams didn't come with any placerbots or pumperbots, only manual generator-powered water pumpers. Seems Kenny's had to press twenty-four of his detainees into placerbot and pumperbot duty because he doesn't have enough custodians and sapienshits to do the work before the hurricane arrives.

Heh. No wonder he and the sapienshits started off OCD as hell and hair-trigger aggressive. Kenny most of all. He may have notched back the custodians' attempts at close-order control, but as I, for one, expected, he had them remove only our handcuffs, not our ankle chains.

Talking or even walking within four feet of another prisoner got you equal parts smacked by a rifle butt or electrolasered, then threatened with return to the cells. So did standing still too long or looking around too obviously. The sapienshits were fastidious about keeping their eight-foot distance from us, too, unless they deemed someone in need of a whack.

Since all that tubedam shit had to get carted out onto the levee, Kenny assigned one group of prisoners to load it onto the camp's pair of pickup trucks while another three groups were sent beyond the outer perimeter fencing to unload the trucks, position the gear, and clear away any sharp debris on the levee crown before the tubedams were laid out. The last two groups—including mine—lugged still more crap out there on our backs.

My scouting during these lugs confirmed the blind rectangle and found a few other blind spots as well. Picked up sapienshit grousing, too, which they somehow think we cannot overhear since we religiously avert our eyes. Thus we know the four custodians out there with us were the only ones still able to cope with the rain, which hasn't stopped for more than a couple hours at a time in days.

Makes me smile. Whoever bought Camp Null's custodian robots got mightily ripped off. The sapienshits say just six remain operational—and only four seemed to benefit from those plasticky "rainshields" that are supposed to keep them functional in a wet environment. One by one, the rest had crapped out over the previous couple of days as they unloaded the helos. "Dunno how many, but too goddamn many" languish in the tech repair facility for lack of spare parts. "And flights've been suspended for the duration."

My conclusion: the sapienshits have no experience managing clusterfucks, and this one's a doozy dependent on dazed prisoners who must perform tasks quickly and effectively in a mercurial environment and with inadequate tools. Plus the sapienshits aren't accustomed to interacting with us anywhere near this much. I think we scare them.

Good.

Initially, Kenny had six sapienshit overseers watch us from their prudent eight-foot distance while he and the two in green ponchos stomped around shouting orders. The four custodians, meanwhile, took up strategic positions between our groups, shifting as we moved around to cover us as we work.

Once we started dragging tubedam shit through the outer perimeter sally ports and up onto the levee crown, both the sapienshits and the custodians began overreacting all over again.

Also good. Because they wasted time, confused themselves even more than us. Controlling us trumped everything, notably anything resembling efficiency.

Fortunately, Kenny talks too much and too loud, so I know—we *all* know—he wants both control *and* efficiency, insisting "those damn tubedams" will, by god, run all the way round the several thousand feet of levee that enclose the "camp." This means folding together the ends of tubedams by the hundreds to connect them and then pyramiding them—five rows on the bottom, four in the second layer, followed by layers of three, two, one.

To stabilize this pyramid, we thread strapping over-under-over around the tubedams and then tie the strapping to three-foot-long augered eyelet ground anchors that we've screwed into the soil at five-foot intervals using a steel drive rod. Once filled with water, a single tubedam widens to almost two feet and rises to about fifteen inches high; each fill requires us to drag around generator pumps and attach and detach heavy hoses.

Assuming the people doing this have a clue, the completed tubedam pyramid will stand slightly more than six feet high and measure about ten feet across at the bottom—which is just about all Camp Null's fourteen-foot-wide levee crown can handle. Kenny also wants a second smaller line of tubedam defense along the landside toe of the levee embankment, at the inside edge of the levee soak ditch, to contain seepage and protect the camp's nine seepage pumps.

So (surprise!) I did some counting. Adds up to more than 1,800 tubedams, some 3,600 anchors, thousands of yards of strapping. We haven't been told anything about the amount of time this will take, but I know from Del how quickly tubedams install, especially compared to sandbags. With twenty-four people, it ought to be a three-day job, and I'd bet plenty that's all the time Kenny's gonna get. Whether he likes it or not.

❖

Three days…

After all that time trapped in a hotbox with nothing—no tools, no options, no fucking air to breathe—I was deluged by the possibilities of *Outside!*, but they jumbled and tumbled and unraveled into anarchy. Too much time in that mind-squashing steel box; I was overwhelmed.

Every time I stood on the levee's crown today, I wanted to run, take my chances in the vast marsh beyond the levee. Just go—yes, now, go *go GO*…

I faked staring down at the crown's single-lane gravel road, glancing here, glimpsing there while I hauled sixty-pound rolled-up tubedam upon tubedam, searching for another road, the one leading to that sliver of survival's light.

Beyond the levee stretch wetlands that appear downright walkable at low tide, but in fact the ground is squishy-soggy and, besides, alligators lurk in the grasses. At high tide, the grasses disappear almost entirely in seawater that swells at least three or four feet up the marsh side of the levee embankment. Gators there, too.

Occasionally, isolated higher-elevation remnants of Parris Island—a couple with wind turbine colonies, most with decaying, overgrown ruins—interrupt the salt marsh.

Nearest of these, about 150 yards to the north, is the old depot headquarters building and its wind turbine neighbor. From what I could see, the levee encircling that area has deteriorated quite a bit, as if some nostalgic effort to save the old headquarters has been forsaken.

Farther off, the open waters of the Broad River to the west and the Beaufort River to the east meander south to join up at Port Royal

Sound, wider than I remember it, soon to be inundated with a ridge of water that will rise *how high* out of the Atlantic?

Nope. Not that way.

Three days…

Run. God, it burned, the way I wanted to run…

Of course, un-fucking-questionably, running would be suicide, by bullet from the sapienshits' tower or by alligator or drowning in ankle chains in the vast marsh.

So, so close. I was outside, breathing in the open air, but I could see no path to that sliver of light. Even if some miracle relieved me of the collar, I saw only a parade of dead ends.

Custodians playing zone defense well enough by midmorning that, despite some erratic moments, one of them always has a clear, no-miss shot at every one of us.

Levee cams monitoring the entire marsh beyond the camp—so no one can escape unseen just as no one can approach unseen.

A small, cam-free dock off the west side of the levee tempting us with a couple of fast shallow-bottom motorboats tied up there, but the watchtower has a clean line of sight, as does my old Echo Company squadbay, which, if amenities like barbecue grills, umbrella-shaded tablesets, and a Confederate flag offer any hint, is now where the sapienshits reside.

So how many dead ends is that?

Once upon a time I was capable of imagining, concocting a plan, thinking it through. Once upon a time I always fucking had a fucking plan. But this morning it stayed beyond my reach, heckling me.

"What the fuck is wrong with you, cunt?" the bitch sneered eventually. "Been out here for hours and you haven't even made eye contact with anybody. Like that scraggly forty-something woman up ahead who keeps looking over at you. Cuz you can't do this alone. You goddamn well *know* that!"

Bitch had a point.

Beneath a jittery sapienshit scowl, I followed the scraggly forty-something back across the helipad to the pile of tubedam crap our group had been ordered to transport. Somewhere along the way, the woman glimpsed at me, then at the bundle on the ground between us, and I answered with a what-the-hell chin jut.

Seconds later, we simultaneously breached the four-feet-apart rule and scammed our sapienshit by "misunderstanding" our most recent order—to each carry another rolled-up tubedam out to the north side of the levee this time rather than the south side. We got it part-right by heading north, but instead of tubedam rolls, we'd grabbed either end of a heavy bundle of ground anchors.

"Stop!" the sapienshit hollered. This paralyzed not only everyone in our group but four more prisoners in the group nearest ours. At the edge of my vision, I noticed a custodian speeding toward us, three of its appendages swinging spastically to keep eight of us under constant threat of one of its weapons.

"You two!" yelled the sapienshit. "Turn around!"

In utter silence, we executed half of a slow, stumbling about-face, looking as blank and mystified as possible.

"What's the holdup?" shouted one of the green-poncho sapienshits.

"Fuck it," our sapienshit growled, then yelled at us again. "Go on. Go. Everyone move it!"

As we shuffled away, eighteen inches per chained step, I heard over my thundering heartbeat our sapienshit order the custodian to stand down. He had to say it twice.

"Nice," the woman murmured to me as we shambled toward the north side of the helipad. "Y'oughta be in pictures."

"We're on two cams right now," I murmured back. "Northeast corner, southeast corner—'bout a hundred and twenty yards from each of 'em."

"Screw the cams. My kingdom for a chance to flip the kill switch on those Vederes," she snarled in a whisper.

"Those what?" I asked.

"Vederes—the robots."

"You mean the custodians?"

"Yeah. They're all Vederes—worst custodian model ever made," the woman huffed, out of breath. "So of course it's the most popular."

I slowed down. "You know where their kill switch is?"

She offered a wisp of a smile. "Name's Magenau. Who the hell're you?"

"Gwynmorgan." I meant to merely glance, but I ended up staring. Not because there was anything in particular about her to stare at. It was because I'd abruptly begun to wonder about Philippa Flynn. No, no, this is somebody else, I reminded myself. Magenau, not Philippa Flynn.

"Hey!" Magenau growled too loudly. "I got no time for anybody's zombie shit. Twist your head on straight or stay the fuck away from me."

"Sorry." I forced my gaze to the ground several feet ahead and made a point of speaking very softly. To set an example. "Just wondered if you know somebody named Philippa Flynn. Maybe run into her here."

Magenau snarled, still too loud. "Never heard of her."

I tried again. "Know the date?"

"Second to last day of my life," Magenau muttered, "unless I get real clever real fast."

"Third to last by my reckoning. Tell me where the Vedere's kill switch is."

"Tell *me* how you're gonna get the hell outta here, Gwynmorgan."

I pretended to scratch my chest just below my collar's end rings. "No point in trying shit till this is gone."

"After that?"

"Well-aimed ground anchor, assault rifle, shitloads of luck," I said. "Thought about a truck at low tide when the road's not overwashed, but—"

Magenau said, "Tide's ebbing now."

"Yeah. Well. Some crazy damn fool will probably try it. But it's a no-go. Truck needs to be facing the ramp over on the northwest side of the levee. Even then, anyone who manages to drive it away'll get shot to hell inside thirty seconds." I angled my head leftward toward the dock. "The boats're just as bad. But I bet you know all that, right?"

Magenau said nothing, kept her gaze grounded.

"So, I guess, if we can't get out we need to take the place down," I mumbled after a few more steps. "Starting with that power substation we passed on our way out here. Which, as I said, will require an assault rifle off one of the sapienshits."

"Ooh, 'sapienshits.' I like it." Magenau didn't miss a beat. "That's a bingo on the substation. Bullets optional if we know the access code, probably need co-conspirators for a diversion, and I'd love a fully charged electrolase—"

I interrupted. "Custodian two o'clock."

We went silent, eyes down, as the machine rolled close, the lenses in the cylinder at its "head" slowly spinning and contra-spinning behind the tinted armorglass covered by its plasticky rainshield. "Detainee-ss, halt!" it demanded.

We halted, the 150-pound bundle of anchors suspended between us. We didn't drop the bundle or put it down or budge, since the morning had already taught us to respond to a custodian's order absolutely literally. As in "halt" means cease moving. Not a twitch.

After a very long thirty seconds, the custodian made another sound. "DETAINEE-SS, PROCEED!"

"See?" Magenau whispered when we'd moved on far enough. "That's how fucking much time it needs to work through its damn algorithms. God, it actually struggled over the plural for 'detainee.' Twice. Pathetically slow learners, those Vederes. I doubt that rain thingy's been doing it any favors either."

She lowered her head farther to keep her grin from the cams monitoring the helipad; the closest was still a hundred yards distant, but hi-res enough to pick out a pimple. "The more we behave out-of-pattern, the slower they'll go," she said. "Whaddaya bet we can get 'em to stop altogether?"

I told her about the custodian in the infirmary that no longer responded to commands, how Infirmary Woman figured it's because custodians don't like profanity.

"Really? Triggered by a spoken command?" Magenau frowned when I offered an I-guess-so shrug. "How'd she deal with it?"

A pause, I recalled.

"Probably overfitting themselves right into a state-space explosion," Magenau said.

I'd heard of overfitting and state-space explosions—somewhere back when I had a real life. I tried to sharpen blurry recollections of Dana and Lily at the dinner table explaining machine intelligence basics to Evvie, then her sisters.

"You mean," I said after some mental rummaging, "as the custodians do their self-learning, they screw up what's important, right? Because they've handled too narrow a range of functions for too long."

Magenau's head hinted a nod. "Works okay till they're given a novel new task," she said. "Say, babysitting two dozen detainees suddenly hustled outside to plod all over a levee. Then they're not sure which move to make."

"Explains why I feel like that one wanted to electrolaser us."

"Yeah, cuz it did." Magenau flung me a crackling look. "Think of their novel new task as a goal, which is composed of a bunch of sub-goals. Plus they have new priors—"

"Instructional algorithms, right?"

"Yep. Those algorithms explicate *a priori* conditions that define and limit the machine's state space—y'know, the set of all possible states of a machine. Typically, these higher-level conditions are defined by a human programmer. Then the machine self-learns its own lower-level conditions by lots of trial and error."

Probably because of Lynn's stories, this always made me think of legislators waxing grand with big, new, vaguely worded laws that bureaucrats carry out by creating niggling little regulations that eventually tend to overreach. Can a custodian succumb to mission creep?

Magenau's lips curved then, but her eyes reminded me of granite. "And therein lies our hope."

"Tell me."

"If the custodians' programming is sloppy—and we see plenty of signs it is—those new goals and priors have not overwritten the old ones. Instead they've been tacked on. And depending on *how* they've been tacked on, they can mess up the existing hierarchy of concepts that are based on the old goals and priors. The new goals and priors end up causing a rush of too many additional options—more than the machines' algorithms can handle because they lack enough of the right kind of inputs for sufficient trial and error."

"You mean they don't get enough practice," I said. "Lack of experience."

"Mathematically, they end up in what's called a local optimum."

"Like getting stuck in a puddle." I had to hide a smile then. "Which means in the real world that performance suffers, right?"

Magenau dipped her head in a minimal nod. "Or stops altogether, like that custodian in the infirmary. It'll go down differently with each machine. If their algorithms' solution happens to produce a conflict—do A *and* do not-A—they can behave quite erratically, the ultimate local optimum. Means it's refresh and reboot time."

"Yeah. That's happened with the custodians here." I told her what Infirmary Woman said about how the custodians would stop recognizing IDs, attack staff, about how the sapienshits inserted new program modules and desiccant packs in the machines. "But the woman in the infirmary said once in a while it still happens."

Magenau had gone slitty-eyed by the time I finished. She spoke almost absently, as if reciting. "Like most robots, custodians are best suited for a narrow range of frequently repeated actions." She tossed me a quick look. "Whaddaya bet the custodians came here already secondhand? Multiple layers of root goals and priors. Easy to mess 'em up."

"And you know all this *how*?"

"Used to take 'em apart," Magenau whispered. "To figure out the best ways to hack 'em. Between you and me, I'm shit-kickin' good at it."

We shut up again as we neared a simple, cam-free gate—one of those with only microphone, speaker, and keypad—located between the helipad and the area just north of it containing the solar panels and the power substation.

But no cam, no matter. Because thanks to the trackers built into the collars around our necks, the sapienshits' software knew our location. Precisely. So when we were a couple yards from the gate, a machine voice ordered each of us to state our ID number. Magenau and I obeyed and the gate promptly swung open as a "DETAINEES PROCEED" emanated from the loudspeaker. It was the third gate I'd seen—and the second I'd passed through—with no cam, only audio commo and keypad.

Ten yards ahead of us stood the solar array, its panels mounted high enough on concrete footings that Magenau could walk upright beneath them (I had to duck slightly). Hardly more than thirty unimpeded yards away, to our left as we proceeded beneath the solar panels, stood the power substation. We were in the northeast corner of the camp—a fenced-off area some 250 yards long, maybe 30 yards wide harboring critical infrastructure, and not a single camera anywhere.

On the other side of the solar array, we encountered the sally port that cuts through the camp's three layers of outer perimeter fencing. Just like on the south side, it, too, has keypads alongside the higher security of pervasive cam coverage. And here, too, cams monitor the extended tracts of the fenced no-man's-land the sally port traverses; we're visible on three separate cams while we move through, including a CL160 in the dome above the sally port's middle gate.

Then, just as on the south side, comes the blind rectangle—first, a twenty-yard span from the outermost sally port gate to the soak ditch, then about five yards of levee embankment rising six feet to the levee crown, where, about halfway across, the cam coverage resumes.

Sounds better than it is, however, since much of this area can be seen quite clearly from the watchtower. But there *are* places where other structures block the watchtower's view. Just gotta get these goddamn collars off…

I spotted a stretch like that along the south side of the levee. On the north side (where it fucking matters, as far as I'm concerned), the solar array's thirty-inch concrete footings provide several small hiding places entirely out of sight of either watchtower or cams, and there's a blind spot up on the levee crown where the power substation structure interrupts the watchtower's line of sight for about seventy yards.

"You *do* know trying to shoot up the substation will just get us killed sooner instead of later, yes?" Magenau asked as we dumped the bundle of anchors alongside a pile of tubedams we'd created at the edge of the northside levee crown.

Fine, I thought, I'll play. "Got an alternative?"

Magenau's lips never moved when she murmured, "Did you know some of those digits on the custodians' appendages contain tools? Like screwdrivers, pliers. Hard-wire cutters. Did you know those tools can be extracted and detached by any human with appropriate access?"

We were split up before I could reply—back to carting tubedams in single file, four feet between us. I felt light-headed. Shit! The custodians carry hard-wire cutters...

The next time I had a chance to team up with someone and secretly communicate, the guy refused to make a sound, wouldn't even sneak a peek at me. After his earlier electolasering, he was simply too terrified not to obey *them*. That's when I understood what Magenau meant by "zombie shit."

After a while (hard to tell time in the rain beneath thick cloud cover), the custodians settled down some and the sapienshits began to ease up on both the four-feet-apart rule and their insistence that our groups of four remain strictly together. I figure their automated tracking of our collars means the sapienshits on the levee don't have to pay so much attention to our *individual* whereabouts since the software alerts them to anyone out of bounds.

Means they can focus instead on haranguing us to work harder. It also means we can move around somewhat more freely, which I proceeded to do.

A depressing experience, because at least half the detainees out there today were zombies—too afraid or too zonked *not* to mindlessly obey. Even so, six of us who are still whole-brained managed to find each other and decide we better damn well trust each other.

I discovered Ozawa the hydrologist next and asked him what I'd already asked Magenau. "Know anything about why you're here?"

He said what Magenau said. "Kidnapped."

Ozawa's an academic who, by his own description, couldn't resist what was supposed to be a quick but ridiculously lucrative corporate research contract. "Except," he said, "those dicks weren't buying research," just a credential to glue onto "findings" they massaged past all recognition. The day after he emailed a buddy asking about lawyers who could find a way to void a research contract, he was snatched on his way to work.

A while later I encountered Maddie Small, who is, well, quite small, and Ozawa found Rosario Finlay the physician. Magenau soon showed up with Creel, a lawyer who's represented the Wilderness Web Coalition and has worked with Del. Creel recognized me. Don't know how yet; information comes in small, purpose-built bites out on the levee.

What I do know is that none of them have ever heard of Philippa Flynn, though Maddie Small remembers hearing a woman screaming soon after she got here. "Five menstruations ago," she said.

❖

The moment that bonded the six of us with whole brains went down not long after we introduced ourselves. Started when Magenau, I think, or maybe Creel, saw the opportunity and Rosario and I jumped in, too.

Essentially, we pulled a four-woman version of what Magenau and I had done earlier with the bundle of ground anchors, only this time our target was a generator pump. Even though two people could've carried the damn thing, we put on our best hunched shuffles and each grabbed a corner.

This move inspired the loudest, assholiest of the sapienshits, who stood closer to us than all his brother sapienshits, to swing his rifle off his shoulder and point it at my face screeching, "WHAT THE *FUCK*?!"

Goddamn, I thought as I froze and stared into the small black hole bearing the bullet that would kill me, sure as hell called this one wrong.

Mouth open wide behind his surgical mask, the sapienshit seemed stuck for the longest time. Finally, he gushed an oddly protesting "*Ah! Ah!*" before he lowered his weapon, blinked wildly, and sputtered in a near soprano, "J-J-Jus—hell's bells, all of you just get it the fuck *done*!"

Then he waved us on without another word.

We were shaking so much, gasping so hard, that no one could

speak; a few feet behind us, Ozawa and Maddie Small, paired off to carry a load of ground anchors, were almost as freaked out as we were. But we sensed a breakthrough, walked the shit we carried nice and slow at least 300 yards to the levee under attentive but distant eyes and cams, talking surreptitiously the whole way.

After that, we agreed. The more we act shuffly and hunched and zombied, the more they'll let us Just Get It Done. Our other consensus: as long as we make it seem random or accidental, we can gradually maneuver ourselves into working near pretty much any detainee we want.

Not freedom certainly, but sure as hell it gives us some leeway.

"We should spread out," I suggested to the others. "Look for anything and anyone else that can help us."

They agreed.

"Then we try as best we can to get back together in, y'know, a while," said Creel. "Compare notes. Come up with a plan."

I wanted to go north with Magenau to better scout the area around the power substation, but Maddie Small angled for that slot and I opted to avoid conflict. So Rosario and I went south, Ozawa east, and Creel west. We were searching for weak spots, exploitable patterns, other detainees with sanity, knowledge, ideas, skills.

Creel brought us Perez and Sarr. Ozawa dug up Grodinsky. Magenau and Maddie Small met Cintron. We became a gang of ten, sort of. I say "sort of" because, hell, how can I be sure about these people, especially these last four guys? Sarr and Cintron strike me as a little wild-eyed. Who's to say one of 'em won't screw our chances in a moment of panic or despair or rage?

For survival purposes, I'd say Magenau offers the most. She started out as an electrician upgrading power grid facilities so, as she says, she knows how to sabotage them. Somewhere along the way, she got into hacking—"for the hell of it, y'know?"—and developed an expertise so deep she made a living off it for five years before her politics and the feds caught up with her. Her handle, CharlieTann, is infamous enough that I remember Dana and Lily mentioning it.

Magenau believes the feds hired somebody to grab her because they can't prove shit but are eager to make her work for them. She's been interrogated here at Camp Null in ways she can't bring herself to describe. "But it's been a while since they've messed me up. Three menstrual cycles." She worries some that she's lost her hacker's edge because "I've been in this slimy shithole too fucking long."

I'm hoping Magenau and I can sneak unseen into the power substation. I'm hoping we find in there a comlink I can use to contact Del and Lynn and get help—step one to freedom. I'm hoping Magenau's able to bring down the power in the camp so we, the prisoners, can overtake the damn sapienshits before they're able to kill us.

And yeah, yeah, I know it's a little unspecific about how the hell unarmed prisoners in ankle chains and zapper-tracker collars overtake sapienshits and robots with automatic weapons.

What can I say? You embrace the odds, which range from overwhelmingly against you to utterly impossible, you marshal your skills and strengths, juicing yourself as best you can so you'll be able to see and seize opportunity, you sketch a plan that's really only a starting point from which you try to envision multiple alternative moves ahead. Jamie be nimble, Jamie be quick.

Then there's Creel, who grew up close by, "in a Gullah swamp near Penny Creek," and used her brains, brashness, and shot-putter brawn to slog out all the way to law school and a well-respected expertise in eminent domain issues. She met Del in the early stages of *the* Wilderness Web eminent domain case—the one Warrick van Gelderen attempted and failed to appeal to the Supreme Court.

"I was whisked right out of a hotel restaurant into a great big blank," she said, "and woke up in yellow spandex."

I imagine Creel could be quite helpful should those of us who haven't zombied find a way out of here and into the surrounding low country. Say, in some or all of those boats docked over on the west side of the levee.

Took me longer to appreciate the talents of Maddie Small, even though I liked her right off because she asked me to repeat Philippa Flynn's name, said she thought the woman she heard screaming that time deserved to have a name. "Y'know, in my head, when I remember that screamin', she's a whole person, not just a sound that's hard to hear."

Maddie Small is young, a street kid runaway who adopted New York City but not some of its more common vices, like pharma and prostitution—an achievement that requires a good deal more than luck.

"I steal," she confided. "In an' out quick, quiet. From your pocket, your house, your car. All kindsa currencies these days." She claims to have lived "all over," but home is Manhattan's Freedom Tunnel. "We got our own secret passageways an' chambers offa there like you wouldn't believe."

Maddie Small says she was grabbed because she ducked left when she should've ducked right. But she was chased in the first place, she believes, because she witnessed something one night on Riverside Drive "up near a Hundred 'n' Seventh."

"What'd you see?" I asked.

"Buncha old rich dudes drunk as shit, talkin' shit. I didn't hear shit, but I hadda run like hell anyway from the hired help when they spotted me." She shook her head, still unable to quite believe it. "Bastards *got* me."

Guess I feel kind of protective of Maddie Small (she reminds me of me), though I had real doubts at first about how much I could trust her. But I know now.

Rosario the physician (but don't call her Dr. Finlay) certainly brings a useful set of skills to our situation. She's another whistle-blower, involved with a human rights group that caught one of the big pharma-nutrition conglomerates using food bank programs to test new drug-infused alt food products on clueless poor urban populations, then diddling less than optimal test results. Hasn't been here long—a few weeks, she says.

"Burying me won't stop anything," she declared in a raspy, determined whisper while the two of us lugged a crate of tubedam sundries—poly sheets, rolls of ducktape and strapping—on the south side of the levee. "I've seen to that—"

She was interrupted by yelling first—male, deep-throated, angry—which was quickly followed by a turgid burst of loud, sharp cracks I knew to be fire from multiple automatic weapons, all from our right, west of us, out of sight behind the sapienshits' squadbay.

Then came sirens and orders from a distinctly human voice that trumpeted over multiple loudspeakers, creating a shrill, dissonant echo. "Detainees!Detainees! FaceFace downdown onon thethe ground!ground! HitHit thethe dirtdirt *now!now!*"

Rosario and I hadn't waited. We both dropped the crate and dove aysap for the meager cover of the nearest seepage pump house about ten feet in front of us.

A sapienshit ran by shouting to no one in particular, "Detainees! Hands on the backs of your heads!" A heartbeat later, another sapienshit lumbered wordlessly past us, soon followed by a custodian that kept us in its purview.

"What happened?" Rosario asked.

"Low tide," I answered.

❖

His name was Castillo, and his run for it on the west side of the levee was doomed, of course. I hadn't met him, but Magenau told me she talked with him just before he bolted; she thought he was okay, not at all zombied. "Then, when he saw that truck unattended and all ready to go, he just lost it."

She described how damn fast he scrambled in, threw the truck into manual, drove it off the levee crown and down the ramp a hundred yards before intensive sapienshit weapons fire stopped him.

"Truck got shot all to hell," Magenau reported, giving me a quick, grim look. "Only way to retrieve it was to send a bunch of us out there to push it back in here. I ended up at the driver's side door, doing the steering. Castillo's blood and brains were everywhere."

She didn't say anything else then, but I sensed she had more to tell.

I heard the rest later, once Kenny put us to work laying out tubedams. He decided to erect them starting near the southwest corner of the levee and moving eastward. Intermittently shoulder to shoulder on the levee crown as the rain resumed, Magenau and I put down the rows of five tubedams needed for the bottom layer.

We were, in effect, at the spearhead of the effort, farthest east out ahead of the others, who worked behind us filling the tubedams we'd laid out and placing then filling new layers on top of ours. Since the rest of the prisoners were behind us, so were the custodians and all but one sapienshit, giving us the opportunity to communicate in choppy intervals.

With a smile tiny and sly, Magenau got right to the point. "The cellblocks over there and the sally ports in that nasty fencing around it are three-factor autokey secured," she said.

I nodded. The only high-level security I've seen in here is in and around the squadbay cellblocks. It's seriously hard-ass. Sure as hell no keypads.

"But," she continued, "*everything else*—and I mean anywhere there's a keypad, understand?—can be opened with the same ten-digit keycode. *All* the doors and gates in this dump. Even the outer perimeter sally port gates. And the code?" She gave her head a minute shake. "Security satire."

"How the hell do you know that?"

"Castillo's gift."

"Say what?"

Cynical as she is, Magenau has this notion that when someone dies a gift emerges from it, not necessarily or even usually material, sometimes recognizable only in hindsight, years later. According to Magenau, though, Castillo's gift appeared immediately.

"While I was steering that awful, bloody truck," she whispered, "I saw the edge of a piece of paper sticking out from beneath the driver's side floor mat—a crib sheet describing how to open any gate in what the sapienshits call the 'secondary perimeter.'"

That means any Camp Null gate or door where there's a keypad, Magenau repeated. Like the gates near the substation. Like the fucking door of the substation, which *does* have a keypad, oh by the way.

And the paper, the crib sheet?

Magenau memorized it, then immersed it in a pool of blood under the driver seat, making it unreadable. "So the sapienshits think no one saw shit."

I remember looking skyward as I silently repeated the keycode Magenau recited, letting the rain slap my face, tempt my tongue while the tiny tremor of awakening possibility hummed outward from my xyphoid (the body's tuning fork, don't you think?).

Powerful knowledge if it's real—yet of little value because of the collars around our necks tracking our every move, threatening a zap for any mismove.

Inevitably, visibly, each of us began to face a terrible truth: *Day's almost done and you're going back into that cell tonight. Maybe the sapienshits will let you out of your cage tomorrow. Maybe not.*

Every one of us who still had any significant mental capacity— "not too decompensated," as Rosario says—couldn't stop thinking about it. You're going back into that cell tonight. The urgent awareness of it was on every sentient face and a few zombie faces, too.

I feared for us as we continued assembling tubedams along the south side of the levee, as our gang of ten managed to pull off a raggedy version of what Creel had proposed—reconvene—and it became clear that we were out of skills, out of tools, out of ideas, out of options.

You're going back into that cell tonight.

So why did Magenau seem almost pleased?

"Are you shitting me?" she responded when I asked. "Look at that bioware. They're acting more freaked out by the minute. Impetuous. Unpredictable. And the custodians are about to make one fuck-ass mess."

I followed Magenau's negligible head tilt westward to the tubedam pyramid. Its six-foot height extended a couple hundred yards, but she was indicating a point on the levee crown where the pyramid had just been topped off about a hundred yards behind us. Between there and where we stood, prisoners worked on both sides of staggered tubedam layers while the sapienshits and custodians scrambled to maintain a visual on all of us at once.

Not easy, since the tubedams claim most of the levee crown. The remaining space—an uneven, rain-thrashed two-foot ribbon on either side—leaves barely enough room on the crown for the custodians to negotiate.

When the tide's out, they compensate by taking up positions below us on the marsh side of the levee embankment. But as the incoming tide claimed the levee's marshside embankment, the custodians had to retreat to the land side.

I watched the last custodian still on the marsh side lurch toward us on its three "legs," taking the shortest route to the levee's land side while its three armed appendages waggled threat at the seven prisoners behind us on the narrow marshside strip of levee crown.

Every one of those seven prisoners kept glancing around as they minced and skittered in search of the best instance of spacetime to make a run for it. Through storm-riled, chest-high water. In ankle chains.

"Robo," warned Maddie Small from her position on the marsh side fifteen yards closer to the custodian than Magenau and I. Incredibly, she didn't draw back as the machine approached.

Damn, I thought, Magenau's right.

Before I could tell her so, it happened.

❖

Still AF134.

Actually early AF135, in the deep middle of the night, and I'm way too wound to sleep.

Because I let them bring me back in here. God, I obeyed and came back in here—all on the bet that the damn cell doors will open again in the morning...

Keep telling myself: after what happened on the levee late today, we have a chance. Slim. But a chance.

And whatever chance that turns into I gotta lay at the feet of Maddie Small.

Or maybe she did it with her hands. Happened so blink-of-an-eye fast I can't be sure. All I know for certain is that she held her ground as the custodian retreated up the embankment toward her, came real close to her, too close, but still she didn't back off. And then somehow the custodian was arcing sensors-first right into the water, taking Maddie Small with it.

At the very same instant, two prisoners behind us on the marshside of the tubedams scrambled into the water, making their run for it, and almost all eyes turned to look at them. Except my eyes. And Magenau's. We focused on the water about four or five yards from us where the custodian wriggled and gurgled, Maddie Small wriggling and gurgling beneath it.

To our west, meanwhile, two more prisoners wigged out, slipped, tumbled down the embankment into the water, and frantically attempted to splash out again.

This kept sapienshit and custodian eyes oblivious to Maddie Small caught underneath the immersed custodian. I could see only her arm and thought she was drowning, so I scrambled toward her. The custodian could not right itself, but Maddie Small emerged after a few seconds, spurted toward my outstretched hand, and I yanked her onto the levee crown.

By then, loudspeakers had erupted with sirens and shouted orders while the three remaining custodians, all now on the land side of the tubedams, galumphed back and forth, weaponized appendages menacing, and the sapienshits yelled at us and each other.

I pulled Maddie Small to the ground next to me, wrapped an arm around her diminutive body, and crawled with her closer to Magenau, who lay belly-first on the land side of the levee crown, at the edge of the blind rectangle.

The two escaping prisoners each tried to wade-swim for different clumps of sea grass poking through the high water, their yellow spandex surprisingly difficult to spot. As I watched, I remember thinking *Well, at least Caprice has given them rain and fog and choppy water*.

Ten, twenty, thirty seconds, more, more passed as they swam away. Briefly, I envied them, thought maybe they'd pull it off and I'd be the fool grubbing here in the dirt of Camp Null, coveting their getaway, their freedom. And then the sapienshits started shooting at them.

One of them dove underwater at the first shots; when the other took a bullet mid-spine, I couldn't watch anymore and inched farther onto the land side of the levee crown.

"Got suh-um fuh ya," Maddie Small mumbled as she slipped an object under my nose. I had to stare at it for a couple seconds before I comprehended. Somehow she had liberated one of the dunked custodian's digit tools—a combo pliers-wire cutter.

"Holy shit, Maddie Small," I remember gasping. "Holy *shit*!"

"How d'you wanna do this?" she asked me, eyes wide and serious.

Jeezus, I had so many questions, none of which mattered, at least not then. Maddie Small had given me her stupendous prize, her trust, her faith that what I'd propose would be the best we could do. I glanced at her, at Magenau; they were waiting for me.

"Uh—"

I lifted my eyes to see several rounds puncturing the water within a few feet of the second escaping prisoner. Not much time, not many options. I glanced toward the cams—yep, we lay just inside the blind rectangle. Glanced toward the watchtower—yep, as long as we stayed down, we were out of its sight, too.

So okay. I turned to Magenau. "We clear?" I asked her.

"Yeah, clear," she answered a few heartbeats later. "No sapienshits. No custodians. Do it."

I grabbed the stolen custodian wire cutter, unfolded it, and started talking as I reached for Maddie Small's collar and went to work. "Gonna cut a link on the underside—just one, so the break will be hidden by the adjacent link. When I'm done, don't pry it open. We gotta wait." I halted and looked hard at Maddie Small. "Promise me."

"Yeah. Promise."

I cut a single link in Maddie Small's collar, talking the whole time.

"Plan is to get Magenau close to the power substation, where she can pop off her collar, get inside the substation, and knock out the electricity. You"—I caught Maddie Small's gaze—"and I will be ready to divert their attention away from Magenau. That's when we pop our collars."

We'd cut more collars, too—Creel's, Rosario's, Ozawa's, the others'. Later on, as the moment of the diversion approached, we'd use the wire cutter again to cut our ankle chains. And we'd take the place down, by god.

As I spoke, they nodded; I inched next to Magenau, cut a link in her collar, too. Then I handed her the strange tool and she cut one of the links in my collar before handing it back to me while I wondered, *Where am I gonna hide this thing?*

About the time I decided on my shoe, the second escaping prisoner floated in the water maybe thirty yards off the levee. Two more dead. The sapienshits sent a couple of prisoners out there to retrieve the two bodies and a couple more to extract Maddie Small's custodian diving partner. The rest of us were ordered not to move.

Even before the custodian had been dragged out, one of the sapienshits wailed something about four missing custodian digits. Next to me, Maddie Small snorted defiantly.

When Kenny ordered all custodian digits recovered NO MATTER THE FUCK WHAT! I knew tragedy had struck.

If the wire cutter was found anywhere near us, the sapienshits would carefully check every collar, every ankle chain. Sure as hell our collars' severed links would be discovered.

And sooner rather than later. Amidst much splashing around the broken custodian, the other sapienshits started standing up prisoners one by one to be scanned.

Facedown on the levee crown, I admit to begging Caprice as I picked a moment when, I hoped, all cams and eyes were still focused west, away from Maddie Small and Magenau and me, so I could toss the custodian's wire cutter digit back into the water undetected but *please please please* close enough to the custodian hulk.

As I prepared a fast, ground-hugging sideswing, Maddie Small swiped the wire cutter from my hand with a quick whisper, "I'm closer to the water," and did the deed herself.

A good throw, apparently unnoticed. All we could do was hope the software and bioware instantly analyzing the marsh-facing cam data would dismiss the quick dark flash of something small whooshing across the bottom of the frame. A bird maybe, or an artifact of the cam integration technology...

The wire cutter's splash hadn't yet dissipated when a sapienshit turned around and ordered Magenau, Maddie Small, and me to our feet for a head-to-toe scanning.

I held my breath as I stood. Had Maddie Small's toss really gone unseen? Did the wire cutter land close enough to the broken custodian? Or will the sapienshits guess the truth?

Waiting in the rain to be scanned, I commanded myself to *bree-*

ee-eathe and not think about what comes next if the sapienshits detect the severed link in my collar or Maddie Small's collar or Magenau's.

Caprice smiled then, in that double-edged way she has. We'd lost the wire cutter much too soon, but the sapienshits retrieved it—the last of the missing custodian digits—right before the scanner reached us. The relief oozing off the sapienshits was palpable, and they relaxed.

So the rest of their scanning—including of the three of us—was half-assed. One by one, we were cleared and berated back to work. My legs trembled for a long time after that.

But I'd come up with a plan. All we gotta do is dupe the sapienshits into giving Magenau the only assignment that'll grant her access to the north side of the camp and the power substation—gofer duty.

The gofer wheels around a water container from person to thirsty person and fetches shit to and from every-fucking-where. So once Magenau can move toward the substation as part of her job, we make our move.

I figured we had a shot—no question Kenny planned to work us as long as there's light. Which Kenny did, especially since he'd killed three prisoners and had to use up precious time retrieving those four lost custodian digits.

I estimate we laid down almost 300 yards of Camp Null's tubedam pyramid today. But we never did get Magenau assigned to gofer duty.

Please please please let us have just one more day to try.

CHAPTER ELEVEN

Six hundred thirty-five days

AF150.
Saturday, August 1.
18:56 hours.

Until this afternoon, I believed today is AF135. It's not. I lost fifteen days.

I'll get to that, mostly, but first things first. I've calmed down enough now for first things first, beginning with this morning when, yes, the sapienshits let me out of their steel trap.

Let out the others, too, except for Maddie Small, whom I fervently hoped was still alive, hoped had revealed nothing about our collars or our plans. Seemed like a good sign that the sapienshits didn't pay me or Magenau any particular attention, but you never really know.

Day two on the levee began pre-dawn early with Kenny's crude, threatening references to yesterday's killings, but he also wholeheartedly sacrificed the security of regimentation to the need for speed, especially since he'd replaced Maddie Small and yesterday's dead with four clueless and comparatively unproductive new prisoners who, I'm pleased to say, claimed an inordinate amount of sapienshit time and attention.

In rain slowly surrendering to swaths of fog, high tide lapping near the top of the levee, we picked up where we left off about eighty or ninety yards shy of the levee's southeast corner. Our gang, of just nine now, picked up where we left off, too—though only Creel, Rosario, and Ozawa knew at first that Magenau and I could remove our collars.

I was hopeful. We had what we needed even without Maddie Small. Just a matter of getting Magenau assigned to gofer duty as the tubedam installation proceeded along the eastern stretch of the levee, since we'd need her in position by the time the tubedams rounded the levee's northeast corner.

As gofer, when the time was right she'd be able to move through that sally port near the power substation without raising suspicions. When the time was right, our marshside diversion would pull all eyes and cams 180 degrees *away* from Magenau as she neared the substation, and she'd pop off her collar, ditch it, run unseen and untracked beneath the solar panels to the substation, enter using the access code she calls Castillo's gift, contact Del, and sabotage the Camp fucking Null power supply while we wait for help.

Best time for this, no question, would be low tide, just as tubedam construction along the east side of the levee approached the northeast corner. This was also when only one of the three remaining custodians out on the levee would be located landside and would be easily lured by our diversion from persistently tracking Magenau. The other two custodians, meanwhile, would be marshside keeping the six or eight prisoners at work there sufficiently intimidated. Cuz hey, as we've all learned, detainees get a little crazy when they work the marsh side.

Looked like we'd also get help from the increasingly dense fog, which made controlling more distant prisoners especially challenging.

Great plan, except Magenau could not wangle gofer duty.

The tide had ebbed and was rising again, rising in tandem with our desperation as construction neared the levee's northeast corner.

Soon—shortly before the leading edge of tubedams rounded that corner—Kenny would order the marshside custodians to relocate landside. And once construction turned that corner and proceeded along the north side of the levee, the sally port and the power substation would lie within everyone's field of view. So certain anomalies—such as "What happened to the gofer?"—become impossible *not* to spot. Any diversion at that point would have to be bigger, badder, inestimably more dangerous and deadly.

Soon, too fucking soon, we'd be out of time.

Yet the damn sapienshits would *not* let Magenau anywhere near the gofer job, which seemed to be reserved for unambiguous zombies. Hell, it was all we could do to keep her at the front end of the tubedam construction with me and Creel and Ozawa, where we rolled out, lined up, connected new tubedam segments—and had just started on a new section that would turn that fateful northeast corner.

In back of us, layers of orange rose from flat to water-filled bulbous upon more bulbous in staggered lines that continued for more than a hundred yards before reaching the full tubedam pyramid height of six-plus feet.

We needed a Plan B. Pretty damn quick.

That's when the three of them appointed me Chief Fix-This Officer. They never spoke a word. Just looked at me, three sets of eyes asking So Now What?

I guess Plan B Pretty Damn Quick had been inventing itself for a while as I watched the fog billow into almost opaque sheets that wreathed sensuously, mockingly around all that orange—the snaking lengths of tubedams, the sapienshits' ponchos. Like a striptease. Now you see it, now you don't.

"What's wrong with you?" Creel growled as she bent over to join up yet more tubedams. "You look almost happy."

"Got an idea."

"Entertain me."

"Y'know that blind spot up ahead where the power substation blocks the watchtower's line of sight," I reminded her, twitching my head to indicate the north side of the levee about three tubedam lengths in front of us. "Extends about seventy yards—also goes all the way down the embankment, to and through the sally port, right to the substation door."

Creel arched her back, rotated her shoulders, and rolled her head, allowing her to briefly scan around us. "Plus there's the blind rectangle," she whispered once she resumed her squat in front of me. "No cam coverage on the land side of the levee crown."

"Yep," I agreed. "Which leaves the sally port cam dome and the two north side perimeter fence cams."

"Which *means*—" Creel's eyes narrowed. "Your blind spot's not blind at all."

"Unless I shoot out the cams before Magenau's within their range."

"So," said Creel, her tone descending toward incredulity, "your diversion—the one where you magically acquire a gun without attracting any attention—comes first."

"Sort of," I replied. "Our diversion goes down as planned: y'know, marsh side of the tubedam construction at the very back end—and it goes down while the back end's still on the east side of the levee. But it'll have to be sustained longer than we figured. Minutes rather than seconds."

Sarr and Cintron had already volunteered for this duty and would be directed by Rosario, who somehow managed to keep herself stationed midway along the hundred-yard tubedam construction zone, always on the marsh side. A good ole gator scare, the three of them had decided.

"Bunch of us scream real loud," Sarr had proposed, "then tear-ass south along the levee crown far as we can get from the north corner, screeching all the way. So they chase us, of course, but they're also eyeballing the water, and they're scared—"

"And hey, maybe somebody else panics," Cintron added with expert tag-team timing. "Maybe loses control of a hose that's maybe, y'know, pumping away under full pressure. Kinda pressure that'd knock a sapienshit right on his ass, y'know?"

Their fury-fueled enthusiasm would be exactly what we'd need.

"You're talking about a whole lot more than a few minutes." Creel's eyes had gone slitty again. "Where the hell will *you* be?"

"Up ahead of here in the blind spot with Magenau," I said. "When Sarr and Cintron toss it in the fan, Magenau and I both drop to the ground like they want. That's when we remove our collars. I whack the nearest sapienshit, take his weapon, shoot out those three cams—the one at the sally port, the others along the perimeter fencing. Probably also a sapienshit and custodian or two by then, depending on visibility."

"So Magenau can open the sally port gates by entering Castillo's keycode into the keypads," Creel said. "Then she heads for the substation."

I nodded. "Once she's through the sally port, she's off-cam for the thirty yards to the substation door. And I'll fucking blow away anyone who tries to stop her."

I didn't mention how, for all we knew, Camp Null might go into lockdown the nanosecond any cam is damaged, forcing Magenau to hit the dirt while I attempted to shoot away any uncooperative locks without spraying shrapnel all over her. How if this plan worked even a little bit I'd probably end up killing somebody and a bunch of us would very likely get ourselves shot all to hell. How, no matter the fuck what, I would not allow myself to be locked in that steel box ever again.

But Creel knew. "Doing this has implications," she said, solemn and lawyerly.

"So does not doing it, Counselor."

For a long moment, Creel stared at me.

"Best time'll be when the leading edge of tubedams extends about seventy yards west from the corner," I said.

"Okay, Lieutenant," she murmured finally. "I'll head back there and let 'em know. And since I spent years scamming my brothers and cousins with false gator alarms, I'll stay there and share my expertise."

"Creel," I whispered, "tell 'em to fucking hug those tubedams as they make their run south. The sapienshits all know Kenny'll flay anyone who shoots holes in his precious water balloons."

She winked at me, then stood and waved to the nearest sapienshit that she needed to pee, took a few steps, and promptly fell over a newly rolled out tubedam near the marsh side of the levee crown.

It was a masterful performance. She emitted a squeaky yelp as she grabbed futilely for the tubedam to halt her clumsy roll nearly into the water now risen to lap less than two feet below the earthen levee crown. While she scrambled back up to the crown, she surreptitiously signaled Magenau and Ozawa about who should go where.

"Get yo' ugly ass away from there, godfuckindammit!" screeched the sapienshit, who waved his electrolaser in a fitful loop.

Especially hunched and obsequious, Creel scurried eastward as Ozawa abandoned the hose he held and backed farther away from us, behind Magenau, who now stood closer to the sapienshit than he did.

"You!" the flustered sapienshit hollered. "Get up here."

Ozawa gaped, petrified in place while Magenau trotted forward. Judging from the sapienshit's gesture, I suspect he meant to bring Ozawa forward, but after a weary double take, he shrugged and didn't intervene.

I made myself *bree-ee-eathe.*

The next move would be Creel's, and I hoped to hear it rather than see it. As we finished off the bottom layer of one tubedam segment and began the next, bringing us fifty feet closer to our escape window, I conveyed Plan B to Magenau, who nodded. After that came the waiting.

And the prepping. While Magenau snuck glances at what would be her route down the embankment, through the sally port, and to the substation, I started timing the sapienshits' circuits.

❖

They'd developed a way of watching us on Day Two that relied more than ever on automated central detainee collar tracking. Two petty morning mishaps showed how anytime a collar violated their parameters—like, say, trundling down the marshside embankment farther than about two yards—alarms sounded and the unfortunate detainee's collar zapper got activated (suggesting yesterday's shootings were about sapienshits' love of live target practice rather than lack of alternative).

Out on the leading edge of the construction, the sapienshits patrolled a circuit—an orange poncho, or occasionally a green one, always ambled well out ahead of us to linger until another approached from behind and they switched positions, generally at what I guessed to be twenty-minute intervals or longer, depending on how much time they devoted to hassling somebody along the way or gossiping with another of their kind.

The landside custodian served as their backup, but since it had more than just us to monitor, it tended to stay about thirty yards behind us. A second custodian on the land side, elevated high on its three "legs" for the duration of high tide to maintain its view of marshside activities, lumbered back and forth a hundred fog-faded yards away on the levee's east side. The third custodian remained on the marsh side and was invisible in the fog.

Kenny had become a more regular visitor, though he never stayed long; at least his one-of-a-kind blue poncho made it easy to see him coming amidst all the orange tubedams.

Magenau and I spent what had to be at least an hour waiting and watching the sapienshits and custodians we could make out in the fog, our eyes telling each other precisely where they were every fucking second, and I kept a ground anchor within quick reach, furtively nudging one along as we worked.

By the time we'd progressed to the blind spot, waves of opaquing fog wafted by us from the southeast. A few minutes after a new sapienshit sauntered out ahead of us, I heard a genuinely terrified screech—"*Ga-ator!*"—followed by another person screaming, and another, and another.

"*Gator! Right there! Gator!*" they wailed. "*Help! Shoot it!*" All from somewhere around the corner on the marsh side of the levee. Jeezus, I thought, maybe there *is* a gator over there.

The sapienshit out ahead of us swore loudly, colorfully. Magenau and I knew he wouldn't run toward the commotion until we'd firmly planted our faces in the dirt, so as the alarms bellowed we did just that.

I twisted open the broken link on my collar almost before I hit the ground. Because I was gonna get my hands on that fucking assault rifle or die trying. And if I didn't die trying, I intended to keep the damn thing until I was dead or free.

But, dammit, the dude just stood there. And stood there. Even when the commotion escalated.

Just before the sapienshit finally began his reluctant trot eastward toward the ferment, following the two nearest custodians, Magenau signaled. She, too, had emancipated herself from her collar.

We wanted the sapienshit to pass by us along the land side of the levee (just outside the levee cams' range), so we'd inconspicuously staged a bunch of rolled-up tubedams on the marsh side of the levee crown, and our ploy worked. The sapienshit loped along the land side right at the bumpy edge of the crown, obeying Kenny's edict not to step on the tubedams.

Thank you, Caprice.

I grabbed my ground anchor, raised it to trip the sapienshit as he came alongside me—and fucking missed!

Fast as I could, I yanked myself upward, figuring I'd leap for his lower legs and tackle him from behind. But east of me, Magenau managed to trip him with her foot, so my tackle hit him higher and slammed him hard into the ground.

He emitted a single rough grunt as the rifle he hugged across his chest punched the air out of his lungs, and he and I slid a little down the landside embankment. After I pounded his forehead into the ground twice, he went limp.

I glanced up. Both custodians continued to stomp away from us, moving east toward the fray. Lucky again.

I pulled the sapienshit's boonie hat over his eyewraps so his ops center couldn't use the cameras in them to see what was happening, then started dragging him the few feet back to the levee crown, where we could stash him behind the leading water-filled tubedam that ran on the land side a staggered six feet ahead of the tubedam next to it, and just inside the blind rectangle.

Racing against the moment when the custodians' cams would do a 360-degree sweep and notice us, Magenau and I got the sapienshit and ourselves scrunched behind the tubedam, and I rolled him, wrenching off his orange poncho so I could liberate that rifle, while Magenau went for his keychain.

We did not speak—too likely that his eyewraps continued to transmit audio—and we worked fast; in seconds, his out-of-pattern movements would attract notice and then response.

Once I had the rifle, I folded the sapienshit's boonie hat around his eyewraps, stripped them off, and used the rifle butt to smash them, which obliterated their live-link to the sapienshits' ops center. Meanwhile Magenau used the sapienshit's cuff key to remove her ankle chains.

"Go!" I whispered when I saw she'd freed her feet.

Before she could respond, a howl, then another and another spewed toward us from the east—the diversion intensifying again. Magenau and I both peeked eastward.

Yes, Rosario remained at the outer edge of the levee corner seventy yards from us, barely visible through the fog. From her spot, flat on her belly by then, she had a view down both the east and north sides of the levee. She was the event's conductor; we were instruments in her orchestra. She'd motioned for more brass and percussion on the marshside back end hoping the sapienshits and custodians would focus there rather than notice us.

And it worked.

So Magenau didn't go; instead, without a word, she unchained my ankles and used both cuffs to deftly hogtie the sapienshit—right wrist to left ankle, right ankle to left wrist—while I took possession of his electrolaser, stuffed his surgical mask deep into his mouth as he roused so he wouldn't be able to yell, and pulled a couple of empty tubedams over him.

To our east, visibility was dropping fast; I could no longer discern either the custodian or Rosario. To our west, we could still see maybe 150 yards.

"Here," I said to Magenau, handing her the sapienshit's orange poncho. "Might fool the perimeter cams if I miss 'em." She'd just pulled the poncho over her head when the loud cracking of gunfire from the far side of the tubedams sent us ducking. I held out the sapienshit's electrolaser. "Take this, too. And pull the spandex up to your knees so its yellow doesn't show."

She handed me the sapienshit's cuff key as she accepted the electrolaser with my reminder about its limited range in fog, then began her run down the embankment to the north sally port. I had the time Magenau needed for her hundred-yard dash to position the first assault rifle I'd handled in more than a decade, then find and eliminate my three targets.

At least I was familiar with the weapon. It was the same E19 model I'd so often used in the Corps. I aimed tight, made myself *bree-ee-eathe* toward that still point between exhale and inhale, and—yes.

Yes.

Yes.

Fucking yes.

Through the rifle's smartscope, I watched the sally port cam dome explode—the cam that mattered most because an orange poncho alone would never fool it.

The first perimeter cam was tougher. Only a few degrees farther to my right, only some fifty yards farther away, but the cam itself was smaller and a thick ribbon of fog obscured it for a tense god-knows-how-long until the fog eased, like a languid wink, and I found it, focused, *bree-ee-eathe*...and—tap. Again the rifle punched proudly into my shoulder. Two shots. Two kills.

After that I swept hard left about 130 degrees to find the second perimeter cam, just visible on its pole sixty yards distant. Another easy target. Three shots. Three kills.

God, I remember how huge the rifle's reports sounded. Each one seemed to elicit shrill, indecipherable howls from the east. After the third shot, I searched once more for Rosario, who was scarcely visible, but I could make out no sapienshits or custodians. A new surge of fog seemed to be coming toward me from the east, obscuring even the orange of the tubedams.

Certainly a good thing because if they could have seen me, by then every sapienshit in Camp Null would have been strafing my location. Instead I heard only shrieks from the east.

And then I saw it—one of the custodians, less than thirty yards away on the landside embankment and coming fast straight for me.

I'd been told by Magenau where a bullet would do the most damage to a Vedere custodian (its control system at the base of its sensor array), so I fired a fourth time and watched the machine's appendages contort and shake before it toppled slo-mo down the embankment into the soak ditch.

I think that round was the most satisfying I've ever fired in my life.

❖

I'd have continued shooting, but fog shrouded everything farther away than the now defunct custodian, maybe twenty-five yards off. I saw no other custodians, no sapienshits; hell, I had to scramble westward down the embankment to (just barely) keep eyes on Magenau as she punched a thumb into the keypad at the first of the three sally port gates.

Everything depended on those gates opening despite their cams and sensors being shot to hell. Finally, I had to ask: What if the gates don't open? What the fuck is Plan C? And do I have enough firepower to kill every sapienshit in this hellhole?

Fact is, I wouldn't hesitate to kill them all rather than get locked in that cell again. And I'd already experienced the sublime pleasure of taking down a custodian.

It was probably only seconds, but god, it was excruciating. At last the first gate opened for her, and then the second and third gates opened before the first gate closed. All three slowly swung wide fucking open. Incredibly, they stayed open. And Magenau was running again. The orange of her poncho quickly disappeared in the fog still thickening around us.

I scurried farther west so I could cover her. Saw her reach the substation door, punch numbers into the keypad, and—oh god *yes!*—the door opened and in she went.

Goddamn, I wanted to backtrack to the sally port and follow her. I'd told her how to contact Del and Lynn when she found the comlink she assured me the substation would have. Deepest down, though, I wanted to hear Del's voice myself.

I hesitated about which way to go long enough to realize that the pole I could just make out to my right carried one of the marsh-facing levee cams. I descended onto my backside, one knee up to brace the rifle, then aimed it, cuz what the hell...

Five shots. Five kills.

As if in response, more rifle fire burst from the east, accompanied by more screams and shouts. That's when the sniper in me kind of took over.

I crouched low and ran back toward the custodian I'd shot to retrieve the wire cutter I knew it carried. Ten yards before I reached it, I passed the zombie assigned to gofer duty, facedown and terrified. Next I saw Perez, who gave a thumbs-up as I passed him. By the time I got to Ozawa, the clamor now so near to the east seemed to be over.

Just ahead of me, the custodian I'd shot didn't move. Magenau had warned that it might still be dangerous, though, because of "opinionated independent circuits" in its appendages. So I approached with care, as she'd instructed; twice I had to duck spastic flailing to reach the right switches inside the right compartments. Once I toggled them, all twelve digit tools from the custodian's top two appendages dumped onto the ground at my feet.

I scooped up wire cutter, another cuff key, electrolaser, the automatic pistol (remarkably ergonomic once it's unfolded and snapped into position), and scurried back to Ozawa, who was nearest, to cut him out of the collar on his neck and unlock his ankle cuffs. I offered him the pistol, but he preferred the electrolaser.

Perez next. "Holy shit," he muttered as I liberated his neck and feet. "Creel was right about you." I handed him the pistol.

Ozawa wanted to retrieve the terrified gofer, but I was more concerned about getting back up to the levee crown aysap. I'd seen Grodinsky there with two others, lying next to a water-filled tubedam where, if the fog permitted, I'd also have a line of sight to Rosario.

Yet before we could move in either direction, Perez whispered, "Down! We got company."

Ozawa and I flattened again and followed Perez's point. Easy to miss at first, but then I saw what he'd spotted: another custodian hardly more than twenty yards south of us ghostily visible through the outermost perimeter fence's chain links.

"Ooh," I remember whispering, "lots of company." Three or four yards behind the custodian came two ponchos, one orange, the other green.

Before I could aim, the custodian fired at us, its bullet zinging close enough to leave a burnstreak along my right forearm.

"Jeezus," Perez wheezed.

I fired back and the custodian went down.

Six shots now. Six kills.

But we were entirely exposed. No cover, no concealment.

I watched the two sapienshits duck low, their weapons rearing upward to vaguely point in our direction, and then they swung away, one leftward, one rightward.

What the fuck? They can't see us? Are they so accustomed to tracking us as icons on their eyewraps' virtual maps that they can't see *us* lying here? They haven't noticed the rifle I'm fucking pointing right at them? And—and what? They figured the shot came from somewhere else?

Fast as I could I targeted the orange poncho (easier to see)...*bree-ee-eathe*...and as he pivoted slowly to his right, offering himself up, his rifle in full profile before me, I shot the goddamn thing from his hands and mangled his arm in the process. He screamed, adding his scream to the sum of screams spouting once more from the east, and then folded squirming to his knees.

"Spread-eagle on the ground," I ordered the green poncho. The dude whipped his head and rifle in tandem from side to side, apparently more disoriented than ever. "Yeah, *you*, green poncho. Do it *now*."

And—thank you, Caprice, thank you, thank you—he did.

"Use all these cuffs to wrap 'em up good," I whispered to Ozawa and Perez. "Destroy their eyewraps, and don't forget to strip that goddamn custodian exactly the way Magenau said. I'll be topside." I motioned to the levee crown. "Getting Grodinsky and the other two."

About thirty yards shy of the northeast corner, I found Grodinsky and more zombies. Well, to be fair, a zombie and a semi-zombie, Cindy, whose mind was reviving and was determined to stay close to Grodinsky even before I got her unchained.

"Hear that?" Ozawa said a few minutes later as he scrambled up the embankment a step in front of Perez, urging the trembling gofer ahead of him. No more gunfire, but the shouting and screaming persisted. "Oh god," he groaned, "those are getting-zapped screams."

Hear what?

"Shit, Oz," I said, realizing. "No sirens."

"Power's down!" Perez blurted.

Ozawa almost shook his head. "Siren power, anyway."

Imprudent to assume their cams and sensors are also down, I agreed. We need to stay in the blind rectangle as much as possible so the sapienshits can't track us.

The others also agreed, even the two zombies, encouraged along by Ozawa. "No sirens," he repeated. "Reason for cautious hope."

Seven of us unchained now, plus Magenau. With the haul from the sapienshits and the second custodian, our booty consisted of two assault rifles, two automatic pistols, two wire cutters, a green poncho, a somewhat bloody orange poncho, two small knives, and more cuff keys and electrolasers than we knew what to do with.

And the time had come to use it all.

❖

So okay, soon I'd likely be killing more than cams and custodians. I was already thinking about how, since visibility, which was certainly not our friend, had begun to intermittently assert itself. Although sometimes I could see no more than eight or ten yards in front of me, in other moments I could make out the perimeter fence line as much as a hundred, even 200 yards off. And what I could see changed dramatically, unpredictably from one second to another.

The watchtower stood about 350 yards away, still hidden by the fog that, thank god, also hid us from the watchtower sapienshits. But for how long?

And if—when—the fog abandons us, where do I want to be?

The marsh side of the levee, I decided—where Creel and Sarr and Cintron had spawned our diversion, where we could hide behind the water-filled tubedam pyramid Kenny would be loath to shoot up.

Those of us not already over there would have to cross a fifteen-yard stretch along the levee crown that would be visible to the watchtower sapienshits as soon as the fog lifted sufficiently. Which is to say: anytime.

And around the corner where we were heading lurked sapienshits as well as the last "outdoor" custodian and maybe Kenny. Plus god knows how many prisoners who might or might not be alive.

"Perez, you got our backs," I whispered. Hoping he really had been in the army like he claimed, I'd already given him the other rifle (and the other wire cutter); now I handed him the green poncho.

Grodinsky, who clearly did have military experience, volunteered for the bloody orange poncho and the other pistol. Ozawa as well as everyone but the two zombies carried a electrolaser and a cuff key.

We were ready, and visibility to our west-southwest, where the watchtower stood, hadn't improved enough to expose us. So I gave the signal and, to my immeasurable relief, we crossed that exposed fifteen-yard stretch along the levee crown unaccosted. We all made it to the two-layer tubedam segment and hunkered behind its concealing thirty-inch height. I'd worried that an advanced long-distance microwave-infrared integrated sensor array in the watchtower might pick us up, but either such an advanced sensor array didn't exist at Camp Null or Magenau had disabled it.

Just twenty yards now from the corner around which we could hear little. From my position, I saw only one human form: a body in yellow spandex where Rosario had been, facedown, hands cradling the head. Probably her, but I couldn't be sure. Whoever lay there didn't move.

Bile burbled from my stomach to sting my throat. Was Rosario dead? Who else was dead?

I quite distinctly remember my thought as I stared at her lying there, the edges of her blurring so very slightly, the world behind her obscure, unreal. *If my mistakes are that bad, I won't live long enough to suffer for them. Caprice's gift.*

We crept eastward to the next tubedam segment where its three layers rose almost four feet high. This put us less than ten yards from the corner. Around us, the ever-fickle fog began to thin even more. Momentary streams of near clarity grew longer, the puffs of opacity shorter, less frequent. Increasingly, the orange contours of the tubedam pyramid stayed visible for at least 200 yards before everything faded into soft white-gray.

So okay. The moment had arrived—that still point after the end of before and before the beginning of after.

Now you see it, now you don't.

My now stilled like that, *shh*, and I split—the watcher watching the rifle-ready doer, who crawled the final feet eastward to an all-or-nothing ad lib at the levee's northeast corner. And then two things happened at once.

Up ahead, Rosario moved. Her hands signaled (gotta love a tomboy army brat): Blue fucker—that would be Kenny—stationary fifteen yards south of her position. Robo seventy yards south of her position, moving north fast.

Aaand that's an Oh Shit.

Simultaneously, right behind me, Grodinsky nudged my foot with electric urgency, pointing southward. Didn't know yet what he was pointing at, but yeah, I could already feel it—another Oh Shit.

Wondering all the while how fast a marshside custodian can traverse seventy yards, I poked my head over the tubedams to follow Grodinsky's point. Six yellow human forms scattered along the landside embankment, the closest maybe a hundred yards south of us, all of them flat on the ground, all of them facing away from the tumult.

They'd been running. They'd been stopped and dropped. Not one of them moved. Not even a little.

Whereupon that old regiment of needles quick-marched up my spine. Yes, I'd spotted a sapienshit, too. Difficult to discern in his orange poncho as he perched on an orange tubedam above where the prisoners sprawled. Looking down at them, guarding them, I thought. He hasn't fucking seen us, I thought.

And damn if Perez, maybe fifteen yards west of me, didn't stand up in his green poncho and give this sapienshit a high single-hand wave with his rifle.

No! No no *NO!* I wanted to scream. To stop time. To kick Perez's ass into fucking orbit.

But then...

What was it about the way the sapienshit returned Perez's wave?

I realized he believed Perez was alone—one of his green-ponchoed supervisors appearing out of the fog to lend assistance.

"Cover Perez," I whispered to Grodinsky.

As I scuttled the last few feet east to the corner, Rosario signaled again. Robo fifteen yards and closing. I slid onto my belly, swung the rifle rightward into position at my shoulder, and slithered up against the bottom-most marshside tubedam.

I didn't have a plan, only hope.

Hope that Magenau had managed to take down the sapienshits' commo in addition to their cams and sensors (which would help explain why I wasn't dead yet).

Hope that encountering an untracked detainee cuddled up with an assault rifle against one of Kenny's sacrosanct water-filled tubedams would be so anomalous for the custodian that it'd produce a state-space explosion—and hesitation. Just for one fracking heartbeat. That's all I'd need.

❖

It happened so damn fast. All of a sudden I found myself on an insane, face-melting ride with a fucking maniac—only the maniac was me.

Before I had any chance to aim, the custodian loomed high above me, way closer than I expected. Several of the digits in its two front appendages pointed at me, apertures open, so I yanked on the rifle's trigger and held it, releasing an extended burst of rounds that did the necessary damage.

I was up on one knee before the custodian finished capsizing, my rifle aimed south down the marsh side of the tubedam pyramid where pretty much all at once I saw Kenny hunched fifteen yards back (just like Rosario signaled) raising his pistol at me while, well behind him, a sapienshit trotted toward me, rifle still swinging upward from prone yellow spandex to aim at me, and three more sapienshits much farther away unceremoniously dropped the motionless yellow-clad bodies they'd been dragging to turn toward—you guessed it—me.

I shot Kenny first, then the sapienshit coming up behind him.

"Weapons on the ground!" I yelled at the other three.

Two of them froze. I shot the one who didn't, inspiring Messrs. Frozen to toss their rifles and obey my command to spread-eagle.

To my right, I heard Perez holler at the sapienshit guarding the prone prisoners on the landside embankment. "That's right! Weapon the fuck down, asshole! On the floor now and do *not* fuckin' *move!*"

I passed word to Perez to disarm and secure the sapienshit, then move those prisoners aysap, before the fog lifts. No place was safe, but I figured low-profiling alongside the perimeter fence near the solar array—hidden from the watchtower's view—had to be an improvement over lying exposed to the watchtower on the eastern embankment.

My god, I thought, we got all eight sapienshits and Kenny *and* their three surviving outdoor custodians. Good thing I was already on one knee, because I shook so much I'd have fallen had I been standing.

Do not relax, somebody in my head whispered. Because there had to be others, right?

But where?

Sapienshits had to be sneaking along the south side of the levee at that very moment, right? Unseen on the other side of tubedams. Could pop up any fucking second 300 yards in front of me, firing away.

No cover or concealment from the south on the levee's eastern marshside, so I stayed hunched on one knee and kept eyes on the 300-yard span littered with a wrecked custodian hulk, a couple of writhing sapienshits, too many prostrate bodies in yellow spandex—and waited for more sapienshits to show up in the fog-faded space ahead of me.

But the fog-faded space stayed empty.

I had Grodinsky watching to the west, the other direction from which sapienshits were likely to approach, so I told Ozawa, still crouched low between me and Grodinsky, to take the wire cutter from my waistband and remove every detainee collar, unlock every detainee ankle chain on the marsh side—cuffing up sapienshits and collecting their weapons as he went.

"Gonna have to take up arms, too, Oz," I told him. "We need a defender down at the southeast corner to watch for sapienshits coming at us along the south side. Cuz till then, our only eyes in that direction are mine. Which isn't good at all."

He wasn't happy about it, but he nodded, said he'd use one of the sapienshit rifles. He started out by liberating Rosario, who lay behind me.

She sounded okay, seemed okay as she accompanied Ozawa

south along the marshside. They moved with impressive speed, Ozawa snipping collars and shackling sapienshits while Rosario unlocked cuffs and triaged the wounded.

Careful to stay low behind tubedams and out of sight of the watchtower, I tried to *bree-ee-eathe* as I dared a glance rightward. Ten yards away, Grodinsky rested his pistol on the tubedam he peeked over, orange on orange but for a few streaks of sapienshit blood.

Good, I thought, he understands to avoid the watchtower's line of sight. I asked after Perez. "Has he got everyone moved yet? Sapienshit hogtied?"

"Yes and yes—an' I bet I'm gonna get a ri-i-ifle," Grodinsky singsonged back.

He would. And just in time, too.

Out ahead of Grodinsky, the northwest corner of the levee made a pallid appearance, and I could see the ramp near the main gate that had tempted Castillo to his death. No question I'd be able to see the watchtower, and vice versa, if I stepped a few yards westward and stood up. But neither sapienshits nor custodians approached from the west, and I heard none of the light, menacing whir of drones. *Where* the hell were they?

Rosario's soft voice filled my left ear. "Sarr's dead. Shot. Cintron was shot, too, but it's minor and he's ambulatory. I used one of the sapienshit medipacks to bandage him. He kept one of the sapienshit rifles and is staying down there with Ozawa." And both Ozawa and Cintron had taken orange ponchos, she said, then drew in a long breath. "Cintron wants revenge."

"Creel?"

"Tonic-clonic seizure from a collar-zap and electrolasering. She's postictal now."

I asked about the six other prisoners.

"Two shot dead." Rosario did her doctor best to control herself, but she hummed with compressed rage. "The others were collar-zapped. The blue fucker's alive, too, though not quite kicking. But he'll survive."

"Kenny. Good. Can he talk?"

Rosario almost smiled. "Oh my yes."

"And the other sapienshits?" I asked.

"Ozawa trussed up the two uninjured as well as the one you wounded, who'll recover just fine. Slick job killing his rifle instead of him." Then Rosario sighed. "The other one's dead. Sorry."

She'd gathered a trove of sapienshit goodies into the other green sapienshit poncho and distributed the water bottles and candy bars to Creel, Ozawa, Cintron, and the other prisoners. The remaining sapienshit weapon, ammunition packs, keys, comlinks, medipacks, Kenny's blue poncho—and one last bottle of water—she brought to me.

"Ozawa said the sapienshit eyewraps are offlink," she told me as I passed the rifle to Grodinsky, then snugged Kenny's pistol into my waistband. "They're blind out here."

And still all clear on the levee's south side, according to Ozawa's hand signal.

"I want to check those six prisoners down by the solar array," Rosario declared.

"Not a good idea," I objected as she donned Kenny's blue poncho. "You can't get there from here without exposing yourself to the watchtower for almost fifty feet." I pointed west. "Right there."

She patted me on the shoulder, stood, and walked crisply—did not run—across that exposed fifty feet. Walked like the goddamn sapienshit in charge. In eerie, unmolested silence.

Which left me with the echo of her voice. "The other one's dead. Sorry."

Sorry.

One dead by my still profoundly talented trigger finger. Another echo, this one from long, long ago, whooshed by...*Fucking Annie Fucking Oakley.*

The other one's dead. Sorry, Fucking Annie Fucking Oakley.

No, Jamie, murmured someone who sounded a whole lot like Del, *not yet.*

Not dead yet.

I made myself focus. Nobody coming at us from either side; nobody sneaking in across the marsh behind us, around us. Nope. Way too easy. Not done yet.

❖

I watched Creel stumble to her feet about thirty-five yards south of the corner where I crouched and decided to give her a hand. The zaps she'd endured messed up her motor skills, and it wouldn't take much for her to tumble into the drink right behind her.

But instinct told me not to leave the northeast corner for long. As

I steered her back there, she halted next to Kenny and proceeded to half fall on him as she attempted to yank him to his shackled feet.

He'd been handcuffed, too—hands behind him, just like he'd done to us; I'd winged him in his right shoulder and he obviously didn't like pain, so he was easy to control, even for postictal Creel. And, more determined and less unbalanced with every step, she clearly wanted to do this herself.

She pulled Kenny up and shoved him in front of her until I said, "Watchtower."

After that, Kenny had to shuffle forward on his knees. And, yes, I will confess to indulging in a moment of unadulterated schadenfreude, though I sure as hell didn't smile. I was a shit long way from smiling.

While Creel plunked onto a water-fattened tubedam, I kept Kenny on his knees. I guess he'd seen enough at that point not to squawk—though he didn't conceal his effrontery that we'd dared to resist his righteous power.

I decided to start out small. "How many in that watchtower over there?"

He smirked.

Considered electrolasering him, but recovery can be unpredictable, especially for someone already dealing with a bullet wound, albeit a minor one. Sure as hell could've enjoyed the venting a few slaps and kicks would provide—

But I resisted.

"Kenny, Kenny, Kenny," I said, noting how his eyes flared when I spoke his name. "It's *over*, and you, mister boss man, have a shitload of Nullsplainin' to do." I made sure my voice stayed far steadier and more relaxed than I felt—in preparation for saying what I hoped but did not know to be true. "Because we've got help on the way."

"Fuck you, cunt," Kenny replied.

"I'm doing better," Creel announced. "How 'bout I go get one of the others?"

I nodded and, without a word, closed the four-foot distance to Kenny, grabbed his shirt, and whipped him forward so he hit the ground face-first with a yelp I found far too satisfying.

"We'll be waiting for a few minutes while she drags one of your subordinates up here," I told him. "So, unlike anybody else, you get a second chance at our one-time-only offer."

I kept my voice low, soft. "Very brief window of opportunity, though. The ten-nine-eight kind you assholes like so much. Do the countdown in your head, *Kenny*. And after a little bit I'll ask you again. Maybe I'll shoot you again if you decline. Haven't decided. Cuz it's my turn now to get away with bloody murder, *Kenny*, and shit, I am sorely tempted."

Kenny grunted and wiggled some, which struck me as a complaint. I had to *bree-ee-eathe* to ignore it.

Way down the marsh side of the levee, Creel had selected one of the uninjured sapienshits and now shoved him toward me. Unaccustomed to being shackled, he stumbled. Creel hauled him upright and shoved him forward again.

"Three-two-one, Kenny," I said. "How many in the watchtower?"

"You'll go down for this, you cunt-fucking goddamn dyke *bitch*," Kenny seethed.

I didn't bother replying, and my silence seemed to bother him. He sputtered another round of unimaginative, "cunt"-infested threats that soon wilted into whiny protest. "This is a gummint contractor facility. We're—we're *authorized*, y'know. By the fuckin' DHS!"

Can't say I was surprised to hear it, but I gaped anyway. Before I could respond, though, Grodinsky's voice interrupted. It was shaking. "We got two—no, three, four—four sapienshits a-and, oh god, two custodians at the substation. Wanna get in, looks like."

Until then I didn't know I still had that sort of fast-forward in me. First glimpse and I realized I needed a clearer line of sight to the substation, one not obscured by the sally port's heavy, shot-blocking gate structures. I was already running full-tilt past Grodinsky as I told him to take the corner and shoot any sapienshit who fucking twitches. Bent low along the marshside embankment, my feet in the water, I ran west across that fifteen-yard chasm where I could be seen from the watchtower—and fired upon.

God, did I run. Because, unlike Rosario, *I* got shot at.

A few of the watchtower's rounds bit into the ground at my feet, some whined past my head, and I felt the heat of one or two—all of them chased a second later by the sharp, echoing crack of the rifle. By the time I made it to the blind spot and bellied onto the levee crown, the four sapienshits messing around the substation had split up.

Only a single custodian and two black-clad sapienshits remained on the north side of the substation where I could see them. One pounded in frustration at the substation door, which failed to open after he entered the keycode into the door's keypad. The other hustled him aside and called for the custodian to remove the door.

Grateful that the OCD bitch in my head had earlier nagged me into swapping my rifle's nearly depleted ammo cartridge for a full one, I aimed at the custodian. An easy shot; I followed up with two or three more to make sure. Before I had a chance to target the two sapienshits now jumping and cringing and ducking as the custodian withered in front of them, I heard gunfire south of me.

Perez had dashed a hundred yards from the perimeter fence to one of the soak ditch pump houses and was firing on the other two sapienshits and their custodian, who'd been attempting to enter the substation from the south side. I could see Perez but not what happened to his targets. Sure as hell I heard it, though, and so did the two sapienshits on my side of the substation. When I ordered them to drop their pistols (the only weapons they carried) and do a face-plant, they obeyed. Quickly.

Behind me at the corner, I heard Grodinsky's *woot!* and my stomach three-sixtied. Only one way he could see that we'd prevailed: he was out of position, visible to the watchtower.

And he paid for it even before I could shout a warning.

Perez was taking fire from the watchtower, too; I saw him curl fetal-tight behind the pump house's concrete foundation, unable to return fire.

The sound of Grodinsky's final grunting cry replaying in my head, I scrambled to my feet and ran farther west, because the only way I could fucking shoot at that fucking tower was to expose myself to fire from that fucking tower.

Didn't go a goddamn inch farther than I had to for a clean shot, slid fast onto my belly, and fired every last round in my rifle at the gun slots in the windows of the tower's top floor, hoping I'd guessed right about where those sapienshit rounds came from. At some point, Perez joined in. When finally I stopped and he stopped, the tower's top floor of black glass had entirely disappeared.

Nope, I thought quite calmly, not bulletproof after all. And nobody there returned our fire anymore. But the shooting continued. As best I could tell, it came from even farther south than Perez.

Oh. The southeast corner. Near Ozawa and Cintron. Who must need help.

Yeah, okay, so I should get up now. Now. Get up. Get. Up.

I didn't, though. I couldn't.

Then came the pain. It burst flamethrower hot out of my right thigh, raging through my calf, stabbing deep into my hip, up my spine.

It bullied the air out of my lungs and pounded its burning fury against the top of my head from the inside, determined to blast my head off.

❖

I have no idea how much time I lost. I simply found myself thinking "thirteen." Clinging to "thirteen" like it would help me hurt less. Until, in slo-oh-*oh* motion, I remembered. My count of sapienshits killed or captured had reached thirteen. Thirteen accounted for…must be more here than that…get up…

When someone spoke my name, I realized I lay on my belly staring at water droplets clinging to the battered grass a foot from my face. My right hand held the pistol I'd earlier tucked in my waistband; now the weapon pointed vaguely at the substation, though the shooting had stopped.

"Easy." Rosario's voice came from above me where I couldn't see her, and someone stroked my back. "I need to turn you over."

"Over?" I managed to ask.

"You're bleeding and I don't know why," Rosario said. Like discussing the weather.

"Leg," I tried to say. Got shot, I tried to say.

"Ready?" Rosario asked somebody.

"Ready." Ah, Magenau's voice, strong and calm. Magenau's okay.

And then I was on my back writhing, wondering why my leg hurt so much. Hell, that very leg had been shot before. But not like this.

While Magenau shifted me to my left side, Rosario extracted a folding knife from a small duffel bag she'd somehow acquired, flipped the knife open, told me to hold still, and cut off my right pant leg.

She quickly peered, poked, then produced wound pluggers and a compression bandage while asking me about pain, about numbness. I responded with grunts that seemed to burble out of me in time with the volcanic throbbing in my leg.

"Well, you've been damn lucky," she announced, frowning at my right thigh as I moaned. "High velocity, no tumbling. Perforated, exit wound's not too nasty. Moderate cavitation, but it looks like the bullet missed your femoral bone and your femoral artery."

She then stopped up both holes and tightly wrapped my thigh.

"Okay," she said, pointing at my leg. "That needs to be cleaned out, treated aysap for the infection that's already begun, then elevated."

"Grodinsky," I said, hoping.

Rosario sighed, shook her head, sighed again. Grief exhaled. Then she pointed at my nose. "You need to be hydrated. So to the infirmary with you. Magenau's volunteered to be your crutch."

Gotta say, Magenau didn't look to me like she volunteered. But there was no one I wanted to hear from more than her. Besides, Rosario had already trotted off with some woman in yellow spandex I didn't recognize who'd acquired a video camera and was recording as they jogged.

"What's that woman doing?" I asked Magenau.

"Don't get me started," Magenau snarked, and reached down both arms to me.

Standing up was nasty enough that we were halfway down the embankment before Magenau's repeated statement of the obvious truly registered. We'd taken Camp Null—rounded up all the sapienshits, the custodians had been neutralized—all of them either shot up or shut down.

And yes, yes, yes, help was on the way.

"Did you talk to Del?"

Wet and muddy (as were we all), Magenau smiled—the first real smile I ever saw on her face—and nodded. "Said two hours, maybe three, till help gets here. Fog's been slowing them down."

"All the sapienshits and all the custodians?" I asked again. "For sure?"

I made Magenau say it all again, and even now the numbers replay in my head like a damn mantra. The thirteen sapienshits I'd already counted, two who ventured along the south side but were stopped by Ozawa and Cintron, one "incapacitated" by Magenau's substation machinations, another who never made it out of the watchtower, and the last two who attempted escape by boat, but Kenny had disabled the boats and Cintron and Ozawa soon overtook them.

Nineteen sapienshits in all. Just nineteen. Three of them dead now, the rest cuffed up in that central courtyard where we started yesterday morning and, ha ha, now *they're* in chains, not us. And don't worry, Creel has a couple of wholebrains watching 'em, keeping 'em separated, making sure they don't pull any shit.

"And commo's down, right?" I asked.

Of course, Magenau's head moved up, down.

That had been the plan and Magenau executed the plan: Once

in the substation, use its comlink to contact Del just long enough to convince her you're not a goddamn crank and tell her where we are. Then cut electric power, which would also kill Camp Null commo. Because, as we'd learned from overheard sapienshit grousing, to keep Camp Null commo secure, *all* commo was routed through either the landline node in the substation or cell and satellite transceivers on the watchtower roof. No "civilian" comlink services allowed.

"Though," Magenau added, "it's hard to believe *somebody* hasn't cheated. Perez and a couple others are foraging over in the squadbay where they live." Then her shoulders hitched beneath my arm into a don't-get-your-hopes-up shrug. "But it's a mess."

She meant the fire caused by electric arcing caused by her substation machinations.

We'd reached the helipad; ahead of us, people in yellow spandex trickled out of the cellblock squadbay through two sally ports, the gates now flung wide open. A few cried. Too many were zombied. They all gaped as they beheld *Outside!* Not one of them was Maddie Small.

"Magenau," I said, "We gotta find Maddie Small."

She gave me a look I was too befuddled to care about. I felt her shoulder shrug again, doubtful beneath my grip. "Rosario said—"

"I can handle it," I insisted, hoping she didn't notice the wince I couldn't quite mask. "Won't take long."

Magenau's tone gave away that she did notice. "Let me know when you change your mind."

We entered the cellblock squadbay through its center doorway. At the bottom of the stairs, we encountered Creel already organizing everybody. Step one: identify the wholebrains and urge them to help the less able outside, into misty air sublimely fresh compared to inside.

"Seen Maddie Small?" Magenau asked her.

Creel's face creased into a deep scowl and she told me I needed to go to the infirmary, pointing the way.

"Is Maddie Small there?" I asked.

"Haven't seen her yet," Creel said. "But the cells upstairs still have people locked inside—"

I find it hard, now, to describe how important it had become for me to find Maddie Small. Something about balance. My balance, the world's balance. Something about balance.

"Gotta go upstairs," I said to Magenau. "Help those people out."

A few feet away, Creel shook her head. "You're crazy, Jamie."

Magenau didn't move. "I need to get you to the infirmary and then go retrieve the sapienshits' backup box."

"Please."

"Jeezus, Gwynmorgan," Magenau muttered. But she acquiesced.

"Tell me again," I said as I tortured myself up the stairs. "Y'know… how you did…the overvoltage."

"Bypassed the circuit breakers and a few varistors, diddled the voltage controllers, goosed a transformer, kicked up their generator." Magenau's lopsided grin gave away how much she reveled in reciting her tale. "Produced wonderful long-duration arcing. Fried commo first, then cams and sensors and that foul collar tracking system, then their robot recharging stations. Heh. Shorted out a shitload of Vederes."

"Kitchen, too, right?"

"Fried it all to a fare-thee-well circuit by fucking circuit. Except the infirmary. And that appliance box with all their backed-up data." Her grin evaporated and she blew out a deep breath. "Now it's about getting the hell outta here before the feds show up."

"The feds?" For the first time since that long-ago morning in November, I thought about what comes after the steel cage and the beatings and the pharma and the forced labor. About having to explain why I killed yet another human being with an assault rifle.

"What'd you think, Gwynmorgan?" Magenau shook her head. "You'd just go home? Kick back, have a beer and a finger-lickin' good time, head off to work in the morning?"

All I could do was stare at her. I'd thought only about *being* home—nothing about how I'd get there from here. Nothing about having to account for myself to strangers along the way. "Fuck," I bleated. "I don't want to deal with any of that."

"Yeah, well, pick a side," Magenau said. "People like me just want to disappear and be left alone. Then there's people like Creel and Rosario and Ozawa—bent on saving the world and ready to lead the Candid Camera brigade."

We'd at last reached the top of the stairs. A second videographer in yellow spandex (who turned out to be Ozawa) recorded Cintron helping a prisoner creep unsteadily out of a cell. I wanted to suggest a third category to Magenau—the blank-eyed souls who may never find themselves again—but I struggled to form a coherent sentence. Cuz, oh god, my leg was being immolated anew every time my heart beat.

"You gotta lie down," Magenau said.

"No," I insisted. "First I find Maddie Small." Because I'd decided. If Maddie Small was dead, I would kill Kenny Bouchard before help arrived to stop me.

❖

The seventh cell door on the right.

By the time I reached it, Magenau had already handed me to Ozawa (literally) and hurried off to recover the sapienshits' backup box. With his help, I'd defied the nausea induced by the sight and smell of the cells and opened two, encouraging forth their disoriented occupants, who faltered at the prospect of stepping into the corridor.

At the seventh door on the right, my turn came to falter. I knew, somehow, Maddie Small was in there. Have no notion why or how—I just knew. As I leaned on him, Ozawa shoved the key in the lock, turned it, pulled the door open. We saw no one. He moved to step inside, but I reached out and stopped him.

"Let me this time," I said. "And don't record it, okay?"

Ozawa dipped his head, almost like a bow, and backed away.

"Hey, Maddie Small," I called out softly. "We did it. We're getting outta here."

Silence.

She had to be in the inner cell, the door to which had opened automatically when Magenau took down the power, but I couldn't see her. Holding first onto the outer cell door frame, then the elliptical, I hobbled to the door of the inner cell.

Still no one.

"Aw, Maddie Small," I murmured, "where'd you go?"

Seconds passed, more seconds, while I staved off a compulsion to vomit at the sight of the scratches on the wall alongside the empty bunk. Then, oh so briefly, the scratches along the back wall jiggled...

Ignominious

I was standing in my own cell.

I think I gasped or gagged or maybe just tried to *bree-ee-eathe* as I clung to the door frame, horrified unto dizziness. I wanted to run, couldn't run, I was stuck, locked in here forever, no I can turn around and leave anytime I fucking well want, I can, I can, can't I?

A tiny sound interrupted my graveyard spiral—a sound that didn't come from me. Or from Ozawa. It came from beneath the bunk. When

I heard it again, I lowered myself onto the floor ass-first—and there she was: Maddie Small, as tiny as her sound.

I thought it was a good sign that she was curled up facing me rather than with her back to the world. "Hey, Maddie Small," I soothed her, and reached out my hand, which she stared at.

Finally she said, "Hey, Jamie Gwynmorgan."

"We beat 'em," I told her. "Thanks to you."

Her eyes shifted slowly to my leg. "You got hurt."

"So did you," I said. "Lemme see."

After a lo-o-ong minute, Maddie Small used her shoulders and hips to wriggle out from under the bunk; her hands were grotesquely swollen, deep purple, fingers obviously broken. "They zapped me, smashed my hands."

A sapienshit collar still circled her neck, and not the one I'd cut yesterday. It was a new, intact collar. Maddie Small had been found out, yet she convinced the sapienshits she'd used the custodian wire cutters she'd "found" only on her own collar. And she had revealed nothing of our plans.

We commiserated for a bit about how much her hands and my leg hurt, how scary it was to get zapped, how hungry she was, and all the while Maddie Small inched closer to me, until she allowed my hand to rest on her thin shoulder and she leaned into me.

"Would you cut it off again?" she asked, her head easing back against my chest.

"I'd be honored, Maddie Small." Ozawa handed me the wire cutter he kept in his waistband, and soon I had her freed and agreeing to go to the infirmary so Rosario could treat her hands.

"Just so you know, Maddie Small," I told her before Ozawa took her to the infirmary, "what you did makes you a hero. Twice over."

By then, Ozawa had both promised to keep Maddie Small out of the video recording and helped me from the floor to the bunk. As I was figuring out how to get to my feet by myself, I remembered Audy. Right behind me within arm's reach, tucked away in Vesica the Gap.

I removed Audy as always, careful to replace Vesica's clever cover so it's invisible, ready to be discovered by the next prisoner, and followed Maddie Small to the infirmary.

Rosario had found a small generator spared by Magenau, who got it running. And she'd found a couple of liberatees (like that? made it up myself) with medical training to help her. Soon they had me showered, wound compressioned and debrided (to my steady chorus of fuckfuckfuck), leg elevated. There's some almost-real food in my belly and a needle in my arm delivering fluids and antimicrobial liposomes.

I've traded yellow spandex for green infirmary scrubs—though Creel made sure her videographers documented me all grubby and bloody in detainee yellow being helped along by you'd-never-know-it-from-those-images Magenau.

The fog has returned and is thicker now than any time all day, so I'm not surprised that our rescuers are late. This has made some of the liberatees very nervous, but perhaps it's not a bad thing.

At least it's given me a chance to adapt to the news that today is Saturday, August 1, not Friday, July 17. This I learned from Kenny's old-fashioned analog calendar watch, given to me by Cintron, along with a ball-style neck chain, like for wearing dog tags, onto which I slid Audy.

I've been relieved of duty as Chief Fix-This Officer in a quite gentle and entirely unspoken way, though either Creel, Rosario, or Ozawa keep me apprised of what's going on. I like that they want me to know, and I'm grateful they don't want me to decide anything. Because right now my leg is on fucking fire and I need most of my energy to keep from screaming.

Anticipating a future they see better than I do, Creel, Rosario, and Ozawa have used this extra time to make a record of who's here, and in the process get most everyone agreed on a way to stay in touch. I know Creel wants more, but she's smart enough to settle for simple, basic liberatee commo.

Which, I suppose, is why Creel has emerged as our leader. I like that, too. Truth is, we all kind of looked at her and asked So Now What?

First thing we heard from her was a warning. "Although we've made contact with friends who will spread word we're here, we have reason to believe—" She raised her hands so her fingers could mock quotation marks. "We'll be 'rescued' by some flavor of law enforcement, probably federal. We also have reason to believe that this facility has been operated by contractors working for the Department of Homeland Security."

"Who told you that?" several people around me wanted to know.

Kenny Bouchard, said Creel. Behind her, Cintron, Ozawa, and I nodded; we'd heard Kenny say it, too.

Creel zipped through some useful legal tips (conversations with your attorney, physician, pastor, and spouse are privileged and these people cannot be compelled to testify against you; ultimately, you cannot trust anything law enforcement officials say because they are allowed to lie to you, although it's a crime for you to lie to them; and the biggie—unless you are under arrest, you cannot be legally detained, though DHS is famous for doing it anyway).

She went on to describe habeas corpus, even quoting the Constitution. "The privilege of the writ of habeas corpus shall not be suspended," she said, "unless when in cases of rebellion or invasion the public safety may require it." This means whoever's holding a prisoner can be required to produce that prisoner in court along with proof of authority to detain; if the court deems there's a lack of authority, then the prisoner must be released.

So Creel thinks we could need writs of habeas corpus to get the hell out of here…

Rock. Quagmire. Hard place.

That's what we're looking at now, all fifty-nine of us almost-liberated detainees. Reason enough, says Creel, for all fifty-nine of us to speak with one voice.

But a sizable contingent want to bolt before help arrives—too many (at first) for the pair of boats tied up at Camp Null's small dock.

"I'd go this minute," I said to the dozen or so people around me, "if I could get away from that fucking hurricane in time. But I can't, not without a helicopter."

Nevertheless, last I heard nineteen liberatees want to find their own way out and avoid anything official—among them not just Magenau but Maddie Small and Perez, too. Can't say I blame them—even though, as Creel made clear, "you better already know how to get by in the darker corners of the shadow economy."

❖

Almost nine o'clock now, according to Kenny's watch. Twenty-one hundred hours. Close to dark outside.

I made a deal with Rosario that as long as she didn't try to shoot me up with pain pharma, and if she let me stay near one of the infirmary windows (we're in the staff part with real windows you can see through), then I'd resist this slithering sense of claustrophobia and endure here hooked up to her IV.

So that's where I've been for the last couple of hours. Most everyone around me is asleep or, like Maddie Small, drugged into silliness to ease the pain.

But not me. I'm wide awake and trying to absorb what Rosario just mentioned in passing—the date. The whole, full date. And, of course, I counted how long it's been since I was grabbed. Last November 6 to August 1—*plus a year*. I haven't lost almost nine months. I've lost almost twenty-one months. And I still don't know why.

Six hundred thirty-five days since I've seen Del, touched Del. I wonder who will show up here any ole time now. How officious will they be, how many more days will I lose to explanations and writs and god knows what bureaucratic bullshit before I get home to Del? Or will I be charged with homicide for shooting that sapienshit? And maybe I killed the one who died in the watchtower, too...

Right now nothing around me feels quite real, not even these people I see when I open my eyes or the sounds of their sleep or the smells of their fear.

Nothing feels quite real except Audy. So that's what I've been doing for the last couple hours—talking to a little black stick hanging from my neck while I try, try to *bree-ee-eathe*...

CHAPTER TWELVE

Wend catawampus

AF151.

Sunday, August 2.

Don't know the time—zero dark some-damn-hour, emphasis on *dark*.

I'm still trying to wrap my diminished capacity around the shit that's gone down since I woke up. It was one of those sneaky sleeps that gets you believing you're awake, but actually you're *dreaming* an awake that's not *this awake*…and then your eyes open to Del's dimly lit face inches away, all worried, tears streaming down her cheeks, her warm-sweet breath ragged, almost gasping.

This awake was out of time, out of place, tenuously illuminated by skittering flashlights. I'd left off at Camp Null's infirmary, my shot-up leg hoisted, too tired to talk to Audy anymore, gazing into the dark beyond the window near my gurney…

And then I'm looking at Del, inhaling her sublime scent, wondering how I got to her and where am I now and what now *is* this anyway? Or maybe I'm dreaming it all. Maybe *this awake* is a dream, too.

I remember blinking slowly, doubting Del would be there when my eyes opened again. But she *was* there. Older, I thought. Eyes even kinder than I remembered them. Tired and drawn, yet more beautiful than I'd ever seen her.

Of course, her presence sucked all the air out of my lungs. Then I felt her touch, feather-slight and electric along my temple, my jaw. Are you real? her touch asked me, hesitating. *Please please please* be real, it begged.

So I smiled. Tried to anyway. Tried to speak. Del, I wanted to say. Del.

And maybe I did, because a low yowl of a sob tumbled out of her as she huddled against me. I wrapped my arms around her. And realized I hadn't lost time at all; I still lay on that gurney.

Del had come to Camp Null.

What.

The.

Fuck.

Which is pretty much what I said to her when she stopped kissing me to take a breath.

"First dibs," she replied, grinning through her tears.

Really. That's what she said.

Before I could ask what she meant, Creel appeared and handed her a comlink into which she soon murmured, "How long?"

Magenau's voice echoed in my head then. *What'd you think, Gwynmorgan? You'd just go home?*

I glanced at Creel, gazed at Del, and I knew. They had a plan. Which is to say, Del had a plan and had already enlisted Creel. I glanced at Creel again—yep, an eager recruit. I wondered how long ago Del had arrived and how many others had already joined her cavalry.

Odd moment, that one. Like crowds converging on a convoluted intersection, everyone trying to wend catawampus to some sort of resolution. And I was all of these madding crowds—the lost crowd pursuing the distant pulse of almost-forgotten arousal, the weary crowd desperate to just go home, the confounded crowd seeking explanation, the raging crowd demanding justice. All of the crowds of me chaotic, exhausted—and gridlocked.

"How complicated will this get?" I asked Del once she handed the comlink back to Creel.

"Very."

I asked what happens next.

"We scoot the hell out of here."

Home? I didn't say it aloud but I suppose my face gave me away.

"Tennessee next," Del said. "Then I'm not sure yet. Then home."

And oh, god, I remember how my need lifted me toward her scent, exhaled my plea—"Tell me the rest between kisses?"—and how she answered with two soft syllables, uh-huuuh, delivered deep into my mouth on her hungry tongue.

❖

The rest. God knows how long it'll take for me to learn the rest. So far it's kinda like untangling a twenty-one-month knot—most recent snarls first, with glimpses of earlier kinks yet to be unraveled.

Pretty much the first thing I found out: Del had been on a boat heading to Parris Island when Magenau called her from the substation. "I'll explain all about 'why a boat' later," she said between chunks of increasingly urgent conversation with Creel and someone on the other end of the comlink she and Creel kept passing between them. "The point is, we're maybe an hour ahead of USCP and SLED and I gather from Leta that—"

"Whoa." I brushed Del's cheek to slow her down. "What's USCP, what's Sled, what's Leta?"

"US Capitol Police, which is leading the only real investigation into the abduction of a United States senator's family member—that would be you. South Carolina Law Enforcement Division, essentially the part of the local state police that fields a SWAT team. And Leta is Taletha Creel's nickname."

"Creel doesn't look like a Leta. Or a Taletha." I kept my eyes on Creel but I wasn't thinking about her name. I was thinking about soon being surrounded by special ops cops and a shitload of questions, starting with "What the fuck happened here?"

Del came closer, a crease forming between her eloquent eyebrows. "Tell me, baby."

"I shot at least four people today," I confessed to that crease, then made myself look into those bottomless eyes of hers. "At least one of them's dead."

She nodded, flicking a glance toward Creel, who still spoke quietly into the comlink.

Shit, she already knew. Because, shit, it was the first goddamn thing she heard when she got here.

Then I'm not sure yet. Because if my detention has been legal all along, I'm a criminal for killing at least one someone, maybe another, and injuring others in an illegal escape attempt.

Then home. Because Del can't bear to deprive me of hope even when no hope is warranted.

"Hey." Her hand raised my chin so I'd look at her. "You are not the bad guy here."

"Yeah?" I muttered. "So who the hell is?"

"Long, long story," she answered. "And we're only just getting to the denouement."

❖

Del had arrived at Camp Null with several others, including Creel's brother and cousin ("their boat"), an attorney from the ACLU, one of Lily and Dana's best security people, Pilar ("*you* try saying no to my sister, I dare you"), and two journalists—Vivian Velty, still famous after all these years, and her much younger camera guy.

By Ozawa's count, "Rescue" showed up three and a half hours later. Del used those three and a half hours to set up our transport out of Camp Null, haggling an arrangement that keeps us together as far as Tennessee, where we'll all undergo police interviews.

Word of the plan didn't travel; it simply *was* everywhere at once. Like quantum entanglement. Not surprising, then, that maybe two-thirds of the way through those three and a half hours, Magenau, Perez, and several others showed up at the infirmary to announce their departure.

Magenau did the talking. "We're leaving," she declared. "Taking the two sapienshit boats right the fuck now."

Del and Creel explained that a helicopter ride to a little town in Tennessee would pull everyone well out of the hurricane's path, that no one would be under arrest.

"You won't be in anyone's custody," Del said. "The helicopters are private, on loan from, well, let's just say a strong supporter of the ACLU."

She told them the ACLU attorney accompanying her has maintained contact with a DC federal district court judge who issued a habeas corpus writ for me even before Del's boat docked and was about to issue writs for all Camp Null detainees based on the list of names Creel and Rosario put together. "At this very moment, we're ninety-nine percent on our way to getting Judge Byrne to sign off on it."

Eleven people simultaneously shouted "NO FUCKING WAY," and Magenau turned to the gurney next to mine. "Hey, Maddie Small, you coming?"

"Jeezus, Magenau," I protested, "you know you can't outrun the storm in a boat. And with those hands, Maddie Small's gonna have a hell of a time trying to swim."

Magenau ignored me, but Maddie Small did not. Slowly her head pendulumed toward me and she offered a pharma-high smile. "Wha' 'bout you, Jamie Gwynmorgan?"

I smiled back. "Ever been in a helo, Maddie Small?"

That's when Del dove in again. "I get that it's hard, but—"

"You don't get *shit*," Magenau snapped; she held tight to a canvas bag I hadn't noticed before. "Some of us—"

"Stop!" Voice raised, Del rose from her perch on my gurney and squared her shoulders to face off with Magenau. "Listen. To. Me."

And Magenau hesitated.

"Here," Del continued, "is the abbreviated version, which is all we have time for now. What's gone down here comes under federal jurisdiction, but these cops who are on their way are sympathetic—"

"What the fuck does *that* mean?" Perez demanded.

"Short answer: they're not from the Justice Department or DHS," said Del. "We have reason not to trust Justice or DHS. These guys on their way here are feds—but they're US Capitol Police responsible to the *legislative* branch only, the Congress *only*, and they're working on Jamie's kidnapping."

"Lucky Jamie," sneered Magenau. "So why the hell do you need habeas writs?"

"Because I had no idea when I left Charleston to come here that you guys were freeing yourselves," Del replied.

"A writ of habeas corpus would be the only other way to get a prisoner released," Creel pointed out.

"And the only prisoner name I had was Jamie's," Del added.

Magenau looked feral. "Well, we're not prisoners anymore."

"But," Del reminded her, reminded us all, "your breakout or takeover or whatever this is changed everything. People died."

"It was a take*down*, Del," I said, "which most of the prisoners here had nothing to do with. They were locked in cells and probably not even aware of it till it was over."

"A-an' the s-say-*sa*pienshits were bad first." Maddie Small frowned and nodded for emphasis when Del looked over at her. "Very *mee-ean*," she added. "Shot people dead fuh tryin' to run when they coulda just collar-zapped 'em."

"Exactly right," I said, reaching a hand to Maddie Small's shoulder. "I figured they'd kill us tomorrow—once we finished putting together their tubedams."

Del leaned over and kissed me, but her words were for the others. "I understand how you want to take off on your own. But what happened here has to be accounted for, and if you leave without doing that, then you give the FBI and DHS the excuse they need to declare you persons of interest in an active homicide investigation and to then chase you down. You also give the, uh, sapienshits control of the narrative, which will turn into some version of 'if they're innocent, why did they run?' If you run, you destroy your legitimacy and your credibility. If you run, you *lose*."

Face contorting, Magenau slammed a fist onto my gurney, no doubt the surrogate for Del's face. Yet Del didn't flinch. Instead, she delicately touched Magenau's rigid forearm.

"But if you stay," she said in a gentle hush that stilled everyone, "the habeas corpus writs we're obtaining for every single person detained here can protect you—even though a few of you managed to make the writs moot."

Perez pounced. "Protect us how?"

"Deterrence," Creel said. "Prevents the FBI or DHS from detaining us again."

"Hell." Magenau almost spat. "They can *prove* any accusation they decide to lay on us. Doesn't have to be *real*, for chrissake. Easy enough to support whatever they're gonna hang on us by diddling their surveillance data and sapienshit testimony. You're a lawyer, Creel. You know that."

"But *not* so easy given that the little box in your bag carries all their *undiddled* surveillance data," Del countered. "And *not* so easy once a first-rank journo posts clips about habeas corpus writs for you and fifty-eight others held in undisclosed detention on Parris Island. Undisclosed even to you, it seems. Who here was ever told by anyone you were under arrest?"

Seventeen detainees in that large infirmary space and every single one, including me, including Magenau, shook their heads.

"So no," Del went on, "you will *not* be taken into custody when USCP gets here, and you will *not* be taken into custody in Tennessee. Your presence here signifies that you were abducted, and your attorneys, who are waiting for you in Tennessee, are getting you safely the hell outta here. That's the deal we're making."

"You know what?" Magenau said. "I believe you *think* that's the deal you're making. Maybe even the judge thinks so, too. And you *think* you've got the momentum. But I don't trust the FBI or DHS or the Secret Service or the fucking GX Men not to divert your damn helicopter to god-knows-where and grab us any-thefuck-way. They make their own rules, Professor."

"At this moment," Del replied, "Judge Byrne is being presented with evidence that impugns the FBI's integrity in this matter, outright damns DHS, and shows that Jamie was illegally abducted, not legally detained."

"Ooh," Magenau gibed. "Lucky Jamie again."

"Lucky all of you." Del's gaze shifted from Magenau to Perez to the man next to Perez and each of the others as she spoke. "It means the Camp Null staff is involved in Jamie's kidnapping, and now they've shot her. This gives the Capitol Police cause to arrest them, *not you*. Which is why it's the Capitol Police on their way here right now, not the FBI, not DHS. In effect, the Capitol Police become your bodyguards."

"For how long?" somebody asked.

"Depends on when they talk to you," said Del. "They'll interview every single person they find here, including me. That has to happen somewhere else because of the hurricane—also part of the deal, which is to say, the judge's order. Tennessee's the choice for a bunch of reasons and the judge agreed because we did all the logistical work faster than anyone else. And, frankly, because I have connections. After USCP is done talking with you, you're free to decline the offer of a ride home."

"So the FBI and DHS just give up and go away?" Perez's voice pitched high with disbelief.

Del's head shifted slowly back and forth. "Oh no. For the next thirty-six hours or so, this is about the abduction of Jamie Gwynmorgan. But by Monday noon, the stench of scandal will be stinking up Washington, and both the FBI and DHS—especially DHS—will be dancing as fast as they can. Ladies and gentlemen, all hell is about to break loose."

"Which means some of us," Creel added, "will be called to testify at Congressional committee hearings and, I hope, before a grand jury and eventually at a few criminal trials. I, for one, can't fucking wait."

She paused and looked at Magenau. "But you know what? If you guys don't want your faces all over this, we can keep you in the shadows. Lawyers can be useful like that, and for this one we have a free legal ride. We need cameras on this, but Vivian Velty will respect your no-faces no-voices thing. Plenty of others are already spouting away, so your absence will go unnoticed."

"Rescue will be here soon," Del told them. "And we've gotten word that within eight or nine hours, wind speeds will be too high on the barrier islands for helos to take off. Best way out of here is on a helicopter to Tennessee within the next two or three hours."

"Shit," Magenau groaned. "*Shit.*" She didn't say anything else but I knew we were thinking precisely the same thing: if we had waited just a few more hours, no takedown would've been needed because Del was coming with a writ of habeas corpus—and only one of those was sufficient to blow the lid off Camp Null.

Del saw it in our eyes, I guess. "No," she said to me, then to Magenau. "No. You could not know how close we'd gotten."

Creel seconded, all lawyerly. "Those of us out on the levee today risked our lives doing what was necessary to escape and survive our abductors," she insisted. "Yes, out of necessity some of us used deadly force, but none of us used force except in the face of imminent harm. And none of us used excessive force. Which means that, unlike the sapienshits, our actions were not criminal."

"So we go to Tennessee and get out of the helicopter, and what next?" asked a man standing near Perez, one of several people I didn't know.

"You meet with the ACLU attorneys who'll be waiting for us in Tennessee, or you can call your own attorney. Together with your attorney you sit down to be interviewed by the Capitol Police—an interview that'll be video recorded," Creel explained. "You say *nothing*, sign *nothing* without your attorney present and advising you."

"After that?" the man persisted.

"The lawyers'll end up doing the first of many press conferences," Creel replied, "with some of us volunteering to serve as, y'know, color commentary—the more the merrier, as far as I'm concerned. We also make sure we have a secure and private means to keep in touch with each other, so can we stay apprised of what's going on—"

"And so we can send up a flare if we need help," I said.

"Mmm." Magenau sounded skeptical but distinctly less grouchy. "Don't mind that flare part, Gwynmorgan. But as the man said—" Her head angled toward the guy next to Perez. "And then what?"

"Well, I plan to scoop up my girl here and take her home with me," Del said. "And while we put our lives back together, we watch."

"For what?" Perez asked.

"To see," Del answered with a calm smile, "who has the audacity to walk into Judge Byrne's courtroom and argue that your detention in this hellhole has been legal."

❖

Twenty of them altogether. The first fifteen scurried off an unmarked military surplus helo in full tactical regalia (including automatic assault rifles), helmet lights swiping erratically across the darkness as they crouched and pivoted, weapons ready to fire.

Propped on a set of Camp Null crutches, I watched them from the edge of the parade deck with all the other detainees. Fifty-nine of us—even battered, shaky Maddie Small—lined up shoulder to shoulder in front of the high-security triple fence around the cellblock squadbay. At the southern end of our long, mostly yellow spandex column, Ozawa, Rosario, Cintron, Perez, and Cindy the recovering semi-zombie had solemnly set out our seven dead comrades.

"We should all be together for this," Rosario had declared to a soft murmur of agreement when Cintron and Perez carried out Castillo's body, followed by Ozawa and Cindy carrying Grodinsky.

Impressive, I thought. Creel, Rosario, Ozawa, and Cindy had created a genuine sense of fellowship and even a kind of loyalty among fifty-nine strangers, most of whom had never seen each other before their cell doors opened a few hours earlier, many of whom were mentally precarious. They lined up in small clutches of new affiliation, helping each other. Like people who've been through a disaster, I thought. Humanity at its best.

Camp Null's nineteen sapienshits lay on the ground before us, too, the sixteen still alive facedown, cuffed up, and squirming. Between us and their chained ankles, Cintron and Cindy neatly arrayed every weapon we'd used or found. And out in front of all of this stood Del and the ACLU attorney as well as Creel, erect and proud in filthy yellow spandex.

When Rescue's helo lights became visible maybe a quarter mile northeast of us, Vivian Velty and her cameraman, who hadn't stopped interviewing and videoing since they'd arrived, positioned about a hundred feet from us and ran two cams. One recorded Rescue, the other our reactions as the helo landed, as the SWAT guys emerged and succumbed to obvious confusion upon finally getting a good look at us.

"Oh, how fucking appropriate," grumbled Magenau. "'Rescue' doesn't have a clue." Canvas bag held to her chest, she stayed with Maddie Small and Perez in the shadows a half step behind me, Rosario, and Ozawa.

"Maybe they realize we got journos here," Perez muttered. "Oh yeah, look, they get it. That's right, Leo, freeze for the cameras."

Which is exactly what happened. While assorted helmet lights jittered around Creel's yellow spandex, Del waved to one of the last people off the helo, a man in a dark windbreaker bearing large yellow letters—USCP. He waved back, and as she, Creel, and the ACLU attorney walked toward him, I stopped breathing.

Oh dear god, just one jumpy finger, one brief burst of bullets...

But I needn't have worried.

Unable to hear anything over the helo's racket from so far away, I watched Del work and forced myself to *bree-ee-eathe*. Every move she made, I could tell, had been arranged, negotiated. She already knew this guy, I could tell, and she introduced the others with that spectacularly effortless grace I've always loved to behold. And oh god I ached with the joy of watching her, of knowing I'd soon touch her again, be touched again. By her. By *Her*...

Rescue Leader shook hands with them and, as they turned and approached us, Del handed him her comlink; hands cupped over both ears, he listened for longer than he spoke, somehow hearing over the din what was said to him, his body bending oh-so-slightly forward at his waist. Like a bow, I thought. Yep, Del had done it. Rescue Leader would behave, even though what he found—and what he'd do next— wasn't anything like what he'd initially expected.

They took away the sapienshits first, and not to Tennessee. Two more transport helos came for us less than an hour later. Del and I boarded the second one, along with Maddie Small, Magenau, and Perez, among others, just as the wind started to develop serious attitude.

God, I'd forgotten how fucking noisy these things are. I can only hope Audy's been able to pick up the sound of my voice over the damn rotors. Certainly I'm not disturbing Del, who is, incredibly, sound asleep next to me, her head snugged into my left shoulder, her hand claiming my arm.

I'm too wound up to sleep. Too untrusting. Our bird's supposed to be headed for an airport on the Cumberland Plateau. ETA two hours, give or take, which means we'll land there around first light, so I'll be able to get a look from the air, make sure what I see matches what I've been told.

A small airport, Del said, but with a hangar big enough for interviewing and even briefly housing fifty-nine rescued abductees in need of a chance to call home and a real shower and real clothes and real food and a lock-free place with cots to lie down on for a while. A small airport, but with a 6700-foot runway close to an interstate and eighty-odd miles equidistant from Nashville, Chattanooga, and Knoxville.

"Oh," I remember saying to Del just before we boarded, "so lots of escape routes."

She smiled and found a way to make kissing someone on crutches intensely arousing before she replied. "You taught me well, my sweet."

❖

AF152.
Monday, August 3.
02:36 hours.

Considering how little notice the people out there on the Cumberland Plateau were given about dozens of wretches landing in their midst, the hangar's setup was impressive. I think this contributed to its effect on Magenau, who gave it all one quick glance and decided it was a sign that USCP was reneging and that we'd end up in chains again.

Reluctantly, I halted my shamble toward a table laid out with bread and sandwich meats and potato salad and what looked like jugs of lemonade. "Has anyone *said* you're under arrest?" I asked her.

"No." She snorted. "But they didn't last time, either."

"Was Vivian Velty there last time?"

"You have way more faith than I do in her ability to slip packets through the baleen."

"The what?"

"Baleen—a big fuckin' filter like whales have so they can extract plankton or krill or whatever from their gargantuan gulps of seawater." Magenau said this with exaggerated patience, though she managed not to roll her eyes. "Been going on since before I was grabbed. Two years anyway. First sign came when a big-fucking-deal hack just never got reported in the media, even though the hackers notified multiple news venues. After it happened twice more, we started sniffing around, realized somebody was doing very targeted data filtering."

"The baleen, I presume," I said. When she nodded, I asked who was behind it all.

"The whale, of course," she replied, shaking her head at me.

"Ah. You think a government—*our* government—did it."

"Whaddaya suppose CISA's for?" Magenau pronounced it sigh-suh like she wanted to spit something evil out of her mouth.

"You mean that law?" I managed to guess. "The, uh, Computer Information Sharing Act?"

Magenau humphed an affirmative.

Lynn once compared CISA to how the IRS corners retailers and bosses into doing its tax collecting. CISA forces network service providers to monitor customers' metadata and message content for anything that might even remotely be construed as terrorism-related, and then "share" what they find. And under CISA, network providers can't be sued by anyone whose private data gets sucked up for the great government whale.

But according to Magenau, CISA's merely a cover for much worse.

"Usually," she explained, "messages that are CISA-flagged get delivered to the recipient, since the feds' terrorism criteria are so broad and generate so many false positives. Halting message transmission has always indicated that the feds are ready to make arrests. They show you the warrant authorizing seizure of the message that was never delivered *after* you're in custody. But the baleen is different—"

I guessed again. "The messages about the hacks you mentioned were never received, but the feds never busted anyone either."

Once more, Magenau nodded. "Not a huge step from CISA-style monitoring to swallowing information outright." Her gaze began to methodically traverse the hangar. "When we first saw it, we wanted to learn how it works, engineer around it—probably by bypassing network provider monitoring. The network's splendidly uncontrollable redundancy is a beautiful thing." She sighed. "As a whole, anyway. But at the edge? Not so much. And at any given endpoint? Not at all."

However, before Magenau and her crew could test their hack—

She raised her arms and shrugged. "This."

"So you think Vivian Velty's video clips and news reports aren't getting disseminated."

Magenau shrugged. "I think CISA both enables and hides a covert mechanism designed to disappear any information the well-connected want disappeared. I think that mechanism is used to manipulate what the public sees, hears about. In the case of individual messages, it's done near the endpoint. When it's about interfering with broad dissemination, I think they're messing with the edge as well as endpoints. Gotta be done carefully," she said. "To keep it from getting noticed except by the sort of people they can make look like crazies."

"They," I interrupted. "Who?"

Magenau scowled. "CISA requires network providers to 'share' with the Department of Homeland Security."

DHS. Of fucking course.

"And Vivian Velty might be running all around here doing interviews, babbling at her camera lens," Magenau snarled on, "but I sure as hell haven't seen her face or Creel's or that ACLU dude's on any screens yet. One might regard that as too coincidental to be a coincidence."

My stomach began to cramp. Magenau had been right about plenty, why not this?

I looked around for a screen somewhere in the minimalist hangar temporarily transformed into an ad hoc disaster relief facility. The local Red Cross had been enlisted (with a handsome donation, I discovered later) to arrange cots and long tables with food; showers and shitters occupied one corner, medical triage another. (The cops and lawyers took the only spaces separated by walls and doors.)

No video screens anywhere, though. So let's find somebody with a functioning comlink, I proposed.

But Magenau balked—at staying inside, at eating anything, at remaining within conversational distance of another human being—and insisted on walking in circles around an adjacent parking lot where, she made a point of shouting out from a hundred feet away, there were *no* reporters, not a one.

I left her muttering there when my ACLU lawyer showed up to usher me ahead of the rest through a routine in the hangar that struck me as a compromise worked out between the lawyers and the LEOs.

Best part was that Del got to stay close by through most of it. Second-best part was that I got to drink halfway decent lemonade and eat a real ham sandwich and chocolate during the medical tech's quick once-over, followed by a sort-of shower and hospital scrubs in my choice of five colors. Del picked navy blue.

"So have we appeared on Candid Camera yet?" I asked her in a whisper as soon as we had any privacy.

"Not that I'm aware." She spoke slowly, her face darkening with each syllable while she helped me pull on the scrub pants. "And Vivian kind of growled earlier when I mentioned GNN had nothing up yet."

"Magenau may be able to help," I said. "If she hasn't already done a runner. Try getting 'em together."

While Del did that, I declined an unenthusiastic offer to rest on a cot for a while before my USCP interview, even though I hadn't slept much for...how long? Thirty-six hours? Two days? No matter. I was still way too adrenalized to sleep.

Plus I wanted to get the interview over with, since I'd be separated from Del for its duration, and I damn well needed to know if news of Camp Null was really being disappeared. Because if it was, all fifty-nine of us reappearing detainees might find ourselves swallowed up yet again. How could I test Magenau's theory about whether we were free to go following our interview until the interview was done?

My attorney was comfortingly protective, while the cops—two detectives—remained meticulously polite. I know too well what hostile interrogation is like; these two conducted a non-hostile interview, albeit a very, very thorough one.

And, god knows, I wanted to tell my tale. I'd lost a lot to pharma and the disorientation of solitary confinement, but I was gonna make damn sure these detectives knew about Philippa Flynn.

Hadn't anticipated that they'd want me to fork over Audy, something I resisted, though I allowed them to make a copy of the Philippa Flynn entry at the beginning, which they did in my presence since I refused to let Audy leave my sight.

After a couple of hours, I had to shade my eyes. Outside the large window about three feet from me, blazing neon-bright blue sky tyrannized the Plateau's flat landscape. The sun's death rays ricocheted off vehicles and flagpoles, eager to blind me. Frantic, phosphorescent green shimmered rebellion in the over-trimmed shrubbery, in stands of trees distant on the far side of the air wriggling above the runway's sweltered pavement. Inside was almost as bad. A glaring beige banality of razor lines and machined patterns throbbed all around me.

Took me by surprise, having to stare like that at the worn, scratched steel tabletop to keep calm. Out there on the levee after so long inside, I'd wondered if *Outside!* would get to me. And there was a moment as we first stood shackled on the helo pad, when the pre-dawn dark had retreated and the space around me felt so big big big, and yeah, I was afraid. A feral, physical terror. I shoved it down, that afraid. Shoved it down and it stayed down, y'know? And I thought, hey, not bad, stronger than you look.

But *Outside!* on the levee had been fog-infused, near-sighted, gray-vague. Nothing like Tennessee, where color super-saturated so intensely that it stung, it sledgehammered, it set off bolts of lightning that slashed through the grime-infested tunnel in my thigh deep into my hip, up my spine. I felt impaled on an electric spike whacking the inside of my skull.

My lawyer suggested a break, but I wanted to keep going, wanted to be done. "Just gotta close my eyes," I said to them. The detectives rustled and stirred some with the instinct to object. They study you when they probe, eager to speculate (and project) about every detail of you, real and imagined. But I suppose my vulnerability tempted them; they agreed, kept the lights down, and on we went, over it and over it until they were engorged.

By the time I left that room, many of the others who'd been out on the levee were already through interviews conducted by other cops, and several had departed, some alone, to meet up with loved ones elsewhere. A good sign, right?

I found Del deep in quiet conversation with Creel, Rosario, Ozawa, and a couple of the lawyers, the phrases "press conference" and "should be in DC" floating around them. A good sign, right?

As soon as she noticed me, Del broke away from them to tell me, at double-speed, that Dana was coming to get us "in the big plane" and we'd be able to take eight others besides the two of us. "Pilar'll stay and give Creel, Rosario, and Ozawa a hand, make sure they get home from Washington okay. Magenau's coming back with us."

"Wait," I pleaded; Del seemed almost buoyant, but I needed to know for certain. "What about Candid Camera?"

"Oh yeah, yeah, Vivian and Magenau did it," Del whispered. "Something about asynchronous packet distribution." An odd expression skimmed across her face as her speech slowed to normal. "They, uh, make *quite* a pair."

"So," I asked through what must've looked like a wicked shit-eating grin, "it went from zero to press conference in *how* long?"

Del also smiled. "Two hours, give or take." She reached up, the palms of her hands cupping my face, and her eyes, dark unto infinity, brightened with tears. "I never stopped looking for you. Not for one single minute." Then she kissed me, and I was taken again by the scent of her, the soft, caressing warmth of her skin, her sweet breath.

This was the moment I first believed I'd be able to go home, and it made me effervescent. I felt myself lifting, lighter and lighter...like I'd been caught in the bubblenet churned up by a pod of baleen whales guzzling vast quantities into their prodigious mouths...

And then Del had me around my waist, having tucked herself under my left crutch. She swept the crutches from my hands and, with Rosario's help, swung me onto a nearby cot.

"You need to sleep, baby."

I started to say something that was quickly lost in another kiss. It's deliciously easy to get lost in Del's kisses.

"I know someone who might like a ride," I said eventually.

"Yep. She's over there." Del pointed to a cot a few yards away where Maddie Small lay curled up asleep. "You two can talk later. Now close your eyes."

I obeyed her. It felt so good to obey her.

Although I had no intention of sleeping.

Del was holding my hand, stroking my arm, finding one way after another to touch me while she continued her conversation with the three people—Creel, Rosario, and Ozawa—who'd become the leaders of the fifty-nine freed detainees of Camp Null. I wanted to revel in Del's touch, listen to them discuss how the future into which we'd all be swept would play out. I heard Del say "committee hearings during the August recess" and, after a bit, Creel's voice, something about a special prosecutor…

I had no intention of sleeping, yet I startled awake to a sound, the excited chatter of people in the next room. Except there was no next room, only the hangar where the light streaming through the building's side windows had shifted, softened, and the echoes rang hollower. I was alone on the cot and the hands on Kenny's watch had shifted, too—ahead almost three hours.

I scanned the hangar in search of the people whose voices I could hear; a few seconds before they appeared at the edge of the screened-off medical area where I lay, I recognized Dana's voice, Del's voice. And Lynn Hillinger's. Lynn appeared first, just as I'd hiked myself up on my elbows. So I got a full-on, ten-feet-away view of her seeing me for the first time in twenty-one months.

Gotta give her credit. She masked it well. But it scared me, what her face told me she saw.

Anyway, she hurried to my cot, slid onto her fifty-eight-year-old knees, and hugged me. No words, but she didn't let go her hug, and I felt her back heaving beneath my arms. We held on for a while, our respiration synchronizing.

When she finally rose, she kissed my forehead—our old ritual. Tears slipped from her eyes and followed smile lines down her cheeks as her expression kaleidoscoped between elation and sadness, triumph and fury. "I'm so sorry, sweetie." She glanced at my thigh. "I'm so sorry."

"Why would you be sorry?" I asked just as Del appeared beside her.

"Because it took us *so* long to find you," Lynn answered. "And because I'm one of the people entrusted to keep this kind of shit from happening in the first place."

"But you did it, you found me," I said to them both. "And—" I tried and failed to blink back my own tears. "I'm so grateful—"

They held me, Del and Lynn both, and my sense of time slipped away again into the surge of relief released, until—a few seconds later? twenty minutes?—this moment came when Del and Lynn began to help me onto crutches.

Dana appeared then; her face, too, grimaced involuntarily at the sight of me before she could mask it. The plane, she told us after I got a long, felt hug from her, was fueled up and ready to go.

Maddie Small and Perez were among our passengers. We dropped them off with a couple others in New Jersey—at Teterboro, not so far from Maddie Small's end of New York City.

Can't figure out what it is about Maddie Small that gets to me. I worry about her, want to help her in ways I know she'll reject, should reject because they're wrong for her, but I can't see clear to what's right for her. Or maybe I do see and I don't like it.

For what it's worth, I've made sure as well as anyone can that I'm able to find her, that she's able to find me.

"The lawyer dude says money won't be a problem for a while now," she told me. "Got me a doc an' a place to live an' even this comlink." With a wrapped hand, she nudged the slightly oversized pendant on a sturdy ballchain around her neck, but her grin was sly as she confided, "Me an' Perez're gonna share the place. Long as he behaves."

I, too, had acquired a special comlink, which I think of as the Null-link, and I held it up to hers and clicked it. "Now you're my first deets."

"You're my first, too," said Maddie Small, and there was that sly little grin again. "'Cept fer Perez."

She'll be okay, I tried to convince myself as we said good-bye.

CHAPTER THIRTEEN

The Entangled

AF152.
Monday, August 3.
15:18 hours.

I wasn't gonna bother with Audy anymore. Cuz, hey, it's over, right?

Got the hell out of Camp Null. Dodged Hurricane Elmer. Waded through yesterday's LEOs and lawyers. Endured the hospital's scans and tests and another scour-and-vacuum of the hole through my thigh where a nerve has been declared "traumatized" and yes, that's why it hurts so fucking much. Oh, and I'll need surgery soon to help regenerate muscle tissue lost to the bullet.

But no complaints. Would've been far more painful to have had to participate in this morning's First Press Conference. I confess I hoped Hurricane Elmer would track a little farther north and shut down Washington, DC, but it seems Caprice wants the first episode of the Camp Null Show to enjoy maximum media attention.

Now I'm at Great Hill. Been here for maybe four hours, the first three of which were swept into the wondrous whirlwind of family, all shouts and tears and hugs and squealing kids and more hugs. Something only females can do, like when elephant clans reunite.

Something only females can do even when they're grieving.

You see, Mary's gone now, her death last May still a disorienting black hole around which we all quietly orbit. Everyone else has had three months to become accustomed to the chasm of her absence, but I've had only the few hours since Del and Lynn told me shortly before the end of the flight home.

And yeah, I dreamed it, but I struggle anyway to believe it. I keep expecting Mary to appear on the stairs, in a doorway, eyes gently twinkling. Soon after I arrived, I felt her hand on my elbow and turned to greet her, hoping against all reason the way I did once after my mother died, but no…no.

I think it showed, this clench of missing Mary that broiled in my gut, and I saw their own mourning rouse again. Yet I also saw them treasure the beauty dwelling there in our grief—missing Mary is a gift because Mary was a gift, and they included her as they embraced me.

"Mary knew you'd come back to us," Lily said.

"Mum would be so, so pleased now," Rebecca told me while Robin—now officially Dr. Hillinger—wiped tears from her eyes at the mention of her grandmother's name.

They suffused themselves into me, these remarkable women, with touch and attentiveness and food and laughter. And music. For the first time in twenty-one months, I listened to Del play Mary's baby grand. "I'm a little rusty," she said before she perched on the piano bench exactly the way I'd tried so often to recall. And then she played—not rusty at all to ears long accustomed to dissonant buzzing. She played all my favorites and, inevitably, I cried.

"Happy tears," I explained to a concerned Evvie as Del finished with *Canon in D*. "The happiest tears ever because finally I get to be with all of you."

Evvie frowned. "Mum and Dee say we have to go to camp tomorrow." Her gesture included her sisters, who also frowned. "For the rest of the four weeks." They were supposed to leave for camp yesterday, but wanted to be here to greet me this morning, and then they wanted to chuck camp altogether.

"I won't be much fun for a while," I assured them. "Stuck on crutches and going to the hospital every day to get my leg cleaned out so it can heal."

They would come with me, the twins declared. Hold my hand. Help make it better.

I thanked them as tears filled my eyes again. "But I thought you *wanted* to go to camp?" I said, and their expressions gave away that I'd guessed correctly. They'd all been eager to go till they found out I was on my way home.

I promised to be here when they got back, promised to answer all their questions. "We'll talk as long as you want," I promised.

Evvie sighed. She knew when she was beat. But she made me reiterate my promises, which I did, one by one, as Del sat close against me, keeper of my must-stay-elevated right leg, and I savored each majestically mundane, irreplaceable moment, unique in all the multiverses, each one so beautiful it hurt.

And just for a little while I was swept in, able to glimpse again the elegantly simple secret in plain sight that so often we cannot see: *everything* is beautiful. I watched every movement, attended every moment, aching with awe. I tried to stay right there the whole time. I tried.

But shit, everybody blinks.

And sometimes a blink is all it takes.

One blink among many, apparently innocent, and *bang!*—now I glimpse an expanse of rusted steel, and suddenly I'm trapped in the elliptical machine's enslaving motion, legs circling, circling, arms pulling-pushing forever. The odor of sulfurous decay fills my nostrils, impossibly humid heat sucks the air from my lungs.

I cringe as this other real closes in, threatening to overtake the real I've only barely dared believe might be possible. Helpless, I watch these opposing reals slide through each other, slipping, twisting between foreground and background.

One blink among many, apparently innocent, and *bang!*—I'm losing track of which real to hold on to. Just. Like. That.

Of course, I have a preference. I yearn for the real that's close and warm and sparkling with Del, with Lynn, with Rebecca and Robin and Lily and Dana and the kids and the deep, familiar comfort of Great Hill.

But I've wanted that for such a long time, and every time just as I fall for it and let myself embrace it—another *bang!* and I hear Caprice's snigger in the relentless buzzing, smell my body's pungent anxiety. And behind what I hope hope hope I really see, the sweating, rusting steel taunts...

Ignominious

I blink again and maybe again until I can see Del almost clearly. I keep my eyes on her, clutch tight to *her* real, hoping it won't disappear altogether the next time I have to blink.

And then—

Then Del swoops in, yanks me out of Ignominious's grasp. She's decided I'm tired and it's time for me to lie down for a while before dinner.

Now, after my laughably clumsy trek upstairs (even *with* the help of the elevator), for the first time in almost two years I'm in "our" bedroom at Great Hill where Del has left me for "just a couple minutes, I'll be right back."

I can tell the room's changed some—new coat of paint, new window shades, new bedspread—and I still can't look too long at *Outside!* and all its vibrating colors and there's this little black audiostick on the dogtag chain around my neck...

And yeah, yeah, I know. I shouldn't need Audy—

But as I lie here in "our" room, I have a sense of being a ghost. Weightless. Placeless. Floating in a swirl of pasts near and pasts far and this tenuous present, a blink away from Camp Null's sweltering, buzzing steel box.

The effect is dizzying. I realize I'm marooned in my very own version of the Tetris effect. Vestibular illusions. Positional and optical and auditory illusions.

So okay: yeah, I *am* tired.

But goddamn, been here, done this. After my time in the wrong fucking war, I spent years getting my head screwed on straight. So I know the mindfucks, I know how to fight them.

Even so, the mindfucks are damn convincing, and I'm definitely not ready to close my eyes yet. Blinking, though, is unavoidable. And goddamn, I do *not* like how wiggly it all gets sometimes.

Right now, for instance, I can hear the twins scampering and giggling down the hallway outside our door while I pick up the faintest scent of South Carolina magnolia and can taste copper—or is it blood?—in my mouth. When I close my eyes, I see my mother's face and the shadowed figure of a dead six-year-old girl.

So how many reals is that? Two? Three? Four?

For just a little too long as this happens, I must seriously consider the possibility that all reals are created equal—a personal version of quantum entanglement in which I am the Entangled, too easily devoured by whichever reals happen to face up after Caprice tosses her dice.

But I don't want to believe that.

I want to believe there's one real that's more truly real than the others, and I have the capacity to keep hold of this more truly real. With touch when Del's around. With words when she isn't. So I'm holding on tight to Audy and talking away.

❖

AF153.
Tuesday, August 4.
02:54 hours.

Can't sleep.

Del is out cold and I didn't want to wake her, so I've come down to the great room via the back stairs (on my ass slowly, crutches sliding on the stairs alongside me—very dignified).

Now I'm observing.

Think of it as a test. Another check on whether I'm imagining being at Great Hill with everybody, imagining safe. Because it feels really good, maybe too good to be more truly real.

I mean, consider what Del did earlier.

Her "be right back" took long enough that she apologized when she returned. She also wore that particular squint I already associate with her wanting to talk (still, again) about Camp Null, but she chose instead to curl along my left side and nuzzle close, careful to dodge my right thigh.

"Ah, Jamie Gwynmorgan," she murmured in my ear, "I have *missed* you."

I think I made some sort of sound, a moan. No way I could muster actual words to convey the depth of my sense of deliverance, my undiluted joy, my incandescing lust. I tried to tell her I love you, Del, I love you. I reached for her, with my hands, my mouth, my rocking ravenous clit—

Which was a mistake.

Betrayed by touch, and goddamn, it hurt. From the tips of my right toes to the hair on my head, in the time it takes to snap your fingers I was flung from live-wire turn-on to thrashing agony.

Every doc who's seen my thigh has warned me about these episodes of breakthrough nerve pain, and I have meds, painkillers, to ease it. For me, though, the painkillers are worse than the pain; I leave the meds in their bottles.

So it's about enduring the body slam. In that moment, as I gasped to keep from yelping while the lightning bolt clamped around my thigh and stabbed up my spine into my head, Del spoke soft and close to my ear.

"Yes or no?"

I managed a "no." No pharma. Not surrendering yet.

Thus I plunged into the crippling torment of the next two or three minutes. A fierce, all-consuming eternity that just seizes you, and you're entirely powerless—heart pounding, gulping air, sweating, desperate to move to escape the pain but afraid even the smallest twitch will make the pain worse. Been a damn long time since anything has hurt as much.

"*Bree-ee-eathe*," Del whispered slow and rhythmic while I battled an overbearing urge to scream. "*Bree-ee-eathe* as loud as you need to…"

And while she held my hand and gazed at my chest, she began a hum, a soft almost-melody that kept rhythm with the rasping beg in my breathing. Her hum hypnotized me, and when I finally retrieved the presence of mind to tell her so, she laughed softly and said it must be getting better now, huh?

This is when I realized where her other hand had gone, what her pianist's fingers were doing between my legs.

Did I mention that Del is ambidextrous?

And then I heard a voice, Del's voice but maybe not Del's voice because whispers can fool you when your eyes are closed, y'know?

"Tell me what turns you on."

I mumbled something—didn't I? I wanted to answer "Relief," but wait, wait—"Anticipation of relief…"

And she said, the laugh lilting through her words, animating her exquisitely delicate touch, "We were made for this, you know."

Truth is, I *don't* know or possibly I just don't *want* to know; either way, I don't care because oh my god how I came and came and came. It was the purest sexual experience I've ever had. Free of burden or question or doubt. I surrendered not to pain or painkillers but to the beauty of Del's voice, the grace of Del's more truly real touch.

Afterward, I laughed, in the sort of delighted-surprise way people do when their ticket wins the lottery, and Del said it was the first time she'd seen me laugh since *before*.

"You haven't forgotten *any*thing," I told her.

And she got *that* gleam in her eyes just before she insisted I close mine again. I obeyed and felt her kiss, her murmur on my cheek, and then, even before I had a chance to say "my turn," I was asleep.

My turn came when I woke up a couple of hours later and looked over and, yes, Del was still there, sleeping, beautiful. If she's more truly real, I told myself as I stared at her, she'll let me touch her awake, she'll let me undulate her into awareness, into arousal, into orgasm.

And she did, just as I'd imagined so many, many times.

❖

But, like I said, maybe too good to be true.

Somewhere during my awkward hobble from our bedroom downstairs to my first real dinner in twenty-one months, I realized how much I wished all the Camp Null shit was behind me.

Don't get me wrong. I want to know what happened—why I was grabbed, how Del found me. And sure as hell I want to know what's gonna happen next.

But I'd prefer to watch it from afar, on a screen maybe, while I figure out how to keep hold of Del's more truly real and resurrect my life.

Cuz hey, I don't have a job anymore (the small outfit I worked for was absorbed by a larger firm almost a year ago) and I need to renew my professional license, which will require racking up some professional education hours. Plus I can't even start physical therapy for another three fucking weeks.

Anyway, best I can tell, I'm stuck in a ringside seat at one hell of a fight that's pulled in Del and Lynn as well as Rebecca, Lily, and Dana. Unquestionably, it's all escalating big-time now. And I'm struggling to understand both the plot and the cast of characters, having arrived, as Del said, at the denouement.

Thus I had no idea who "Shirley" is.

After a convoluted description which included more than one "I'll fill you in on that later," I realized Shirley is Infirmary Woman.

Who happens to be superstitious as hell, thank god Caprice human nature dumb fucking luck Caprice god*damn* you Caprice…

According to Del, when New South and that custodian wheeled me into the Camp Null infirmary after I collapsed last March, Infirmary Woman noticed the scars on my hands, souvenirs of a long dead enemy—and beheld Stigmata.

And couldn't stop thinking about Stigmata. Infirmary Woman, Shirley, started to dream about the damn scars on my hands. Found herself so haunted by the confounding knowledge that this *woman* with Stigmata was locked away in the next building that she quit her job.

But that wasn't enough. Infirmary Woman Shirley had to tell someone about it, even though she'd signed a quite draconian non-disclosure agreement with LSI.

(What's LSI? I asked, and Del said, "Just possibly the pot of gold at the end of the rainbow," but I don't know what that means yet.)

Anyway, despite LSI's non-disclosure agreement, Infirmary

Woman Shirley backed herself into becoming a whistle-blower. First tried to keep herself anonymous, but got ignored by all the muckrakers because she had no video for them. Eventually, she hit on the idea of talking to a minister. Not her usual Sunday preacher; instead she chose a stranger—a young woman fresh out of divinity school, ripe with idealism, committed to maintaining clergy-penitent confidentiality.

After some rumination, the young woman minister called a friend, also a minister, who happened to be involved in the Women's International Sanctuary Exchange, and this friend called Leta Creel's brother, who'd been in touch with Del for months.

Thus did Del learn of "Camp Null" early last Saturday morning during a face-to with Infirmary Woman Shirley in Charleston; after leaving some lawyers behind to take Infirmary Woman Shirley's deposition, she hooked up with Leta Creel's brother and cousin. On their way to Parris Island, she got Magenau's call from the Camp Null power substation.

I learned this in Lynn's study at Great Hill, where she and Del had sat me down in order to catch me up and compare notes of their own.

"Christ," I muttered. "Sounds like Camp Null is at the heart of some secret undisclosed detention industrial complex."

"Yeah, pretty much," Lynn said. "And now that we've found you and a couple other people we were hoping to locate—" Lynn closed her eyes and pulled in a breath; I noticed a tiny quiver in her eyebrows, but her voice was ice-edged. "I am going to raise holy hell."

She and Del talked gobbledygook government acronyms that were lost on me, except for D...H...S.

Then Lynn looked my way. "We've told the Homeland Security directorate in question to send over the people best able to explain to us what the hell Camp Null is," she told me. "They'll be appearing before the Judiciary Committee during Thursday's hearing, after testimony from Taletha Creel, Rosario Finlay, and Oscar Ozawa."

I think maybe I ventured a small smile because, thank you thank you, my name was not mentioned.

Lynn nodded like she read my thought. "And when the DHS people attempt to explain why all of you were detained, their answers will be inadequate. Which is all we need."

"For what?" I asked.

"To attract the number of votes required to convene a special select committee on federal threat identification and detention practices,"

Lynn answered. "It'll pick up where our own committee investigation leaves off."

Ah, I thought for one brief moment, a break till September, maybe even October. Then someone said "depositions" and, yet again, "testify."

"They'll just call us terrorists," I mumbled.

Lynn reacted to that. "They can try." She didn't smile. "Hell, they *will* try. But they'll fail and the committee will continue its hearings right through August. We've already amassed plenty of evidence. Now we'll share it with the world for the next three weeks. Everyone will keep watching right through their vacations. We'll get our select committee, and with a fat bipartisan margin, too, about a month after the Senate's back in session. As we speak, the smarter rats are grasping that the game of musical snitches has begun."

Del and I came upstairs around midnight. I watched her slide into sleep, watched our room until I fell asleep, too, and woke in a rusty buzzy steel box remembering my spectacular dream: taking down Camp Null, kissing Del, a helo ride to Tennessee and an interminable police interview, arriving at Great Hill. I lay in a narrow stinking bunk, sweating, dirty, alone with the fading remnants of my dream.

I closed my eyes again...*please please please...*

Then I blinked. And blinked and blinked and blinked. Still the rusty buzzy steel box held me, owned me, while my dream of Del's real fluttered farther and farther away from me. I blinked again. And again. *Please please please...*

And then I woke up.

Again.

Del lay next to me asleep, but our room seemed smaller than before, the ceiling lower, closer.

Caprice tossing the dice, I guess, but it damn well begs the question one more time: Which real is *really* more truly real?

For now, if I can lie on this cushy sofa in this expansive space with its high ceiling, its wall of windows that'll display a distant ocean vista in the morning's light, and if I can close my eyes and *bree-ee-eathe* and when I open my eyes, I'm still right here in this great big great room, then yeah, I'll start to believe Del's real really *is* more truly real.

CHAPTER FOURTEEN

Tell me how you found me

AF154.
Wednesday, August 5.
16:20 hours.

In between the bouts of serious discomfort over the last two days while the tunnel through my thigh gets scraped clean, I've learned about what Del and Lynn and the rest of the clan and others, too, have been doing for the last twenty-one months.

How the FBI guys took charge soon after I was abducted and how they seemed optimistic, which gave everybody hope.

How they'd agreed I'd been abducted by professionals—very slickly and efficiently—for ransom or some sort of extortion.

How the family—god, yes, *my* family (saying that still gives me goose bumps)—was advised to stay low-profile while they waited to hear from the kidnappers. No talking to the media, no talking to much of anybody.

How after two weeks and no contact from the kidnappers, no demands, the investigation hit a wall.

Del believes that during those two weeks, the LEOs really tried to find me. She described their efforts as "way beyond pro forma," but the longer they came up empty, the more helpless everyone felt.

Except for Lynn. Lynn was angry.

"She kept repeating 'This smells,'" Del said of her. "She never really articulated how or why, but she was so worried it had to do with her. Early on, we all kind of thought it had to do with her."

Then somebody, probably a LEO, leaked news of my kidnapping to the media. As soon as the world knew I'd been grabbed, everything changed.

Lynn, a third-term senator with the power, as chairman of the Judiciary Committee, to dig deeper and darker than most, immediately sent staff investigators quietly sniffing around. They didn't get far, though, because they had no starting point other than "Hear anything about who kidnapped Senator Hillinger's favorite ex-marine?" And besides, if I wasn't dead already, any incautious move might get me killed. Del described Lynn as pacing a lot, chewing on her lower lip. "And, of course, she sent Springer trawling."

Meanwhile, headlines spawned several fake ransom and extortion demands, each of which had to be pursued, each of which wasted time and resources. "Twice we thought it was real and we were so full of hope." Del's voice went hoarse. "But it wasn't real."

Weeks became months, and the trail, such as it was, went stone cold.

By then, Del had made below-the-radar contact with her friends at the Wilderness Web Coalition, the women's sanctuary underground—and Cecilia Danta.

"Wait," I demanded. "You said—"

"Cecilia Danta. Yes."

I wanted to gripe about that, even though Cecilia Danta's minimal presence in our lives has been entirely my own doing. I don't like thinking about Cecilia Danta because then I have to think about my mother, and I'd rather not.

Del saw my bitch coming and shushed me with her eyes so she could recount how the Wilderness Web Coalition people had been briefly overrun with FBI agents who, according to Del's friends, treated them like criminals, threatened to return with warrants (on what grounds no one was sure), then went away and didn't come back.

But neither Del's women's sanctuary friends nor Cecilia Danta heard from the FBI at all. This gave Del hope because it meant there were people, organizations, possibilities the LEOs had missed.

"We had to consider siccing the FBI on the women's sanctuary people and Cecilia," Del said, her eyes glistening too much. "But I decided before we did, I'd talk to them—all of them—myself, one by one."

"You vetted them?" I asked.

"Not formally, but yeah, I did. Painstakingly. And, as the FBI guys would say, I ruled them out." She inhaled deeply. "Then I enlisted their help. They were, every one of them, eager to help."

Del also tried to persuade the FBI to let her see their files. But they refused.

She lowered her head and her voice. "Some junior special agent working our case got so irritated at me he blurted that the FBI believed you were dead, even though no evidence at all of your death, and certainly no body, had been found." Her voice cracked then. "I lost it. Went off on him big-time, which trashed what little rapport I'd managed to build with those people. Because I damn well knew you were not dead. I just *knew*."

By early March, four months after I'd been grabbed, the FBI's interaction with Del consisted of a perfunctory call to her once a week to find out if she'd heard anything.

Lynn and Springer, too, were coming up empty. Del described how rattled Lynn was. "She'd do this tight circle in the study mumbling, 'No trace anywhere. Who could pull that off?'" Del said.

"People with deep pockets for deep purposes," I remarked.

Del stared at me. "That's what Lynn said, almost verbatim. She also commented that they must have government agency people somewhere colluding with them. People we have to assume are very skittish. Which meant any wrong move on our part could cost you your life. On the other hand, the FBI had written you off, so finding you was up to us."

At that point we were here, in our room where I am now; I pulled her close and she squiggled into my shoulder as she described how "that awful time" drove her into her own bottom-up investigation.

"I took the lead," Del said, "but it was very much a group effort. Family in the largest, richest sense."

Lynn had her own shortlist of likeliest colluders—moguls with means and opportunity—so she went off to sniff out evidence and to cultivate allies, notably judicial ones.

"I guess," Del said, "she was already suspicious of DHS and the FBI. I think she also had her eye on Judge Byrne as an ally even back then. Maybe the US Capitol Police, too; she got them to open an independent investigation into your abduction within a few days of the news leak to the media."

Meanwhile, Springer and Del coordinated the efforts of several private investigators, who mostly went over familiar, trodden ground, but with special focus on government contractors with "the relevant skillsets." Del shook her head.

"Yeah, I know," I commiserated. "There are *so* many."

"Like I said, a really awful time—until we got lucky."

"Caprice," I murmured.

"Cecilia, actually."

Okay, I admit it. I pouted. I snarked. "So—on a first-name basis with Friday's Sister now, are we?"

"I needed all the help I could get." Del's voice went low and her eyes clamped me in place with the Look. "Cecilia Danta offered to sniff around in places where no one else can. The private investigators are either clunky or smarmy. The FBI people march in all officious and menacing. Cecilia's people get you high, and while they're giving you a spectacular orgasm they're telling you how extraordinary you are in precisely the way you most want to hear it. Who do *you* think finds out more?"

Del called it the one-part-per-million whisper, something not even Springer had picked up. It came from an investment banker visiting Cecilia's New York establishment who got prodigiously drunk and dropped a vague, slurred brag about being big shot enough to have heard from "a *verrry* connected fellow" of a secretly revived undisclosed detention program designed to "stop fuckin' traitors before they can commit treason against our great fuckin' country."

Shhh. UD is *baa*-ack.

Before your time? Don't remember? Well, Del remembers. Born of amendments to the National Cybersecurity Protection Act passed more than twenty years ago just after that series of post-pandemic datawipes, blunted ten years later when the Supreme Court declared most of it unconstitutional.

Since then, undisclosed detentions are supposed to be extremely rare and subject to strict rules. First of all, it's called Classified Administrative Detention now and it must always be explicitly approved by the president, always reviewed by a National Security Court judge who interviews the detainee, always in response to a concrete threat to national security, always short-term, always continuously court-monitored.

"The guy at Cecilia's was a one-off, tagging along with a friend of one of her regulars," Del recalled. "No record of his name, nobody remembers which bank he said he worked for. Shitty video. So, literally, all we had in this dark, silent forest was a whisper. Might as well have been a bullhorn blaring 'This Way!'"

As someone briefly swallowed by the government's pandemic-inspired, "emergency immunization research" quarantining, Del had no trouble believing undisclosed detention is alive and well. Yet she *knew* only that there was rumor of a stealth UD program.

Del believed, as did Lynn, that if such a program existed, an amorphous government agency with a banal name surreptitiously tended it, bestowing upon it a stolid acronym, farming out its dirty work to (repudiable) contractors. Which meant that somewhere out there, if such a program existed, despite its obscurity, it was leaving some sort of trail that could be found and followed.

Cecilia counseled patience, promised to immediately convey whatever else might slobber out of her clientele. But eliciting such information is an extremely delicate art, especially if you don't want the elicitee to understand what's going on.

"We worried that if we publicly snooped around about a UD program, we'd put you at risk," Del said. "If in fact this UD thing was even what took you. So all we could do is listen."

And then—

"Caprice this time," I guessed.

"Yes." Del's smile was minimal, wily. Mmm, turns me on, that gleam-in-the-shadows smile of hers.

"Go on," I said. "I can be titillated and listen at the same time."

After only minor further interruption, I learned about a no-notice penetration testing contract with the Justice Department's Management Division (the admin guys). Lily and Dana had lowballed Callithump's bid when they realized the contract would, in effect, "let them in the building," so their whitehat security team could take a leave-no-trace crack at FBI systems where my abduction case files were stored.

Dana and Lily run a very talented crew, so soon the Callithump whitehats had everything—all the FBI's so-called assessments and predicated investigations linked in any way to my abduction.

"You guys committed a felony," I said.

"Maybe. Maybe not." Del hitched her shoulder a little defiantly. "Lily and Dana are very careful. And they know how to write a contract."

"Bullshit. You committed a felony." I kissed her for the zillionth time. "My god."

"I deny everything," she murmured into my kiss. "And I'd do it again in a heartbeat."

❖

FBI assessments and investigations go way beyond interviews; they get into informants, surveillance on a vast and scary scale, grand jury subpoenas and testimony—all targeting a person. Everything and everyone around that person gets rooted out, ransacked, then written up in reports infused with assumptions and speculation.

The feds dug into me all the way back to Hyannis. They knew about my mother, my time in the Marine Corps, in school, at GKN, at the bridge. In one note, an agent pondered how I managed to help Pethra get jobs on the Artemisia Center project without *visible* criminal wrongdoing.

Yet they missed shit, too. Del found no mention of Cecilia Danta or my illicit shuttles of desperate women between Sapphira Honeyjohn and the Rosies. (Heh. Seems my camdodging really did beat the FB-fucking-I, apparently more than once.)

According to several heavily hyperlinked documents, the FBI concluded that *who I knew* rather than *what I did* probably prompted my abduction.

"As you might expect, most of their stuff concerned potential threats to Lynn and how you might be used as leverage. They identified only a few related to Dana and Lily, since Callithump's been so low-visibility for so long." Then Del went quiet; what she hadn't yet told me filled the space around us. Tears welled in her eyes. "It was something Evvie said while Lily and I were talking one day. 'What about you, Auntie Del? Where's *your* Bad Guys?'"

I imagine Evvie in that moment. Too young to know so much, worry so much. I can see her face. I want to hug her and tell her how sorry I am for becoming the example Caprice used to teach her what happens here on Planet Vagary.

"Evvie nailed it," Del said. "But I couldn't know that for, well, until I found you three days ago. Everything I did for sixteen months was a shot in the dark. Built off a whisper in the forest and a wild guess."

She started by reexamining the few FBI assessments and

investigations where her name appeared. Turns out every one of them linked to earlier FBI attempts to connect the organizations she's involved with—most notably the Wilderness Web Coalition—to some sort of domestic terrorism.

"Damn, Jamie, they *so* don't like environmental activists," she told me. "We actually found email threads in which FBI supervisors advised private enterprises about WWC activities and made suggestions concerning how to challenge WWC initiatives."

"How very iron triangle," I said.

"Oh, it gets worse."

Del smiled anyway and described other email threads between FBI supervisors and an FBI "WMD coordinator" speculating about how much of a threat the Wilderness Web Coalition poses. Since the closest the WWC comes to weapons of mass destruction is expertise in eminent domain law, that all went south pretty quickly for "lack of predication."

As it happens, though, the mere presence of those three letters—WMD—in proximity to one's name on an official document serves as reason enough for further investigation.

Neat trick, huh?

In fact, the FBI's view of Del was so negative that when I was abducted they had to do a one-eighty and investigate people they'd been helping. And they did—up to a point. Agents' notes show they initially poked around a good number of Auntie Del's Bad Guys—people eager to shut down the WWC and even trash her personally to dampen her effectiveness.

But the investigatory pace remained sluggish, little or no follow-through, and after a couple of months, the reviewing FBI supervisor canned every one of those lines of inquiry.

Even so, once she'd examined the FBI docs "penetrated" by Callithump, Del reckoned my abduction was about her, not Lynn.

To figure out who her enemy might be, she built two lists off the FBI files.

The first list included individuals, companies, trade groups, even elements of the government—all those who expressed interest in shutting down her or the WWC or any of the other like-minded people or groups mentioned in the FBI's documents.

The second list consisted of people like herself whom the FBI had investigated at the prompting of those on the first list.

Then she cross-tabulated the people on the second list with public data—behaviorals mostly, some demographics—and soon found cluster patterns.

The air vacated my lungs as I listened to her.

"So, *what* happened to these people who dared to oppose Auntie Del's Bad Guys?" I needed her to say it again.

Del gazed at me as she synopsized. "Some bonkered into psychosis or hopeless drug addiction or early-onset dementia," she said in a near monotone. "Couple of comas—brain dead. Others suffered sudden premature, fatal heart attacks or strokes. Or died of unnatural causes like accident, suicide, even murder. Some were—still are—just missing. Forty-three people in clusters that have significance values way beyond chance variation."

Then her voice broke. "Oh god, Jamie, I-I thought I'd lost you."

❖

"Tell me how you found me."

We were alone in the car and about to start back to Great Hill after today's thigh gouging appointment. Instead of answering me, Del grabbed the shirt I wasn't yet accustomed to wearing, suddenly gulping back sobs, curling anguished into herself. "I'm so sorry it took all this time. I'm so, so sorry..."

I embraced her as much as the car seat and my leg allowed. "No no no, baby," I murmured between kisses I nestled and snuggled onto her. "No sorries. You found me." I chuckled some while I planted more kisses. "I mean, already on your way to Parris Island when Magenau called you? Someday when we're really old, we'll do the math, figure out the odds of that."

Slowly, she calmed, and eventually she could smile, taking control first of herself and then the car's conn. As we headed home, she described how excruciatingly slow her progress was.

"The clusters helped me believe I wasn't crazy," she said, eyes on the road, voice brooding. "And, god, I had my suspicions that some FBI people helped out certain of their corporate 'constituents' with discreet, off-the-books referrals—but we actually had only correlation, not causation."

She'd identified several corporations associated with a disturbingly high number of dead or gone or bonkered, yet any attorney could easily argue coincidence. And innocence. "Besides," she said, "we had nothing that gave us any way to *find you*."

So she was stuck again—until a second penetration hack by Lily and Dana's people. "And," she added, "a little more, uh, undercover work by Cecilia."

"Wait." My thigh had started to burn.

"Yes," Del said. "Cecilia again."

So okay. I admit I needed calming down.

Del commanded me to *bree-ee-eathe*, skewered me in place with those eyes, and talked about how Lily and Dana's second penetration scooped up the documents and data at the ends of all the fourth-, fifth-, and sixth-order hyperlinks tentacling from my abduction case files.

Mostly these turned out to be more FBI files—primary documents concerning both Auntie Del's Bad Guys and the dead or gone or bonkered. This led, eventually, to what she called "*the* crucial trail of clues."

It was buried in the case files of a mining company supervisor whose wife reported him missing. His body was discovered days later in a neighboring state (hence the FBI's involvement) and he was declared a suicide, but his wife raised hell because, she claimed, her husband would never kill himself.

This banal case hid a hyperlink jackpot. The supervisor died a few weeks after he met with an environmental journalist the FBI had tracked via CISA monitoring. Also, two months before the supervisor's "suicide," the mining company's chief security officer had groused in an email to an FBI agent about the tribulations of claiming employee data theft when the employee threatens to counterclaim whistle-blower status and where were the legal lines, anyway?

The agent responded by offering to make introductions with "a friend" in the Department of Homeland Security. "To help you handle difficult personnel issues without media meddling," the FBI guy wrote before including a DHS email address.

"Right there," Del said, her voice grim, her face set. "I knew I had to drill down right there." She paused. "But if those guys hooked up, it happened offlink and off-record."

There was, however, a new trail to follow—into DHS, beginning with the DHS dude on the other end of the email addy. He worked in something called the Infrastructure and Resource Protection Directorate, which is a pretty big target. Has its own deputy undersecretary—one of those connected, dangerous people who glides between senior federal appointments and succulent private-sector gigs.

Not much of a trail, but, as Del commented, "Not the end of the trail either."

From behind a well-constructed anonymity cloak, Del sent certain bits of the dead mining company supervisor's FBI case files directly to Lynn's committee investigators. Lynn responded by charging into the DHS Infrastructure and Resource Protection Directorate—sideways. Like a crab.

"So you never told Lynn about the Callithump penetration hack of the FBI?" I asked.

Del shook her head. "I'd already shown her my information on those forty-three dead and gone and bonkered people without mentioning how I developed it. And she didn't ask, since she's not stupid and is scrupulous about keeping herself walled off from anything Callithump. As for anonymous leaks, well, how they're regarded depends a lot on the nature of the evidence."

Lynn found the FBI case files about the dead mining company supervisor compelling enough to order the Senate Judiciary Committee's investigators to, as she put it, "chew on the edges" of the DHS directorate. No interviews, just probe its programs, low-key and low-profile, for whiffs of overreach regarding CISA and data surveillance. *Only* data surveillance.

Anything more direct, Lynn feared, would endanger me. And not just me. "What happened to those forty-three people on my second list showed so much damage," Del said. "We were just beginning to sense the scale of what was happening."

In her own pursuit of the DHS dude whose addy appeared in the FBI email thread, Del hit up the Callithump penetration testers one last time before their Management Division project concluded, hoping they could worm their way over to the DHS dude's contact list.

"They did me one better. I got his email addy list in order of who he emailed most. They pulled whole profiles, too. For a little context, they claimed. But really they were showing off how they could penetrate DHS via Justice systems." Del was grinning. "And about twenty contacts down, I saw a name I recognized."

"Who?"

"Walter Welch."

I should've remembered him immediately, but I didn't; after all, I met the man only once about a million years ago in a previous life.

After a blink or two, I flashed on that distant August day up on the ninth floor of Burton's building on Morton Street, flashed on Walter Welch's face as Isaac Franklin sycophanted all over him while Burton turned away toward the stairs, toward that fucking heart attack.

I never saw Walter Welch again; he moved to the rear that day when the shit started to fly, then later pulled some spooky action at a distance to help Isaac try to screw me out of an engineering career.

Welch now works in the bowels of the Department of Homeland Security's Directorate of Infrastructure and Resource Protection. He's a Supervisory Procurement Manager for Collaborative Development Initiatives at the directorate's Risk Reduction Coordinating Center, a DHS creation with limited authority to undertake inherently governmental functions. So Welch is there to farm out those functions to appropriately vetted contractors.

"You went after him?" I asked.

"Well, he came to our attention before we quite got that far."

A teensy uh-oh gurgled up my esophagus. "Say what?"

"Cecilia," Del said evenly while her eyes pinned me yet again.

Seems Walter Welch is one of nineteen people on Del's Bad Guys list who are also among Cecilia's regulars. And Walter Welch is by far the most garrulous.

I watched the light in Del's eyes flare. "Our Walter is known to have a certain sexual penchant." She said it the French way, up in her nose, pulling the collar of my shirt as she came closer. "So I took a chance and called Cecilia again. Because I would not—I will not *ever*—hesitate to do *anything* to get you back." She half turned in the driver's seat and kissed me. "Now *bree-ee-eathe*, dammit."

I obeyed her. It felt so good to obey her.

"So," she asked me after maybe a minute, "you ready for the rest?"

"Yes, please."

Walter Welch has been one of Cecilia's customers for ten years and currently has a standing weekly appointment at her Washington place. Cecilia's six-foot-three ebony Amazon in red leather, who'd become his favorite, knew well how to work him. Milk him, Cecilia called it.

I tried not to wince as I listened, imagined. My mother used to say things like that. Dress like that. I swallowed my Kill-'Em-All! war cry and focused.

Turns out Welch was babbling about all kinds of helpful shit that they had no way of recognizing or understanding. Not for more than four months.

"It was Springer who found the missing piece," Del explained. "Did you know she still chums the DC bar scene for what she calls brag trash? The men mostly but sometimes women in lower bureaucracy jobs who know all kinds of shit and just can't stand *not* to swank about it after the third drink."

Last fall, Springer emerged from one martini-soaked evening at a Georgetown watering hole with a DHS acronym—DTAN—that neither she nor Lynn had heard of. Springer wondered if she'd *mis*heard; upon asking about it in the bright light of the morning after, the fellow who mentioned it freaked and pretended not to know what she was talking about.

Soon enough, Lynn's committee staff learned that DTAN stands for Data Threat Analysis Network, which at first seemed to be strictly what the DHS people kept insisting it was: a pilot implementation of super-technical CISA rules about monitoring cybersecurity threats.

"And suddenly," Del said, eyes flashing again, "I understood that's what Walter Welch had rambled on about when he was at Cecilia's— Deetan. All about how much higher-visibility he'd become thanks to Deetan. We thought Deetan was a person, not a fucking acronym."

Yet an acronym that had nothing to do with undisclosed detention or the dead and gone and bonkered.

"We were so depressed—DTAN appeared entirely aboveboard," Del recalled. "But Lynn had never heard of it. That's when she let loose her committee staffers, who started interviewing DHS people about DTAN, how it generates its 'products,' who uses them, and why hasn't anybody mentioned any of this to Congress?"

I peered at her. "So what's DTAN actually do?"

"Vacuums up results of automated information sifting of just about every network provider out there and uses it to compile observations, analyses, predictions, and speculations into profiles," she said.

"You," I said. "Be easy enough for them to use DTAN to surveil someone like you."

"Oh, DTAN profiling does way more than that," she replied, eyes ablaze. "In real time it filters just about all data communicated anywhere by anyone, identifies what its masters deem to be threats—and reacts. Sometimes that means preventing delivery of a message, or disrupting a comcall. More broadly, DTAN can also stymie dissemination of news items, has been used to alter content. It's especially effective at disrupting video."

So Magenau's baleen is real, happening right now.

And though it provided nothing new about disappearances in general, much less mine in particular, Del said, "With DTAN I felt closer—just a little closer."

She decided to feed information from Lynn about DTAN to Cecilia in the hope that the Amazon could use it to bamboozle more out of Welch. Which the Amazon did; a mere three or four lines of coke and Walter Welch is a talker.

Over more weeks and then months, he dribbled brags about DTAN that revealed its evolution from filtering datastreams for threats to "cleansing" datastreams of the information DHS constituents deem "challenging"—information that also sometimes prompted requests for a "solution."

"He actually said that?" I asked. "Requests for a 'solution'?"

"He did." Del was nodding again, her face hardened into a grimace. "Heard the recording myself. And in the very next sentence, Jamie, he handed us the grand prize," Del said through gritted teeth. "DTQ."

The Domestic Threat Quarantine "pre-pilot test-bed program," one of several Collaborative Development Initiatives. When I asked what that really meant, Del said it means pretty much anything DHS wants it to.

For his part, Welch laughed that "test-bed" means they don't ever have to mention it to Congress. Easy to see why they don't want to. DTQ is undisclosed detention without court review or monitoring. And I'll personally vouch that it's sure as hell not short-term, either.

So Cecilia's recordings confirmed Lynn's assumption that federal officials and a coterie of well-heeled corporate and trade group constituents have colluded—are colluding still—to use information gleaned from DTAN monitoring to identify who needs to be "TQed," as Welch put it.

"That was last May," Del said as the car turned into one of the Great Hill garage bays. She made no move to exit the car, instead stroking my chest, nuzzling into my shoulder. Still making sure I'm real, I thought. "God, it took so, so long. We didn't dare spook him because at that point he was our only source of information. Our only hope of finding you. Nine fucking months of working that *asshole* man."

Del gave everything Cecilia collected on Walter Welch to Lynn, who now had "blackmail-worthy, piss-your-pants evidence" of UD revived, and probably worse. Certainly, Welch's brags hinted at worse: lives obliterated out of irritation or resentment, to cover mistakes, to spare inconvenience.

"We didn't want our Walter to have a clue about us," Del said. "If you were among the 'TQed,' then one wrong word from him to the wrong person and you'd be toast—maybe everyone who'd been 'TQed' would be toast."

So Lynn held back, made sure her committee staffers continued to focus only on how DTAN staff implemented CISA rules, and she left Welch alone. Just Springer and a couple of Lynn's most trusted aides conducted a covert investigation of DTQ.

Then, in early June, Cecilia's Amazon sucked one more critical brag from Welch: the name of the contractor handling DTQ detentions—Lazaretto Services Inc.

"We started stalking Lazaretto—LSI, as they call themselves," Del explained. "Privately held, run by its main stockholder, a retired colonel named Strauss. *Very* cozy with DHS—lots of Immigration and Customs detention contracts. And a special talent for leasing mothballed military facilities, of which there are a great many, at breathtakingly cheap prices."

By this time, Del's "we" comprised an informal network of a dozen or so people, including Leta Creel's brother, linked by their compulsion to continue searching for those they'd lost. When this crew learned about LSI, they decided to check out each of the company's lease sites.

Took a while, since LSI holds twenty-odd leases on former military installations, though in mid-June Creel's brother attempted to drive to LSI's Parris Island lease site. He got no farther than the beginning of the causeway several miles distant from Camp Null, where he was turned around by a locked gate and an unfriendly rent-a-cop. Three other LSI locations around the country had similarly forbidding security, so Del's "we" focused on these; Creel's brother took charge of the effort to get a look at the Parris Island site.

As of early July, he'd made three boat trips close enough to lay eyes on what turned out to be Camp Null. When he attempted to approach the dock on the camp's west side, he was waved off by "some kind of law enforcement" in another boat. Undeterred, he decided to fly a drone over the place, which he did more than once. Illegally. And saw only old squadbay buildings, one dude ambling to and from a truck, and nothing but an overabundance of razor wire to hint its secret purpose.

But Creel's brother had also spotted the marked, dredged channel leading to the Camp Null dock. So when the friend of Infirmary Woman Shirley's new young pastor called out of the blue, he was primed, and on the afternoon of AF150, he and Del were en route by boat when Magenau called.

For twenty-one months, she'd never stopped looking, never stopped believing I was alive. And the fierceness that drove her hasn't abated just because she finally got me back. On the contrary, my presence seems to rev her up. Del remains affronted in the most basic and profound way by what happened to me, to both of us. She's after them now, she and Lynn, too—whoever "them" turn out to be.

I, by contrast, am still blinking like a buffoon. I kissed Del and kissed her when she said "Thank god Leta had already told me you were okay before I saw you lying there unconscious." I wanted to never blink again, much less close my eyes—never relinquish the sight of her for even a blink's hundred milliseconds.

I told her I love her. I thanked her over and over for not giving up on me. I could not touch her enough, could not inhale the scent of her enough. And I finally felt like I was home, I'd made it home.

Chapter Fifteen

What game is *this, anyway?*

AF154.
Wednesday, August 5.
21:05 hours.

I'm noticing I have this tendency to drift; the actual sensation of it resembles floating. Almost as if I'm not entirely back to earth from yesterday's damn surgery pharma. I become numb and hollow and separate when I drift, which has happened more than once since I departed the rusted steel box, but nothing like just a little while ago.

We were in Lynn's study, only Del and Lynn and I, shortly before Lynn left for DC and the Judiciary Committee hearing she'll preside over tomorrow.

Which is to say, the two of them popped up and down—sitting standing pacing sitting, and again! like overwrought jack-in-the-boxes—while I remained leashed by my leg to the sofa, a kind of mascot of what's become their Larger Purpose.

For Lynn, ever the legislator, this has taken the form of four goals: use the sensation of the Camp Null scandal to protect the ex-detainees from further government detention or harassment, get the courts to declare DTQ and DTAN unconstitutional, chase down the worst of the corruption that enabled DTQ and DTAN in the first place, and make as many new laws as necessary to plug the holes in the old laws.

"Regarding this matter," Lynn said, echoing what Del and Creel told us before we left Camp Null, "the entirety of executive branch law enforcement and intelligence operations is suspect."

Not because they're *all* corrupt but because corruption's capillary action enables it to flow unpredictably into bureaucracies' narrow, unseen spaces. Which means it can show up anywhere, anytime in apparent defiance of reason and gravity.

"Fortunately," Lynn said, "Judge Byrne is a constitutionalist who gets mad as hell when she sees evidence of the executive branch illegitimately nibbling at judicial and legislative powers."

So now, as Creel predicted, the judge is likely to appoint an independent special prosecutor, who in turn is likely to request and be granted a special grand jury to investigate how Camp Null happened and who's responsible. Yeah, it's a thing; a federal judge can do that if you piss one off enough. And this one, I gather, is on a tear.

In effect, a judge will make sure what happened at Camp Null gets genuinely investigated and any wrongdoing impartially prosecuted. Lynn thinks appointment of a special prosecutor could happen as early as mid-September. Downside: I'll probably be subpoenaed to testify at least once sometime over the next several months—though not before Lynn's committee, unless I want to (um, no thanks).

By the way, did you know that grand juries can subpoena and consider evidence that's been illegally obtained? Like from illegal search or seizure. Or, say, from an anonymous whistle-blower passing on certain classified FBI files to a special prosecutor.

Which will make hiding behind the State Secrets Act just a little tougher for the people who've brought us DTQ and Camp Null. Their secrets, beginning with Vivian Velty's images of bedraggled Camp Null detainees, are already splashing unimpeded across media sites worldwide; tomorrow they'll be openly discussed within the wood-paneled walls of Dirksen Senate Office Building Room 226—in front of live-broadcasting cameras.

"The game of chicken," Lynn said, rubbing her index finger along her lip, "has begun."

She meant with the fracking White House, which she described as off-balance because it has failed to rise above the fray. "Two—count 'em, *two*—cabinet secretaries have stepped way over the line," she said.

"You're referring to the attorney general, huh?" I asked.

"Upton Ford, yes, and ole Buck Ayars over at DHS, too. So—" Lynn waved a hand, palm up. "Of course—" She waved her other hand. "The president's first instinct is to bury the mess and bully *us*."

Thus the White House has threatened to demand all things Camp Null and DTQ be moved to the National Security Court, where proceedings are secret, classified, hidden from public view. Upton

Ford's Justice Department will argue that "special needs" exceptions to Fourth Amendment search and seizure warrant requirements justify both preventive undisclosed detention programs like DTQ, the legitimacy of a place like Camp Null, *and* use of technologies like DTAN to keep information about programs like DTQ under wraps.

"I hate this," I remember muttering as the throbbing in my thigh intensified. "I fucking hate this."

"Jamie, look at me," Lynn insisted. "If they push—which is risky for them—we have strong counter-arguments—"

I shrugged; my Nulled brain was not yet ready for such complexity.

"And I *will* turn this into a goddamn Constitutional crisis if I have to," Lynn vowed.

"Good," Del said. "Because without judicial oversight, those who've been detained have no means to challenge their detention." She perched on the edge of a chair looking particularly female-feline-ready-to-pounce. "For anyone in DTQ detention, the rule of law and the rights of due process simply vanished. Even so, the wrong National Security Court judge could quash your hearings or force them into classified closed-door session."

And they were off, two thoroughbreds running together, and relishing it, too, in a way I never saw *before*. Soon they were prancing around each other, splendidly balanced in their eager barycentric motion, discussing maneuvers, making plans.

I confess I'm hopeless with these two women; I get the most wonderful warm melty feeling, and I will not only do what they want, I will do what I *think* they want. In those rare moments when Del and Lynn disagree, I am a lost soul, forlorn unless I can find a solution that satisfies them both—or unless they very explicitly and expressively agree to disagree and make up. This afternoon, they were entirely in sync. And they were a joy to behold.

I stopped being aware of particulars as they discussed legal arcanities and whose deputy undersecretary assistant pooh-bah claimed what in which message. I simply delighted in the sight of them, the sound and motion of them. This is what luck looks like, I thought as Lynn half turned to give Del a quick hug, and their conversation came into focus.

"...Vivian's Camp Null video has certainly helped, too," Lynn was saying to Del. "I had my doubts about that decision, but you *so* made the right call. And you—" Lynn smiled at me—almost like her old smile. "You got CharlieTann to trust you."

Did she mean Magenau? I wondered.

She did.

That's when I found out Magenau handed Lynn the Camp Null backup box she'd been so determined to take with her after sparing it from her overvoltages. I also found out Lynn had her hired as an independent contractor reporting to Judiciary Committee investigators.

"Magenau's hacking for you?" I asked Lynn.

Short answer: yes. Since the plane ride out of Tennessee.

Lynn seems disappointed, though, with the data coming out of the Camp Null backup box, which recorded every detail of the camp's activities but includes almost no data related to LSI. Interesting that detainees are referred to only by ID number. No names anywhere.

Fifty-nine of those Camp Null ID numbers now do have names; a look at the record of Detainee 2076 shows I arrived at Camp Null a year ago last February—so for three months I was held somewhere else, which suggests the existence of at least one other detention site.

During a facecall today, Magenau said the backup box shows plenty of orphan ID numbers—signifying a person once held at Camp Null who remains unnamed. Now dead? Still alive? One of Magenau's assignments is to find out.

And oh yeah, there goddamn well *is* a helo list, begun a couple years ago. It has four columns: flight ID, detainee number, departure date, departure time. Never a return date or time. And only two detainee numbers were ever removed from the list. One was Detainee 2076.

Me.

Made the mistake then of allowing myself to drift again—indulging too long in attempts to match up strands from those lost months of memory-maybe-delusion. By the time I managed to return to Del and Lynn, they were discussing Magenau's work with Lynn's committee investigators.

"…If we can't get access to that LSI database soon, we'll have to slow things down," Lynn was saying. "Seems Bouchard has the means, but he's balked at telling us. And god knows how long it'll take without his help. Plus the FBI wants him yesterday, and the Capitol Police are nearly out of excuses for holding him."

I told her about New South. "I know he survived the takedown because I heard his voice afterward." I relayed how he bragged in the infirmary, the big deal he made about beating Bouchard at poker, how this got him a job at Camp Null.

"If he's still in custody," I said, "*I'll* make a bet that you can persuade him to roll on ole Kenny inside five minutes. Could help turn up whatever might inspire Kenny to cooperate."

Reaching for her pocketcom, Lynn gave me a quick little salute and flashed her famous grin. I hadn't seen that grin in more than twenty-one months; kinda brought tears to my eyes as I grinned back.

❖

AF155.
Thursday, August 6.
01:52 hours.

Can't sleep. Again.

Don't know why it took me so long to come round to it, but today I finally asked Del about money. As in how the hell has she been supporting herself for the last twenty-one months?

She answered me like she was confessing a sin. "A few small engineering projects. Produced a course—just one, but it's doing well." Her shoulders had slumped a little, as if her attempt at a shrug ran out of steam; she seemed suddenly worn out. "And I, uh—"

"You borrowed money," I guessed. "From your sister."

"Lily and Dana refuse to call it a loan," Del told me. "Don't even try to argue with them about it."

"How much?"

"Too much." Del shook her head, and when I persisted, she persisted right back. It will be discussed later, not now.

Later hasn't happened yet, but I've calmed the part of me that squirms at the prospect of being bailed out, even if it's "just an accident" or "beyond your control." I recognize Caprice's two-edged sword, starting with my getting grabbed off the goddamn street and disappeared, very likely by mistake—*by fucking mistake!* How's that for shit luck?

But wait. Because I got grabbed, Del did not; Del was spared, thank you, Caprice, thank you, because I freak the fuck out just thinking about Del locked away in one of those corroding steel boxes…

And I, daughter of prostitution, of rape, of murder, I survive in more or less one piece (though admittedly the pieces rattle some).

True, my leg hurts all the fucking time, my job is gone, and I won't be able to even attempt to make a living again for at least a couple of months.

Still, I've got solid backup, I'm playing with a net. How the fuck unlikely, and how the fuck wondrous lucky, is that?

Ah, not over yet. Caprice twists the sword again because when one plays with a net, one can play for higher stakes, more dangerous consequences, and nobody understands this better than Del. That's what the Wilderness Web Coalition is all about.

Hell, that's very likely what my twenty-one-month detention was all about, too. I watched Del this evening after Lynn and Rebecca left for DC and saw someone who's realized the safety limits of her net. By luck and luck alone was she spared; by luck and luck alone I was not. This has chastened her.

And it's done something else, too...

I watched Del this evening and recalled last Sunday morning, recalled how she stood a couple feet in front of me at the entrance to that hangar in Tennessee, how she nodded almost imperceptibly as she first perused the setup. And now I've finally found the wits to wonder aloud who the hell paid for it all.

The Red Cross in lavish mode. The well-organized defense fund that burst forth, like Athena fully grown from the head of Zeus, to assemble several helos on a few hours' notice and fly dozens of us through the night, to hustle a squad of lawyers onto the Cumberland Plateau early on a Sunday, to arrange for the parade of small jets that ferried most of the other detainees all over hell and gone, to even provide modest stipends for those on the edge, like Maddie Small.

"A few weeks before I learned about Shirley—your Infirmary Woman—and went down to Charleston to talk to her," Del told me, "I knew we were close to what we thought might be thirty or even forty detained people. I hoped—oh god, how I *hoped* you'd be among them. But I didn't *know*. Yet as a member of a senator's family, you were the only one the Capitol Police were looking for, and it wasn't clear how far they'd pursue what they might see as an ancillary situation."

So she contacted the ACLU and lined up some resources without revealing much in the way of specifics. "I told them lives were at stake, that it was risky to divulge details too soon." She blew out a breath. "The people there know me, but let me tell you, I had to do my very best dance to convince them I hadn't lost my mind."

I stared at Del as she swung off the bed in our room and walked to the window. She wore her favorite jeans, faded and softened with age, and snug. Her T-shirt was snug, too. She looked tired and tense. And strong and so, so beautiful. And I said, "I'd have paid to see that dance."

She kept her back to me and continued to gaze out the window. She didn't say a word. Which is when I grasped that somebody *had* paid to see that dance.

"Who?" I asked her. "Whose deep pockets for deep purposes?"

"Jonathan Armstrong Archer's."

Goddamn.

I hadn't seen the man since I was twenty-one, since that final time I wore a Marine Corps uniform. After that, whenever I encountered his name in the media, I tapped it away aysap, and then as the years passed I noticed it less. So he's an old man now. But maybe not out of the game. Which begs the question: What game *is* this, anyway?

Even though I never had anything more than unfounded conjecture, I always took Jonathan Armstrong Archer as a bad guy. The kind of guy who exploits a war that gets children killed and makes monsters of teenagers too poor not to enlist in the military—and for what? For shareholder returns. For a fat addition to his already outrageous hoard. For another half-inch on his inflating dick while all dicks about him wither.

Del turned around to face me. "I know what you think of him," she said, her backlit face difficult to read. "But he's always supported the kind of work I do—" She extended her arms, palms up. "The work *we* do. And yes, the guy ran mining and fossil fuel extraction and processing companies, but back in the day he called us in to clean it up, remember?" Her hands flopped to her sides. "And he claims he's got a thing about the Bill of Rights."

I really didn't know what to say. There's even the possibility that my mouth was hanging open.

So Del kept on talking. "Anyway, Archer's pretty much given blank checks to the ACLU and the Null Relief Fund."

Quite suddenly, I felt molecular tired, like all the itty bitty parts of me were too fatigued to bother holding on to each other anymore.

"I'm not a fool, my sweet," Del said as she returned to sit on the bed and find a way to touch me, starting with my left forearm. "I can believe Archer has his ulterior motives. I don't care. What happened to you and all the other people locked up in that place is an absolutely unacceptable abuse of power."

Her touch, translated: she will not cower, she will not retreat; she will use any weapon at hand.

I imitated her palms-up gesture, a warning. "Might makes right."

Del's eyes fired; she was strengthening, energizing before my eyes.

"There are many kinds of might," she said softly, calmly. "Archer's was instrumental in getting the right attorneys working on a habeas writ for you at the right moment."

And then she gave me the oddest look.

"There was this moment last Saturday on the boat after I took Magenau's call, this moment when it sank in," she almost whispered. "I was on my way to you at last—*you* for sure. But you were being shot at. You might already be dying. Or dead. And we couldn't see three fucking feet in front of us. I called the USCP contact I had and he scrambled a team immediately, ordered us to stay back and let his people handle it. But his ETA was worse, much worse than ours."

"So you ignored his orders."

She answered me with a kiss.

❖

AF155.
Thursday, August 6.
04:37 hours.

Del took Springer's comcall a few minutes ago and put it on speaker.

"Escalation, although negotiations continue," Springer announced, apparently while she was getting dressed. "Looks like Upton Ford really is damn fool enough to argue that DTQ is legitimate."

In about two hours, Ford himself will appear before Judge Byrne seeking to quash a passel of Senate Judiciary Committee subpoenas and pull everything into the National Security Court, behind the black curtain, prior to today's Judiciary Committee hearing, which starts at ten.

"Let me guess," Del interjected. "He'll claim that although some of the detainees may have been confined erroneously, current statutes empower the government to hold any person suspected of 'terrorist connections' for up to seven days without benefit of a habeas corpus proceeding, and as attorney general, he may extend that period to six months, renewable indefinitely."

"Quick study, Professor," Springer said, then pointed out that the law has never been tested in the courts because it's hardly been used. "Justice toyed with it twenty or thirty years ago but backed off in the face of a real challenge," she said, since it probably fails several Constitutional standards.

Del observed that a challenge will take years to resolve. "I know Archer's willing—even eager—to pay the costs of that kind of battle, but somebody with standing and a hell of a lot of stamina has to be the defendant."

Springer agreed. "Starting with a perp walk in handcuffs."

I wanted to know why wouldn't every person detained claim they were *erroneously* detained, given that the government acknowledges such error is possible?

"Every person detained *will* claim that," said Springer. "And to counter such claims, the government will say it must turn to classified information, which is why they're also arguing that any case related to DTQ—indeed, any mention of DTQ at all, such as in a Senate Judiciary Committee hearing—should be restricted to the National Security Court, since even some of the legal precedents that apply to DTQ detentions are secret."

"So let me get this straight," I said. "Secret proceedings will be conducted to decide if, for example, I have broken a secret law I can know nothing about because, well, it's a secret. Yes?"

"Yes," Springer answered, sounding like maybe she was beginning to regret her promise to Del to keep us updated on all things Camp Null.

I didn't give a shit, kept on going. "And since my secret crime is to have been *suspected*—not proven, merely *suspected*—of having 'terrorist connections' by accusers who are not required to show themselves or the source of their suspicions against me, and given that no process exists by which I can even know these accusations much less refute these accusations, I will of course be deemed guilty. In secret. After which I'll be shipped off to a secret prison. And that's the good news because at least this time you'll know what the fuck happened to me."

Silence.

Wow. I'd nailed it.

And what I'd nailed is terrifying. I just lay there, leg in perpetual elevation, another shot of pain from it shunting up my back, slamming the inside of my skull. I just lay there listening to the *please please please* don't lock me away again in a prison cell. Not ever, ever fucking ever again.

Springer's voice yanked me back. "Wait. Gotta take this call."

So, to the rhythm of *please please please*, we wait while Springer takes that call…

❖

AF155.
Thursday, August 6.
05:10 hours.

For once, someone besides me has (sort of) blinked: Attorney General Upton Ford. Next week he will informally recognize that I was "taken into custody" by mistake.

"His office will claim DHS contractors thought you were someone else," Springer told us. "Someone whose name they'll declare classified. They'll grant you should not have been detained, Jamie, while maintaining that the effort to detain the person they mistook you for was legal."

"They thought I was Del," I retorted. "So in effect they're asserting the right to detain Del secretly, indefinitely, without charge or recourse because they've finally found a way to invent an uncontestable 'suspicion' that she has 'terrorist connections.' Truth is, they're afraid of Del and the Wilderness Web Coalition."

"Hey, Preacher Gwynmorgan," Springer protested wearily. "I'm the choir here."

"You're the messenger, Springer," I snapped back while a red rage tightened my gut, wrapped a band of steamheat around my head. "Message received loud and fucking clear."

❖

AF155.
Thursday, August 6.
06:20 hours.

I'm by myself in our bathroom while Del has gone in search of more coffee. She'll be a while because she'll down a cup talking with Lily in the kitchen before she makes her way back up here with cup number three and I scold her for it, as in, "Three? Seriously?"

Alone in the bathroom, I realize I haven't looked at myself in a mirror yet. Not directly, full on. Not since *before*.

I know I've lost weight. Twenty-four pounds sucked away since my last *before* physical, one of the nurses told me, and I was not overweight back then.

Bree-ee-eathe…and wait till later to ask yourself why the prospect of simply looking at your own face bothers you so damn much…

So okay, I stole a glance.

And it didn't kill me.

Looked again, longer this time…

Mmm, I look older. Gaunt. Sickly pale, almost gray skin. Hair like somebody chopped it off with garden shears, then dyed it with mud. And those eyes—who the hell *is* that?

CHAPTER SIXTEEN

Invisible enemies

AF156.
Friday, August 7.
23:43 hours.

No dreams last night, no waking up drenched in dread. Only a brief flash of rusted steel before Del's real took over. Altogether a decent rest, and just in time, too, because the last couple of days have required a certain stamina.

Yesterday morning, Judge Byrne sent Upton Ford's Justice Department packing. The Senate Judiciary Committee hearings will proceed, she ruled; whenever classified information is discussed, the hearings will move behind closed doors, as is standard. We heard from Springer that after Ford sniffed around informally about how the DC Circuit might respond to an appeal, he backed off. For now anyway.

So the hearings are under way. We've had two long days of them so far, displayed gavel-to-gavel on every screen in the study at Great Hill and accompanied by all manner of detailed critiques.

Quite an education, accelerated by the family backchannel to the chairman of the committee and intermittent commentary from Del that starts with "Ah, now watch what she does next..." Means I'm putting this together faster than the typical prisoner just out of solitary confinement who's drowning in sensory overload.

I know, for instance, that with Magenau's help the committee's sleep-deprived data forensics team has pried loose plenty from the Camp Null backup box and even LSI's corporate vaults (yep, both New South and Kenny Bouchard wilted last Wednesday). Meanwhile, Judge Byrne has ordered that subpoenas from the Judiciary Committee be honored by DHS, the FBI, and the attorney general's office.

I know, too, that a planned second round of subpoenas was served this morning on thirty-seven private sector organizations. "Targeted according to what we learned from DTAN-related files subpoenaed earlier," Lynn said before leaving for Washington, a small gotcha inflecting her words, teasing her mouth. "As well as information supplied by some, uh, anonymous sources." (I'd swear she and Del exchanged a nanoglance.)

Been fun seeing Del get so excited in that victory-at-*last* way that can sweep up people when they've been in a hard fight for too long. They're tired but goddamn angry, so they celebrate passionately when even the most minor of turns finally finally finally goes their way.

Before I can join that struggle, however, I need to achieve a better foothold in Del's real.

Came a moment today, for instance, when I blinked, and suddenly I'm splayed flat on my back on the levee at Camp Null, unable to move, and all around me the Judiciary Committee hearing's sport continues—

I hear Lynn say to some DHS bureaucrat, "Oh, I see another acronym here, Director Biggs." And I can tell she's about to spring her trap. "'DTQ,'" she says. "That's Domestic Threat Quarantine, is it not?"

I see Senator Hillinger edge slightly forward in her chair, follow her relentless squint—and then cannot stop ogling the white flecks of dried spittle at the corners of Director Biggs's mouth as I slide into numb and hollow and separate.

The committee's investigators have been at this for many months, gathering data, compiling evidence. Lynn already knows who will say what, and it will be dramatic and damning. A spectacular show.

And you know what? It won't be enough. That's already obvious—to me, anyway—after two days of hearings and the harbinger spittle at the corners of Director Biggs's mouth.

I read once about how as human societies become larger and more complex, we turn to rituals of human sacrifice—the scapegoat—to reinforce our societies' hierarchies and power structures. And that's what'll happen here. Because without their hierarchies and power structures, people freak out.

Nah, Lynn, you can beat on Director Biggs and people like him all you want, and you'll bring him down—which he'll deserve, in my humble opinion. You may even nail Upton Ford or Buck Ayars. Hell, maybe even that asshole in the White House.

But those truly responsible, the invisible enemies, will stay invisible. They may have to sidestep once or twice; they may find their net worth dinged a bit. But they'll remain unaccused, not because their actions are condoned but rather because their actions are quite willfully *not seen at all*.

So a new question looms: How do we—Del and I—protect ourselves from the impune who may well attack again?

One way: bolt like I've heard Magenau's going to once she's finished "working for the Pollyannas," as she says. After that, she'll "do it straight for a while" and become a Callithump contractor.

"The price of getting my ass to Uruguay free and clear," she said.

For Magenau, Uruguay's an obvious choice. It's "the Internet's Switzerland" and has a habit of providing political asylum to all manner of whistle-blowers whose cyberleaks violate laws and regulations in other nations.

Magenau called her plan "the path back to anonymous." And lectured me because she thinks I'm crazy. "Jeezus, Gwynmorgan—a *senator*? You should know by now to stay far away from the vainglorious rich. They'll grind you the fuck underfoot, even when they think they're helping. You'll end up as collateral damage—*again*, Gwynmorgan. Don't let 'em fool you twice."

Well, I dispute the notion that Lynn is vainglorious, but if it were up to just me, I might give Uruguay a try.

I made a joke of it when I brought it up.

"Uruguay!" Del laughed the syllables.

And then her smile went serious and she touched me—a gentle, wordless, caressing reminder that we're playing with a net, remember? Lynn's protection, the family's significant financial resources, and don't forget Judge Byrne's habeas writs and the ACLU's attorneys and all those fracking headlines and, yeah, even Jonathan Armstrong Archer.

Plus people like Creel, Rosario, Ozawa, Cindy, and some others have offered themselves up as media fodder, so the Null detainees have already become enough of a cause célèbre that our defense and help funds really can pay for defense and help.

But I don't like invisible enemies. The scout/sniper still entangled with the rest of me believes *I'm* supposed to be the invisible enemy.

So, to be unseen by thine enemy, first you need to know who the fuck thine enemy is.

"Forty million companies worldwide," Springer remarked a few days ago. "Forty thousand of them transnationals of which fifteen hundred have interlocking ownerships. And of those fifteen hundred, just a hundred and fifty companies—mostly banks—have so tightly and pyramidally interlocked ownership that they function as a single super-entity in control of almost fifty percent of the world's entire corporate wealth and the vast majority of the world's 'real' economy. Oh, and three of the top five of those companies are privately held."

And seeded by plenty of old money, too. Roots all the way back to Charlemagne's grandfather and the Rajputs.

Yeah? "So who's king?" I asked.

Half a dozen people in the study at the time and nobody answered.

"C'mon," I needled them. "Start with the boards of directors, right? Ten or twelve per board times a hundred and fifty, but figure overlapping membership of, say, twenty percent. So, let's estimate thirteen hundred in the upper reaches of the worldwide corporate nobility. A subset of that is interconnected enough, powerful enough to be part of the king's court. That's maybe three, four hundred? Then a small inner circle of the superconnected—fifty, possibly only twenty or thirty. And one of them's the king. C'mon, who's the king?"

"We all have our theories," Rebecca mumbled while Lynn remained silent, seeming to prefer a detailed study of her hands. I have the feeling she wishes I wouldn't think about it.

Mmm, an invisible king with power aplenty to surpass the limits of any delegated authority. Exercising the power to disappear me and scores of others, the power to kill me or not as the whim takes him—that's more than the delegated authority of a president or a general or one of those bank barons. After all, delegated power *shows*, and it's not limitless.

Whaddaya bet he's got a certain charismatic personal appeal, this invisible king, a real believable guy good at exploiting some expertise he claims legitimizes those kingly ideas, especially the smellier ones. This attracts admiration, loyalty, envy. Followers.

Add in an ability to significantly reward—and significantly punish—so he can reinforce the "right" thought and action, reinforce admiration and loyalty while repressing all that envy. And yeah, a king is born. Invisibility is just our culture's version of royal ermine.

I can't tell who's crazy—me for asking who's king (and silently wondering if it's Jonathan Armstrong Archer) or them for looking at me like I'm crazy because I expect an answer.

No wonder I can't get past numb and hollow and separate.

❖

AF159.
Monday, August 10.
04:15 hours.

Woke up a few minutes ago from, well, I guess it was a dream. But it seems like a whole other real running in uncomfortably close parallel to the one I'm apparently occupying now.

In this other real, I lie facedown on the levee crown thinking I should get up now. Now. Get up. Get. Up.

I didn't, though. I couldn't.

Then came the pain, a burning rampage from my thigh up through my body, blasting right out the top of my head, but I managed to think "thirteen" anyway. *Ohh* yeah, thirteen sapienshits killed or captured...

I heard a woman call my name, and for a millisecond I thought *Del*; then I knew like a sigh, *No, not Del*. But I thought I should open my eyes, which was harder than I expected, though what I saw, finally, was exquisite—these delicate droplets of water clinging to broken blades of grass inches away, waves and shades of reflective greens and grays.

And she said "Jamie" again. "Jamie."

I realized I'm on my belly, pistol in my hand.

"Easy," she said, and I recognized Rosario's voice coming from on high, beyond where I could see, and someone stroked my back. "I need to turn you over."

"Over?" I managed to ask.

Rosario said, "You're bleeding and I don't know why." Like discussing the weather.

"Leg," I tried to say. Got shot, I tried to say.

Rosario said, "Oh god," and shouted, "Hand me that strap!" and the pain in my leg exploded all over again...and then I felt no pain and my vision dappled toward darkness and I knew.

Femoral artery...just seconds now...

And then I blinked my way from that nothingness to my tenuous foothold in Del's real, remembering something I read somewhere about dying. How you slip into a kind of waking dream-state and then, as death nears, neurochemicals in your brain suddenly surge, how all the different regions of your brain synchronize and its electrical activity becomes coherent. Like a goddamn laser.

I think maybe I know what that's like. You sweep out of time, out of place as your awareness winks and blinks through the reals toward the darkness, and who's to say which real is more truly real than any other? Or how long any of them lasts…

❖

AF167.
Tuesday, August 18.
23:25 hours.

With Magenau's help, the data forensics team Lynn let loose on all those subpoenaed files keeps zinging out all kinda gruesome shit about the Domestic Threat Quarantine "pre-pilot test-bed."

Best compared to a set of Russian nesting dolls:

The Department of Homeland Security hides…

The Directorate of Infrastructure and Resource Protection, which hides…

The Risk Reduction Coordinating Center, which hides…

The Collaborative Development Initiatives section, which hides…

The Domestic Threat Quarantine Pre-pilot Test-bed, which hides seven years of detaining no fewer than 289 US citizens and outright killing ninety-nine—the seven who died on the Camp Null levee as well as ninety-two others who were never seen alive again for reasons that do not appear in LSI records or any DTQ data seen so far by committee investigators.

The bodies of forty-four of those ninety-two people, plus the seven Camp Null detainees killed out on the levee, have been identified. Forty-eight remain missing—including Philippa Flynn. Of the 190 who survived, DTQ released 101, but they were left so badly broken either physically or mentally or both that eleven have since died.

Eighty-nine of us have shot, run, walked, wheeled, and/or limped our way out of DTQ detention—fifty-nine of us from Camp Null and another thirty detained at a second LSI site.

The media, always wisecrack-challenged, has nicknamed the other LSI detention site "Camp Void"; its detainees were retrieved three days ago by the US Capitol Police at the behest of the Senate Judiciary Committee, which has them staying at a resort in "custody" on material witness warrants, most hunkering with their families "until things calm down."

"We're pushing the boundaries," Lynn admitted. "I'm not sure a Senate committee has ever requested that the Capitol Police execute a material witness warrant. Debatable legality. But at least those people are protected while we slow-waltz through the courts." She never explicitly said who or what the ex-detainees needed protection from.

Probably Upton Ford. Certainly not the DTQ nomenklatura. Not anymore.

The guy in charge of DTQ—some "well-connected up-and-comer" named Bainbridge—had, like Robert ("Just Call Me Bubba") Strauss, invoked his Fifth Amendment right to shut the fuck up. By contrast, Walter Welch made a deal at the speed of light.

"We were told the test-bed showed promise as an anti-terrorism tool," Welch said, still swaddled in the bean counter's illusion of a safe bureaucratic distance. But then he sniveled, "I don't make decisions about what DTQ pays for. I'm *told* what to pay for."

Downright breathtaking to watch Senator Hillinger show what in fact DTQ bought—how many grabbed, how many ruined, how many killed.

I thought I'd girded pretty well, but the shit I'm hearing about the helo list sends shivers right through me. All thirty-seven people on that list are among the forty-eight missing, according to the committee's data forensics crew, which has managed to match up 289 DTQ detainee ID numbers with names. (I don't know what it means that Philippa Flynn isn't on the helo list; she's among the eleven missing by some other means.)

One name and detainee ID number at a time, Lynn has exploited the Camp Null helo list to spectacular effect. First, she got one of the sapienshits to repeat the "rumor" so pervasive at Camp Null that it even seeped through the barrier of automation and silence to reach those of us who erected tubedams out on the levee: yes, detainees on the helo list damn well *were* transported 200 miles off the South Carolina coast and "we'd just say they were dropped off."

By then I could no longer look at the screen, but the dude's voice rubbed me wrong from the first syllable; I recognized its chafe against the horrified hush that overtook Room 226. Fuckin' A—New South. Talking snide about dumping detainees in the goddamn Gulf Stream.

Room 226's hush flustered him, it seems, because he started to kind of blame-babble. "The helo crew'd say that, so what the hell, we all said it. 'Let 'em pick up their own ride on the way down,' we'd say."

His tone oozed resentment. *All* the sapienshits saying it made it okay to say, okay to not object, okay to maybe even get off on it a little, and now somebody's changed the rules? How come nobody told him?

I wanted to bite open his carotid artery all over again.

Good news is I'm not the only one. New South's testimony has incited a fresh round of exclamation-pointed headlines and intensified demand for a Special Senate Select Committee. "Joint criminal enterprise!" has actually become a rallying cry.

Now, as the world contemplates what it feels like to be thrown out of a helicopter 3,000 feet above the Atlantic Ocean, members of the Judiciary Committee grill DHS personnel, DTQ contractors, and executives of DHS's so-called corporate collaborators. Lynn's especially gifted at using carefully researched and crafted questions to link a missing detainee to events in which the witness du jour has somehow participated.

Many I-do-not-recalls and whispered exchanges with attorneys later, Bubba Strauss isn't the only one invoking the Fifth.

AF178.
Saturday, August 29.
03:50 hours.

Okay, I admit it: I'm flailing.

Every fucking night I dream about a different bad guy, though Upton Ford and Buck Ayars have been figuring prominently. And every fucking night, the night's bad guy makes some sort of move on either Del or me.

Just now Philippa Flynn woke me up talking about that Georgica Corporation audit board meeting and warning me about Bubba Strauss. Neural payback, I guess, after learning that Bubba and Buck are old buddies from once upon a time and still belong to the same very private Texas hunting club. Also, what a curious coincidence that Buck Ayars sat on Georgica's board before he got tapped for the DHS post.

And why the hell is Philippa Flynn one of those eleven detainees who are so *missing* compared to the others?

"It's weird, y'know?" I keep saying to Del. "Why doesn't anyone know what happened to them?"

"Patience," Del soothes. Which is what everyone keeps repeating. Patience.

But it's taking too long! I know I've been out of there for less than a month, but I also know that for however long this shit takes I will be numb and hollow and separate. And I don't want to be numb and hollow and separate anymore.

Would help to be able to go home, all the way home. But at this rate, Del and I'll never get back to Birch Lane.

Because, much as I want to sleep in my own bed, I am (yeah, I admit it) afraid that the unstoppable invisible "they" will take Del. "They" already tried—just dumb luck it was me instead.

And sure, DTQ's dead and bunches of DHS minions are scurrying for cover. Yet the attorney general continues to assert, backed by the full force of the federal government and a nervous president running for reelection, that he has the right to grab Adele Sabellius anytime anywhere and hold her without probable cause or charge for as long as he wants just because he can state that he "suspects" her.

Seems Upton Ford hasn't quite worked up the gumption to send federal agents after any of what everyone now calls the DTQ survivors. Maddie Small, for one, remains unmolested; I know because I checked on her—and warned her.

The view here in the rarified atmosphere of Great Hill is that we're all quite safe. But goddamn, that strikes me as, yeah, vainglorious, and I worry how long Del and I would remain unmolested in our little first-floor two-bedroom in Belmont.

So, much as I'd like to scratch that itch we both have to go home to Birch Lane, I believe we're a whole lot safer in the vainglory of Great Hill.

Del, on the other hand, finds the prospect of returning to Birch Lane very tempting. Might her presence there goad Attorney General Ford into having her detained, thus launching that Constitutional test case she discussed with Springer not so long ago? And might such a test case seduce our invisible enemies into revealing themselves?

Goddamn, I can't tell you how fiercely I do *not* want to learn the answers to those questions.

But I shouldn't be surprised that what Del needs and what I need are deviating.

I, too, have four goals: get my thigh—and my mind—healed enough that I can make love with abandon, renew my lapsed professional engineering license, find the kind of work as a structural engineer that'll lead me back to design projects, and become invisible to my enemies.

Meanwhile, Del craves a chance to blow the roof off what she calls "that den of poisonous powermongers so dominant they don't even have a name."

It's a tribute to her power—and to my hunger for her—that

those words didn't paralyze me on the spot when she said them as she climbed into bed and wreathed herself around me. I let them slip away, water through my fingers, and after we made love I slipped away, too, into the special, nourishing sleep that only happens when Del lies beside me.

But I'm wide fucking awake now.

CHAPTER SEVENTEEN

Fleshtime

AF183.
Thursday, September 3.
23:33 hours.

Last Monday, I was deemed fit for surgery (inflammation receded, no infection). The doc Rebecca selected had an opening this morning, and despite some screw-ups with my medical records (how the hell can *all* the copies of my *before* blood and DNA data disappear?), the extracellular matrix procedure that'll help regenerate the muscle in my thigh has been done. It's day surgery now—nothing like the biggish deal it was the last time parts of me had to be scaffolded together again. Back in the day.

I'll heal more quickly now, not least because I'm finished with wound scourings and vacuumings and can begin physical therapy tomorrow.

And I'm feeling good because I won't have to deal yet with a rehab place full of people, since fleshtime with strangers is not my friend. I get too jaggedy when someone's behind me and I don't know what they're doing.

So Del's arranged for a week of physical therapy at Great Hill. Her generosity extends to saying that my jaggedness isn't the reason, she just wants to make sure I'm doing everything right. "And not overdoing it."

God, she has been patient with me. Never once has she suggested I stay at Great Hill while she zips off to Birch Lane without me. Could've done that, coming and going at will, any time during the last five weeks. But she didn't; she's been with me the whole way. If leaving me here tempts her, she gives no hint. And yeah, I'm on the lookout for that hint.

Actually, Del has made me feel needed—a remarkable feat since I'm close to useless.

Thus I was babbling thank-yous again, still pretty loopy from the surgery's knock-you-on-your-ass pharma as we returned to Great Hill from the hospital and found ourselves pulling up to the house as Lily and Dana and the girls, just returned from camp, were trudging backpacks inside.

"Ready?" Del asked.

I think I grinned. "Do I have a choice?"

Turns out I did.

Because even though Del has seen it only a couple of times, she knows I am downright bizarre when I am drugged all to shit, and this afternoon I was drugged all to shit. So she got the kids to regale us with their camp stories and their camp artifacts. Even got them to teach us their camp songs, which she accompanied on the piano.

Only later, after I had time to sober up some from the pharma, did the kids and I talk. Lily and Dana have a house rule: try to be as optimistic as possible, as gentle as the moment requires, but don't lie to their children (and someday I'll describe how they managed to account for Santa Claus, who's a gender-adventurous girl, by the way, without ever fibbing).

To my surprise, our conversation went on for several hours but seemed to slip by too quickly. I answered every single question they posed. As they sat cross-legged in a semicircle at the foot of the room's best leg-propping sofa, Evvie, Alex, and Remy posed them all.

They seem so much older—made older still, I suspect, by the effects on them of what happened to me. Evvie's thirteen now, much taller, breasts blossoming, far more serious than I remember, and she led her ten-year-old sisters through their Q&A of me.

It was unnerving how often I found myself honestly saying "I just don't know, I can't remember." But I think I did all right.

Del stayed at the piano for the duration, sometimes playing it to lighten things up or to give me a breather. And she answered questions, too. Ones that clearly traversed old territory, like why anyone would want to kidnap their Auntie Del. Soon we were talking about why some people dislike the Wilderness Web so much that they'll do things like try to kidnap a person who's especially good at showing its value.

Remy said, "Maybe you should stop now, Auntie Del. Maybe then they'd leave you alone."

"Oh, Rems," Del answered, leaning toward her with a smile, "remember how I said once that would be like letting a bunch of people with big wrecking machines start tearing down the houses near the railroad tracks. And how people living in houses far away from the tracks don't notice anything at first, but then—"

"Like what's happened to the elephants," Evvie reminded her sisters.

"And polar bears," Alex chimed in. "And the butterflies and the bees."

"Yes," Del said, "and I still want to do everything in my power to prevent it from getting even worse." She gazed at me with eyes gone abyssal black. "But I'm extra careful now about making sure we stay safe."

All three kids nodded in earnest unison. This, more than anything, is what they wanted to hear. And what I wanted to hear. I eased into the sofa, still a little high from the pharma, as Del beckoned the kids away from the seriousness of our conversation with laughter and fingers that boogied across the keyboard. The twins, then I'm-too-old-for-such-foolishness Evvie bounced up to dance along until even Dana and Lily joined in.

I watched, I laughed, I let my good leg tap and swing to Del's playing and felt stronger than I have in a long, long time.

❖

AF197.
Thursday, September 17.
23:40 hours.

Del and I have returned to Birch Lane.

Meanwhile, Magenau's SkulkWorks, which is what everyone's calling the dig into all those subpoenaed Justice Department, DHS, and corporate records, has found something in common between Philippa Flynn and the other ten missing detainees who never showed up on the helo list. Their medical records are either partially or entirely missing, not unlike what happened to my medical records. Whatever that may mean. Lynn isn't going to be asking about it at the committee hearings until she damn well knows what answers she'll hear.

The SkulkWorks also confirmed that Attorney General Ford did not lie. I *was* grabbed by accident. It *was* supposed to be Del.

No answer, though, to another question: How come Detainee 2076 got pulled from the helo list? Why bother to keep an accident, a mistake, alive for twenty-one months?

Possibly because my accidental abduction delivered to its still-unidentified sponsors something almost as effective as disappearing Del. It shut down her work on the Wilderness Web Coalition by getting her to divert virtually all of her prodigious energy to finding me.

As for keeping me alive, I can now see three why-the-hell-nots. It was low-risk, since DTQ had proven sufficiently invisible and untouchable; it was also low-cost, since the well-disguised bill for my room, board, and mindfuck pharma went to the taxpayers; and the ability to show proof of life on demand gave them ongoing potential to manipulate Del and Lynn.

But Caprice turned on them. I got away, made it home. So how do Del's enemies stop her now?

Not even the invisible king and his oligarchs can bend their own rules far enough to constrain her without subverting their sociopolitical charade (this is a democracy under the rule of law, *really* it is!), which they need to wield power while staying safely beyond the mob's awareness.

Nor can Del be out-argued, since she's right about the facts, about the science, about the future. Ad hominem attacks backfire because she's brilliant, a charming master of riposte whose classic, unadorned beauty and spirited candor make her fun to watch, and make her cause fun to get excited about.

There is no countermeasure to Adele Sabellius.

No wonder her enemies cheat.

I grew up with cheaters, albeit much poorer ones. Rich or poor, however, there's a common theme: their furtive ravening for a higher spot on whatever hierarchy enthralls them. Look and you'll see their willingness, eagerness even, to keep on doing anything they think they can get away with. Because no matter how much they have, it's never enough. They're addicted.

Gotta say, though, when it's scaled up like *this*—

This is definitely *not* my neighborhood and, jeezus, talk about ay-fucking-symmetric. Del and her save-the-wilderness friends versus whole swaths of the federal government handmaiding for a corporate oligarchy that has shitloads invested in the man-rules-nature paradigm. And that's just *this* country.

How much does Del threaten her enemies everywhere now that,

in this country, DTQ has been laid wide open and we're hearing from minions who did the dirty work and the wet work as they scramble for cover, deflecting what blame they can where they can?

"Oh come on," she said when I worried aloud that "they" will come after her again. "If nothing else, with all these nefarious test-beds and exploits like DTQ now exposed, I suspect I've never been safer. You either."

"You know damn well the pricks responsible for it all will diddlybop off unscathed," I replied.

I didn't have to remind her of Magenau's grumpy facecall earlier complaining about the oldest trick in the CEO book: LDL, let's discuss live, the executive suite's favorite messaging acronym, hider of secrets, collusions, deals arranged on a handshake far from any cams or microphones.

So what, I bitched, if you keep mining all the data in those subpoenaed files, keep discussing the patterns and meanings lurking in who sent what when to whom. You'll just keep getting that same dull corporate drip drip drip of LDL.

Magenau hasn't given up, Del declared, then kept talking just a little too fast about how Magenau's currently in the throes of algorithm-refining, according to Springer, and everybody's optimistic, yada, yada.

But I know Del's sense of letdown when I hear it.

Fact is, LDL confers deniability and, so far anyway, it has quite successfully shut down Lynn's committee investigators' ability to incriminate anybody anywhere above mid management.

I was still a half-second away from blurting, "This ain't Kansas anymore, Dorothy, and I'm shit-scared they're gonna come here and arrest you," when Del spoke first, anticipating me in that uncanny way she has, backlit by the dining room window's southern light, arms spread, palms up, not quite beseeching. "I know what you think of…"

I admit I kinda don't remember her words after that because they don't matter. "I know what you think of…" really means she intends to risk her life regardless of what I think.

I interrupted her. "They will put you in a steel box, Del, and you will *not* survive."

This, at least, shut her up.

She clasped her hands in front of her and bowed her head. Behind her left shoulder out the window, the sun peeked from the day's cloud cover and lit up the apple trees alongside the house. A good crop this year, ready for picking soon—and suddenly I wanted to smell our apples and started moving toward the back door almost like a regular person now that I need only a cane.

"I can't allow that kind of threat to stop me," Del said, her head still bowed. "They've stopped me long enough."

I left the edge in my retort. "So you *want* to be a martyr?"

She didn't answer immediately. I clunked along another couple of steps. Then, "No. I want to make a difference," she said. "I want to put all my skills and insight and personal power into making a difference."

"This *particular* difference, you mean—the Wilderness Web Coalition." I wasn't asking.

"Yes." She lifted her gaze to meet mine. "It's like coming upon an injured person in the street, helpless and bleeding," she said. "Some people can walk on or stand back staring, but I know how badly I'd be haunted by what I didn't do, by seeing somebody injured and helpless bleed to death right in front of me *because I did not act*." She smiled tentatively; her eyes flashed for a nanosecond. "I know you appreciate the risks of regret avoidance. I've seen the medals."

Shit. She'd told me this many times in many different ways over our years together. And she wasn't the only one; I remembered that dream I had in the steel box, the one about Mary and those epileptic seizures.

"I'm gonna go smell the apples," I told her.

She followed me outside like an errant child. And for the first time I understood. She won't do it anymore if I don't agree. Then she actually said the words. "I will give up the Wilderness Web unless you tell me not to."

I stared at her, searched her face. Yes, she means it. Yes, it's real.

I took my time before I replied. Because I was so...damn... tempted. Yes, she'd do it. She'd stop. But what would it cost her?

I took a moment to *bree-ee-eathe...*

"No, Del," I said. "Don't give up the Wilderness Web. Or the Rosies. Don't give up any of it."

But I bargained, too. "How you make a difference has to be different now," I told her. "Otherwise, you *will* end up a martyr and then I'll get whacked taking out whoever whacked you, and god help your cause then because I'll set it back at least a hundred years. Besides, you promised the girls you're careful now about staying safe. I've already managed to re-up my concealed carry license, but we damn well also need to layer on more security around here."

And she said yes. Del is extremely talented at saying yes.

❖

AF213.
Saturday, October 3.
02:20 hours.

Not even a week back at Birch Lane and they arrested me—the FBI, I mean. Might've been worse if Maddie Small hadn't broken pattern and sent warning that they'd tried to grab Perez and missed. The two of them are in hiding now. Maddie Small didn't say where, but my bet's on the Freedom Tunnel.

The next morning I spotted two guys in a car down the street. Just two guys sitting in a car. But it's a private street and they hadn't been there when Del left maybe half an hour earlier.

Odd how what seemed even then to be my irrational hysteria anticipated so precisely what would happen. I guessed who they were, knew what they wanted. Considered the possibility I was merely being surveilled. Until I recalled Mary's story—the moment when she looked away from the epileptic seizure in denial promising to act if it was still happening when she looked back...

I figured if they'd come to arrest me, they'd eagerly barge into our place, use arresting me as an excuse to rifle through everything. But if I'm on the street, they might opt to pick me up right there and leave our place alone. I took a few seconds to stash some things in the wall safe—my wedding ring, Audy, my high-security bracelet comlink, my pistol—

Oh god, I held that pistol and contemplated what arrest would mean. Sure as hell, without hesitation I'd kill them if that act could keep me from getting locked in a cell again. But it wouldn't. So I faced my real choice: Del or death.

I chose Del. Secured the pistol in the safe, sent her a warning text, secured the house, and departed unarmed.

Which seemed to surprise them. With help from my cane, I actually fast-walked past their car and made it around the corner onto Waverley Street before they managed to turn their vehicle around, catch up with me, flash their little FBI cards, and yes, fucking arrest me, handcuffs and all. On a bullshit material witness warrant.

To freak me out, they held me incommunicado for what turned out to be almost twelve hours by hauling me down to Rhode Island and slow-processing me into a municipally run prison that incarcerates miscellaneous federal detainees—people dragged in by the FBI, DHS, the US Marshals, the Navy, a local Indian tribe.

Three days later, I became a habeas corpus writ two-timer, thanks to a federal judge in Boston who found the information on the government's warrant "misleading."

I was home for about fifteen hours when they showed up again. Arrested me again, hauled me back to Rhode Island again, this time on a federal complaint: murder of two federal contract employees during performance of their duties—oh, and three counts of attempted murder.

This time around, it took six days to get me out.

I was told how lucky I was not to be chained up and dragged back for a little fleshtime with a judge in South Carolina. Instead I had my first taste of teleconference justice, during which the government claimed I may present a terrorism risk. No evidence or probable cause, you understand. Just get some *pee*-niss of a US Attorney somewhere to *say* it—"uh oh, terrorism"—and a cloud of presumed guilt lowers over you.

In my case, this meant the US Attorney didn't have to show why I should remain in custody. Instead, I had to show why I should be granted bail. I'd be there still but for my attorney's ability to poke holes in the government's case and Lynn informing the judge she'd post a hundred percent of my eight-figure bond right then.

I feel like I'm living on the point of a spear that's about to impale me. Federal law prohibits media from disclosing my arrest. My deets now reside in a database of domestic terrorism suspects and will, I'm told, remain there even if the charges against me are dropped. Oh, and don't expect to ever again travel commercially, not if it involves checking ID. I also face the possibility of civil seizure of my assets even if I'm never convicted of anything.

Everyone says not to worry, don't be intimidated, the charges *will* end up dropped, your deets *will* be expunged from the terrorism blacklist. I just smile. They mean well, and I appreciate the sentiment.

But shit. Déjà vu all over again. Twice.

Now Del and I are back at Great Hill, and I'm wearing a fucking monitor bracelet around my ankle, restricted to a three-mile radius from where I'm standing. In those nine days in custody I was stripped and cavity-searched eight times, and for 122 hours I was trapped in a seven-foot by ten-foot maximum security cell with a 200-pound paranoid psychopath who never shut up.

Been free for a few days but still all I wanna do is sleep. And still my eyes refuse to close.

Doesn't help that since I was released I've heard other former Camp Null detainees are being hassled, too. The sizable number of them who were whistle-blowers are scared they'll end up "manninged," as Creel calls it—locked away for crossing one of the many arcane legal lines that make whistle-blowing at least difficult and costly and at most life-destroying.

Besides me, others will likely be accused of terrorism, too—especially those supporting environmental causes and asylum reform—and face long, expensive legal battles and possibly prison sentences.

Retaliation, Lynn calls it—focused on me first because "that bully of a president" is trying to get her to back off.

"He wants us satisfied with a ceremonial slaying of DTQ that includes sacrificing Bainbridge and Biggs on the bad-guy altar, and he'll toss in some lipstick-on-a-pig rule tweaks that do nothing to end undisclosed detention," Lynn fumed in a single breath as she circled Great Hill's kitchen island. "Oh, and DTAN is sacred now, so leave it untouched, drop the hearings like a hot potato, and absolutely forget about convening a select committee."

She stopped suddenly and looked at me like she just realized the implications of her words. "And that prick chose you to be the messenger," she almost whispered. "I am so sorry."

It was one of those moments when Lynn makes me all squiggly. I am at once burningly in love with her, ready to die for her, feeling mothered by her, protected and protecting, awed and achingly aware of her vulnerabilities, aware even of a blindspot or two.

But this time I was also light-headed; all the colors of the world were slightly washed out. And I said, "Mmm, you told me about this once, didn't you? About responsibility for—how'd you put it? 'For our excellent fortune.'"

As I think back on that moment, I finally comprehend the almost-cruel irony I didn't intend or understand. But I guess everyone else grasped it. And Lynn felt it, of course; I can see that now. She rounded the kitchen island to stand in front of me and almost touch me as she apologized again.

I shook my head, told Lynn no, no need, and tried to explain. "Mary and I talked, and I think I'm starting to get what her story about the recurring epileptic seizures means. Same kind of deal with us, y'know?

In our version, I get slammed somehow and you end up apologizing for it. Yet there's this way that it really is beyond our control, but it also may be a test."

Curious moment, that. Lynn gaped. Which is saying something, since Lynn doesn't gape. I oughta explain that better, I thought, but it's still light outside. After 122 hours locked in a box with a lunatic, I craved *Outside!*

So I excused myself—probably a bit oddly because at this point they were all gaping like Lynn, but, well, what the hell. And I went outside, started along one of the easy walking paths east of the house.

After a few minutes, Del caught up with me and asked if I'd like some company.

I said, "Your company—always. But I have a request."

She ran her hand down my back and kissed my shoulder as we walked—more carefully than usual, I realized, because I'd jumped earlier when she touched me. In prison being touched is—dangerous. I wasn't entirely home yet.

I made my request—"Please let's not talk about any of *that*"— and halted, turned to her; yeah, she knew exactly what I meant, and her expression gave away that not talking about it would take effort. "Please, Del."

We walked along for a few steps in silence, her right arm laced through my left, and then she said, "Yeah, you're right. That's a very good idea."

I persuaded her to walk down to the beach with me. Two miles to the sand, two miles back, all of it beautiful. I commanded myself: notice it all, soak it up, remember, remember so when you close your eyes it stays bright and crisp and real.

I close my eyes now...and...not bad. I'll go on the same walk tomorrow, go on that walk and other walks every day I have, noticing, remembering. Cuz eventually they'll come for me again. No way to stop them. But I know I won't be able to do it another time. (How many is it now, Mary? I think I might be beating your record.)

I can almost see what'll happen. I'll be in custody when I take myself out—with as many sapienshits as possible—and all that I'm noticing and remembering in this golden hour will fill the very last instant of my life.

CHAPTER EIGHTEEN

Normal

AF225.
Thursday, October 15.
21:25 hours.

Ever watch chess champions play each other? Even if you're like me and understand the game's basics, in only a few moves two highly proficient players will leave you wondering what the hell just happened. And what the hell is going on now. As for what might come next—forget it.

Welcome to my world, where I'm standing here, thumb up my ass, leaning on a cane, trying to catch up. Goddammit, I'm watching as fast as I can.

About ten days ago, anonymously leaked news of the arrests of nine Null campers broke from the bottom up, when the first of several pic-n-paragraphs appeared on all the right affinity feeds. By that night, the credentialed media, which could not legally report the actual arrests (every one of us, apparently, "may present a terrorism risk"), *did* eagerly report details of a sudden gush of gossip about the arrests of nine Null campers. And have kept on reporting.

The effect was immediate, and public uproar about our arrests seems to have prompted a phase transition of sorts.

Started with the Senate's nearly unanimous vote last week to establish a Select Committee, named exactly as Lynn proposed—the Select Committee on Federal Threat Identification and Detention Practices—and given all the power the Senate can muster, including appointing Lynn its chairman.

The very next day, one of Judge Byrne's colleagues granted an injunction requiring the Department of Homeland Security to immediately show compliance with provisions of the National Security Act's rules of Classified Administrative Detention, especially as regard Notices of Detainment, which are issued by the attorney general under his power to detain any person suspected of "terrorist connections."

As the media's obsession about the rules of Classified Administrative Detention and NoDs peaked over the weekend, Lynn said, "Okay, we pounce at Tuesday's hearings." Monday, she believed, would be too soon. "We want as many voters as possible knowing that each of those two hundred eighty-nine DTQ 'disappearances' started with a criminally corrupted NoD."

I am witnessing a grandmaster at work. During yesterday's Select Committee hearing, Lynn got one midlevel DHS employee to admit that the Justice officials responsible for NoD oversight actually have nothing to do with "our NoDs." Justice sign-off has always been automatic—literally—as was DHS sign-off.

"Robo process, robo signature," said Bainbridge, the DTQ pre-pilot test-bed manager now desperate for an escape hatch. "The NoDs come from our collaborative partners. We just tick a couple of boxes and send them on to our contractors for fulfillment."

Oh my god, Lynn had a field day with that.

By "fulfillment" you mean carry off by force and imprison the person named in the Notice?

Yes.

By "collaborative partners" you mean the various organizations—corporations of all sorts, government entities at local, state, and federal levels—with whom you cooperate on matters related to security and threat amelioration?

Yes.

Did you review the evidence and documentation your collaborative partners provided in support of their requests for Notices of Detainment?

"Uh, well, usually there was no documentation, just the NoD. These are trusted partners. Their word is good enough."

Lynn demanded access to all Notice of Detainment records from both the Justice Department and DHS; by day's end both had balked, asserting the data is classified.

This morning, Judge Byrne dismissed the complaints against three of the arrested Null campers and appointed an independent special prosecutor to investigate possible government misconduct involving DTQ, DTAN, and related activities.

This afternoon, my attorney called to tell me all charges against me had been dropped. No indictment, no more ankle monitor, my deets purged from the terrorism database, no civil seizure of my assets, Lynn gets her bail money back.

And I get my life back.

❖

AF231.

Wednesday, October 21.

23:15 hours.

We've returned to Birch Lane. For good, I hope. For real.

Yesterday, I inquired about normal. As in, "How long, do you think, till our lives get back to normal?"

That's when I discovered I have two heads. The second one, which I neither feel nor see, seems to snuggle just to the left of the one I call home, and Del stared at us both, back and forth from me to the other me, then said she didn't know when. She focused on a tablet screen, dragged her eyes away to gaze at the other me, and added, "It'll be a while, I suspect."

Years. She meant—means—years.

I responded with my favorite thousand-yard stare and asked if she'd like a sandwich. I'm still underweight, so Del approves of me consuming as many sandwiches as possible.

"I picked up a baguette earlier, and at least one of those avocados should be ripe," she encouraged. But right on cue she declined a sandwich of her own, claiming the need to prep for a strategy facecall with what I (privately) call the DTQ289 Club: Creel, Rosario, Ozawa, Cindy, a few others I don't know, some ACLU people, plus Archer and a couple other "influential contributors."

The meeting would be tense, I already knew, because now it's the Senate Select Committee's turn to hit the LDL wall. Also doesn't help Del that I've become a rather grumpy Survivor; the last time I sat in on one of these confabs, I made just-a-joke about DTQ289 franchises.

Oops.

So when Del rose from her desk to touch me and remind me to touch her, I spotted the hint, in her eyes mostly, but also in the sweep of her hand along my forearm. She'd prefer I not attend the meeting.

So okay, this was a relief.

Yet it bothered me because I should be at Del's side, at Lynn's side, up to my elbows in the DTQ289 battle, easily able to sustain a burning desire for Justice. If Del doesn't want me there, I have failed. Too weak, too neurotic.

Too.

Fucked.

Up.

Thing is, I spend my nights, well, elsewhere. Every morning I have to fight my way out of that corroded steel box and back to Del's real—*every fucking morning*. Sometimes I need to just fucking turn off Camp fucking Null. I need normal, even if it's only a pretense.

And I crave the mundane of it, y'know? The way the living room looks in the midday light, the feel of clean laundry fresh from the dryer, Del's scent on the pillow next to me when I get into bed first.

So I decided to embrace my sense of relief, made sandwiches for both of us, and sent Del off with hers to prep for her meeting.

"Gonna do my exercises," I told her.

I've made immersing in Del's real an extension of the physical therapy routine I still go through twice a day to heal my thigh. Not unlike the KIMS games we trained with back in scout/sniper school—only now I watch, notice, remember normal.

Del helps, too, when she manages to set aside yet another manic analysis of the day's assorted thrusts and parries and talk about stuff like the wetlands restoration project she somehow finds time to work on, or the latest micro wind turbine technology, or how good Dana's mushroom soup turned out. Hell, that's almost normal, right?

The docs say the hole in my thigh is healing a little faster than normal. Even so, it reacts to *everything* like a goddamn Greek chorus— changes in temperature, time of day, the way Del kisses me, touches me, the effects of even a little exertion as well as all emotions of every type.

Other sorts of healing, meanwhile, seem to be progressing slower than normal—like how I'm doing with fleshtime. Which is to say, not so well, at least by the standards of those around me.

This is where I seem to bump into the limits of normal and have to face the possibility that what those around me regard as normal is, well, *not*.

I mean, I seem to be the only person not on the security staff who understands that *anything can happen* when one shares actual physical space with other human beings, especially strangers.

Hell, *anything-can-happen* happened to me just last month, during my second stint in that Rhode Island lockup. I had to very nearly kill my psychotic cellie to stop her from killing me. After eighty-four hours of muttering and shouting demented nonsense, she decided I was a demon sent by an alien race to steal her brain, and she jumped me. I believe her plan was to rip my head off, and she was big enough, strong enough, terrified enough to do it.

God knows how I managed to wriggle free enough of her grip to reach her neck and push, grope, push until my fingers found her carotid artery's baroreceptors. She weakened, went woozy, and I broke loose.

But then what? She'd be just as fucking crazy when she regained full strength, and I sure as hell couldn't go anywhere. So I got her onto the lower bunk, cradled her in front of me, and talked to her as she came to, pressed her carotid as soon as she flipped out again. This went on for hours—talk, press, talk—till cellie had an epiphany and decided I was an angel sent to soothe her.

None of the sapienshit "staff" in that shithole ever intervened; either the cell's cameras had failed or we served as entertainment through two shifts. If that poor tortured soul had moved on me two seconds earlier than she did, I'd have been dead in a matter of minutes.

No, no, fleshtime with strangers requires a trust I do not have, cannot imagine having. Give me a nice, hyper-resolution comscreen any day. I'll forsake the fleshtime cues everyone's on about these days for the comfort of knowing nobody can coldcock me or shoot me or shove a knife between my ribs.

Fact is, except for Del and the crew at Great Hill, I kinda don't want to talk to people anymore. Of course, I realize this has, uh, implications for how I'm going to earn a living.

So I stalled. Tunnel-visioned on re-upping my Professional Structural Engineer license because I could do the professional development and continuing education requirements via comscreen, which also has distracted me from DTQ289 shit.

Now I actually have more hours than I need, and as of last week my PSE license is renewed—though for reasons I haven't figured out, it took me a while to tell Del.

But I do claim one victory. Today I stopped stalling.

While Del and her compatriots helped each other grasp the limits of Justice for those whom the rules are designed to exploit, I cajoled myself into beginning an onlink job hunt. And this evening I showed Del my new PSE license, let her know I'd started looking for work.

She'd come back from the front lines weary and discouraged, yet she rallied for me, lit up like she used to, and as I watched her do it, I turned on in a way I hadn't turned on since *before*.

She'll be out of the bathroom any second now, bathed in the hall light, the supple naked edges of her glowing as she walks slowly toward me, syncopating her tease to the rhythm of my invitation…

Goddamn, I love Del's real. Which just might be as normal as I'll ever want.

❖

AF244.
Tuesday, November 3.
03:05 hours.

The era of DTQ civil lawsuits has begun, which made a deposition inevitable, I guess. My attorney managed to stave it off until I'm not in anyone's prosecutorial crosshairs anymore, something which took just long enough that I dared hope it might never happen.

But it did. And it may not be the only one.

Beats testifying in person in a courtroom or at a hearing, so I suppose I have no business bitching. But screw it, I'm bitching, even though I did okay till near the end, till Assistant US Attorney Sorensen's question—"How did you manage to convince yourself that the people detaining you at Parris Island intended to kill you?"

His tone hovered between contempt and disbelief. His tone pissed me off.

I decided to clarify the question. "You mean, sir, the people who abducted me, drugged me, beat me, and held me incommunicado in solitary confinement for so long I didn't know the date or time of day? You want to know the reasons I believed the people who treated me like *that* had murderous intentions, *sir*?"

Assistant US Attorney Sorensen glowered. So I blasted out my reasons in one profanity-laden salvo.

Because I heard panic in Philippa Flynn's screams, in her message saying they were gonna kill her, and I was shit-scared enough to believe her. Because I guessed what the fucking helo list was even before we overheard the guards out on the levee. Because the assholes who made sure I never saw anything suddenly didn't care what shit I saw out on the levee. Because I witnessed those guards kill people when they didn't have to and then get off on it, and I believed I'd be next, that's fucking why.

I might've been yelling by the time I finished.

The conference room lights I'd hardly noticed before had grown blindingly bright; the room remained silent for an inordinately long time after I finally shut up. Just about when it seemed too many seconds had ticked by, I heard Philippa Flynn, her voice low and dire, talking way too fast. I heard her fear, her effort not to panic as she faced her death.

Then someone said thank you and called me Ms. Gwynmorgan. After which Philippa Flynn said, "Jamie, I've been abducted and I believe I'm going to be killed."

And I realized—omigod, Philippa Flynn's talking to *me*. So I asked her, "Where are you?"

But it was Del who answered, her voice coming from the seat beside me, her hand on my shoulder. For a second, three seconds, longer, oh god for too much longer the rusted sweating steel box snaked into Del's real, coiled around it, through it. Both of them alive, claiming me, both at once.

Yeah, entangled again.

And for a second, three seconds, longer, spacetime took yet another twirl and I was back in that Rhode Island lockup, in that instant when I realize the crazed woman I'm confined with in this tiny, unescapable cell is already moving, already about to twist my head right off, and she's got that extra half-step on me she needs because I let myself become too distracted by Philippa Flynn's brave fear.

The crazy woman has me by the neck, slams my head into the cell's concrete wall, squeezes off my airway. I'm suffocating, my neck is being wrenched too hard, too far. I am about to die and I am helpless. It is happening, it is as real as Del's voice coming from the seat beside me, her hand on my shoulder...

So much for normal.

CHAPTER NINETEEN

Single point of failure

AF252.
Wednesday, November 11.
15:15 hours.

Got a note from Magenau this morning. Handwritten, came by snail mail.

She's gone. To Uruguay, I assume, though she didn't say.

Thus endeth, well, something. Certainly the best of the data analysis, pattern discovery, and insight that moved this Camp Null/DTQ bullshit along so fast.

It was Magenau who matched up most of the DTQ detainee ID numbers with the names of actual human beings—no small feat. (Even now, four of those eleven missing detainees not on the Camp Null helo list remain unnamed.)

It was Magenau who sniffed out the court-admissible evidence that ties no fewer than twenty-three private sector companies to almost two-thirds of the disappearances and assaults executed by DTQ contractors—some going back seven years to when Domestic Threat Quarantine was Buck Ayars's newborn pet.

And it's Magenau who connected the dots between one of the eleven missing detainees and that private hospital in Puerto Rico. "Part dumb shit luck and part slog," she called it.

Dumb shit luck because, more than a year ago, rampant billing fraud at the hospital attracted a surprise inspection that generated a report which included, probably accidentally, appendices full of minute patient detail just waiting to be unearthed by a Magenau data dig.

The slog part involved a two-step. First, despite all eleven detainees' medical records vanishing as completely and mysteriously as the detainees themselves, Magenau finally found an old, overlooked DNA sample from Detainee 2104 (not Philippa Flynn, which is some good news).

Then, only last Thursday, she discovered those same Detainee 2104 DNA markers buried in one of the appendices of that inspection report about the private hospital in Puerto Rico. "Part of the record of an organ transplant surgery in which Detainee 2104 was the donor," she'd told us. Curiously, the organ recipient's identity seems to be lost in a blur of data errors.

Creepy to think about, since the medical data of several DTQ289 survivors—including me—also seems to have been messed with, like somebody tried to obliterate our records in the various databases where they reside. Detainee 2104 sure as hell makes me wonder why.

Plenty more to this story, which Magenau thinks will scale into Chapter Two of the DTQ epic. Her words, "Chapter Two," and "scale" as a verb, as in *balloon*, or maybe *explode*.

Meanwhile, Chapter One is pretty much over. And Magenau is, as she said, "outta here."

Ah well. Not bad for a hundred days' work.

Already some of the largest companies in the country have issued mincingly vague acknowledgment of employee "violations." One CEO after another has sworn he knew nothing. And good luck proving otherwise, thanks to LDL. No question that, done right, Let's Discuss Live can keep a pooh-bah out of prison.

Did I mention how I said weeks ago it would fucking go down like this? *Exactly* like this?

Anyway, Magenau left me a good-bye gift—a link that onioned to a secret super-encrypted site just for me, set up to make me thrice-prove who I am before it would open. When it did open, I found the information she'd amassed in answer to the only question I really care about: Who used DTQ to go after Del?

Four names. See below.

Copy and save what you want. Site will automatically be removed and ex-wiped upon your exit.

I skipped over Magenau's final little lecture about the dangers of proximity to the rich and skimmed for the four names she promised.

As you'll see, only one of these people currently serves in a government post—

Just one? Seriously?

Buck Ayars, who is the least of your worries.

I gawked at the screen as a white-noise roar filled my head, squeezed the bridge of my nose. Where the hell was Upton Ford? C'mon, Magenau, where's the fracking president, for chrissake?

Made myself *bree-ee-eathe* and scroll on.

So okay, I expected to see Buck Ayars on the list. The Secretary of the Department of Homeland Security who conceived and deployed an illegal undisclosed detention program that killed more than a hundred people over two presidents' administrations, a guy who may yet harbor hopes of snaring the presidency for himself the next time around, in five years—he damn well deserves the number-one slot.

But the second name—Rafael Vicario—took me by surprise. Springer once called him "Machiavellian as hell." He avoided federal prison for his role in the attempted coup in Cuba twelve years ago by betraying a gilded selection of his Pentagon friends and surrendering a minor slice of his sleazily acquired fortune as well as his law license and his reputation.

He kept plenty, though. Enough to be an eager if unofficial greaser of palms the whole time. As has his son, Julius, whom I encountered once or twice back when I worked for Burton Neal and who triggered the pernicious events that backfired and ricocheted into the Artemisia Center and the resulting design competition that resurrected my dead-on-arrival career (oh the pickling irony).

So although Rafael Vicario isn't supposed to have any kind of clout these days, Magenau contends that he "owns" both Upton Ford and the president and has deep hooks into Buck Ayars, too. Clearly assembled from data hacks (which I'd wager Lynn knows nothing about), Magenau's evidence trove reveals a Vicario who harbors dreams of an Ayars presidency during which he will at last fully restore himself to his former grandeur.

I was thinking about how Rafael Vicario might be a pretty good candidate for invisible king—until I scrolled down to the last two names on Magenau's list and suffered the mental equivalent of cardiac arrest.

Warrick van Gelderen, CEO, Georgica Corporation.

Marvin Este Malik, Chairman of the Board, MetraGlobal Bank.

Of course.

God knows how long I stared at that screen.

Of fucking *course*.

Caprice has been screaming it at me since AF1—using Philippa Flynn's voice. "Senior assistant vice president of investment risk management at MetraGlobal Bank in New York...a Georgica

Corporation audit board meeting...been abducted...going to be killed..." All uttered into a device bearing MetraGlobal Bank's logo. The same device I'm talking to right now.

Must be five years since the only time I ever saw either one of them. They were together when Del and I encountered them right after Georgica lost out to the Wilderness Web Coalition in that Ninth Circuit eminent domain appeal.

And god, they were nasty. While Marvin Este Malik smirked, muttered, his greedy gaze undressing Del, Warrick van Gelderen attacked her with a pit bull snarl that made it clear he'd rather slap her than form words to shout at her.

I immediately despised van Gelderen not only for his bullying but for assuming he had a right not merely to denigrate Del but also to brazenly menace her the way he did. I despised him for the way he used his voice, his scowl, his body to barge through several layers of interpersonal distance to *declare!* all manner of crap four inches from Del's face.

I remember contemplating his testicles when he got close to her like that. The angle and force of my kick. I remember shifting my weight, preparing. One more inch, asshole. Just one more.

Maybe he sensed me doing that. But it was Del, coolly riveting in black silk and unflappable feline grace, who held me back as she stared right at him, amused, never raising her voice. Vir triumphalis, memento mori.

Certainly Vir Triumphalis Junior and Senior detest Adele Sabellius. If someone had asked me which of them was likelier to go after her, I'd have pointed to van Gelderen.

After all, Georgica Corporation got its ass wiped by the Worldwide Web Coalition in court. Not only that, Magenau has excavated uncountable volumes of backup communications data that irrefutably link DTQ and Georgica Corporation.

Among the threads of tactical commo between DTQ staff and contractors and lower-level Georgica employees, one message thread in particular strengthens the case against Georgica. When the DTQ contractor grabbed me by mistake, word of this blunder traveled under its own subject header—Error61141 Resolution. The resulting thread bears timestamps that shadow such milestones in my abduction as getting hustled from one vehicle to another and arrivals at and departures from several intermediate detention facilities.

Then there's the LDL-laced directives and responses carrying occasional oblique references to the tactical stuff which traveled to and from Georgica's upper echelons. Legal careers will be made arguing how many oblique references to abduction and murder dance on the head of the pin labeled Beyond Reasonable Doubt.

Even worse for Georgica, the company dude in whose in-box these various message threads intersected—LDLs from above, the more incriminating tactical commo from below—has snitched on his bosses.

This guy testified that, in a meeting, van Gelderen described mediating Georgica's cooperation with the Department of Homeland Security "at the highest levels" and explicitly approved "active collaborative sponsor involvement in the DTQ pre-pilot test-bed."

Of course, van Gelderen denies this, as do all the others present at the meeting in question. So it's a he said–he said, and the guy in the email crosshairs—who's also Georgica's now-disgraced and fired chief security officer—has lost, has been anointed Georgica's fall guy, and soon will be arrested. Meanwhile, all those layers of LDL insulate van Gelderen, so he's free and clear, where he will stay.

But understand, Magenau wrote, *van Gelderen is just a pit bull doing his master's bidding.*

She believes Marvin Este Malik is the dude in charge—of son-in-law van Gelderen, of Raphael Vicario, of Buck Ayars. Of the whole frackin' planet, it seems. And therefore Marvin Este Malik either commissioned or, at the least, signed off on Del's (failed) abduction.

In Magenau's view, Ayars and Vicario hate the Wilderness Web Coalition because it impedes their political ambitions and financial returns, and van Gelderen hates it for successfully demanding more ecologically responsible Georgica operations and planning. But Malik's hatred has tipped into something fanatical. Marvin Este Malik obsessively rejects the Wilderness Web Coalition's right to exist and believes his efforts to destroy it by whatever means he can muster are entirely legitimate.

To illustrate, Magenau included a secretly recorded video of Malik at an informal, very private Lakeside Talk during which information and opinion not available to the public gets shared among select members of the king's court. (Well, okay, Magenau didn't call it the king's court, but I've double-checked the names of the people she identified in the video, and that's damn well what it was.)

In what turns out to be a rare recording of a man who relishes secrecy and privacy, Malik didn't outright say he aided and abetted DTQ, but he sure as hell cheered it on in principle, asserting that anyone who seriously prioritizes environmental issues is a terrorist and we all know what should happen to terrorists. He sounded a lot like Warrick van Gelderen did five years ago when he was bloviating at Del.

Ah, but has Magenau *shown* that Ayars and Vicario and van Gelderen and Malik used DTQ to go after Del? Ayars may be a slam dunk, but what about these other three guys?

To be clear, I don't expect Justice. I don't even expect justice, which takes generations. What I want in this my only life, right the fuck now, is to fucking *know* who our enemies are.

Magenau's secret site riffed on too-familiar caveat. *The evidence is circumstantial. A fast-talking lawyer, a pinch of perjury, and presto! Not guilty.*

Circumstantial, yeah. But this jury—the one I behold in the mirror—can damn well believe those two sore loser pricks I saw years ago trying to bully Del decided to take a crack at disappearing her. And maybe disappeared Leta Creel, too—to put a crimp in that same eminent domain case van Gelderen screeched at Del about. Hell, maybe Senior Assistant Vice President of Investment Risk Management Philippa Flynn learned too much at that Georgica Corporation audit board meeting and one of them disappeared her, too.

Whatever they've actually done, they've gotten away with it. Viri Triumphalis.

At least they're all thoroughly off balance. Fingers are pointing, Congresspeople are publicly shouting at each other and at cabinet secretaries and at their CEO buddies. The pace of resignations has picked up.

So far, van Gelderen has glowered through two appearances before media microphones and cameras claiming ignorance, like all the others, having delegated day-to-day operational responsibility to focus on strategic concerns, blah blah.

Meanwhile, all of DTQ's former "collaborative partners" are making large, splashy donations to relevant charities. The ACLU perhaps. Or the Wilderness Web Coalition. Georgica Corporation has contributed generously to both.

It'll play out like this for months to come, probably for years in some courtroom or other, but it's fucking finished.

So okay. I know who tried to grab Del. I know why. I know they've gotten away with it. No doubt they'll want to try again, but abducting Del has never presented higher risk or lower benefit.

So okay.

I was just about to exhale when I scrolled into one more missive on Magenau's secret site:

A final thought, Gwynmorgan, before I ghost.

All signs point to you getting nabbed by mistake. It really was supposed to be Del. But don't forget—at some juncture they decided to keep you. Records show that, starting about a year ago, most of us at Camp Null, including you, were given a series of medical tests consistent with donor-recipient organ matching.

We don't know who sought these tests. Maybe one person or group, maybe several. But based on what we've learned about Detainee 2104, I believe it's plausible that at least some of us still alive may have been targeted for organ donorship.

If investigated, this possibility will probably turn up a whole new set of crimes and culprits. Your senator promises such an investigation is under way, but take it from me, it'll be a while before that special prosecutor finds squat.

Then, on a line all its own in large letters, I read

So watch your back

❖

AF257.
Monday, November 16.
11:15 hours.

At least Del is safe from Malik and van Gelderen. For now. Kind of.

"Yeah," Lynn said over the weekend when she described the deal that's gone down this week. "It's never enough. But it's a hell of a lot more than they wanted to relinquish."

I nodded, smiled, and silently debated whether "it" constitutes a Hobson's choice or a Morton's fork. Gotta admit, though, Lynn achieved the four goals that were almost the first thing I heard about when I got home—protect the DTQ detainees, blow up the DTQ and DTAN programs, expose the corruption that enabled them, change the rules so that at least this road to hell is blocked off. For now. Kind of.

"We can *prove* relatively little," Lynn explained last Saturday.

"But we subpoenaed people like Ayars and Ford and their good friends Rafael Vicario and Warrick van Gelderen to testify further. And we sent word that our questions would become increasingly antagonistic, that we'd do our best to corner them into pleading the Fifth just before having to explain themselves to the special prosecutor and his grand jury."

I noticed how she never mentioned Marvin Este Malik. Nope, she said when I asked about him, he's too well-insulated; having a son-in-law who runs a company caught in the DTQ morass just doesn't count, no matter how dirty the dude's hands really are.

The consolation prize: Lynn's bill rolled through both chambers like a snowball down a mountainside. Hardly anyone voted against it, and yesterday the president signed it into law.

"It's legislation all those guys would normally do *anything* to eviscerate—" Lynn's smile remained understated, though she let her satisfaction show. "But we got it through intact. As thorough a clean-out of DHS and Justice as we'll see in our lifetimes."

Has a few nice touches, too, assuming it's actually enforced. Some semi-decent cover for whistle-blowers. Makes Classified Administrative Detention genuinely rare again and highly regulated and monitored. All sifting of transmitted data requires a warrant reviewed and signed by, count 'em, two separate National Security Court judges. The whole section of DHS where DTQ and DTAN were squirreled away is gone. The Congressional Office of Special Investigations gets a lot more clout, too, including an oversight division.

"And the president won't be reelected," Lynn predicted. "He thinks he can recover because the indictments will stay low-level and he's been told that grand jury's under control." She rubbed her hands together and singsonged. "But he's been told wro-ong. So Upton Ford will end up bitch-slapped out of Washington. And several Friends of Buck as well as Ayars himself will be indicted."

But not Rafael Vicario or that slimeball Warrick van Gelderen. I confess I regret not taking the chance when I had it to kick van Gelderen's nuts into his throat...

"The president's attempt to shield Ayars was a serious miscalculation," Lynn was saying as I drifted back from contemplating that kick. "A single point of failure that'll cascade all the way into *next* November."

Next fucking November.

I wonder if I'll be past this shit by next fucking November. If the goddamn depositions will be done with by next fucking November.

Because somehow I just can't pull off what Lynn has, what Del has, which is to turn everything that's happened over the last two years into part of their mission.

And hell, maybe that's the problem. I don't have a mission. Just a life I'd like to lead in anonymous peace.

❖

AF264.
Monday, November 23.
23:40 hours.

Like anything, everything Camp Null, I should put Audy away and forget her, but I still prefer to keep her close, on a cord around my neck, ready to talk to soft and quiet, easy to check if I want, when I need to. Cuz, goddamn, there are these moments when I lose my bearings. Not that I forget; I just don't trust what I remember.

Del notices, of course. I see her eyes flick to the cord just visible under my shirt, I see her try to mask her—what? Concern, maybe. Worry.

For Del's sake more than mine, sometimes I leave Audy in the drawer. But sometimes—well, okay, most times—I need to keep her closer than that. Around-my-neck close. Makes finding her in the dark easier. Like when a nightmare wakes me and I slip out to the living room with her to talk about it. The good news is that, more and more, I can curl up holding Audy and do nothing more than listen to an earlier entry. I have a few that help me *bree-ee-eathe*.

Or sometimes I listen to nothing at all and merely hand-charge her, reminding myself I have her close. Just in case.

Cuz the nightmares have gotten worse lately. More frequent. Del says it's the stress of job hunting. Says don't worry about going back to work yet.

And I say what about the bills? What if the only work I can get is in Timbuk-fuckin'-tu since nobody around here will touch me with an invar staff? And she says don't be silly, you *will* get work, and besides we're doing okay, and I thump the goddamn cane I still need to lean on and say, hey, *you're* doing okay but I'm doing shit, I feel like a kept woman.

And she smiles, oh god she smiles *that* smile and slinks up to me where I'm busy ranting in the middle of the living room and makes contact from our thighs to our hips to our breasts, and her soft scent engulfs me, and her breath heats my ear as she whispers, "Work on your portfolio, my sweet—starting tomorrow."

Then she kisses my neck and I'm instantly molten and her hand slides up my suddenly shivering left thigh. "Right now—" She tugs at my jeans crotch seam as she steps backward toward the bedroom. "You're needed—" Another tug, another step. "Else. Where." Two tugs, two steps, lots of kisses.

Moving backward, by proprioception alone she undulates us scissor-legged to the bed, our eyes fluttering open only briefly to glimpse each other as my kisses follow hers, and she's laughing and the music of her, the exquisite, zealous touch of her fill me until I burst with orgasm and moans and laughter and then—

Then she surrenders to me very, *very* slowly.

God, how I love remembering that.

❖

AF306.
Monday, January 4.
01:13 hours.

A while back, Del said I should add something fresh to my portfolio, find a competition or a request-for-proposal and submit a design that becomes my most recent work sample, so it's obvious I'm up to speed, ready to roll.

Since I decided to keep it local, I had to root around some to turn up a small project with a doable proposal submission deadline. I put together the design concept and then, for a couple of reasons, I think, I've spent way too much time honing and revising.

One reason: even though my submission's a long shot, the work of it is keenly satisfying, steadying—a kind of immersive training in normal. I'm having fun.

The other reason for what amounts to stalling: I'm not sure how to craft the submission's front end—the part where I have to sell the prospective client on why they should award their project to me.

So okay, decision time: Who am I?

That wandering structural design engineer with an odd name? Oh yeah, one of those terror detention people who slicked a get-out-of-jail-free card from all that publicity—but hold on, where there's smoke, right? No wonder some lawyer or other is always including her on a list of "persons of interest we shall be rigorously deposing." No wonder she can't find a job.

Or do I present myself as a company? A sole proprietorship, to be sure, but a company that might have contractors or even employees, not to mention clients. JG Design|Engineering LLC, perhaps.

I picked door number two. As of last week, JG Design|Engineering LLC is an actual entity in the world. As of this morning it has—I have—professional liability insurance (which ain't cheap; if I ever get a project, I'll be lucky if the fee covers the premium). And as of three days from now, JG Design|Engineering LLC will have made its first submission.

I wonder how much Del understood about what would happen when I chose a project to chew on. Often of late I've slept the night through. Almost every day I go outside for a walk and recently even a run. In the last week I've ventured down to Trapelo Road with its stores and traffic and furtive avarice—and returned intact, without my nerves flagellated.

Today I even left my pistol at home, went for a run unarmed, and here I am, back again unaccosted.

❖

AF331.
Friday, January 29.
02:40 hours.

Haven't seen any response to that RFP submission yet, but I survived another deposition and actually got a callback on a job I applied for a while ago.

This morning I donned a monkey suit (the navy one with drapey pants and a short jacket that Del says makes me memorably leggy) and went through a whole battery of interviews with what turns out to be a reasonably impressive design-build firm in Boston. I was there for four hours and, best I can tell, I did pretty well.

"So what's bothering you?" Del asked.

I told her I'd be surprised if they offered me the job.

Her eyes shadowed for a few seconds. "Uh-uh." She started to put down her tablet and was about to move closer. "Something else is bugging you."

Nope. Not ready yet. I quick-marched from the living room through the dining room to the kitchen, putting the kitchen counter peninsula between us. Del ambled after me to alight on one of the bar stools, where she watched me, waiting.

So I shrugged.

"Oh, I see," she said after a couple more seconds. "You don't *want* this job you say is the perfect job for you."

I shrugged again and let my eyes follow the bare branches of the apple trees outside the kitchen window. Easier than looking at her while she undressed my catatonic psyche.

"Too much power handed over to too many people too often and for too long, huh?" she offered, her tone laced with just the right amount of I-know-the-feeling.

"I should want it, but I don't," I told the apple trees as twilight darkened them. At the far right edge of my vision, Del didn't move. I could tell she was staring at me.

She said, "It's okay with me if you, uh, take the lower offer from JG Design|Engineering LLC," and winked when she caught my eye.

"Del," I said, "we'll be frackin' broke. We'll end up in all kinds of debt—"

She shook her head. "We'll be fine."

And right then I knew. Not the specifics. Just that there was something she hadn't told me yet, a something that changes the whole damn picture. "What?" I demanded.

"We're okay financially, Jamie."

She had moved round the counter and closed in, gently turning me toward her. Here it comes, I thought.

"Check this out." She handed me her tablet, which displayed our updated household financials—balance sheet, cash flow, income statement.

Aaand *wait* a minute. "This shows your income as almost twice what it was two years ago." I squinted at the screen. "Doesn't it?"

"My newest course is doing well, but the bump comes from speeches mostly—booked through next autumn, and more coming in every month," she answered.

Events. In public. Where people can hurt her. I tried not to scowl. Del soldiered on. "Well-paid speeches to people who can afford it. Seems I'm in demand these days." She nudged my arm. "Certainly an excellent per-hour rate, plus a spiel I'm pretty smooth at delivering now. And I don't have to pander."

I refused to be placated. "Who's paying for your security?"

She pointed to a line item on the spreadsheet. "All expensed—yes, realistically—along with travel. See?"

Damn. She'd kept her promise about boosting security.

"You need time, baby," Del said to me then, almost whispering, her fingers tracing my hairline, her gaze calming the churn at the center of me. "God knows, I owe you that."

I saw tears in her eyes just before my own tears made everything go bright and doubled and wet.

I said, "I'm sorry."

She said, "Me too." We hugged, held on to each other for a long, long while. And I realized I'd been resenting the whole time, from the day I was grabbed on Thomas Street to that very moment. Resenting how the life I had was gone, and give it back, dammit! That was mine! *My* life. Give it the fuck *back*!

As I hugged her, I gave up *before*. Like Alby and Awa and Luce and Biz and Mary and Philippa Flynn and so many others, my *before* life is dead.

But unlike Alby and Awa and Luce and Biz and Mary and Philippa Flynn and so many others, I get a new life. A new life with Del in it, Del who still loves me, still wants me.

So okay, I've decided. JG Design|Engineering LLC it is.

For real.

❖

AF393.
Thursday, March 31.
16:50 hours.

About six weeks ago, the public media channel did a special on government transparency—after all, it's presidential election season— that included a segment on DTQ and Camp Null and mentioning me while they ran video from years ago of me in dress blues at that White House medal ceremony.

Maybe two weeks later, JG Design|Engineering LLC acquired its first client—a mid-size Boston design/engineer/build firm seeking help with classic structural engineering shitwork. Coincidence? Or pity work from someone who remembers me from my days with Burton Neal? Either way, it's work and I'll take it.

This last Monday, I picked up client number two, also a mid-size design/engineer/build firm, but this one's in Providence. Theirs is a more interesting project—well, a small portion of a more interesting project on which I'll be busting hump in hopes of attracting larger-scope work in the future.

Meanwhile, one RFP response remains in the wind, though I'm not hopeful. Did I mention my first two submissions didn't make the initial cut?

So, two clients. Almost like a real company. Too bad JG Design|Engineering LLC brings in less than sixty percent of a living. Add on my monthly pension from that medal and I'm a thirty percent kept woman.

Del says don't be discouraged.

Yeah. Well. Besides needing to pay my share of the bills, *I need to work*. I need to do design and engineering to keep that Camp Null shit from leading a parade of flashbacks where one haunt bleeds into another and once it gets going I can't stop it unless I physically exhaust myself to the point where I'm in significant pain.

Or I can go to Del for help.

But—

It's not just that Del's ridiculously busy and often out of the house for extended stretches during the day—even if she's just in the space we've made over the garage so she can do meetings there instead of in the office in our second bedroom, which she has generously declared the global headquarters of JG Design|Engineering LLC.

There's also the risk of addiction. I'm in danger of becoming hooked on her help, simply cuddling forever into a state of being cared for by Del. She's in danger of letting me, too. And god, I'm so desperately tempted, not only because my demons retreat in her presence but also because time spent helping me limits her exposure to the Wilderness Web Coalition's enemies.

Work is how I behave myself. So okay, I find a couple more RFPs, spend way too much time on my proposal submissions.

And life goes on. Del's real goes on.

❖

AF406.
Wednesday, April 20.
22:35 hours.

The nor'easter that's been drenching us for the last four days has at last rolled out to sea. Tomorrow I'll run outside—a different route. Down Thomas Street all the way to Clark Street, right past where I was grabbed. And nothing will happen, by god. *Nothing.*

CHAPTER TWENTY

Rabbit hole

AF439.
Monday, May 23.
03:20 hours.

Maddie Small has surfaced again. And in a really roundabout way, thanks to some help from Magenau, who onioned her encrypted voice message to my usual comlink. No Null-link anymore for Maddie Small; she's convinced it's compromised. But she says she has something she needs to tell me. Something she heard.

"She sounded frantic when I talked with her," Magenau said. "Almost out of control."

So I've sent messages every which way I can think of, but I have yet to make contact.

AF456.
Thursday, June 9.
10:45 hours.

Just took a facecall from a guy named Paul Norman, who runs a design-build firm in New York City called arkIngenium.

His crew's been hired by the Armstrong Institute to design and build a medical education research and conference center that'll occupy about half of a block in Harlem. He wants to discuss involving me in the project design; seems somebody on the Institute's board of directors whose name I didn't recognize likes the look of the Artemisia Center in Boston.

Based on Norman's description, I'd say this is what Burton Neal used to euphemistically call a "personality heavy" project; our job, he'd say, is to identify the architectural glitter and baubles that best flaunt the ego behind the largest donation.

I learned a lot from Burton about how to play this game, and I'm sure as hell in no position to be picky, so play it I will if I get the chance. Gotta say, though, it all feels, I dunno, sort of dissonant.

I mean, hell, I'm an extremely odd choice. I don't have a whole lot of experience leading design of high-profile projects like this one seems to be. Although I worked on taller structures back in the day with Burton and I'm certainly professionally qualified, my own designs have never exceeded nine stories. And while I like to think my stuff is interesting, it's always tended more toward spirals than spires.

Curious, then, the way Norman said, "Given your design expertise, I'm not sure we'll need to bother with an architect for this—if things work out."

So okay, maybe it's another pity job. Guess I'm at the point where I need the charity of pity jobs, because Norman's certainly the best damn prospect I've had thus far.

I've agreed to be in Manhattan next Monday morning for a meeting with Norman and some people from the Armstrong Institute, and all on arkIngenium's tab. I admit, the project sounds interesting, and even if it *is* the result of charity, I'm kind of excited.

Anyway, regardless of the outcome, while I'm there I'll have a chance to take a fleshtime crack at tracking down Maddie Small so I can finally find out what's wrong.

❖

AF464.
Friday, June 17.
14:20 hours.

After one last meeting this morning, I'm finally almost home from New York.

Bree-ee-eathe…

While I was on the train, I looked up the definition of *maze*: A complex system or network of intercommunicating paths or passages that causes bewilderment, confusion, or perplexity.

I thought I'd be in Manhattan for a day, two if things worked out. I ended up there all week and, yes, I've come away bewildered, confused, and perplexed. At least now that I'm in a car driving and alone, I can talk out loud about my week in the maze, try to untangle the experience some before I get back to Birch Lane and lay it all out for Del.

So okay.

I like Paul Norman. And arkIngenium. Overall, the Armstrong Institute people are okay, too, though I wouldn't mind if a couple of the minor players fell off the planet. The big cheese donor "wishes to remain anonymous," but I learned he's anted up the land and the funds for constructing, outfitting, staffing, and generously endowing the Institute's new research lab and conference center. Small nations live on less.

Before I went down there, I had a long what-if talk with Del and followed her advice meticulously. Even so, I doubt it made any difference.

Seems like somebody with clout had already decided. By lunchtime on Monday, I'd been hired to propose a design. Not only are they paying me an in-your-dreams day rate to do it, they say they're open to any design that addresses their needs and complements the adjoining building.

When I told Del, she called this arrangement unusual but not unheard of. It has, however, made me very curious about who, *really*, decided to hire JG Design|Engineering LLC.

Spent the next three days alternating between meetings with the facility's prospective users and other stakeholders, reviewing specs and code issues, doing site visits, and learning nothing about who picked me for this project. All the while, I was leaving messages for Maddie Small. Here's my number, here's where I'm staying, call me, call me. But Maddie Small remained silent.

Until last night. Even then she was silent. What she did was *appear*. Out of fucking nowhere, and right on the street, too. Scared the bejeezus out of me.

I'd declined a ride, opting to hoof the five blocks from the site back to my hotel so I could gauge the walk to the nearest subway stop two blocks away. As I reached 127th Street, I'd briefly pulled off my eyewraps and then made the mistake of glancing rightward up the street and directly into the fierce glare of a late afternoon sun that seemed to be lying in wait. So I was pretty much sunblind when Maddie Small made her move a few seconds after I passed through the sun's glare into the shadow of the building on the far corner.

Suddenly, she was marching close on my right as I walked a

couple feet from the railing of the subway stairs nestled against the building, my eyes still adapting to the shift from dazzle to shadow. Without a word, she crooked her arm through mine so she could swing me into a hard U-turn down the subway stairs while I swore at her and tried to calm my rabid heartbeat.

Thus began what might rank as one of the strangest nights of my post–Marine Corps life.

Starting with, "Kill your locates an' put this on."

In the brief cam-free spacetime of our descent to the station's mezzanine, Maddie Small handed me a wide-brimmed fedora with a prepaid MetroCard slipped into its band.

So okay, we're camdodging. As I clicked off my comlink and traded my khaki boonie hat for her smooth black felt, Maddie Small donned an even wider-brimmed floppy thing she pulled from a small backpack that she deftly diddled into a crossbody messenger bag before we entered the mezzanine cams' purview.

"Keep your tail tight an' close," she murmured. "Gotta do this faster'n usual." She put ten feet and several people between us as we approached the turnstiles.

So okay, I pretend I don't know her as I pass by the cams every-fucking-where overwatching all the place-job people heading home at the same time.

I casually zigged when Maddie Small zagged, moved if she halted, paused while she moved. She led me to the station's lowest level and along the eastmost southbound platform, an arcing ribbon of an island flanked by tracks on both sides, and soon enough we stood about three feet apart, ignoring each other at the platform's north end near a white-tiled back wall embedded with a doorway blocked by a thick, black-painted steel plate that included a keylock but no knob. Two cams recorded us.

Within a couple of minutes, a train rumbled and squealed out of one of the pitch-dark tunnels behind us and slowed into position alongside the platform. As most everyone, including me, began to cluster toward its doors, all the lights in the station flickered off for a two-count.

That's when Maddie Small yanked me from the platform through that blocked doorway, which had suddenly opened. In the tiny slice of time before the lights came back on, she even managed to swing the door mostly shut again. I glimpsed a slab of rough, sooty concrete wall before she firmed the door closed and I stood in abject darkness.

"Spectacular timing, Maddie Small," I said, clicking up my

eyewraps' thermal infrared vision, which I'd earlier flipped to manual mode to save battery power. No big deal typically, but the room had two other doors on two other walls and it all looked fucking identical. I was already hopelessly turned around.

"Couldn't decide if you were being followed," Maddie Small explained. "Not good to hang around out there if you were."

"*You* flicked the lights?" I asked, incredulous.

"Teddy does that," she said as though she was describing the parsing of daily household duties. "I tap on the door to let him know I'm ready an' how quick, then he whacks the lights an' burps the cams. Re-upping takes the cams another six seconds after the lights come back. So we get about eight seconds to evaporate." She signaled me to follow her. "C'mon, we're gonna catch up with him now."

Teddy? I didn't say anything, but Maddie Small read my hesitation. "Perez, yeah." She opened one of the doors and we entered a second room, then repeated this process twice more as she confided, "He's okay. Needs to be needed. Can't do real sex, just a little cuddlin' an' pettin' sometimes. Cuzza what happened there, y'know? 'Tween you an' me, I kinda like it this way. So far it's workin' out for us."

I nodded, sufficiently freaked by the succession of dismal concrete rooms and the smell—mold and some kind of industrial oil—that I found talking tough. My questions about how Perez "burped" the subway station cams were soon eclipsed by *How the* hell *can anybody who survived Camp Null's cells hang out in places like* this*?*

Then I heard Perez's voice. A second later, he came into view. When he shook my hand in the big slappy way some men like, for once I appreciated the gesture. It snapped me out of something that I have to admit now, in hindsight, edged damn close to panic.

"Great places down here," he said heartily. "No cams, no comms, hardly any lights. An' fuh*gedd* about maps. Easy t' get almost anywhere. 'Specially now we got thermal." He tapped his eyewraps.

We didn't linger.

"Got somethin' you need to see," Maddie Small said over her shoulder as I followed her.

"An' hear," Perez added from behind me.

When I asked what, they said they weren't sure about much, but it "seems like maybe we mighta" found out something about Philippa Flynn.

"An' we gotta *show* you, cuz if we only told you, you wouldn't fuckin' believe it," Maddie Small insisted. "We made a video, stashed it at our new place cuz our old place is just too damn dangerous to live in right now."

She didn't mask her disappointment, so I figured she meant the place where the DTQ289 Fund had set her up. But I was wrong.

She meant the Freedom Tunnel. "Not far," she said. "An' we stay under the whole way."

She meant underground.

I admit it. I hesitated. Even with my eyewraps' thermal infrared vision, I am no longer entirely rational in dark, confined spaces, and these two wanted me to stay the fuck down there.

But Maddie Small said her maybe-mighta involved Philippa Flynn.

So okay, I agreed to gird and go with them.

"Goal is to not get killed or caught," Maddie Small said as we set out. "So be ready to keep up if me an' Teddy start runnin' like hell. Means we're aware of someone else down here we prefer to avoid. An' see there? Electrified third rail, so no touchy. Also, you need to move your ass when a train's comin'." She pointed to various get-outta-the-way spots as we walked.

"Worst case," she added much *much* too casually, "you'll have to stand between two third rails an' a couple pillars while trains go by on either side of you. Stay still an' you'll come out in one piece, but you'll be seen, which would be unfortunate."

The unfortunate didn't happen, thank god, and after more than an hour of alternately walking or jogging alongside the tracks and ducking into oddly placed recesses, Maddie Small and Teddy Perez brought me to what they kept calling the Summer Place.

I'm endowed with a pretty decent sense of direction, but I have no notion where the hell I ended up (other than in some unused part of the New York City subway system), nor would I ever be able to find it without their help. All I can say is that the Summer Place is located back-of-house somewhere that's at least a hundred years old and was lost to history long ago.

It's an abandoned service room, eight by maybe fifteen gray and grungy feet. Maddie Small said she'd "inherited" it and its accoutrements, including a woodplank platform with an almost clean double-size mattress topped with sleeping bags. A couple of lights, a hot plate, and a tiny half-refrigerator run off hacked electric power, as does an old flat-screen receiver/media player that's also spliced into hacked internet service. Shelves on one wall hold utensils, bottles of water and juice, cans and plastic containers of food, bags of clothes.

As we sat on the mattress snacking on potato chips and beef jerky and cold root beer, Maddie Small glanced around and said, "Not bad, huh?" She took a long swig of root beer. "Only place right now where I feel even a little safe."

And then she told me why.

She'd accepted the DTQ289 Fund charity as soon as it was offered because she didn't have a choice. She needed time and medical care to heal. But as her hands recovered, so did her restlessness, and soon she was renting out the DTQ289 Fund digs to a prostitute friend while she returned to her Real Home in the Freedom Tunnel not far from 107th Street.

"Wait," I said. "Wasn't that where you were grabbed?"

"Yep." Her slow nod almost hypnotized me. "Went back to the scene of their crime."

"Fuck, why?"

"Need to know who to avoid," she claimed.

I believed her for one of those New York minutes, and then I didn't. But I played along. "So who do you have to avoid?"

Silence. Maddie Small was listening while her eyes skittered around the room. Jeezus, I thought, she's even more paranoid than I am.

"I think we're beyond any eavesdroppers," I said.

"You never fuckin' know," Maddie Small retorted. "That's why we keep movin' around. When we're done here, me an' Teddy'll be gettin' outta Manhattan for a while."

Whereupon she produced a datacoin, seemingly out of thin air like a magician, which she inserted in her media player. "This'll be your copy, Jamie Gwynmorgan—to use how you want, when you're ready."

She tapped on the media player, and the flat-screen flickered into the jittery, grainy gray-into-black shades of thermographic video. "Dual cams mounted into my eyewraps," Maddie Small noted. I noted that she wasn't alone in the video; Perez followed close behind her.

"First thing you gotta know as you watch this," she said, "is there's such a thing as Prohibition tunnels."

As I'd already begun to learn, underneath New York City many labyrinths twist and twine. More than just subway tunnels. Railroad tunnels. Utility tunnels. Steam tunnels. Sewer tunnels big enough to walk in. Even rivers and canals covered over into tunnels. And, of course, all manner of smuggling tunnels.

One of the many parts of the city with smuggling tunnels is the west side of Manhattan, where even owners of mansions once dug underground passages from their basements down to the banks of the Hudson River. At 107th Street during Prohibition, the banks of the Hudson River stood roughly at the western edge of what's now the West Side Line Tunnel—otherwise known as, yep, the Freedom Tunnel.

As I watched the video, Maddie Small narrated. "I've come across a couple other Prohibition tunnels, but only fragments. *This* one, though—" She tilted her head at the flat-screen. "Damn thing's intact. Goes right up to the mansion on the corner of Riverside Drive an' a Hundred an' Seventh. Right under the fuckin' front steps."

Found by accident last year, she said. "Got disappeared before I had a chance to mess with it. But me an' Teddy got it cleared now."

On the flat-screen, the textures of a rough, dirt-crusted concrete wall and a makeshift rope ladder jerked upward as Maddie Small descended, her gleaming-bright hands occasionally poking into view. At the bottom of the ladder, she clicked on an infrared flashlight and illuminated the dark gray walls of an arched tunnel. Narrow, brick-lined, structurally dubious.

I watched the tunnel intermittently incline upward; next to me, Maddie Small eventually said, "Almost there."

Within seconds, I spotted signs that a pile of rubble had been cleared away; bits of it lined the already cramped space.

"It collapsed?" I asked.

"Yep," Perez said cheerily. "Took us a little time to dig it out. Now for about six feet the underside of Riverside Drive is the ceiling—" He pointed to the screen, where Maddie Small's cams showed what a bottleneck looks like from the inside. "Just about there."

After Maddie Small passed through the bottleneck, the tunnel widened again and angled steeply upward, more a runged ramp than steps. Maddie Small's flashlight clicked off and the screen went very dark, except for the dim outline of a gray rectangle.

Turned out to be an overhead hatch in a flat section of ceiling at the tunnel's foreshortened end. Maddie Small and Perez halted; the only sound I could hear on their video came from their breathing.

Then Perez stepped in front to push the hatch open. Slowly. Carefully. Silently. I found myself wincing; I expected the hatch to squeak and groan when he pushed, but it made no noise at all.

"Took us an hour to open that damn thing the first time," Perez said. "So we oiled it up good."

On the screen, he and Maddie Small were climbing into a small, brick-lined utility room with a barrel ceiling—dusty, damp, empty but for a podge of water and sewer pipes, power and commo conduits. A few feet ahead of them stood a modern steel fire door. Perez turned its knob. Slowly. Carefully. Silently.

"This next room's monitored, but it's a stationary cam aimed at an outside door," Maddie Small commented as we watched the video. "That fire door Teddy's workin' doesn't even have a lock. Why would it? They think the tunnel ends at the collapse that we cleared away."

On the video, the fire door opened to a lighter utility room—a long rectangle of a space. The cam Maddie Small mentioned was visible directly overhead, focused leftward at a door with an ornately grilled frosted window. In the light coming through it, I noticed a solar power inverter, a large circuit breaker panel, cable trays, a geothermal pump box, an unused antique gas furnace, and an assortment of paint cans, lumber and piping scraps, and obsolete optoelectronics.

"Our plan was to, y'know, do a little light liftin'." Maddie Small's tone struck me as conspiratorial rather than confessional. "You'd be amazed what people keep in their basements. We'd already scoped the place, knew to avoid the cam by stayin' tight against the rightside wall to reach the security system control and enter CharlieTann's hack code. It was a Saturday night. Place was supposed to be empty. Easy in, easy out."

Before I could ask what she meant by "CharlieTann's hack code," Maddie Small's taut whisper rasped abruptly from the video. "Shit!" On the screen, she and Perez crouched frozen against the room's rightside wall.

Next to me in the Summer Place, Maddie Small did some explaining. "Just beyond that utility room—" She waved at the screen. "They've set up a wine cellar. After that, the main kitchen's on one side, staff bedrooms and bathroom on the other. Then a laundry room an' a secure storage room."

She held up her hand, a signal to listen, and pointed at the screen again just as muffled voices could be heard on the video. Neither Maddie Small's voice nor Perez's. Male voices—two of them, becoming louder, more distinct.

"Scotch is over there," one said. "Look for the Speyfiddich single malt."

"Christ, he wants scotch?" This voice resonated anxiety. "Last time he wanted scotch—"

"Mmm-hmm." First dude sounded weary. "The blood test today shows the suppression shit they got her on ain't working. And they're telling him more stem cell treatments ain't an option. Looks like she'll have to do the whole fucker all over again."

"Shit. Again?"

"Said he wants to be ready."

"Shit. He got a replacement yet?"

"Oh yeah. Next one on the list. Not as good as Philippa. Only four antigens in common. But beggars can't be choosers."

"Fuck. Another live transplant, then."

"Well, he did say it's nobody we know this time."

"Good. I hated having to take down Philippa. One day I'm laughing it up with her about being Irish, two weeks later I'm capping her just so in the right side of her chest. Was fucking nasty."

The voices began to fade. I strained to make out their words.

"Won't be simple like with Philippa, though, huh? Now that the program's been dusted, I mean."

"Don't sweat it, Fred. He'll put together the plan. Like last time. We just have to follow orders. Easy-fuckin'-peasy. And very lucrative."

And then a door slammed. Silence. After a few more frozen seconds, the video showed Maddie Small and Teddy Perez retreating. Slowly. Carefully. Silently.

None of us in the Summer Place spoke as the retreat on the screen continued, until finally Maddie Small turned to me and said, "Could be Philippa Flynn those guys were talkin' about."

❖

"Whose house is that?" I remember feeling heavy with dread as I asked, heavy like I weighed a thousand pounds, because I already knew what she'd say.

Perez answered. "Belongs to Warrick van Gelderen. Called the Malik mansion cuz it was a wedding present from his wife's father."

"Could be Philippa Flynn those guys were talkin' about," Maddie Small repeated.

I didn't reply. I was dizzy and intensely nauseous, salivating like one of Pavlov's dogs. My ears buzzed and my head hurt so much I had trouble seeing.

Next thing I remember, Maddie Small was putting the datacoin containing the video into my hand, and as I looked at it I knew two things: I had to get the video to Del, who'd get it to Creel and the DTQ289 people, and I had to see the Malik mansion tunnel myself, travel it and even try to glimpse inside the house it connects to. So I could say yes, the video *is* what Maddie Small and Teddy Perez say it is, I'm a fucking witness.

"Show me," I said.

Maddie Small grinned. "I figured. You ready to go another layer down to get there?"

"Whatever it fucking takes," I said.

Another layer down meant the sewers. Unlike newer cities, New York's sewer system began as hand-dug channels and natural streams that were flushed with rainwater, and even now much of the city relies on a combined sewage-and-rainwater-runoff system with large tunnels and pipes to accommodate dramatic fluctuations in flow.

"Don't worry." Perez sounded almost perky. "Been dry recently and low tide's around eleven. Drain tunnels won't be even ten percent full."

"Not so bad with waders," Maddie Small added. "Here's yours, Jamie Gwynmorgan."

They were upper-thigh high. I snugged them on, and soon after we departed the Summer Place, we ducked into one of the void spaces alongside the subway tracks and lowered ourselves down an odiferous manhole—right into a beautiful 1890s-era double-barreled brick sewer plenty tall enough for me to stand in. At its deepest, the water reached just below my knees.

Once more, we moved in single file, me behind Maddie Small, Perez behind me, and this time we used a regular flashlight. Once more I lost track of both space and time. I saw no rats, but felt the presence of a few eels—stragglers from the last high tide slithering around my ankles.

Finally, as the sewer tunnel closed in and I had to hunch over as I walked, Maddie Small halted at an opening in the brick arch above us.

"Our exit's right up there," she said.

I scrunched my shoulders and followed Perez into the dark cylinder overhead, up the rungs of a rusted iron ladder and into an enormous cavern. Thirty feet high with whomping steel beams, sixty or seventy feet across, the cavern curved off to the left into oblivion, more oblivion to the right.

This was it: the Freedom Tunnel, smelling of mold and brake dust. Soon as I clicked up my eyewraps' thermal infrared view, I noticed the gray-against-black figure of a rat maybe fifty feet away drinking from a puddle in the train tracks' ballast.

"Keep your ears open, too," Perez said. "Trains come through at ninety miles an hour in both directions and they're fuckin' quiet. Plenty of room here, so stay off the tracks."

As Maddie Small moved in front of me to lead the way, I noticed a rectangle of white paint with three black numerals—115—high on the wall to our left. We were at 115th Street, moving south along the tunnel's two and a half miles of parkland-covered railroad tracks.

Spooky, someone said once about the Freedom Tunnel. I second that. Knowing where I was didn't help, and thermal infrared-enabled vision be damned, I found myself yearning for my pistol. Or at least some daylight.

"There's my old place." Maddie Small spoke so softly I could barely hear her. "Above these beams there's a concrete cap, curves like the underside of a mushroom an' extends into the ground beyond the top of the tunnel wall, but there's gaps an' voids. Lots of 'em."

I followed her point and spotted a ledge between two support beams. Sixteen, maybe eighteen feet up.

"Where there's a void, we can dig under the cap and pop out right in the middle of Riverside Park," she explained. "We call 'em rabbit holes, disguise 'em good on the outside so the assholes don't block 'em on us."

We walked on in silence until Maddie Small stopped in front of a rectangle of white paint with black numerals high on the wall to our left: 107.

Without a word, Perez laced his fingers palms up and braced. Maddie Small gave him her left foot, and he thrust her upward with a single strong sweep from which she sprang high enough to grab something near the ledge and swing herself over. A moment later and about six feet to the left, she attached what turned out to be a knotted rope to the same object—a large rusty bolt embedded high on the wall.

"After you," Perez said as soon as the rope dangled before us. I tested it with a couple tugs, then up I went—to find myself on a concrete platform about five feet deep, twelve feet long, bounded on each side by the massive, rusting I-beams that support the tunnel's concrete cap and the park above it.

From there, we replicated the journey I'd watched on the video by scrunching through a small void between the top of the tunnel wall and the inner edge of the concrete cap—yep, a rabbit hole. But instead of popping up into Riverside Park after passing beneath the cap, this rabbit hole kept descending—into the narrow, claustrophobia-inducing Malik mansion tunnel, which continued eastward for at least a hundred yards.

When we arrived at the bottleneck where the ceiling had collapsed, I knew for sure it was the same damn tunnel as the one in Maddie Small's video. Ahead of me, Maddie Small turned around holding a pair of tight-fitting gloves and a skullcap, which she gave me ("no prints or DNA left behind").

Hands and head properly covered, I squiggled through the bottleneck, then climbed through the iron hatch into the Malik mansion's small outer utility room, noting the pipes, the conduits, the fire door. Same as the video.

We paused, listened. All quiet.

"Stay here," Maddie murmured almost inaudibly. She wisped beyond the ajar fire door to slippy-slide soundlessly along the rightside wall in the next room until she reached the security system controller, where she key-entered the code—"CharlieTann's hack code"—she'd said would override the usual authentication protocols and hang the system ("no recording, no alarms"). Then she scooted out of sight for an eleven-count only to silently join us again in the outer utility room.

"Wait," she ordered, index finger across her lips. We waited in complete silence behind the still-ajar fire door.

And waited.

"Security system's spoofed an' I flipped the circuit breakers for the entire basement," she finally whispered. "If anyone's down here, they'd be checkin' that electrical panel by now. I'd say we're clear."

I followed her into the larger inner utility room with its grillwork door and electrical gear and the old furnace and leftover junk, and, overhead, its now nonfunctioning cam. Again we paused, listened. All quiet.

"You be lookout," I was told when we reached the expansive, best-of-everything kitchen. "No sitting. Don't touch anything." Turns out I'd tagged along on a break-in.

Maddie Small and Teddy Perez worked quickly, noiselessly, never ventured upstairs. They came away with a remarkable number of hundred dollar bills and a cache of ridiculously valuable uncut red beryl gemstones. They ignored a very high-end wristwatch someone left on a kitchen counter.

We exited the way we came, Maddie Small and Perez each carrying a bag of loot and scrupulous to leave the place looking entirely unviolated. Just before Maddie Small closed the door between the wine cellar and the inner utility room, she grabbed several bottles from the wine cellar. "Last of van Gelderen's Speyfiddich," she whispered, then shooed me and Perez to the outer utility room.

She joined us a moment later, having re-upped the circuit breakers and the security system, and we withdrew to the Freedom Tunnel's high ledge. After a few moments consolidating their takings, we retraced our path back to the Summer Place.

"Here," Maddie Small said as she offered me wet wipes. "Gotta make you presentable before we send you topside." She cleaned my face herself, looked me up and down, patting away the worst of the grime. "Good thing you like dark colors." Then she offered me my choice of the red beryls.

I declined, holding up the datacoin she'd given me earlier. "This is all I want from Warrick van Gelderen's house. Thank you for getting it."

"Could be Philippa Flynn those guys were talkin' about, huh?" she asked.

"Yeah, Maddie Small, it damn well could," I told her.

She nodded; I thought she looked…satisfied.

They escorted me to the subway station at 116th Street and we said good-bye in a way that made me wonder if I'd ever see either of them again. "Don't you worry 'bout us, Jamie Gwynmorgan." Maddie Small smiled up at me and gave me a big hug. "Thanks to you, we're set real good for a shit long time."

"Thanks to me?" I asked.

"We knew they do all kinda bent crap there, but we wouldn't have gone back tonight 'cept for you, and I fuckin' guarantee the stash we found was just passin' through. We'd have missed it 'cept for you."

We hugged again. "Stay safe out here, Maddie Small," I said.

"Back atcha, Jamie Gwynmorgan." And with that, they more or less popped me onto the platform in one of the 116th Street station's few cam blind spots.

I blinked, adjusting to the glare, pulled my folded-up boonie hat from a pocket, put it on, and shoved a hand into my pocket to roll the datacoin between my fingers.

Yep. All real.

I could've taken the subway back to 125th Street and ended up two blocks from my hotel. But I'd had enough of tunnels; I surfaced into the almost-cool, humid night air and started walking north, texting Del as fast as I could.

Yes, she'd been worried.

TALES TO TELL, I texted. LDL.

CHAPTER TWENTY-ONE

Always

AF465.
Saturday, June 18.
02:20 hours.

Well, all doubt has been erased. Adele Sabellius married the village idiot.

I told her everything, gave her Maddie Small's datacoin, which she intently watched several times in a row. Then, as she asked me the simplest of questions, came my pathetic refrain: "I don't know," each one slouching me deeper into the sofa in our living room.

What did Maddie Small see that made her think someone might be following you? How paranoid is she? *Were* you followed?

I don't know.

How'd they diddle the lights and "burp" the subway station cameras? What does that even *mean*, "burp" a camera?

I don't know.

What sort of contact does Maddie Small maintain with Magenau? She gets that Magenau *is* CharlieTann, right?

I don't know.

How did Maddie Small know about goings-on at the Malik mansion? Precisely what "bent crap" does she believe happens there? Why'd she decide the place was supposed to be empty the night she recorded the video?

I don't know.

Where will she and Perez go next? How will you get in touch with them? Are they in danger?

I don't know.

Whatever the hell possessed you to stick around and commit a felony with those two? Why the *fuck* did you trust that Maddie Small's security system hack worked?

I don't know.

For that matter, was it *really* Warrick van Gelderen's house the three of you broke into?

I don't know. Show me pictures of the kitchen in his basement. Then I'll know.

And anyway, why would Maddie Small even want to break into Warrick van Gelderen's house, as opposed to, say, Gracie Mansion or Buckingham Palace?

I smiled; I actually have an opinion on that one because I learned a lot about Maddie Small while I was with her in the tunnels. "Maddie Small grew up cheating because she had to," I told Del, "and she doesn't dare trust anyone who's never needed to risk cheating to survive—*or* anyone who cheats for any reason *but* to survive. Plus she believes in revenge."

"So," Del said, "Maddie Small thinks Warrick van Gelderen got her sent to Camp Null…"

Standing abruptly, Del grabbed her super-secure tablet off the coffee table. Her "excuse me a minute" claimed closer to thirty by the time she finished her back-and-forths. With Creel. With Lynn. With Springer. With Magenau. With Cecilia Danta.

"Why the hell are you talking to Cecilia Danta?" I demanded, way edgier than I wanted to feel. Or reveal.

Del ignored my tone and held up her tablet, which displayed a page of the Select Committee's report. "DTQ records show Maddie Small was picked up a year ago last February twenty-eighth. A so-called 'emergency collection.'" Maddie Small's name and detainee number were followed by the neatly laid-out details of her disappearance.

I waited for the *and* I could feel coming…

"And Marilyn Malik van Gelderen underwent her second heart transplant six days later," Del said, her rich complexion paling. "It was—"

"Are you saying you think Maddie Small's *right?*" I asked, nearly shouting. "Of all the Philippas in the world, you believe the guys in that video really were talking about Philippa Flynn who left a message on my audiostick?" I felt a rush of anger, a rush of *NO!*

Del stayed silent and held up the tablet again, which she'd zoomed into a brief celebrity news report about Marilyn Malik van Gelderen's surgery—a live transplant from an unnamed brain dead victim of a bicycle accident.

I counted as I exhaled. The transplant occurred on...AF3. Marilyn Malik van Gelderen acquired somebody's heart two days after I acquired Audy, and I will forever believe it was Philippa Flynn who found a way to fling Audy under my cell door.

"The guy on the video says he shot somebody named Philippa in the right side of her chest," I recalled. "Like in China, where convicts have been executed that way so their hearts can be taken for live transplants. We know nothing about *when* this Philippa was shot, though."

"Which is why," Del replied, "we have to dig out more medical information about both Philippa Flynn and Marilyn Malik van Gelderen. Doubtless Marilyn's is buried in the deepest vault there is."

"And nobody's found Philippa Flynn's medical data either," I mumbled, my *NO!* still gnawing.

Del set aside the tablet, sat down next to me, and drilled me with the Look. "Hence my call to Cecilia Danta."

And then she kissed me. And kissed me and kissed me and kissed me.

Just remembering those kisses obliterates my sense of time and I'm riding a glorious wave of incandescence all over again, melting into Del, melding into her, surrendering my body which is all I am and no longer what I am as I lift and soar and evanesce into her heat.

And she releases a tiny, breathy laugh because she knows, she knows, even though only her lips, her tongue have touched me.

I shimmy a little, thrum a little because, yeah, it's true, I've just come a little and I'm so, so hungry for more.

Later, Del said the most amazing, wonderful thing to me. "I don't want to ever spend another night away from you again. Not even one night. Never again."

I studied her face; tears brimmed in her eyes. "I'll have to go back to New York," I said. "Hell, at some point *you'll* have to go back to New York, and god knows where else."

"I go with you, you go with me," Del murmured in my ear as she wrapped herself around me. She was trembling at a very high frequency. "We find a way, Jamie. Always. Promise me."

I promised eagerly, gratefully, with many kisses. "I go with you, Adele Sabellius, and you go with me. Always."

❖

AF477.
Thursday, June 30.
13:50 hours.

According to all the records, it couldn't have happened in the private hospital in Puerto Rico, but maybe somewhere else, just maybe, Philippa Flynn's heart *was* transplanted into Marilyn Malik van Gelderen. Can't be proven, of course. Nothing can ever be proven when it comes to *those* people.

We know more than we're supposed to, however—thanks to Cecilia Danta, whose power extends to persuading certain medical professionals to share copies of certain medical records which, at first glance, seem pristinely aboveboard.

But—

Can you hear the great big fucking *But*?

But records from *before* Marilyn Malik van Gelderen's transplant show a different donor DNA profile than records from *after* her transplant. Nobody's noticed—nobody cares—since the presence of donor DNA in post-transplant organ recipient blood testing matters only because it serves as the earliest sign of organ rejection.

"Marilyn Malik van Gelderen's donor DNA profile is different from the brain dead bicycle accident victim's," I said to Del when we examined the information Cecilia was able to send us. "So whose heart does Marilyn Malik van Gelderen actually have?"

Del shrugged a who-knows. "Could be nothing more than a clerical screw-up. We can't be sure of anything without Philippa Flynn's DNA profile. To see if it matches the donor DNA in Marilyn Malik van Gelderen's blood tests."

But not even Cecilia Danta can find a record of Philippa Flynn's DNA. Her medical records, like all but one of the eleven missing detainees not on the helo list, are entirely missing. No DNA samples, no blood or tissue samples. Old reports of test results are lost. Nothing remains that can be tested, either; all Philippa Flynn's stuff is long gone. And her only surviving blood relative sailed out of Newport harbor in his sloop a week after we took down Camp Null, hasn't been seen since, and his medical files have disappeared, too.

My current theory: Philippa Flynn's heart is determined to reject Marilyn Malik van Gelderen. Cuz sometimes karma's a bitch.

❖

AF499.
Friday, July 22.
03:05 hours.

A week from next Tuesday, I'm due back in New York for a three-day charette where I'm supposed to present four alternative preliminary design solutions for the Armstrong Institute project.

I'm working flat-out to meet that deadline, which I recognize for what it is: a career-maker—or breaker.

So I wasn't pleased that my attorney tried to claim this coming Monday afternoon for yet another goddamn deposition. I detest depositions. Inevitably, I end up facing off against a barracuda with a law degree and something to unprove as he or she decides to nitpick my testimony to death. I've learned to stay cool, but it's exhausting.

Five minutes after I told the attorney no, Paul Norman called requesting that I "drop by the city" this coming Monday for an afternoon meeting and, later, an "informal, low-key dinner" with the project's "sponsor" who has "decided he wants to run a few ideas past you."

As politely as possible, I suggested we wait until after the charette, at which point the sponsor could weigh in on the alternatives I was developing. And, since Norman brought it up, I came right out and asked who the sponsor is.

The way Norman declined to give me a name makes me question whether he even knows yet himself. Maybe he's eager for what he calls "the pre-meeting" on Monday so he can find out.

Oh, and since dinner will likely run late, arkIngenium will put me up for the night.

Thus did Del and I face our first Always test.

No problem, Del said. "We both go to New York, and I'll have dinner with Leta Creel and some others while you meet your big shot."

I'm not looking forward to adapting the preliminary designs based on the eleventh-hour whims of the project's suddenly involved, still-anonymous patron saint; I'll be doing all-nighters the whole of next week to pull it off, and I'll be spending this weekend prepping as much as possible for Monday's "pre-meeting."

Woke up a few minutes ago wondering again who the Armstrong Institute project sponsor might be. I figure the likeliest candidate is

Jonathan Armstrong Archer—plenty rich enough, plenty egotistical enough, and plenty obsessed enough with his legacy.

But I think what's keeping me awake is the expression I noticed on Del's face this evening, instantly banished when I asked her what was wrong. Yet it returned as soon as she thought I wasn't looking.

CHAPTER TWENTY-TWO

Finitude

AF502.
Monday, July 25.
19:30 hours.
    This afternoon's Armstrong Institute "pre-meeting" was a joke. I presented a sort of pre-charette that produced perfunctory nods and polite smiles but no feedback and no decisions because the sponsor was a no-show.
    "We'll meet him at dinner," Norman said. I watched how he said it and concluded he still doesn't know who our sugar daddy is. Instead he talked about where this dinner tonight will happen—at Comestible, New York's latest ultra-uber restaurant in the sleek high-rise just across the glass-canopied side street from the hotel where Del and I are staying.
    I'm in the hotel lobby now. Del has just departed for her meet-up with Leta Creel, and I'm waiting for Norman. And I admit it: I'm hoping Jonathan Armstrong Archer *is* our sugar daddy. At least I've met the dude, have a sense of his attitudes, his tastes. Which, frankly, could be worse—
    Hey, I see Norman across the lobby. And, jeez, he looks awfully nervous.

❖

AF502.
Monday, July 25.
19:47 hours.
    Shit shit shit I dunno what to do.

If Paul Norman had said it before we crossed that street, before we stepped into the oh-so-private elevator to this oh-so-private penthouse dining room, I sure as hell wouldn't be here now. But Norman didn't utter the words till about the twentieth floor. "Marvin says he's looking forward to meeting you."

I begged Caprice for some other Marvin, any other Marvin. But no, the Armstrong Institute project's sponsor is none other than Marvin Este Malik.

The instant the elevator doors opened, I found him staring at me from maybe fifteen feet off. After a three-count, he turned away, giving no sign he remembers me from the only time years ago we encountered each other.

Even so, every instinct I have screamed at me to run, and my hand reached for the elevator controls, but Norman almost shoved me ahead of him into the dining room lobby and, regrettably, I opted not to make a scene, told myself I'm overreacting.

Yet as soon as the elevator doors closed, a Malik bodyguard took up a position that quite effectively blocks elevator access. Security, he rumbled when I said I needed to return to my hotel room for—for—

I never finished; the bodyguard said just let him know what I need and he'll make sure I get it. Aspirin, I lied. He produced a bottle and asked how many.

Oh god, maybe I'm not really as trapped as I feel. But my whole body's going nuts, like I grabbed a live wire and can't let go.

Bree-ee-eathe…

Only good news is that Malik wants a round of drinks out on the penthouse deck before dinner. That's given me a chance to slip into the restroom for a couple of minutes and pull out both Audy and the little pocketcom I squirreled away in my pants' faraday-sealed pocket (which really does work—their detectors down in the lobby detected nada, since I wasn't asked to drop off my pocketcom there like Norman was).

So whatever happens, I've left this update and texted Del.

Wish I had time to wait for her reply, but at least she knows where I am and who…I'm…with…

❖

AF524.
Tuesday, August 16.
10:35 hours.

I straddle two worlds.

One is Lynn's world, Del's world, swirling with klieg lights and standing ovations and too many bright staring eyes, yet with a center of gravity so warm and embracing that even the thought of it sends a feathery shiver of gratitude right through me. This is a world that should've remained forever unknowable to me, a world I still half expect to wake up from.

Poof. Just a dream.

The other, far darker world baits me, luring, like that time I stood on a narrow beam hundreds of feet above the Big Mystic River, stomach convulsing, dizzied gaze drawn down, down...*I dare you*... This whaddaya-got-to-lose world of Maddie Small and Magenau and Cecilia Danta and so many others is where I come from. Surviving in it requires an endurance/resistance/defiance that suctions me into a continuum of arousal calibrated in ratios of fear and pain.

That which doesn't kill me turns me on, as long as I try hard enough to get it to kill me.

To be aroused, as Mary once told me, is to be alive. And to be alive is power. My very existence is a turn-on because it defies death. Omnipotence enough. To be alive and *will*—to be aroused and *will*—ah, now I'm wishing, I'm desiring, I'm consciously, deliberately choosing to act.

And when my defiance, my *will*, arouses whomever I've defied, anything might happen. On that Monday night twenty-two days ago, anything did happen. Faster than I had time to really understand.

It just fucking happened.

And of course the last thing I should do is babble about it into an audiostick. But shit, I'm having dreams, nightmares, even after all that talking with Del. Last few days, I'm waking up not sure—oh god, I hate to admit this: I'm waking up not sure what's real.

Did I remember that right?

Did it really happen?

Really?

And why do I feel like I'm falling every time I close my eyes?

So—

In the bright light of day, while Del is off in a meeting and before my dreams skew too much of my waking, I'm gonna just say it. I'll risk someone else hearing this as long as *I* can hear this.

❖

That night, there were ten of us in Comestible's private penthouse dining room with its spectacular west-facing view of the Hudson River and New Jersey silhouetted against a too-red sky.

Paul Norman snared me as soon as I emerged from the restroom and led me to be introduced to Malik, who seemed to look right through me—the trillionaire thousand-yard stare—before turning away without even a nod. I'd gone numb except for a low-frequency *no no no no no...*

Mere seconds later, jarringly, Malik wanted dinner served. He took the head of the table, flicked his hand, and his three minions promptly ushered the rest of us to our seats. Mine was as far away from Malik as the table allowed, at the end next to the lowest-ranking Institute guy and across from the most goon-like Malik minion, who wore a glare that just wouldn't fucking quit and a jacket with a distinctly non-anatomical bulge at the waist.

Even before we sat down, I'd wondered why Malik had bothered with a dinner at all, and why the hell he wanted me there. He seemed detached to the point of irritation while everyone except me and the goon across from me tried to keep him interested, entertained, anything to soothe him.

Dinner was perfunctory, though it featured some sort of hoity-toity *very* red meat that I shuffled around on the plate. Malik's goon quickly ate every bite without ever looking at anything but me, which prevented me from rummaging into my faraday-sealed pocket to check the little pocketcom for word from Del.

One can argue, with hindsight, that I missed an opportunity to bolt when I noticed the bodyguard no longer posted by the elevator. The wait staff scurried around clearing the dinner plates and offering desserts, cordials, and scotch and everyone was standing again. I'd actually started edging toward the elevator—

And the next thing I know, Malik has his arm around Paul Norman's shoulder, suddenly hearty and engaged, impeding my path to the elevator. Then off they go, Malik's voice trailing something about "I want to show it to you, it's just across the street in my new office,

Burton Neal's last building, you know…" while Paul Norman croons a chorus of yeses and a Malik minion flutters after them.

Count to three, and another Malik minion started shutting down the rest of us with time-to-go bustles and tones. I felt immense relief; Malik's gone, it's over. I'll get the hell outta here, leave the city tonight, resign the project tomorrow.

God, I was absurdly sloppy then. Even indulged the distraction of privately fuming at Malik because I knew he lied to Paul Norman about Burton Neal's last building, which is in Boston; I should know since I damn well worked on it.

Only when one of the minions spilled some dregs on me and I looked up to find it was just me and Malik's goon squinting at me while we waited for the elevator—did I finally, *finally* get it.

And even then I didn't actually know what I got, just that something's terribly oh-shit wrong with them, not me, and I need to ghost the hell away from Malik's slitty-eyed goon aysap. *Ay-fucking-sap*.

So I try to seem nonchalant (yeah, right), glance around for what I might use to divert his attention—whereupon the elevator does it for me.

As the goon reacts to the elevator's arrival chirp, he turns slightly away from me, and I'm off. A reverse pivot back into the dining room and I'm full-on running with the goon in pursuit hollering, "Hey!" I beeline into the penthouse's serving kitchen, a kind of jazzed-up butler's pantry one floor above Comestible's main kitchen and public dining rooms. It was devoid of staff—which suggests stairs, right? Down to the main kitchen and out, right?

So I'm dodging carts and countertops, scanning the space for the doorway to the stairs, and I make the stairwell, even manage to stiff-shoulder the fire door hard into the goon's face as he tries to rush me. I glimpse him sinking to his knees all grunty-groany, holding his bloodied nose.

But goddamn, I can't go down. Another goon's already clunking loudly up the stairs toward me while Bloody Face wails: "Here, Fred! She's up here!" And then Fred's weapon comes into view. Older, non-electronic—a glick, untrackable, a black market weapon for black market purposes.

At least Fred's nervous. I can tell from the way he holds the pistol, the slow, extra-cautious way he moves. Gives me time to scramble in the only direction left. I remember looking up at the door to the mechanical box on the roof as I race toward it. Thinking I'm doomed if the damn thing's locked. Allowing myself a thin thread of hope when I notice a couple of cigarette butts.

Could it be that Comestible employees sneak up here for a smoke, maybe even keep the door unlocked…?

Yes!

The mechanical box on the other side of the door was more or less what I expected: a steel girder framework open to the sky that encloses the building's mechanical equipment, high walls lining the structure's long north and south sides. A hundred feet dead ahead of me the narrower east side's two-foot-high parapet stretched behind a double row of heat pumps and other electrical gear.

I ducked left between the heat pumps and searched for the egress, another stairway that the building code requires be east of where I hunkered—at maybe eleven o'clock—

Fred wasn't far behind. He started calling out to be heard over the rumble of the heat pumps. "Hey, Jamie, you up here?"

And jeezus, I freaked. Because I recognized Fred's voice. And I don't mean from the evening's private dining experience.

Sounded like he hadn't moved far from the doorway, so I kept heading to my eleven o'clock, nearer the parapet. Crouching behind a large electrical generator, I finally spotted the stairway superstructure. Within a minute, I'd reached the east stairway door.

Locked.

My stomach wrenched then and kept on wrenching. *Man, I am fucked and I can't believe what I'm thinking about* why *I'm fucked.*

"Hey, Jamie," Fred called; he was getting closer but he couldn't see me. "Mister—uh, uh, Marvin'd like to have a word. Got a minute?"

I scrunched low, scooted behind an electrical transformer only feet from the parapet—and looked up to see Fred's weapon about five feet away pointed at my face. I'd circled right the fuck into him.

I forced my eyes to lock on his instead of the black hole at the end of his glick. "Was Philippa looking at you when you shot her?" I asked.

He stiff-armed his weapon, like he wanted to stand as far away from it as possible, as he gaped at me. His mouth opened, but he said nothing.

Slowly, casually as I could, I rose. Fred's weapon and his gape tracked my movement, but the man himself didn't budge while I faced him and began backing away by inches, closer and closer to the parapet behind me. "You supposed to shoot me up here?" I asked.

Only when my calves bumped the parapet did I understand what I was doing, because at last I understood what Malik intended to do with me. I took one more step backward—up and onto the parapet, facing away from the 800-foot drop at my heels, staying on the balls of my feet to counter the building's quite perceptible sway.

"Nah," I declared, answering my own question, "I bet it's supposed to happen downstairs somewhere, huh?"

Fred remained mute and stiff-armed about ten feet from me, his face half hidden behind his weapon. I began to stroll along the parapet, which was maybe a foot wide, stuffing my hands into my pants pockets and doing a little two-step to disguise my right hand's efforts to open my pocket's faraday-sealed compartment.

Finally, he spoke. "Don't do that. You could fall."

"Six of one for me, Fred." I twirled an entire 360 degrees on the ball of my left foot, inducing gasps I could hear even over the heat pumps. "Can your boss use a squished heart if it's scraped off the sidewalk quick enough?"

While Fred swore, I got the seal in my pocket open, clicked up the little pocketcom inside, and hoped I'd turned on RECORD.

"So, lemme guess—" I continued, strolling the parapet again. "You shoot me about here, yeah?" I slapped my right tit hard with my left hand. "A non-mortal wound so the docs your boss has bribed and blackmailed can cut out my live heart and place it warm and beating into his daughter. Way better odds for a successful transplant when it's live like that, I bet."

I could hear Fred muttering during brief lulls in the heat pumps' work. "Jeezus…Jeezus."

Good, keep it rolling.

"Gotta admire the chutzpah," I jabbered. "I mean, to set up a whole cardiothoracic surgical theater with all that state-of-the-art equipment and the post-op rooms and specialists and drugs and backup systems—" I twirled again. "His very own heart transplant enterprise. Fuck, man, right here in this building, too. How many floors?"

And by god, Fred answered me. "Three." He scraped his feet, looked around. "One floor for all the medical. One above, one below for security."

I poked for more. "Labeled as mechanical areas, huh? Hmm… maybe around the twelfth floor. In and out via service elevator to a segregated loading dock where even the cams and sensors out on the street just happen to be down."

"Yeah, well," Fred responded again. "Maximum op precision, minimum personnel."

"Sure, makes sense." I nodded too vigorously, since even my smallest movement upset him. "I mean, how many people can a guy like Malik trust with his daughter's heart, right?"

Goddamn if Fred didn't actually puff up a bit. "Y-Yeah, a-and—" he stammered, trying to reclaim the power he'd been delegated. This effort was interrupted by several large raindrops plopping around us. Fred wiped one off his face—"I got my orders"—and impatiently waved his weapon at me. "So let's go."

"Oh dear, Marilyn must be all prepped and waiting by now, huh?" I said, ignoring the two or three raindrops that landed on my head. "But, Fred—" I stopped, turned to face him, and lifted my arms to receive the incoming rain. "How the hell're you gonna get me down there?"

Once more, Fred went mute. But behind him the door to that locked east stairway swung open, and there stood Marvin Este Malik.

"I'll tell you how, bitch," he yelled as he marched toward me. "You're going to trade yourself for Adele Sabellius. Right here, right the fuck now. I'll let Adele live if you come down from there. But if you choose a swan dive onto West Street, I will make it my life's work to ensure that Adele dies as soon as possible, maybe when she's with her sister and her nieces and the rest of your cunt crew. The kids and Lily first. Then Adele."

I believed him.

He stood next to Fred but never took his eyes off me as he put out his hand, silently demanding the glick. When Fred gave it to him, he stomped a couple pistol-first steps toward me and halted.

"You need to understand I'm not fucking around," Malik growled, then pivoted toward Fred, who stood about four feet behind him.

Fred could see Malik's face, so he understood before I did and backed away, hands rising protectively. By the time my brain got to *Oh shit!*, Malik had fired twice. Fred clumped into a heap, blood oozing from his chest and his forehead.

With a wave of the weapon, Malik dismissed the motionless rag doll that had once been Fred. "And that," he said impassively as he turned back toward me weapon-first, "is what happens to people who steal our goddamn Speyfiddich."

"Oh for chrissake, Marvin, *he* didn't steal your Speyfiddich."

Assuredly, time does not stop, but sometimes it goes radically slo-mo and you recall with vibrant clarity every frame, blink by stunned blink.

"Oh for chrissake, Marvin, *he* didn't steal your Speyfiddich."

I still hear it echo, though she said it only once from the open doorway of the east stairwell. Neither Malik nor I had seen her arrive there, and we both startled at her words resounding above the bluster of the heat pumps.

But Malik startled more. Unlike me, he was moving when she spoke, already half-turned and stepping toward me. At the sound of her voice behind him, which he no doubt recognized, he swung the weapon around at her, but his forward motion pretzeled his legs and he stumbled, the backs of his calves bumping hard into the parapet not two feet from where I stood.

Maybe he'd never have lost his balance if his eyes hadn't first veered to the street below before swerving onto me to flare his outrage. Maybe he'd even have regained his balance unaided. Certainly, I could have reached out to right him—and disarm him, too—with one safe, simple thrust of my hand.

But I didn't.

I didn't.

Instead, I stared into his eyes and gave him the smallest of nudges across the delicate boundary of balance. No more force than a finger tapping the trigger of a sniper rifle.

And over he went, speechless for a bewildered shake, a single plump raindrop splattering on his cheek. Then he was wide-eyed and shrieking. I watched him for the first three everlasting seconds as he fell belly up, saw the unyielding fury on his face, heard it in his *scree-ee-eam*.

Before West Street shushed him, I looked away, stepped down from the parapet trembling and light-headed. Somebody—me, I think—made a sound, incoherent, guttural.

Then I felt her hand on my shoulder. "We should go, baby," Del murmured, her breath warming my ear. "We gotta go right now."

She kissed me, took my hand, and steered me past Fred's blood-and-raindrop-blotched body to the east stairwell, wiping surfaces with her shirttail as she went. We descended two, maybe three floors on foot, then hurried down a darkened hallway into a service elevator.

"This way," she whispered when the elevator doors opened at SB2.

Still holding my hand, she led me through narrow, barely lit passages to a service stairway, explaining that we'd just walked under North End Way to our hotel from the building where Marilyn Malik van Gelderen awaited my heart. Now we were to go upstairs and pretend everything was normal.

"Ready?" she asked.

I nodded, and we climbed two flights into a quiet hallway near the hotel's kitchen.

"Hear that? The bar's still hopping, which is excellent," Del told me. "We can slip in there from here without any cams picking us up, and we won't have to stay long. But when we leave through the front into the lobby, we want to be in as large a cluster of people as possible. That'll go a long way to screwing up any attempts to timestamp our movement tonight."

"How the hell did you figure all this out?" I asked.

She told me how Norman's call last Thursday bugged her, but she couldn't figure out why. How after I'd texted her from Comestible's restroom she'd finally put it together, guessed what Malik really wanted from me. How she had the taxi drop her at the north corner of the Comestible building, where she'd planned to search its loading dock area along Murray Street for a low-profile back way in.

Up ahead of her she'd spotted Malik, alone, no bodyguards, scurrying into one of the neighboring hotel's rear doors. "And thank your friend Caprice he didn't spot me."

Still unseen, suspecting Malik had made sure the cams and sensors around him were dead, Del followed him down to the hotel sub-basement and under North End Way to the Comestible building.

"He took a different elevator to the roof, but I ended up hardly more than a half-step behind him." She inhaled deeply, then shrugged her exhale. "Malik was so determined to leave no trace of what he was up to tonight that, thanks to him, we haven't either."

❖

AF568.
Wednesday, September 28.
11:21 hours.

If I'd had my way That Night, we'd have kept on going. But we stayed in the hotel less than 1,000 feet from where Marvin Este Malik lay splatted on West Street and held on to each other, speaking only in hushed whispers.

Every time I shut my eyes, I was falling, the parapet whooshing away from my clawing hands, my gut twisting its centrifugal groan into my throat. I waited for the cops to come knocking, wondering what I'd tell them, even though Del insisted I simply tell them the truth. "If and when they ask."

Did she realize I tapped the trigger that sent him over the edge?

"You reached for him," Del replied, her obsidian eyes claiming me. "He reached for you. I saw his grip fail. I saw that his fall could not have been prevented. Which is exactly what I'll say to anyone who asks."

Well, it's been sixty-five days and no one's asked yet.

The police and the feds have been incentivized to follow the path of least resistance, Del predicted; they'll find only what's been left for them to find. "Which won't include us."

That Del understood it would go down like this—and I did not—probably explains all you need to know about us.

"I want justice, too," she said to me as I lay quaking in her arms That Night. "But despite what everyone thinks, I'm not a tilter at windmills. Especially rigged windmills."

❖

Malik was found on the street with a death grip on the glick, two rounds fired, shooter's residue on his hand. Took the cops almost half an hour to discover Fred and to realize every cam and sensor in and around the building had been down since late afternoon. This led to a floor-by-floor search that caught Warrick van Gelderen attempting to remove his unconscious wife from what appeared to be an unlicensed surgical facility on the thirteenth floor.

Despite the rain, which got intense for a while That Night, the roof yielded fingerprint, blood, and DNA evidence of Bloody Face as well as Fred and Malik. Bloody Face also left a trail of blood from Comestible's private dining room through the service kitchen and up the stairs. No one on the Comestible staff saw or could explain this or anything else, and Bloody Face had disappeared.

Seems I owe Bloody Face. Had to be his blood smeared all over the stairway doors and doorknobs that obliterated my fingerprints and DNA. Del said it wouldn't matter what the LEOs found, we'd be kept out of it.

Within a day, the cops announced that Fred had been killed by bullets from the weapon Malik clung to and had fired. Exhaustive efforts to find passing drone and even satellite video taken in the area during the evening of July 25 produced zilch. Efforts to locate Bloody Face intensified until early August, when his much-deteriorated body came floating down the Harlem River.

Del acknowledged that the death of the only remaining person who knew I was on the roof That Night helps keep us out of the whole damn thing, but she spat profanity like a marine anyway.

"Reveals plenty about how risk is being perceived these days," she said later, snugging herself almost too firmly around me, like she needed assurance I was really there. "Instability at MetraGlobal and Georgica makes for dangerous times. But at least one of the most dangerous people will be far too busy on defense to consider hassling us."

Recent apologetics involve distraction; Malik family attorneys have been attempting to implicate Bloody Face in both Fred's death and Malik's. But even if that implausible campaign achieves traction, it won't help Warrick van Gelderen.

About three weeks ago, prosecutors hinted that a cardiothoracic surgeon and a nurse were granted immunity for testimony about the heart transplanted into Marilyn Malik van Gelderen 565 days ago. Philippa Flynn's heart, I believe.

Last week, a grand jury indicted Warrick van Gelderen, the medical people caught with him That Night on the thirteenth floor, and even Marilyn Malik van Gelderen. They face a shitload of charges related to attempted organ trafficking, although no one's been able to identify or locate the organ donor. They're also accused of criminal destruction of medical records. But not the murder of Philippa Flynn.

"Not yet," said Del. "Maybe not ever. But at least Marilyn Malik van Gelderen won't be getting *your* heart. Or anybody else's."

Took quite a while to hear anything more from Paul Norman than his cursory text message on July 26 canceling the Armstrong Institute project charette and concluding with "I'll be in touch." I figured the entire project was as dead as Marvin Este Malik.

Paul finally surfaced this morning to tell me that the Institute had undergone a "colonoscopic investigation" of its fund-raising practices and the activities and associations of its employees and members and came out clean.

As did Paul himself. "The police said I'm the last person to have seen Malik alive," he informed me rather breathlessly. It was from Paul that I learned the cops never bothered interviewing the rest of us invited to That Night's bizarre dinner at Comestible, "since the trouble up there started later, after we'd all left."

And yes, the project's a go, Paul said—did I still want it?

I did and I didn't, but I said yes. First rule of the self-employed: never say no, just make sure your yes carries conditions you can live with.

Del approves of my decision. Then she admitted she'd checked out arkIngenium and the Armstrong Institute back when Paul Norman first came around.

I was shocked. "You check out my clients?"

"Only when they give me a certain sort of willies."

Maybe I'm projecting, but I thought her smile hinted that every client I'll ever have will give her those sorts of willies.

"Turned out," she continued blithely, "that arkIngenium and the Armstrong Institute came up squeaky clean." She said she found out later that Malik's money had been filtered through several layers of independent nonprofits, so it didn't show. Ironically, though, that very filtering means the money remains in the Institute's hands.

"You mean you checked *again*?"

"Hell, yes," Del said. "As soon as you texted That Night about Malik being the project patron. Had to do *something* in the taxi on my way back to you."

I'm still waiting for regret, for guilt. But no, I feel only that the world's a better place without Marvin Este Malik in it. Which is, actually, a feeling I wish I didn't have.

❖

AF614.
Sunday, November 13.
06:21 hours.

Ever since That Night, I dream a lot about falling.

Just now woke up from falling tits up, accelerating, thinking *This is it, I'm done...*

And then I lay flat on my back, askew, legs apart. No pain, my hands splayed across my belly, I rolled onto my side and saw that I lay on a sky blue blanket spread out in a grassy clearing. The blanket had white letters on it that took me a bit to put together...

Finitude

Several women sat on the blanket with me, chattering away and playing with a little girl who glanced up at me and smiled. I understood. That's her, Awa, dead by my bullet when she was six years old.

And I counted. She'd be twenty now but for me...

And—

And, oh my god, she smiled at me.

Yet I could not hold her gaze; mine retreated to the blanket's white letters as I was shrouded in the old shame. Awa, dead by my bullet when she was six years old, had paid for my choice. Do what my mother did, traffic in pharma and fuck men for money, *or* learn how to kill men instead. Men who damn well asked for it.

I tried to inhale a breath—to speak? to sob?—but my gut had seized.

Which is when one of the women—was that you, Mary?—said, quite gently, "You can't imagine yourself happy until you can be kind to yourself."

Then I was falling again, tits up, accelerating, thinking *I chose to kill men, and I can handle killing men, but not a six-year-old girl...*

"Stop that, Jamie. Stop. There...is...no...judgment."

The voice, young yet not a child's, spoke firmly, knowingly, from close by, but I saw only fervid blue, and as I kept falling I heard her whisper, "Everything is beautiful when you can bear to see the truth."

And then I woke up.

Chapter Twenty-three

By Caprice's whim alone

AF781
Saturday, April 22.
23:50 hours.

"You know I can't do any of this without you," Del whispered to me backstage tonight as the introductions began.

Only since That Night have I grasped how nervous she gets at events like these, where every word from her, every smile and raised eyebrow and sweep of her hand matters so much to so many. I hugged her long and hard. I told her I love her.

Some people embody a deep power to turn the world. Because these people are both charismatic (they show us what we can *be*) and genuinely visionary (they show us what we must *will*), they inspire those around them with possibility so vividly portrayed that groups, societies, cultures collude to make it real.

Whatever its source, although many harbor ambition for it (too many, and usually for the worst of reasons), such power comes only to a rare few. By any measure, I'm not one of these people. Even Lynn Hillinger, impressive as she is, doesn't have, can never have such power. No one realizes this more than Lynn herself, and I sense she's relieved.

But Del *does* have that deep power, though she remains fundamentally unaware of it even now. I believe this is for the best because power so profound can overwhelm the individual it burdens. Del is better off—we're all better off—if she simply acts in concord with her vision, her truth.

To be alive is power, and if she isn't taken from us by someone's ignorant greed or desperate fear, then the possibilities Del imagines will become real.

I know why now—why Caprice has kept me here in the face of such outrageous odds and, at times, against my will; I understand why Lynn found herself helping me when it would have been far easier, so much more *normal*, to leave me behind. Thanks to Lynn, I'm here now, at this time and in this space, prepared to do everything I can, anything I must so Del lives and thrives.

I suppose I remain unaware, too—fundamentally unable to *be* aware of what caused Del to want me, what keeps her wanting me so many years after she discovered me bruised and shivering that morning. Whatever it is, all I can say is that I am inexpressibly grateful for it.

"I'm right here with you," I said to her as the introduction concluded and the audience rose to its feet, already applauding her. "Always."

I watched her step into the spotlights' glare, her head slightly bowed before their acclamation, her soft smile embracing them while her sparking eyes hinted what was to come.

And, of course, she was magnificent.

❖

AF841.
Wednesday, June 21.
22:19 hours.

Fifteen years ago today, I died. According to any measure, I should've stayed that way. Which means by Caprice's whim alone I've been around for an extra 5,479 days. Not bad for a dead person who can't stop falling.

I'm waiting for Del to come to bed, where we will make love with abandon because at last I can do that, and when we wake up in the morning we'll go to Great Hill a couple of days early and take long walks in the woods.

From where I lie Del passes in and out of my view, pacing in the office across the hall while she talks quietly, earnestly to god-knows-who about god-knows-what. I love watching her in moments like these, when I can revel in her unnoticed.

If you don't hear from me again, trust that it's a good sign—that I am, perhaps, able to be kind to myself, able at last to imagine myself happy.

About the Author

Sophia Kell Hagin's first novel, *Whatever Gods May Be*, won a 2011 Golden Crown Literary Society Award for Dramatic General Fiction and also was a 2010 Golden Crown Debut Author finalist. In addition, *Whatever Gods May Be* won a 2010 Lesbian Fiction Readers Choice Award in General Fiction and received a 2011 LGBT Rainbow Awards Honorable Mention for Best Lesbian Debut Novel.

Sophia's well-received second novel, *Shadows of Something Real*, was published in 2013.

Omnipotence Enough completes the Jamie Gwynmorgan trilogy.

Sophia lives in Truro, Massachusetts, with her longtime love, life, business, and marriage partner. She can be contacted via SophiaKellHagin.com.

Books Available From Bold Strokes Books

A Date to Die by Anne Laughlin. Someone is killing people close to Detective Kay Adler, who must look to her own troubled past for a suspect. There she finds more than one person seeking revenge against her. (978-163555-023-8)

Captured Soul by Laydin Michaels. Can Kadence Munroe save the woman she loves from a twisted killer, or will she lose her to a collector of souls? (978-162639-915-0)

Dawn's New Day by TJ Thomas. Can Dawn Oliver and Cam Cooper, two women who have loved and lost, open their hearts to love again? (978-163555-072-6)

Definite Possibility by Maggie Cummings. Sam Miller is just out for good times, but Lucy Weston makes her realize happily ever after is a definite possibility. (978-162639-909-9)

Eyes Like Those by Melissa Brayden. Isabel Chase and Taylor Andrews struggle between love and ambition from the writers' room on one of Hollywood's hottest TV shows. (978-163555-012-2)

Heart's Orders by Jaycie Morrison. Helen Tucker and Tee Owens escape hardscrabble lives to careers in the Women's Army Corps, but more than their hearts are at risk as friendship blossoms into love. (978-163555-073-3)

Hiding Out by Kay Bigelow. Treat Dandridge is unaware that her life is in danger from the murderer who is hunting the woman she's falling in love with, Mickey Heiden. (978-162639-983-9)

Omnipotence Enough by Sophia Kell Hagin. Can the tiny tool that abducted war veteran Jamie Gwynmorgan accidentally acquires help her escape an unknown enemy to reclaim her stolen life and the woman she deeply loves? (978-163555-037-5)

Summer's Cove by Aurora Rey. Emerson Lange moved to Provincetown to live in the moment, but when she meets Darcy Belo and her son Liam, her quest for summer romance becomes a family affair. (978-162639-971-6)

The Road to Wings by Julie Tizard. Lieutenant Casey Tompkins, Air Force student pilot, has to fly with the toughest instructor, Captain Kathryn "Hard Ass" Hardesty, fly a supersonic jet, and deal with a growing forbidden attraction. (978-162639-988-4)

Beauty and the Boss by Ali Vali. Ellis Renois is at the top of the fashion world, but she never expects her summer assistant Charlotte Hamner to tear her heart and her business apart like sharp scissors through cheap material. (978-162639-919-8)

Fury's Choice by Brey Willows. When gods walk amongst humans, can two women find a balance between love and faith? (978-162639-869-6)

Lessons in Desire by MJ Williamz. Can a summer love stand a four-month hiatus and still burn hot? (978-163555-019-1)

Lightning Chasers by Cass Sellars. For Sydney and Parker, being a couple was never what they had planned. Now they have to fight corruption, murder, and enemies hiding in plain sight just to hold on to each other. Lightning Series, Book Two. (978-162639-965-5)

Summer Fling by Jean Copeland. Still jaded from a breakup years earlier, Kate struggles to trust falling in love again when a summer fling with sexy young singer Jordan rocks her off her feet. (978-162639-981-5)

Take Me There by Julie Cannon. Adrienne and Sloan know it would be career suicide to mix business with pleasure, however tempting it is. But what's the harm? They're both consenting adults. Who would know? (978-162639-917-4)

Unchained Memories by Dena Blake. Can a woman give herself completely when she's left a piece of herself behind? (978-162639-993-8)

Walking Through Shadows by Sheri Lewis Wohl. All Molly wanted to do was go backpacking…in her own century. (978-162639-968-6)

Freedom to Love by Ronica Black. What happens when the woman who spent her life worrying about caring for her family finally finds the freedom to love without borders? (978-1-63555-001-6)

A Lamentation of Swans by Valerie Bronwen. Ariel Montgomery returns to Sea Oats to try to save her broken marriage but soon finds herself also fighting to save her own life and catch a murderer. (978-1-62639-828-3)

House of Fate by Barbara Ann Wright. Two women must throw off the lives they've known as a guardian and an assassin and save two rival houses before their secrets tear the galaxy apart. (978-1-62639-780-4)

Planning for Love by Erin Dutton. Could true love be the one thing that wedding coordinator Faith McKenna didn't plan for? (978-1-62639-954-9)

Sidebar by Carsen Taite. Judge Camille Avery and her clerk, attorney West Fallon, agree on little except their mutual attraction, but can their relationship and their careers survive a headline-grabbing case? (978-1-62639-752-1)

Sweet Boy and Wild One by T. L. Hayes. When Rachel Cole meets soulful singer Bobby Layton at an open mic, she is immediately in thrall. What she soon discovers will rock her world in ways she never imagined. (978-1-62639-963-1)

To Be Determined by Mardi Alexander and Laurie Eichler. Charlie Dickerson escapes her life in the US to rescue Australian wildlife with Pip Atkins, but can they save each other? (978-1-62639-946-4)

True Colors by Yolanda Wallace. Blogger Robby Rawlins plans to use First Daughter Taylor Crenshaw to get ahead, but she never planned on falling in love with her in the process. (978-1-62639-927-3)

Heart Stop by Radclyffe. Two women, one with a damaged body, the other a damaged spirit, challenge each other to dare to live again. (978-1-62639-899-3)

Undercover Affairs by Julie Blair. Searching for stolen documents crucial to U.S. security, CIA agent Rett Spenser confronts lies, deceit, and unexpected romance as she investigates art gallery owner Shannon Kent. (978-1-62639-905-1)

Taking Sides by Kathleen Knowles. When passion and politics collide, can love survive? (978-1-62639-876-4)

Unexpected by Jenny Frame. When Dale McGuire falls for Rebecca Harper, the mother of the son she never knew she had, will Rebecca's troubled past stop them from making the family they both truly crave? (978-1-62639-942-6)

Canvas for Love by Charlotte Greene. When ghosts from Amelia's past threaten to undermine their relationship, Chloé must navigate the greatest romance of her life without losing sight of who she is. (978-1-62639-944-0)

Repercussions by Jessica L. Webb. Someone planted information in Edie Black's brain and now they want it back, but with the protection of shy former soldier Skye Kenny, Edie has a chance at life and love. (978-1-62639-925-9)

Spark by Catherine Friend. Jamie's life is turned upside down when her consciousness travels back to 1560 and lands in the body of one of Queen Elizabeth I's ladies-in-waiting...or has she totally lost her grip on reality? (978-1-62639-930-3)

Thorns of the Past by Gun Brooke. Former cop Darcy Flynn's heart broke when her career on the force ended in disgrace, but perhaps saving Sabrina Hawk's life will mend it in more ways than one. (978-1-62639-857-3)

You Make Me Tremble by Karis Walsh. Seismologist Casey Radnor comes to the San Juan Islands to study an earthquake but finds her heart shaken by passion when she meets animal rescuer Iris Mallery. (978-1-62639-901-3)

Girls Next Door, edited by Sandy Lowe and Stacia Seaman. Best-selling romance authors tell it from the heart—sexy, romantic stories of falling for the girls next door. (978-1-62639-916-7)

Complications by MJ Williamz. Two women battle for the heart of one. (978-1-62639-769-9)

Crossing the Wide Forever by Missouri Vaun. As Cody Walsh and Lillie Ellis face the perils of the untamed West, they discover that love's uncharted frontier isn't for the weak in spirit or the faint of heart. (978-1-62639-851-1)

www.ingramcontent.com/pod-product-compliance
Lightning Source LLC
Chambersburg PA
CBHW021952010726
47494CB00003B/695